# *Vinnie's Wife*

## *Marsha Portnoy*

*Best wishes,*
*Marsha Portnoy*

**Tailor-Made Publishing Group**

www.tailormadepublishinggroup.com
Woodstock, IL

Vinnie's Wife, A Novel

©2014 Marsha Portnoy
All rights reserved

Vinnie's Wife is a work of fiction, and characters, their names and situations are the product of the author's imagination. Any resemblance to persons living or dead is entirely coincidental.

No part of this book may be reproduced or transmitted in any form or by any means, electronic or mechanical, including photocopying, recording, or by any information storage and retrieval system, without permission in writing from the author.

Cover image by Fotolia
Author photo by Jean Schiller

ISBN-13: 978-1-500-96714-7
ISBN-10: 1-500-96714-9

Printed and bound in the United States of America

September 2014
20 19 18 17 16 15 14    1 2 3 4 5

# Vinnie's Wife

## ONE

In the dream Myra is perfectly, perfectly content. And, truly, does she not have every reason to be? Look at that dress someone has poured her into: cabernet-colored silk spilling over every curve. And her hair: expertly tamed into a complicated knot and pinned behind one ear—simply amazing!

Oh, yes, she is elegant; radiant; to all the world the embodiment of an accomplished woman in total control of her life and her destiny.

If only she could figure out what the man in the three-piece suit is doing on the floor at her feet. With his head of thick, silvery-gray hair he reminds her quite a bit of Phil Donahue. And when he tilts back his head to look her in the face, she realizes: he *is* Phil Donahue.

And what he is doing—apparently—is shaving her legs.

She opens her mouth to speak, and in her syrupy dream voice she hears herself say, "What…time…is…it…?" The question's not even in the neighborhood of what she wants to know.

Through his trendy, aviator-style glasses, Phil peers at her earnestly—almost lovingly—before breaking into his slightly lopsided signature smile; and in her sleep, Myra groans softly.

This would not by any means be her first nutty, unsettling dream. (She suspects she experiences them more often than most people do.) One night Elvis himself turned up at the foot of her bed, a young Elvis dressed all in black. There was he: languidly strumming his guitar and piercing her with a blue-eyed stare, begging (with that little hitch in his voice) *love me tender…never let me go. A*nd she: brimming with pity, soggy with desire, helpless to resist.

Another time, she materialized on the fifty-yard line at Soldier Field wearing nothing but a football helmet; and once, decked out in a loincloth and a towering headdress made of peacock feathers, she led President Reagan's motorcade down Michigan Avenue. Other, similar dreams she has managed to put out of her mind altogether, but this is the first ever to feature Phil Donahue.

Which is kind of surprising when you consider that during those long years before Jennifer and Howie were old enough for school, she thought of him as the other man in her life. His program came on at eleven o'clock, right before Bozo's Circus, and she never missed a show if she could help it. And the things they talked about—disease! dysfunction! despair!—the women who were guests, and those who called in to comment, and all their problems, many of them so intimate they had never before been discussed over the public airwaves.

Normally, Myra ran the vacuum during the commercials, but one show in particular angered her enough that she actually picked up the phone and dialed in, and that was the morning Phil had on a panel of women who'd left their husbands and given up custody of their children. In their discussion they kept tossing around phrases like "marital struggle" and "opting for freedom" and "commitment to honesty."

What nonsense! Women's libbers may have been barging their way through the movement's second decade, but some things were still better left alone. In Myra's opinion, mothers with little children ought to be committed to hanging in there, to sticking it out. That is what she'd wanted to say.

Someone put her on hold. While she waited and cleared her throat, Howie slid off her lap. Myra found him at the other end of the kitchen, sampling cat kibble from a plastic bowl. She grabbed him and knocked the bowl away; and then, with the telephone receiver wedged against her neck, she pinned him between her knees and tried to excavate the goo from his mouth with her forefinger. He was still squirming and hollering bloody murder when the phone went *click*. There on the line was Phil Donahue himself, speaking right into her ear. "We're waiting, Caller," he was saying, "are you there?"

"I, uh—" was all she managed to blurt out before the receiver dropped off her shoulder and clattered to the floor. But here's Phil now, in her dream, gliding a safety razor over her bare knee.

"There is absolutely no reason to be nervous," he says gently. "Just tell them why."

"Why?" She is trying her best to understand. "Why, what?"

"Why your husband has left you."

"Oh," she says dully. "That."

Now she gets it. Phil is grooming her for an appearance on his television show. He's planning to put her on stage under blazing lights and ask a bunch of smart-alecky questions. "Myra Greenburg Calderelli," he'll say, his voice ticking with as much exasperation as sympathy, "what in the wide world has gone wrong with your marriage?"

She licks her lips and wrings one damp hand with the other. So this is what she gets for all those years of sitting back smugly and watching other women in crisis struggle to pull their lives back together. "I don't think I could," she tells Phil. "My license has expired. I mean, what if I take the wrong bus..."

She cannot get the words right, but he seems to understand. "Begin at the beginning," he says, stroking her foot and leaning in close. She expects he might kiss her (is actually hoping he will) when without warning—without a word or a sign or even an inkling—the dream suddenly ends. Phil is gone, vanished into thin air; and an angry, frustrated, disappointed Myra finds herself wide awake.

*Rats...oh, rats...*

She mutters, punches the pillow and rolls over, flinging an arm across the empty side of the bed. She keeps her eyes closed and wills herself back into the dream, but it's no good. Phil Donahue and the red dress and the whole sexy feeling have evaporated faster than a splash of gravy in a hot oven. Then come the night thoughts—those marching doubts and terrors she does not have time to deal with during the day—and that cancels sleep for good. Kicking the covers aside, she opens one eye and stomps into the bathroom.

The house is cold and, except for a night light glowing weakly in Howie's room, dark. Myra reaches behind the bathroom door for the navy blue robe with the smell of Vinnie's aftershave on the collar. He didn't bother to take the robe when he left, though he did pack the matching pajamas. The whole outfit was a Christmas present from his mother, who for his birthday had bought him a two week supply of tee-shirts and jockey shorts.

She presses the collar of the robe to her nose. He didn't say where he was going, and the only explanation he offered was that he needed a little time to himself, space of his own; he claimed he had a few things to work out. Myra stood there speechless, holding on to her elbows, feeling as if she had just been beaned by a foul ball at Wrigley Field and afraid that if she moved she'd crack apart like an egg. This could not really be happening but there he was, snapping the suitcase, giving her a peck on the cheek, walking out the door. It closed behind him with a *click, thud*.

The Monday night news had just begun.

There'd been an earthquake in Chile. Floods in Texas. A double murder on the South Side. Another Cook County patronage scandal, this time in the assessor's office. And it was beginning to look like Princess Diana's marriage was also in trouble.

Then the scowling business reporter came on to yammer some more about the latest dive in the stock market, and Myra supposed if she knew anything about the stock market she would have had to be alarmed. But in that regard she was blissfully ignorant, and by the time the weathergirl finished delivering the forecast for a mild, sunny tomorrow, she had regained a little of her senses. With responsibility for two young children, several family pets and a house that does not run itself, falling apart is an option unavailable to her.

And anyway, he called from work early the next morning to let her know he would be by on Sunday. He said he'd take the children somewhere for the day, and if she was running short of cash he'd give her some. She was tempted to gush with gratitude until she realized he planned to stay away the whole week. At that moment, a dozen questions popped into her head, and not a single one could she ask and expect a reasonable answer. Vinnie was king of evasions. Face to face, he'd avert his eyes, mumble, turn a shoulder; on the phone, he would change the subject or rush off.

"I gotta go," he said, and she could picture his discomfort at her silence. "Call me here if you need to."

"Fine." She hung up first so she would not have to listen to the dead hum on the line.

Well, then. Sunday.

She turns on the faucet in the sink, splashes her face and sips from her palm. The water leaves the metallic taste of old pipes on her tongue.

Copper, she thinks.

*Lead?* What has she done with that article on lead poisoning? Probably filed it with the warnings about radon gas and contaminated chicken. She dries her face and goes to check on Howie, putting a hand to his back (yes, still breathing) as he lies curled around his pillow, a plastic action figure in his fist. She wishes Vinnie could see him: holding on for dear life, it seemed. *Look at what you are doing to this poor child*, she would say. *He doesn't really believe you had to go away suddenly on vacation.*

If she were interested in being fair she would have to admit that their son has always had a tendency to be timid and—more often than she cared to admit—annoyingly clingy. Kissing him lightly on the forehead, she is suddenly lonely for the days when he woke in the night and had to be rocked back to sleep.

In Jennifer's room, confronted with her daughter's empty bed, she stands frozen in the doorway for a full ten seconds before reminding herself that Jennifer is spending the night at her friend's house across the street.

Myra lets out the breath she was holding. Feeling her way in the darkness, she comes downstairs to the kitchen, switches on the light and shields her eyes against the glare. Her heart is still beating a little too quickly.

She has not had a decent night's sleep all week, and it's beginning to get to her. The other day, putting away groceries, she discovered she'd tucked her wallet into the vegetable drawer in the refrigerator and left a package of Klondike bars melting on a pantry shelf. And yesterday she took a phone call from her sister-in-law, Loretta, and forgot about the pot of spaghetti on the stove. By the time she finished cleaning up the boiled-over mess and laid out their supper, the children had already polished off half a box of Cheez-Its. They spent twenty minutes twirling pasta around their plates before she gave up and allowed them to leave the table.

Once, not terribly long ago, Myra was the kind of person who had her fingers on every little detail. She drew up lists, kept calendars, saw to it that her family always had clean clothes and the correct amount of servings from the four basic food groups; and lately—on top of everything else—she has undertaken a small business enterprise of her own: selling lingerie at home parties. But now, with Vinnie away, everything has gone a little wobbly, as if the solid ground beneath her feet was slowly turning into goulash.

Possibly, the wobbly feeling has something to do with the amount of caffeine she's been ingesting. The coffeemaker she received for Mother's Day will not work properly if she makes less than four cups, so each morning she drinks her two plus the two Vinnie would have drunk (would have drunk if he hadn't gone off somewhere for some reason she still cannot fathom, though she's been trying for nearly a week). She takes her coffee black with a little sugar and finishes the pot before noon.

It's almost like an act of faith, she has come to believe.

Measuring grounds from the blue Maxwell House can into the Mister Coffee filter basket, she allows herself a brief but satisfying fantasy of him at her door tomorrow morning. He (with the fervor of a man who has only just realized what he almost lost): pleading for her to take him back, grabbing for her hand and pressing it to his lips. And she: allowing an exquisite pause before the slow, sweet embrace. There will be weeping, yes; forgiveness, probably. And in the distance a swell of violins, the faint echo of a horn…

✥✥✥

The aroma of brewing coffee lures her back to reality. She pours a cup and drinks it standing at the sink, watching through the window as the sky turns from midnight blue to misty dawn. (Maybelline eye shadow colors, she muses; she is determined to someday find the perfect shade: one that will bring out the green flecks in her brown eyes without making her look like a vampire.) Across the alley, the houses are still dark. By the time their kitchen lights begin to come on, she is ready to set down her cup and head for the basement.

Saturday has always been Myra's scheduled day for laundry. In their early married years, Vinnie often accompanied her to the coin-op down the street from the kosher bakery in their neighborhood, and they'd spend the morning eating donuts and watching their clothes tumbling together: her blouses and his shirts, his socks and her panties. Marriage was like that, she used to think, a mingling of two lives, a sharing of yourself with the other person so that you became part of one another, so you were no longer just yourself alone.

"What's happening, Vinnie?" she managed to ask just before he went through the door. "Don't you love me?"

He stopped and turned to her, squinting in exasperation. "That ain't the point."

"But I thought love was all you needed—"

"Yeah, yeah. You sound like a Beatles record."

Didn't he realize how much that hurt? Blinking away tears, she gropes for the fabric softener and inadvertently knocks a scrub brush off the shelf. The noise echoes sharply and startles the dog, who has been sleeping by the furnace; and struggling to her feet now, she begins to bark.

"Hush," Myra whispers. She has only a minute or so to get Brownie into the back yard before she loses control of her bowels. The dog has a delicate digestive system, the result of improper feeding by a previous owner. As quietly as she can, Myra leads her up the stairs and unlocks the back door, but now the cats are awake, and from the living room she can hear the tentative mutterings of the parrot, Angelo.

Here's one fact of which Myra is painfully aware: she has a ridiculous number of animals. Years ago, she started out with a single gray tabby that Vinnie had found sitting atop the dumpster behind the Dominick's Finer Food store where he managed the produce department. That was Lucy. They got the dog when Jennifer was a baby, Myra feeling that children and dogs naturally belonged together. Then one morning, on her way back from walking Brownie, she came across a starved-looking white cat huddled inside a cardboard box. An hour later it was still there. The box was empty when she went to check it in the afternoon, but the cat was back that night.

She brought it home and called it Ethel because it ate constantly and seemed friendly toward the other cat. Not until weeks later did she discover Ethel's true identity.

"This is a little boy kitty cat," Dr. Thornberry told her when she took the cat in to be spayed. She could see he was trying not to laugh.

"A male? But he has no—"

"No, of course not. He's already been fixed." He tickled Ethel under his chin. "Yes, Mrs. Calderelli, this fella used to belong to somebody."

Somebody who apparently did not care a speck about him anymore. Myra was indignant. She'd put an ad in the paper and notices on the bulletin board at the supermarket, and no one stepped forward to claim him. "Honestly," she huffed, "I simply don't know what this world is coming to."

"Lucky there are good folks like you around."

"Well, someone has to take responsibility."

"And look on the bright side. You got yourself a free cat." He smiled and handed her the bill, twenty-five dollars for a quick look-see and a couple of shots.

Now Ethel winds around her legs while Lucy paces the countertops. Myra grabs Ethel and shoves a pill down his throat (he has a bladder condition, wouldn't you know, and requires daily medication and a special diet). She lets the dog back inside and wipes her feet with a pair of Vinnie's tattered shorts. She is hurrying to fix their bowls—various kibbles mixed with yogurt or eggs or canned food to entice them to eat the kibble—because in the living room Angelo is growing impatient.

*Son-of-a-bitch!*

He screeches the greeting as she uncovers his cage and opens the door. "I-could-have-been-some-one," she says to him, enunciating each syllable. It's Brando's line from Vinnie's favorite movie, and she has been trying to teach it to the bird for years. He listens with his head cocked, then swings himself out of the cage by his beak and climbs to the top, where he regards her with the bead of his orange eye.

*Besa-mi-o-cu-lo!*

Hopeless. Angelo once belonged to an uncle of Vinnie's who had taught him to swear in three languages. When the uncle died, she took the bird. Well, she had to, didn't she? He still had fifty or so years left on his life expectancy, and no one else had offered to give him a home.

She changes Angelo's water and adds seed to his dish, and then she pours herself another cup of coffee. By now, the sun has come up. In the back yard, sparrows and chickadees dart around a birdfeeder that one of the children fashioned out of an empty milk carton, twigs and yarn. The feeder hangs from a branch of the crooked little olive tree, which stands in the shadow of the maple tree whose brilliant red leaves are littering the ground. She really ought to make a start on raking them today; and later, if she's not too worn out, she might pick up where she left off cleaning and re-organizing the kitchen cabinets.

A moment after lifting the coffee cup to her lips she realizes: she has not yet managed to get going on that load of whites.

෧෧෧

The telephone keeps ringing while she's in the basement, and she has to keep rushing upstairs to answer it. Two of the calls are for Jennifer, who still isn't home. The third turns out to be someone inquiring about a chair.

"Chair?"

"Yep, in the Traders Gazette." A woman's voice grinds at Myra's ear. "The ad says you got a club chair for sale."

She puts two fingers to her forehead and thinks hard. "Oh, yes," she says, snapping to attention. (How could she possibly have forgotten!) "The chair is still for sale." Her voice has dropped a full octave and now sounds resonant with authority. "When would you like to come by and look at it?"

"How 'bout right now?"

"Now would be just fine." She gives the woman her address, hangs up with a measured "goodbye," rushes upstairs to swap the bathrobe for a zippered sweatshirt and a wraparound skirt, and then begins a frantic rush to put the house in some kind of order.

She has been trying to clear out the big front hall closet, and now stacks of boxes and piles of clothing are lying all over the living room. (If she hadn't been so distracted by this Vinnie thing, she would certainly have finished sorting through them by now.) She moves the stacks and piles toward the corners of the room, where she hopes they will be less noticeable, and collects the empty drinking glasses, last Sunday's newspapers, and the several chew bones scattered around the floor. (Amazing how things accumulate if you do not keep after them every little minute.) Twenty minutes later, she opens the front door to a chubby woman with a dark mole above her lip.

Myra leads her up the stairs and points toward the master bedroom where the chair—puffy turquoise vinyl on bent chrome legs—hulks like a sumo wrestler in a far corner.

"That thing any good for sitting in?" the chubby woman says.

"It's extremely comfortable. And the design is an excellent example of classical modern."

The chubby woman says, "Hmmm." She walks up to the chair, pokes at the fabric, bends to examine the legs and then turns and plants her bottom on the seat, her feet springing off the floor as she sits back.

"How much you asking?"

"Fifty dollars." Myra folds her arms across her chest, a little body English to emphasize the firmness of her price.

The chair is not really hers to sell. Vinnie dragged it into the marriage, the only piece of furniture worth rescuing from his bachelor apartment. The morning after he left, after she got the children off to school and cleaned up the breakfast dishes and made a phone call about the Let's Be Lovers party she had set up for the following evening, she put her head down on her arms and gave herself over to several minutes of uncontrolled sobbing. After that, she mopped her eyes and called the Traders Gazette to place the ad.

"That's your best price, I suppose."

Myra notes the challenge in the woman's voice, typical of every bargain hunter she has ever encountered. She needs to gird herself for the coming skirmish, but she's become aware of Howie moving around in the bathroom, and now she hears him calling.

"Mom…?"

Excusing herself, she goes to peek into the bathroom, where she finds him standing on the toilet seat, staring at himself in the medicine chest mirror.

"Mom…?" he says again.

Myra whispers fiercely, "*What?*"

"How come we have eyebrows?" He brings his own together over the bridge of his nose, lifts them and lowers them, and his face suddenly acquires a disturbingly solemn expression.

Howie is at the age when a child's natural curiosity is running at top speed, morning to night, and she knows how important it is to answer all of his questions. Still, with the chubby woman in the bedroom, attempting to turn the chair on its side, she says the first thing that comes into her head.

"To keep the dust out of our eyes."

"That's why we have eye*lashes*. You said. I wanna know about eye*brows*."

"Would it be possible to discuss this later, Howie?"

"Uh-uh." He swivels his head slowly from side to side but keeps his eyes on the mirror.

"All right, then. The reason we have eyebrows is…because…if we didn't have them, how would anyone know when we were surprised?"

The answer seems to satisfy him. He says, "Will Dad be home today?"

"No, Howie. Today is *Saturday*. I told you he would come on *Sunday*. Don't you remember—"

"Missus!" the chubby woman calls. "There's a nick, right here on the arm."

Myra leaves Howie to get dressed and re-enters the bedroom. "A nick, you say? Well, I am not a bit surprised. This chair has quite a story connected to it."

"Oh, yeah?"

"Have you ever heard of the Evening in Paris on Ontario Street?"

"What's that, a bar?"

"A modern art gallery, with the most interesting paintings and sculptures. That chair was part of the furnishings."

"So? It's not worth more than twenty bucks no matter where it came from. I'd have to buy a vinyl repair kit and match up the color and everything."

"All kinds of famous people used to drop by," Myra continues, undaunted. "It was my friend's husband who owned the place, and I'd often get to talk with writers…and artists—"

"And movie stars?"

"Oh…yes. Many movie stars—"

The chubby woman narrows her eyes. "Like who?"

Myra is inventing as she goes. She tries out several famous names until she hits on one that causes the chubby woman's jaw to drop. "*You*? Met Dustin *Hoffman*!"

"He is the nicest man, and he's much taller in person."

"Do you know if he sat in this chair?"

"As a matter of fact, he did. As I remember, he was sitting in it when my friend's husband brought me over and introduced us."

"Oh, my…" The chubby woman comes forward to touch the seat, eyes shiny with reverence. In the kitchen, the phone has started ringing again. Myra waits to see if Howie will pick up, and when he does not she excuses herself and speeds downstairs.

"I didn't call to talk to you," says the voice on the other end. It belongs to Myra's mother, Nettie. "Where are my grandchildren?"

"Good morning, Ma."

"You have a nerve calling me 'Ma' after the way you spoke to me yesterday."

Myra closes her eyes and counts slowly to five. Yesterday, in a moment of weakness, she let it slip that she had not seen Vinnie all week, and Nettie glommed on to that fact like a shark to meat. "I apologize. Really. I'm sorry I yelled."

There is an audible sigh on the other end of the line. Myra wets a finger and wipes a jelly print off the light switch. Nettie's voice comes at her again, smaller this time. "I only asked one question—"

"Ma…"

"—if you called a lawyer—that's all I asked!"

"…you're starting again."

"Sue me. I just wanted to know. I'm your mother."

"I've already told you there is nothing to see a lawyer about. I'm handling things—"

"I know how you handle. Listen, this could be a blessing in disguise. Daddy thinks you should talk to his cousin Sam. For family he wouldn't charge too much."

Myra rubs her eyes. "I have to go. Someone's here."

"Who?"

"A lady. She's going to buy the turquoise chair."

"You're selling off the furniture? Darling, tell me the truth. Do you need money?"

"Later, okay?"

She hangs up. Turning, she nearly bumps into the chubby woman, who is standing in the doorway. "About the chair," she says. "I suppose I could come up with a couple dollars more."

"Yes, well—"

And before Myra can get out another word, the back door bangs open. A backpack sails through and lands on the floor; then Jennifer enters, her hair a wild tangle of curls around her face. "Did Heather call?" she says. "Cause if she did, tell her that I am never speaking to her again." She drops her coat on top of the backpack, kicks off her shoes and heads for the refrigerator.

"Good morning, dear. Heather didn't call."

"What about Amanda?"

"I can't be sure. You got two calls, but no one left their name."

"God, Mom! Whyn't you ask who it was? Did a boy call?"

"I don't know. One of them might have been a boy."

"God!" Jennifer jams a blueberry muffin into her mouth and stomps out of the room, trailing muffin crumbs across the floor.

Myra picks up the coat and backpack and shoves the shoes into a corner. "Hormones," she says.

"None a my kids ever talk to me like that." The mole on the chubby woman's lip is a little brown ball, bouncing over each word.

"It's hell being eleven."

"Back a the hand upside the head. Works every time. Now about the chair. I suppose I could come up with twenty-five dollars."

Myra nods, but now she's not sure she wants to sell Vinnie's chair. Putting the ad in the paper was a crazy, impulsive thing to do. He will pitch an absolute fit when he finds out. "I'm afraid I couldn't take a penny less than forty-five dollars," she says, certain of killing the sale.

"Thirty." The chubby woman stares her in the eye.

"Really, I—"

"Thirty-five…forty…" Her voice has shifted into auctioneer mode. "Forty-two fifty."

Myra sits down at the kitchen table, suddenly exhausted. "Look, why don't we just forget the whole—"

"All right, all right. Forty-five dollars." She opens her purse and fishes for the money. "Lady, you sure drive a hard bargain."

Myra drops her chin into her hand. She has always hated that piece of furniture. Once it is gone, she will no longer have to walk sideways to get to the closet or lug it halfway across the room to vacuum behind it. Who needed a big, ugly chair like that in the bedroom anyway? "I can help you carry it to your car," she says as the chubby woman counts bills into her hand.

Howie appears now, barefoot and shirtless, his jeans half zipped. He climbs onto a chair and says, "Make me pancakes."

"In a minute, Sweetie. I have something to do first."

"I'm hungry."

"I understand, but I have to—"

"Don't bother about the chair. My kid's waiting in the van. He'll get it." The chubby woman gives her a meaningful look. "That boy wouldn't dare open a mouth to me."

Defiant, Myra hooks an arm around Howie's waist—yes, his manners could stand a little bit of improvement, but so what?—and plants a loud kiss on his shoulder.

"Quit it, Mom," he whines, squirming out of her embrace. "You're getting me wet."

❖❖❖

She fortifies herself with another cup of coffee before dialing the number of the dress shop where her mother works. "Roberta's Closet," Nettie croons, her business voice much friendlier than the one Myra is used to hearing. "How may I help you?"

"It's me. Can you talk?"

"Sure. Wait a sec." She puts down the phone. Myra hears the scrape of a chair, and then Nettie is back. "So how's by you, *bubbeleh*," she says, greasing her words in Yiddish inflections, a la Rose Greenburg, Myra's grandmother.

"Ma, you're terrible."

Nettie chuckles. "It'll be a sad day when they pass a law against making fun of your husband's mother. So tell me, did you sell the chair?"

Myra admits she has.

"How much did you get?"

"More than I expected. I told her Dustin Hoffman's *tush* once touched the seat."

"You are your mother's daughter," Nettie says approvingly. Myra allows herself a little smile and waits for her mother to sling the next question. But her mood seems to have mellowed; she makes no mention of Vinnie or cousin Sam, the lawyer. Instead, she turns the subject to an old friend of hers. "Bea Skolnick. Used to be in my poker club. Nice-looking woman, a dyed blonde. I ran into her yesterday at the dry cleaners."

"I don't think I remember her."

"You went out with her son once or twice. Lenny."

Myra thinks of a skinny boy with overly long arms. *Lenny?*

"Don't say it like that. You wouldn't believe him now. A big shot with the Sara Lee company, house in Highland Park, three kids. Remember how crazy he was about you?"

"Please, Ma—"

"Really! Bea told me you broke his heart."

Myra sighs. So there it is again, the insistent rattle she has been hearing for years: she threw her life away on Vinnie when she should have used her head and married a Somebody. In one way or another, it's the quicksand under every conversation.

"Anyway, I told her all about you and the children, showed her a few pictures. And I mentioned that my son-in-law was a mid-level executive for a regional food company."

"Good one, Ma."

"It's not exactly a lie. Why shouldn't she think the best?"

Myra lets her rattle on, knowing that eventually a customer will walk into the store and Nettie will have to ring off.

She fills her cup with the last of the coffee and unplugs the machine. The kitchen is growing warmer now. Golden beams of sunlight slant across the countertops and the floor (which, if she had married Lenny Skolnick, would be inlaid tile and solid oak instead of Formica and linoleum). Sunlight grazes the school papers stuck to the refrigerator and bounces off the gray stripes on Lucy the cat, who lies curled in the basket of folded clothes.

Out in the back yard, Howie is digging in the dirt with a spoon: Howie with those dark, dramatic eyebrows so much like Vinnie's. Jennifer has his smooth olive skin. Myra hoists her feet onto a chair and rubs absently at the stubble on her legs.

What has gone wrong with her marriage?

Nothing.

Nothing at all. This episode of Vinnie's is only a passing madness, and no matter what anyone thinks, she refuses to believe she has thrown her life away. Wouldn't she know in her bones if anything was truly, seriously wrong?

Of course she would.

The coffee in her cup is tepid now; muddy, too. She doesn't want it, but she drinks it anyway, downing it in gulps, like medicine.

## TWO

If the registrar at Loop Junior College had not screwed up her schedule that second winter term, putting her into Philosophy 101 instead of Principles of Accounting, Myra might never have met him at all. She saw no reason to make a fuss over the mix-up since she'd have had to take the philosophy course eventually. And anyway, that first evening of class she had other things on her mind.

Her six-month relationship with Byron Levine, the psych major from Roosevelt University, had reached a critical juncture. Any day now he would be asking her to wear his ring, to commit herself to someday become Mrs. Byron Levine. She was sure of it, and she kept wondering if she could be happy with a man who made her sit through brooding Scandinavian films; who coaxed her to eat things like paella, calamari, escargot; who thought the Chad Mitchell Trio was tops.

On the other hand, he did have a pleasant voice, wavy blonde hair, interesting hazel-colored eyes and a promising future. And he was tall enough that when he took her on a dress-up date she could wear her high heels. She was so busy weighing the pros and cons of Byron Levine she almost failed to notice the boy in the brown leather jacket who followed their instructor, Mr. Karimer, into the room.

From her seat in the back, she watched him coast through the rows of desks, taking his sweet time even though Mr. Karimer was tapping for attention and calling the roll.

"Aronsen!"

"Here."

"Barton!"

"Here."

"Bender!"

"Here."

"Calderelli!"

No one answered to the last name. Mr. Karimer called again. "Vincent Joseph Calderelli?"

Leather jacket boy held up two fingers. "Yo!" he said. Then he slid into the seat right next to hers.

*And here comes trouble.*

Myra knew about boys like him, dangerous boys with cruel good looks and devil-may-care attitudes. Never had she gotten closer than she had to, and she was certainly not about to start now. With careful attention she opened her notebook, uncapped a purple felt pen and wrote the date in shaky script at the top of the page.

The lecture that evening was on thought versus sensation, the differences between the two. Dutifully she took notes, her pen looping and zagging across the page. She tried not to be distracted by the oily-sweet scent of hair tonic that kept drifting her way (Byron Levine, she realized, always smelled of bread) and she resisted with all her might the urge to write down the name Vincent Joseph Calderelli in her notebook and dot the i's with fat little hearts.

The minute class was over she gathered her books and made for the door. Everyone seemed to be leaving at once. Trapped there in the logjam, she detected the scent of hair tonic again, and then he was beside her, saying something she could barely hear, so loudly was her pulse pounding in her ears.

"Pardon?" She angled her head in his direction but kept her eyes focused forward.

"I asked if you want a coffin nail." He held out a box of Marlboro's and flipped up the lid with his thumb.

She took a cigarette because it was simpler than explaining that she didn't smoke. He lit it for her. She exhaled and forced herself not to cough.

"So," he said, "you got a name that goes with Greenburg?"

For a moment she considered giving him a false one; but there, right on the cover of her notebook (if he cared to look) was her full name printed in large capital letters; and so she answered, "M-Myra."

He tested the name on his tongue. They were moving again, walking out the door together, it seemed. Just as she was about to turn and flee, he stretched an arm up against the wall, blocking her way.

"Tell me something," he said, and his voice was like the rasp of a steel file over bricks. "You think your boyfriend would freak out if I bought you a cup of coffee?"

His head was very close to hers: they were almost the same height. His eyes, when she finally looked into them, reminded her of the lake at midnight: calm and deep, with the moon shining over the water. He had very white teeth and a small scar under one eye. His nose looked as if it may have been broken once or twice. He was beautiful—and also vulnerable, a combination so appealing it made her lips tremble.

"I—don't have a boyfriend," she heard herself say as something inside her began to unfurl. At that moment she realized she cared not a crumb if she ever again in her life got to puzzle over another art house film or wonder about the meat in a mysterious ethnic dish, and she offered not a bit of resistance when he took her elbow and steered her out of the building. His touch was like fire, but it was the way he said her name that made her melt: *My-ra*, drawing out the first syllable and holding it in his mouth, as if he were already claiming her for his own.

Now, all these years later, she waits for him, watching the street from her bedroom window. It is a beautiful autumn day and she is full of hope. When the black Cutlass swings into view, she checks her hair in the mirror one last time and comes downstairs to open the door, feeling as jittery as she did on their first date.

She shapes her mouth into a greeting, but Brownie gets to him first, nearly knocking Myra over in her frenzy. She barks and yelps and tries to leap into Vinnie's arms. "Easy, girl," he says, struggling not to drop the cardboard box of fruits and vegetables he has brought. There are oranges, pears, grapes, bananas, a giant head of romaine lettuce, a red cabbage and a bunch of knobby green roots that Myra could not identify if her life depended on it.

"No melons?" she says.

"Maybe next week." He shakes the dog off his leg and carries the box into the kitchen.

Next week?

How much longer is he planning to keep this up? She shuts the front door—*click, thud*—and the noise sends an echo right down her spine.

He comes out of the kitchen and settles himself at the edge of the couch. "Kids ready?"

She takes the wing-back chair. With the mix of emotions running through her, she doesn't trust herself to sit any closer. She is liable to do anything—punch him in the face, fall at his feet...

But no, she could not do either one. That's no way to get anywhere with him. Forcing herself to be calm, she says, "The children will be down in a minute," and adds, "They've missed you."

He ducks his head. "Yeah, well..." He runs a hand through his hair, thinner than it used to be. He's put on weight, too, but he still looks good. What woman could resist him? And she isn't so naïve as to suppose there's not another woman somewhere in all of this.

"I was hoping we could at least talk about it," she says.

"What? You need a few bucks?"

"Not really, but that's not what—"

"Here." He reaches into a back pocket for his wallet, opens it and exposes a wad of bills.

She watches as he lays two twenties on the table, a moment later adding a ten dollar bill to the pile. "You shouldn't be carrying all this money around," she says. "It's dangerous. What if you get mugged?"

He jerks a thumb at his shoulder. "No one in their right mind's gonna mess with me. What're you worrying for?"

"I'm not worrying. But we do live in a big city, you know, with all kinds of people. Druggies. Crazies. They wouldn't have the good sense to be afraid of you."

He looks away. "Stop."

She presses her lips together. Then, refocusing, she says, "I told the children you had to go on a little vacation by yourself. What am I supposed to tell them now?"

He shrugs, avoiding her eyes. "Tell them I'm still on a vacation. Say that sometimes people need to be away from each other for a while."

He glances at her, weaving left a little, then right. Vinnie used to box in Golden Gloves. It was long ago, when he was in his teens, but he hasn't forgotten how to do the fancy footwork, maneuver her into corners, dodge the issues. In all their married years they have never engaged in the kind of serious discussions you see on television talk shows, and she has always taken that as evidence of the strength of their relationship. Now she watches glumly as he jiggles his knee, anxious to be gone.

"Where in hell are those kids?" He stands and hollers their names. "Get a move on, would you!" and in a moment they are scrambling down the stairs and into his arms. "Take us bowling, Dad!" they shout. "Let's eat at Red Lobsters!" Brownie tries to wriggle her way into the happy little group. If Myra dropped through the floor, no one would notice.

She gathers their jackets from the hall closet. Squinting at Jennifer she says, "Is that lipstick you're wearing?"

"I bought it with my own money."

"That is not the point. You are much too young for makeup—Howie, wait! Take your hat. You, too, Jen—"

"They're only going in the car," Vinnie says. "Why're you getting so excited?"

"Excited? Me? These children both had the sniffles last week. You wouldn't know anything about that, of course, being away on *vacation*, but I was here with the vaporizer and the chest rub. I was the one who sat up all night—"

Howie reaches up for a kiss. "Bye, Mom." Jennifer's already out the door.

"Don't eat too many fries. You know how they upset your tummy—"

And suddenly they're gone, their coats half buttoned, their hats still in her hand. Rubbing at the wrenching feeling in her chest, she watches them climb into the car and drive away. She stares down the street, half hoping they'll come back for her; but a moment later she snaps out of it. She has promised Loretta she would meet her for breakfast at Kelly's Deli on Morse Avenue at ten-thirty, and it's nearly that now.

Before she leaves the house she has to shut the bird into his cage, count the cats, send the dog out to the back yard and remember to bring her back inside, lower the lid on the toilet, turn off the bathroom light and Jennifer's radio, check the knobs on the stove and dial down the thermostat.

What else?

She pulls on her coat, and that is when she spots the umbrella tree sagging against the living room window, pleading silently for water.

"I'm late," Myra explains and vows to tend to the plant the very minute she gets home.

❧❧❧

At the restaurant she finds Loretta thumbing through the Sunday Sun-Times and smoking a cigarette. To look at her, you would never suspect she was divorced three times and the mother of three children. Except for a tendency to wear too much jewelry, she appears as normal as anyone else in the place. Myra slides into the booth opposite her, slightly out of breath.

"Something the matter?" Loretta stubs the cigarette into an ashtray. "You don't look so good."

"Just a little stitch in my side. I walked here."

"I could of picked you up."

"To drive me, what, six blocks? Don't be absurd. The walk was fine. Good exercise." She snaps open the menu, and the words swim together. Last night she dreamed her gynecologist, fat Dr. Gurvitz, was chasing her down the street. He had on his blue lab coat and roller skates; she wore a skimpy nightgown and a pair of construction boots with pink laces. She woke up sweating and gasping, and then could not fall back to sleep.

"Why're you looking at the menu?" Loretta says. "You always order the same thing."

"And that is supposed to mean—what?"

Loretta holds up her hands. "Nothing. It don't mean nothing. Boy, you sure are touchy today."

*Anything*, Myra thinks. *Doesn't mean anything*. When will she stop murdering the language? She studies the menu awhile longer. When the waitress arrives, she asks for her usual: a plain waffle and a glass of skim milk.

Loretta orders the Windy City Special. "Eggs fried over easy," she tells the waitress, "don't break the yolks. Bacon real crisp, light brown toast, no seeds in the juice. And bring me some coffee from a fresh pot."

Myra cannot imagine how a little person like her can put away so much food, "Do you ever think about cholesterol and nitrites?" she blurts out before she can stop herself. "And I'll bet you don't even carry a calorie counter in your purse."

Loretta lays her hands flat on the table and stares Myra in the eye. "You're right, I don't. But this isn't about me or what I eat or don't eat. How 'bout you tell me what the real problem is, okay?"

"What makes you think there's a problem?" Myra says, shredding her napkin. "Everything is just…fine."

"Look, you can level with me, whatever it is. Your kids dealing dope? Your mother get arrested? My brother run off with the lady from Mary Kay?"

Myra sucks in a breath and bites her lip.

"Hey, take it easy." She reaches for Myra's arm. "I was only kidding."

All around her, people are buttering toast, forking up eggs, clattering cups into saucers; they're chatting and laughing as though everything in the world was just hunky dory. Myra presses two fingers to her lips. Then she lets the words tumble out.

"He's been gone all week, and it doesn't look like he's coming home anytime soon. Right now he's at the zoo or the park or somewhere with the children, like all the other single fathers. I tried, but I can't get him to talk to me—" She sighs. "Well, you know your brother."

"Jesus." Loretta sits back, taking it all in. "You guys have a big fight or something?"

Myra shakes her head. "We never fight."

"You think he's shacked up with some bimbo?"

"I don't know. Maybe."

"Listen, if you want, I could ask a couple of my friends to follow him after work, see where he goes—"

"No!" She clears her throat. "I mean, this is probably just some kind of mid-life thing. I'm making too much of it. But thanks for listening."

"I get it," Loretta says, lifting her chin and looking down her nose, "you don't wanna know what he's up to."

Myra can feel the heat of her disapproval, but if there is one thing she absolutely does not need right now it's more complications. And anyway, with three failed marriages on her record, Loretta is hardly the person to consult about repairing a relationship. "I'll have to handle this my own way," Myra tells her. "I guess I'll just wait it out."

"All right, if that's what you want, fine with me. But, hey, look on the bright side. You got the whole day off. We can go drop a bundle of money out at the mall, swing by Halligan's later for a couple drinks..."

Myra shakes her head. "I don't know. I probably won't be very good company."

"You're not exactly a barrel of laughs on your best day," Loretta says, offering Myra a friendly wink. Then the waitress sets down their plates, and she gets busy lavishing salt on her eggs, smearing her toast with butter and jam, dosing her coffee with a big glug of cream and three teaspoons of sugar.

*Hypertension,* Myra thinks. *Diabetes. Heart attack.* She cannot help it. She picks up the maple syrup, dots some on her waffle, and puts the pitcher down.

Loretta grabs it. "Get a life, will ya," she says, drowning the waffle. "I never heard of anyone who died from an overdose of happiness."

In the entire Edens Plaza Shopping Center there is nothing Myra wants. Not the electric blue jacket with the buckles and zippers and shoulder pads out to here; not the jungle print scarves or the fake snakeskin boots; not even the real snakeskin boots that cost almost three hundred dollars. It's all just merchandise to her, things to throw away money on and clutter up the closets.

But Loretta clicks along happily in her three-inch-high platform heels, fingering sweaters and blouses, holding bracelets up to the light. "When I'm down in the dumps," she says, "I go out and buy something for myself. Makes me feel better. One time I ran my MasterCard right up to the limit." She says this as if it were some kind of accomplishment. Rummaging through a sale bin of hats, she plucks one out and plops it onto Myra's head.

Myra stares at her image in the countertop mirror: Billy the Kid's sister. "I don't need another hat," she says, removing it and dropping it back into the bin. "I don't need anything."

"What you need is a new image." Loretta digs in the bin again until she comes up with a hat like the one Ingrid Bergman wore in the movie Casablanca.

Myra adjusts the brim, angling it over one eye. "It's not too much, is it?"

"Twelve seventy-five. Plus tax."

"I mean the style. It's not too…extreme?"

Loretta frowns. "You are one hard case, you know that?"

Myra decides to buy the hat and pays for it with one of the twenties Vinnie gave her. (Unlike Loretta, she uses a credit card only occasionally and when the bill arrives she always mails a check promptly.) In her budget for the month she will list the cost of the hat as a medical expense. It wouldn't be too far from the truth: she is beginning to feel better already—and walking into Halligan's later that afternoon, she finds herself smiling at strangers. Maybe the hat has magical properties, she thinks, like Dorothy's red shoes.

While she scouts for a table in a secluded corner, Loretta heads for one in the middle of the room, and before Myra can object she is already setting up camp. She takes off her coat, checks her face in her makeup mirror, wipes a little finger under each eye and flags down their waiter, a slender young man with spiked blonde hair. "Gimme a Seven and Seven, easy on the ice," she tells him. Myra pulls out a chair and asks for a white wine spritzer.

Halligan's is an old neighborhood place on Ashland Avenue that has over the years tried to update itself. Its new owners put in a picture window, resurfaced the bar and hung a few scraggly ivy plants from hooks in the ceiling. Basically, though, Halligan's is not much better than the Tip Tap Lounge where she and Vinnie used to go when they started to date. He got her a fake ID that said her name was Evelyn Delgado, and that she was twenty-four years old. Myra liked that it was not Myra Greenburg sitting in a dark, smoke-filled tavern, Myra Greenburg would never do that, but Evelyn Delgado could drink like a fish and dance to Carl Perkins on the juke box and neck with Vinnie at a back table until two in the morning.

Evelyn Delgado never got a hangover, either, but Myra Greenburg sure did.

"Whaddya think," Loretta says after their waiter has brought their drinks and walked away, "is he gay or not?"

Myra shrugs. "What difference does it make?"

"You gotta know these things. Dating today is a lot different than it used to be."

"Dating? Are you crazy? I'm a married woman with two children!"

"Technically. But what if that changes? What if Vinnie decides he's not coming home?"

"Don't be ridiculous."

Dating? She's getting queasy just thinking about it. She is still wearing the hat, and now she pulls it lower so it shades half her face. A married woman with two children should not be in a place like this, but look at Loretta: she seems right at home. Though she might be a few years younger than Myra, when it comes to scenes like this she is light years ahead. When Myra was in her teens and worrying whether she could French kiss with a boy on their first date and not get a bad reputation, Loretta was already heating up the back seats of boys' cars. On the very evening of Myra's senior prom, while she was floating around the grand ballroom of the Sherman House Hotel in a long periwinkle blue dress, Loretta was at Mercy Hospital giving birth to her daughter, Cara. Sixteen years old and married barely six months!

Now Myra watches her sister-in-law checking out the room—the people scattered at tables, the crowd watching the Bears game on the television over the bar—sees her rise suddenly and wave to someone coming through the door: a lanky man in a dark wool jacket and cowboy boots. He ambles toward them, bends over Loretta and gives her a kiss right on the lips.

"Yum!" she squeals, oozing with delight. Her friend pulls out a chair and levers himself into it. Myra keeps her eyes low and sips her drink.

"Where've you been keeping yourself, Kyle? I haven't seen you since Andy Morgan's barbecue."

"You know me, Lor. I get around." He laughs an easy laugh. Too easy, Myra thinks. She wonders what he does for a living.

"This is my sister-in-law," Loretta says, shoving Myra between the shoulder blades, forcing her to sit up and take notice. "Myra, Kyle."

He grips her hand, and an easy grin creeps over his face, creasing the skin around his slightly bloodshot eyes. "Well, it is a genuine pleasure to meet you," he says in the voice of a radio announcer on a late night station. She murmurs a response and waits for him to release her; but then he puts his other hand on top of hers, trapping it like a sparrow, and she is surprised at the slight thrill that leaps into her belly.

"Kyle's a pilot," Loretta chirps. "He has his own airplane, and sometimes he takes me up in it."

"Is that a fact?" Myra lifts her head to get a better look at him. Every time she even thinks about flying she gets the urge to run to the bathroom.

He explains about the freight service he operates, the little twin engine Cessna he keeps tied down at Palwaukee Airport.

"When're you gonna take me up again?" Loretta says.

"I'm heading to Des Moines tomorrow, late in the afternoon. Why don't both of you come along?"

"Oh, I couldn't," Myra says quickly. "I have to work."

"Count me in," Loretta says.

"Wait a minute. I need your car tomorrow night. Vinnie took the Cutlass."

"Who's Vinnie?" Kyle asks.

"I thought you could stay with Howie and Jen for a few hours until I get back."

"Howie and Jen who?"

"Hey, Kyle, you'll never guess what kind of work my sister-in-law does. Go on, Myra, tell him."

Kyle peers into her face, sizing her up. "A woman with a career, huh? I like that. I'm guessing you're one of those smart lady lawyers."

"Well, no. Actually, I'm an independent businesswoman. I sell a line of products at home parties—"

"Only it's not Tup-per-ware," Loretta chimes. "Not by a country mile!"

"Well then, what?"

"Lingerie," Myra says.

"And those thingamabobs. Sexual enchanters."

"En*han*cers." She can't help but make the correction.

Over in the corner, a jukebox has started to play, thumping out something by Madonna. Kyle bends his ear. "Sexual *what*?"

"Vibrators!" Loretta shouts. "And a whole bunch of other stuff. Some of it is pret-ty kinky, right Myra?"

"Oh, that depends on your point of view, I guess." Her hand is still imprisoned, and now Kyle has begun to knead it with interest.

"Go on, Myra, tell him how you got started in the first place."

She frees her hand and squirms away, fearful of getting in over her head. "It's such a long story, and I don't really think that—"

"It was on account of me," Loretta says, not without pride. "I brought her to one of those parties, and the lady who was showing us all the stuff took Myra off in a corner and told her she'd be terrific in that line of work. Remember? She said you had lots of... whatchamacallit?"

"Poise and self-confidence." Myra takes a sip of her drink, remembering that night and the way Loretta and those women she worked with at S&C Electric carried on like a pack of horny teenagers while she sat among them and pretended to be invisible. Honestly, it was all such silliness; and yet, she liked the idea of having her own business, especially since Howie was about to become a first-grader. Business was the direction she had been heading when Vinnie careened into her life and forced her to take a detour.

No, put the blame where it belonged: she let her classwork slide because she was too busy flashing her Evelyn Delgado ID at the Tip Tap Lounge and other unsavory places. She didn't want to think further into the future than their next date, but she never figured their relationship would last. That late-spring day when he asked her to marry him, she was so startled she could not speak. And then, when she finally choked out her acceptance, tears of relief flowing down her face, she realized how truly miserable she'd been all along thinking that one day she would have to give him up.

Kyle is still studying her face, and now he is leaning into her with his knee. He offers to buy another round of drinks but Myra says, "I should be going. I'll bet Vinnie and the children are on their way home by now."

"You're married?" He sounds wounded.

"Separated," Loretta says.

"Temporarily." Myra pushes her drink away and struggles into her coat. "So are you coming over tomorrow night?"

Loretta slugs back the rest of her Seven and Seven and signals their waiter. "I'm going to Des Moines with Kyle. But you can have the car. I'll send Cara over and she'll watch the kids."

"What if she's made other plans?"

Loretta snickers. "Plans? Don't make me laugh. Tomorrow's a week night, right? She's always home on weeknights, buried in her school books. You wouldn't catch *her* going out and having a good time."

"If there's a problem," Kyle says, trying to get back into the conversation, "maybe I can help you out." She feels his knee again.

"No thanks. Nice meeting you—"

Loretta puts a hand over her arm. "Hey, what's the hurry? Relax. No one's gonna die if you're a couple minutes late."

❧❧❧

"He likes you," Loretta tells her in the car on the way home. "He'll probably ask me for your phone number."

"Don't do me any favors." Myra is driving, taking the longer route in the hope that by the time she reaches her house, Loretta will be sober enough to take over the wheel.

"Aw, lighten up, kiddo. It'd do you good to have a man hot after your body. And Kyle's a real good shoulder to cry on."

"Well, I'm very sorry to disappoint you, but adultery is just not my thing."

"Oh, ho!" She offers Myra a wink of acknowledgement and flips on the radio, and the car is suddenly filled with the voice of Dolly Parton warbling a ballad of heartache and surrender

*…oh you're out there tonight with another…*

Loretta begins humming along. She has never made a secret of her past, the way she two-timed her second husband with the man who later became her third. It shocked Myra to realize that actual people she knew—not just characters in movies and soap operas—did such things.

And yet, every once in a while, she can't help but envy her. How brave she is, how optimistic! Tonight, for instance, if she is feeling lonely, she'll go back to Halligan's for another drink with Kyle. And if the mood should strike her, she'll fall into bed with him. Myra pictures Kyle's long limbs wrapped around Loretta's tough little body, and she swallows the ache in her throat.

The street lamps are on now, and people hurry around in the five o'clock dusk. This is the weekend they switch back from daylight saving time. Night comes on suddenly after the long drawn-out afternoon, and Myra is happy to be going home.

But when she pulls up to the curb in front of the house, she sees that all the windows are dark. "They must have gone to your mother's for supper," she says heavily.

"See? You didn't have to rush. No one even knows how long you been away." She lifts her head off the seatback, ready to slide behind the wheel.

"Maybe I should call over there. You know, just to make sure they're all right."

Loretta sighs. "You never quit, do you?"

"Would you like to come in for coffee?"

"No thanks, gotta go."

"Sure you're okay?"

She nods.

"Well, then…" Myra opens the car door, gets out and pauses on the curb. It seems there is something she's needing to mention. As she is groping to retrieve a thought from the back of her brain—it's almost, almost on the tip of her tongue—a gust of wind comes up, and to keep her new hat from blowing away she has to clamp one hand to the back of her head.

The gesture seems to propel the thought into her frontal lobe.

"And tell me," she almost shouts, closing the driver's side door and bending toward the window, "what kind of a man can make a living flying a twin engine Cessna? Does that not sound suspicious to you?"

Loretta lets out a groan of impatience. "No," she says, buckling her seatbelt, "no it does not. Not at all."

She puts the car into gear and pulls away from the curb, Myra watching as the tail lights of the dented gray Civic fade into the gathering darkness.

Come to think of it, she would not be surprised—not one tiny little bit surprised—if Loretta's friend was using his twin engine Cessna to smuggle dope. ᛋ

## *THREE*

**M**ary Jean Wilson, the least inhibited of the dozen or so women crowded into the small living room, parades across the carpet in a fishnet bodysuit. Amidst all the hooting and giggling, someone calls, "Hey, girl, isn't it getting a little chilly in there?"

Mary Jean grabs her hips and arches her back. "When Stanley gets a load of me in this," she says, nipples winking through the black mesh, "I won't be cold for long!" She makes a final circuit of the room and disappears into the bedroom.

"Thank you, Mary Jean, thank you very much," Myra says. "The bodysuit is number four-fourteen on your order forms. And now we have another fantasy fashion, which…let me see…Betsy has volunteered to model."

A short woman with blonde curls pokes her head through the doorway, and the women chant, "C'mon, Betsy!" as she minces toward them with shivers of nervous pleasure.

"Betsy is wearing our naughty French maid costume, complete with headband and neck ruffle." While Myra describes the black nylon and white lace getup, Betsy prances to and fro, the miniature skirt flouncing over her substantial buttocks with every turn. "When you wear this sexy creation," she says, pausing for effect, "your lover will know that you have the *desire* to *serve*."

The line gets a big laugh, as usual, and Myra chuckles with complicity as Betsy curtsies, French-maid style, and makes her exit.

Now Georgia struts into the room wearing high heels and a nearly invisible gold lamé string bikini. "Not bad for a broad with four kids, is it?" she boasts, and someone retorts, "Yeah, but they're adopted!"

The lively chatter and good-natured bantering have been going on all evening, and the gathering has begun to resemble a big pajama party. The women, most of them somewhere in their thirties, seem comfortable with one another; they work together as waitresses at the same Marriott Hotel. Myra does not know more than that about any of them except for Alice, the hostess. Alice is divorced and lives in this apartment with her little boy, who is being looked after tonight by a neighbor.

As Georgia leaves the room, Mary Jean re-appears, this time in a white satin corset. Her creamy flesh oozes from the top and the bottom of the garment. "Isn't she beautiful in our Heavenly Angel body slimmer," Myra says. "Notice the detailing on the garters."

"Ooh-la-la!"

"Heavenly Angel? No way Saint Peter's gonna let you through the gates wearing that thing!"

"What's it cost, Myra?"

"Twenty-four-fifty. It's listed right there on your order form, top of page five."

"Is it machine washable?"

"It is. But frankly, I would launder it by hand, like any other piece of fine lingerie." Whenever she can, she tries to provide practical information. It pleases her to think she is helping these women improve their lives. When Georgia and Betsy float back into the room in frilly lavender peignoirs, she is gratified to see the dreamy looks on their faces.

"Gosh, I feel so pretty," says the now sweet-and-wholesome-looking Betsy. She bears hardly any resemblance to the woman who pranced around in the French maid costume.

Myra calls for a round of applause for the three brave models, and the women cheer and whistle. While they wait for them to get dressed and return, Alice goes around refilling wine glasses and replenishing bowls of crackers and chips.

"I hope you're all having a good time tonight," Myra says as prelude to the speech she gives at each of these parties.

The women smile and murmur their agreement.

"Because that's what this is all about, really. Fun. Letting go. Having a few laughs. What good is life if you can't let your hair down once in a while, right?"

More smiles and murmurs.

She pauses a few beats and continues. "I think it's *wonderful* that we can be so open about our sexuality. Don't you agree?" She catches the eye of a woman wearing a long ponytail and a thick layer of makeup, who nods enthusiastically. "Yes, I for one am *grateful* I have the *freedom* to indulge my fantasies and desires through the Let's Be Lovers line of *quality* erotic products."

Giving her message a moment to sink in, she sits back and fingers the lucky cufflinks in the pocket of her blazer. The cufflinks belonged to her Grandpa Max, who handed them to her, along with all of his salesman's wisdom, before he died. Myra pictures him traveling a route between Indianapolis and Newark with his cases of costume jewelry, a gentle, self-effacing man who always had time for a little joke, a little schmoozing. "Make first a friend," he used to tell her. "Give a smile, give a kind word. Be humble and polite. That way you will convince and make a customer."

Myra looks around the room at all the friendly faces and says, as if it were an afterthought, "Can you imagine our *mothers* doing this?" As the women respond with a round of conspiratorial giggles, she gets up from her chair to stand behind a long aluminum table that has been set up with other products in the line. "No wardrobe would be complete without the right underwear," she says, holding up a pair of black lace panties. She pushes her hand into the garment, poking two spread fingers through the bottom to demonstrate the crotch-less feature.

"Is this for when you wanna let it all hang out?"

Myra offers a chuckle. "And here is something for that special man in your life. Our red heart G-string with the 'Home of the Whopper' logo."

"Where do the buns go?"

"Hey, mister, not in my oven!"

A roar of laughter sweeps through the room.

The women keep up a chorus of giggles and snorts as Myra holds up the rest of the cut-out bras and panties in rapid succession, working the occasional remark from the audience into her patter. Everyone seems to be enjoying herself. Everyone except a mousy woman wearing a green print dress and a pasted-on smile. Myra notices her sitting off in a corner and wonders if she might be Alice's mother.

"Next we come to the creams and lotions, which are specially formulated to add even more excitement to your romantic escapades." She begins passing around samples of Body Nectar, Pleasure Balm, Wildfire Oil, Joy Jell. The women sniff the jars and touch the lotions to the backs of their hands. "All of them are made from natural ingredients, and they are completely edible."

The woman with the ponytail asks, "Which ones would you recommend, Myra?"

"My personal favorite has to be the banana daiquiri massage cream." She smiles to conceal the lie. Vinnie has flat-out refused to try any of this stuff. For him, sex has always been something fast and furious, to be accomplished in total darkness and at his convenience. But if he were ever to let her take charge, she'd smear him all over with that massage cream and lick it off inch by inch.

She moves now to the other end of the table, where the novelty items are displayed. Candles, gift wrap, Jell-O molds, coat hangers, swizzle sticks, playing cards—all rated X. "Think about giving some of these as gifts for special friends," she says as she winds up the pink plastic penis and sends it shuffling across the table on its little black shoes.

Someone shrieks, "Harvey, it's you!" and the room dissolves into chaos. The women begin chatting amongst themselves, and Myra is afraid they'll lose their focus on the merchandise. In her business, unlike Grandpa Max's, there is no traveling to speak of. All she has to do is walk a thin high wire between decorum and depravity.

"Ladies, *ladies*!" She claps her hands for attention. "Let's take a short time-out and play a game. Would you like that?

"What kind of game?"

"Would we have to take our clothes off?"

She smiles indulgently. "All you have to do is write down some numbers, and when you total up your scores, we will discover who the sexiest woman in the room is. The winner gets a free sample of Captive Eight erotic perfume. Now, you have to be honest, okay?"

"Okay," they promise, good little girls.

"If you are wearing an ankle bracelet, give yourself two points. You can use the back page of your order form."

One of the women writes, while the others listen for the next instruction.

"Give yourself one point if you're wearing white underpants, two if they're colored, and three if they have jungle print patterns on them."

"How many points for not wearing any underpants?"

"Seven," Myra says, happy to have thought of such a quick comeback.

"If you've made love today, give yourself five points. Four if you're wearing your diaphragm. Six if you sleep in the nude." She ticks off several more items, and then the women total their scores. Linda, a heavyset woman in jeans, wins the perfume.

The strategy of inserting the game at this point has had the desired effect. The women have settled down and seem eager for what comes next.

And what comes next is the part Myra always finds difficult: bringing out the vibrators, French ticklers, anal love beads, cock rings, dildoes. Before Let's Be Lovers came into her life, she had never even heard of—let alone used—any of them. But if she is going to do her job well, if she's going to be a consultant for the Let's Be Lovers line of quality erotic products, she has to show them all. So she takes a deep breath and then, in her most competent sounding voice, she begins.

"The items that you are going to see next are extremely unique. They're not for everyone, but they can enhance your sex life in an important way. So keep an open mind. Use your imagination. Put your fears aside."

She reaches under the table for one of the canvas airline bags and pulls out the product referred to in the catalog as Mister Wriggle, an eight-inch long Latex monster of a flesh color so intense it looks as if it might glow in the dark.

The women let out a collective gasp.

"This takes four double A batteries and is guaranteed for one full year." She hands the vibrator to the woman nearest on her right, who examines it carefully. One by one, she brings out the rest of the appliances, and the women pass them from hand to hand. Busy now running their fingers along seams, opening battery cases, testing for weight, they have fallen into silent contemplation. Myra does not bother to look toward the corner of the room. By now, she figures, the mousy woman has probably faded through the wallpaper.

"And finally, we have our Prisoner of Love fur and satin bondage set." Holding up a gift-type box with a cellophane cover, she sneaks a look at her wristwatch.

She has made it through. In about an hour, she will be home.

There have been parties that did not go as well, a few times when someone in the group heckled her all evening or, worse, got up and walked out. You had to expect that kind of thing—that's what the regional rep told her at the training session—but it was always discouraging.

Once, she was actually accused of being a traitor to her sex by a woman who claimed to know Gloria Steinem personally. She called the lingerie "cheesy" and insisted the novelties were nothing but cheap plastic, made to be broken; even the creams smelled rancid to her. No mention of the appliances, but Myra could imagine what she thought of them. And what could she say in her own defense? How could she even begin to explain that what she really dealt in was fantasy and hope, and were those not the flimsiest of all commodities?

"I bet you'd like some wine now," Alice says, coming over to hand her a glass.

Myra thanks her but takes only a sip. She still needs a clear head in case anyone wants to consult her privately. Though that usually doesn't happen, it never hurts to make herself available, and she retires to the bedroom, closes the door, and sits down on the bed.

This is definitely a little boy's room: plaid wallpaper and bruised-looking furniture, shelves and baskets full of toys. Alice must sleep on the living room sofa, which probably unfolds to make a bed. She divorced the husband when she found out he was having an affair with their son's pre-school teacher. Alice explained this earlier, while she was setting up. Myra barely knows Alice and wonders if the woman tells her story to anyone willing to listen.

After a few minutes of waiting, she hears a soft knock on the door. "Come in, please," she says, arranging her features into an alert smile. But her mild expectation fizzles to dismay when she sees who it is.

"I want to talk to you," says the mousy woman, whispering and strangling an order form in her hands. She closes the door and thrusts the paper at Myra, who has to scan the columns twice before noticing the faint mark the woman has made next to the Kama Sutra Special, a kit consisting of a vibrator with four different attachments, a rabbit fur glove, and a pair of handcuffs.

She tries not to betray her surprise. "Are you sure this is right for you?" she asks delicately. "Some of my customers prefer to start off with something less…complicated."

"It's what I want."

"Well…okay." She finishes filling out the order form. The woman volunteers only her first name—Pearl—and her phone number. She pays for the order in cash and wants Myra to call her when the merchandise comes in.

Pearl takes her copy of the receipt and folds it, smaller and smaller, into her hand. She seems reluctant to go. "You won't believe this," she says finally, "but my husband hasn't made love to me in almost three years."

Myra murmurs sympathetically.

"I'm sure women come to you with these kinds of problems all the time. I suppose you know about what men want."

"Oh, I'm not actually a—"

"He won't go to a doctor. I've begged and I've begged, but he says he's lost interest and to leave him alone."

"Well, from what I understand, it's not unusual for some men to go through these little—"

"If I was younger, or prettier, I'd take a lover. I would. But I'm not…I couldn't—" She covers her eyes and lets a sob escape.

Myra rises and places a hand on Pearl's shoulder. "There, now," she says—and thinks what a fraud she is, setting herself up as an expert on romance and seduction when her own husband has not made love to her in…?

She tries to recall the last time he surprised her in the shower, the closet, the middle of the night. Once he came up behind her while she was washing the supper dishes, and they did it right there in the kitchen while Jennifer and Howie watched cartoons in the next room. That was Vinnie's style, and she never complained. But maybe, just maybe, she should have.

In a few minutes, Pearl recovers. "I don't usually get this emotional," she says, wiping her eyes.

Myra dabs at her nose. "I understand."

"You're not going to tell anyone about...this—"

"No, no. Of course not. Everything is purely confidential."

"Because I'd rather die—"

"Please, don't worry." Myra pats her on the arm and opens the door. A few minutes later, when it becomes apparent that no one else needs to talk with her, she comes into the living room, which is almost empty now, the last few women nearly out the door.

"You take care, Alice."

"See you at the salt mine tomorrow."

"Bye, Myra. This was a bunch of fun."

She says good-night and thanks them. Gathering their order forms, her mood lightens a bit as she estimates the evening's sales. It seems that everyone has bought something.

Then the neighbor arrives with Alice's son, all sleepy and confused. Alice carries him off to bed, and when she comes back she begins to fold up the bridge chairs, empty ashtrays, collect glasses and napkins.

"I could make some tea, if you want," she says.

"Thanks, but I'll just finish the paperwork and be on my way."

"No need to rush off on my account." Alice sits down on the sofa, surveys her tiny living room, reaches forward and brushes crumbs off the table and into her hand. "I don't sleep much anyway."

"Lately," Myra says, "neither do I." Maybe it's the hour, or the fact that Alice is a waitress—Myra can picture her in her neatly pressed uniform and quiet shoes, something like a nurse, almost—but she feels she is on the verge of making her own confession. In her line of work, Alice must be used to offering small comforts: a cup of coffee, a willing ear. Myra could get a week's worth of grief off her chest right now. She lets out a small snort and says, "Husbands."

Alice seems to take that as her cue. "Yeah, tell me about it. You know, if the bastard had just dropped dead one day, it'd be hard, but at least I'd have the memories. I'd be able to say, 'Well, we had six good years.' But divorce? That wipes away everything. That's as good as saying the whole marriage was just one big goddamn waste of time."

Her bitterness is a little appalling. Alice mentioned that the divorce has been final for several years now, but apparently she is still in a world of hurt. Sympathizing, Myra tries to offer a few palliative words. "I can see you're a strong woman," she begins, "and I'm sure that someday you'll be able to put all this behind you, and then you can—"

"You're still married, Myra, right?"

She hesitates, then nods.

"So you wouldn't have the slightest idea of what I'm talking about, would you?"

"Oh, but I can certainly imagine—"

"Did you see? I ordered one of those string bikinis. After I lose a few pounds, I'm gonna have my picture taken in that suit, and then I'm gonna send it to the bastard and his twiggy nothing of a new wife, just in time for Christmas. In a big frame. And the card's gonna say, 'Eat your heart out, Schmuck!'"

The hard glitter in Alice's eyes tells Myra that any further conversation would be pointless. "I'm sure the suit will look terrific on you," she says, hurriedly gathering her papers. She packs up the airline bags, breathing shallowly all the while, as if Alice's bitterness might be contaminating the air.

At the door, she turns, feeling she should offer the woman some teaspoon of consolation. "Your little boy is very cute," she says. It's not enough, she knows, not nearly enough, but it's all she can think of to tell her.

"Yeah," Alice says, "he's a real sweetheart. Best thing in my life." She tries to grin, but her voice is so filled with despair, so lacking in anything resembling joy, it sends Myra spinning away, down three flights of stairs, with her cumbersome bags and her own gnawing dread.

She opens the hatch of the Civic, throws her things inside and speeds away, through empty streets, to the refuge of her own lonely bed.

## *FOUR*

The orange cat turns up on Thursday, the same day that Myra's new ad appears in the Trader's Gazette. This time she is looking to get rid of a bunch of old records and magazines, some fishing gear, an electric space heater, an assortment of ashtrays from various bars and restaurants, and a box of rusting tools. The ad says "Make Me An Offer" but she'd almost be willing to give it away for free, just to have it gone from her sight.

The stuff is Vinnie's, mostly, and it's an absolute shame the way he let it accumulate in the little spare room in the basement, which she'd had her heart set on someday turning into a sewing room. Once she learned how to sew, she could make clothes for herself and the children and save the family a bunch of money. Vinnie—impractical as ever—wanted to put in a pool table and shelves for his collections. It was a waste of a perfectly good space, she insisted: with a big pool table, there would not be enough room for a sewing machine, or a cabinet for her supplies, or a work surface for cutting out her patterns.

They argued about it for days, but anyway, as it turned out, they never got farther than smearing a primer coat of paint on the walls and having Vinnie's uncle Aldo measure the floor for linoleum.

Howie comes home after school with the orange cat in his arms. Myra is on the telephone, giving directions to a man who wants to see the space heater. "We can keep him, Mom, can't we?" Howie says.

"Farwell Avenue, a few blocks north of Pratt. A white house with green shutters."

"Can we? *Please*?"

"Yes, that's right."

"Oh, boy! Thanks!"

"Wait a minute." She hangs up the phone. "I was *not* talking to *you*. Where did you get the cat?"

"Jeremy found him in his garage. He told me I could have him."

He hoists the cat onto his shoulder. It's a long, skinny animal with slippery legs. She takes it and sets it on the floor. "Did you stop to think it might already belong to someone? It's probably just lost."

Howie doesn't answer. He opens the cabinet under the sink and drags out a bag of kibble, scoops up a handful and holds it under the cat's nose. Myra watches as the animal jerks down the food, and even before she stoops to run her hand over its back, she knows how bony the poor thing will be.

The cat arches itself into her touch. "It's very friendly," she says, lifting the tail.

"He's a boy, Mom. I seen his balls."

"Well, I'm sure if we take him to the shelter, they'll find him a good home—"

"No! He's mine! He loves me!" Howie throws himself on the floor. "You can't give him away."

"Don't be difficult." She gets up to swing the kitchen door closed, stopping Lucy and Ethel in their tracks on the other side of it. "We already have enough cats."

Howie sniffles loudly.

"They wouldn't get along with this one. You know how Lucy is."

He reaches out blindly and strokes the orange fur.

"And besides, we cannot afford any more vet bills right now." As she is speaking, she hears Jennifer hollering in the living room.

"I hate school! I hate Mr. McGrath!" She shoves the kitchen door open and flings her book bag on the floor. "He marked my history paper down a whole grade just because it was a day late."

"Oh, honey, that's too bad." She tries to put an arm around Jennifer's shoulders. "I'm sure that was only his way of emphasizing the importance of turning in assignments on time—"

"That's it, take his side! How come everything's my fault!" She slumps into a chair. "Can't you write him a note?"

Howie starts moaning again. "*Why* can't we keep him?"

Myra's head is beginning to throb. "Now, listen," she says, watching as Ethel and Lucy creep into the room. Lucy she manages to grab in mid-step, but as she's reaching for Ethel, the dog bounds in, and in a single swift motion the orange cat launches himself off the floor and onto the countertop.

"Where'd you get the cat?" Jennifer says.

"I found him, but Mom won't let me keep him."

"Now listen, I explained why we can't—"

"No, Brownie!" Howie shouts. "Don't hurt him!"

The dog is working her nose along the counter's edge when the cat strikes, a quick pop accompanied by a blood-curdling yowl. The dog yelps and backs into a corner, and Myra rushes to comfort her. "Do you see what I'm talking about? This is simply *not* going to work."

Jennifer scoops up the orange cat. "Don't be mean. You should let Howie keep it."

"He can live in my room."

"Absolutely not!" She takes a deep breath. They are ganging up on her, these same children who only this morning were so at odds they had to eat breakfast in separate rooms. "Now look, we already have too many animals. Who will be responsible for this one? Who's going to—"

She is talking to the backs of their heads. "Sweet kitty," Jennifer murmurs as they saunter through the doorway.

"He's probably got fleas," Myra grumbles. She is so angry she grabs the phone and dials Vinnie's number at work—when their father tells them no, it's *no*—but halfway through the first ring, she hangs up. How can she even think of getting him involved? That would be as good as admitting she's not able to handle her own children. Well, she will just wait until morning. When they go off to school, she'll simply encourage the cat to depart on its own.

❧❧❧

Toward evening, an older couple comes to look at the phonograph records. Myra leads them through the living room, stepping carefully around Jennifer, who lies sprawled on the carpet in front of the television set. "I hope we aren't having meatloaf again for supper," she says, busy copying out math problems into her notebook.

"When I was a boy, we had to do our homework in our rooms," the man says. "With the door closed. No television for us."

"When you were a boy, Teddy, they'd hardly even invented radio." The woman smiles at Jennifer. "Pay him no attention. He's an old fool."

"Now, Bunny—"

On the television screen, Theo Huxtable points at his sister and utters something hilarious. Laughter gushes from the set.

"The records are in the basement," Myra says, turning to go down the stairs.

"Got any Perry Como, dear? I was always a big fan of his."

She shows them the boxes with the record albums and leaves them to browse. "Supper," she mutters, wondering where the afternoon has disappeared. The kitchen clock tells her it's already almost six.

Between the telephone calls from the ad and the commotion over the cat, the subject of meal planning hasn't even entered her head. The refrigerator yields only two wobbly stalks of celery, half an onion, a bowl of leftover noodles and a small carton of banana yogurt. Most of what Vinnie brought her is gone—except for the red cabbage and the green knobs, and what is she supposed to do with those?

There are probably some carrots and leeks in the backyard garden, though it's too dark to go digging for them now. She might have made a hearty soup, or a casserole topped with melted cheese. If she had any cheese. But digging through the pantry, she does manage to find a small can of shrimp.

Okay. She can do something with shrimp and vegetables and noodles. It will be a challenge, whipping up a decent meal from practically nothing. Too bad Vinnie's not here to appreciate how resourceful she can be.

She recalls the day they planted the garden, his hands on the spade strong and brown, the four of them working in the warm dirt under a glorious May sky. The children poked seeds into the soil: three rows of beans—slightly uneven—little hills of squash and cucumber. Myra tied the baby tomato plants to stakes while Howie made a joke about using T-bones instead of sticks, and even Jennifer laughed. After supper, they sat out on the back stoop, dirt under their fingernails and sunburn over their noses, and watched the sun set.

It had been a wonderful day, cut out of the fabric of ordinary days and preserved in her memory. When they put their minds to it, they could be as happy as anyone on The Cosby Show. She should have taken pictures that day for proof.

"Peel that onion under water, dear, and you won't have tears." The woman has come up from the basement with an armful of record albums, and the man follows, holding something behind his back. "That's a nice collection you've got there. Torme, Bennett, Sinatra, all the greats."

"Thanks," Myra says, wiping a sleeve across her eyes. The records came from the same uncle who had owned the parrot.

The man looks around the kitchen." I don't suppose you have any cookbooks you want to get rid of?"

"Oh, Teddy, you've got at least a hundred old cookbooks cluttering up the house."

"Well that's nothing compared to her old records. Keeps 'em going night and day, can't get a minute's rest." He snaps his fingers in imitation of castanets. "Sometimes I find myself doing the tango in my sleep."

Myra smiles. What a funny couple they are. She imagines them at home, the wife in the living room swaying to her music while the husband whips up a soufflé in the kitchen. "You must have an interesting marriage," she says.

"Oh, we aren't married. Bunny is my sister."

"Can't you see the resemblance?" They turn their heads to show identical profiles: a smaller and larger version of the same spigot-shaped nose and double chin.

The woman offers Myra four dollars for the albums. As they are leaving, the man presses a five dollar bill into her hand. "For this," he whispers, flashing a faded copy of Playboy magazine. "It's a classic. The one with all those pictures of Jayne Mansfield taking a bath."

❧❧❧

*Woof-woof. Woof-woof-woof.*

Angelo is working on his impersonation of Brownie barking at the mailman. On television, a woman testifies that she has become a new human being and found true meaning in life thanks to Jenny Craig diet centers. And the phone has started to ring.

Six forty-five. It's Vinnie, calling to check up on them. Myra pours oil into the sauté pan and shouts into the living room, "Someone answer that, please." He never has much to say to her beyond *So, how's it going?*

Howie jumps for the phone, but Jennifer beats him to it. "Hi, Dad?" she says breathlessly. "Uh-huh. I got a B on my English test. Uh-huh…uh-huh…"

"Lemme talk, I wanna talk," Howie chants.

Myra tosses the vegetables into the pan.

"…and Howie found this cat—"

"I wanna tell him!"

"How-ee, Jen-ni-fer," she sings, just loudly enough to be heard on the other end of the telephone wire, "let's wash up for sup-per." She adds the shrimp and the noodles, and wishes that Vinnie could hear the delicious sizzle.

"What's this?" Jennifer says, peeking over Myra's shoulder.

"Noodle surprise." She flips the mixture in the pan several more times and then divides it among their three plates.

"This all we get?"

"Have some crackers." Myra turns to Howie, who has just hung up the phone. "Didn't Dad want to speak with me?

He shakes his head. "What's this stuff?"

"Mom says noodle surprise."

"Well, did he ask you to give me a message?"

Howie shrugs. "I need ketchup."

"Did he even mention my *name*?"

"Nope."

Frustrated, Myra shovels up a forkful of noodles. Tomorrow, she will answer the telephone herself, and when Vinnie asks *How's it going?* she just might haul off and tell him.

The doorbell rings. She gets up to answer it, chewing slowly and trying to determine whether it's too much garlic powder she has put in, or too much oregano. After *shushing* Brownie and looping a restraining finger through the dog's collar, she opens the front door to a tall man standing on the stairs.

"I hope I have the right place," he says, coming forward a step. "Are you the party that advertised the space heater for sale?"

His voice seems to drip from his nose. He is wearing glasses with dark rims and a long, black overcoat, and he gives the impression of having been rained upon, though—as Myra can plainly see—the sky is clear and bright with stars. She swallows and motions him inside.

"Oh, I do apologize. I see that I am interrupting your dinner. I would have been here much earlier, but I took a wrong turn off Clark Street and ended up in the middle of the aftermath of what was apparently a multi-vehicle accident. Traffic was backed up for a mile—oh, hello young miss, young sir…"

He follows her through the kitchen and down the basement stairs, talking all the way. Myra flips on the wall switch in the spare room and points to the heater, which is sitting on the floor next to Vinnie's green metal tackle box. On the weekend they were supposed to finish painting the room and pick out flooring and maybe even shop for a cozy chair, he got an invitation to go fishing. And to her amazement, he went. To this day she cannot look at that tackle box without getting upset all over again.

"I assume the heater is in working order?"

"Of course it's in working order!" she snaps, inserting the plug of the heater into a socket high on the wall. "I would never sell something that was broken."

She turns on the switch, and the coils behind the safety grill light up, giving off a smell of singed dust. The man bends and spreads his fingers over the grill. "Yes, this is perfect, just what I need." He smiles. "I will give you three dollars for it."

For a moment, she's tempted to tell him what a new heater would cost, and this one has never been used. She can't even remember why Vinnie bought it, unless it was a gift from one of his buddies, an appliance that just happened to fall off the back of a truck. "You're getting an awfully good deal," she says, anxious to be rid of both him and the dusty contraption.

The man takes out a handkerchief and blows his nose. "I could also use a warm blanket, if you have any for sale."

"Sorry, no blankets. How about a nice tackle box?"

"I think not. I'm afraid that I have never been able to fathom the pleasures of fishing."

"It's a stupid sport," she agrees.

In the kitchen, Howie and Jennifer are spreading peanut butter on their crackers. Ethel sits in the middle of the table, attempting to spear a shrimp with his toenail.

"You could at least have eaten a few bites," Myra says, trying hard not to feel defeated. She dumps the cat on the floor and carries their plates to the sink.

The tall man examines them as they pass under his gaze. "I must say, that looks delicious. Quite gourmet, in fact."

"Gourmet? Not really."

"An Oriental recipe, then, perhaps?" It seems he is having trouble taking his eyes off the food.

"I really hate to throw this away. If you would like any—"

"How kind of you to offer, and I accept with gratitude." Setting the space heater on the floor, he takes the plates from her and brings them back to the table. "And if it isn't too much trouble, I would very much appreciate a cup of hot tea. I'm dealing with a wretched head cold that I cannot seem to shake."

Myra watches as he sits down and picks up a fork. She can hardly believe this is happening: a perfect stranger seated right here at her kitchen table, digging into the children's supper.

"This is quite good," he says, chewing.

"I may have overdone the oregano."

"Not at all. I think you've put in just the right amount."

"Well," she says, pleased at the compliment.

Jennifer and Howie are poking each other, snickering and staring at him as if he had just leapt from the pages of one of their storybooks.

She hisses for them to behave, finishes fixing the tea and brings the cup to him. He takes it in both hands and lifts it to his lips. Then, with a shake of his head, he sets the cup down again. "You must think me a complete dolt. Here I am, enjoying your marvelous cooking, and I have not even introduced myself." He stands and extends a bony hand. "My name is Haskell Reed."

From the oddly formal way he speaks, Myra half expects him to click his heels and bow. She introduces herself and the children, who mutter and stare at the floor, suddenly and exasperatingly shy.

"Say 'hello,'" she coaches.

They giggle. A drool of peanut butter escapes from Howie's mouth and lands on her shoe. The table is littered with cracker crumbs.

Haskell Reed seems not to notice. He finishes the first plate and starts in on the second with hardly a pause. Myra wonders who he is and where he came from. This would be a funny story to tell to Vinnie when he came home tonight.

If he were coming home tonight.

Which he is not. She lets out a small, unhappy sigh, reminding herself for the hundredth time today of her predicament.

The children slip away, and then she is alone with this stranger, this Haskell Reed, which sounds suspiciously made-up. (What sort of mother would give an innocent baby that kind of name?) She hurriedly finishes the rest of her supper and then gets busy at the sink, keeping watch out of the corner of her eye. It was a mistake to have invited him to eat. He looks all right, but these days, who knew? He could be planning some hideous crime right this minute. Instantly she pictures herself lying on the floor in a puddle of blood, Vinnie bent over her body, pressing her lifeless hand to his heart.

It would serve him right.

She wipes her forehead. In her agitation, she has worked up a good amount of steam and soapsuds. Pulling another dish from the basin, her elbow knocks into the figure at her side, and she gasps.

"Oh—I'm so sorry if I startled you." He hands her his dishes. "I guess I should go now. It would be awkward trying to explain my presence to your husband when he comes home—"

"He's not coming home." She shuts off the water and grabs for a towel, wiping her hands, her face.

"Ah, well, I hope the late Mr. Calderelli didn't suffer a lingering illness—"

"He isn't dead. Did I say he was dead?"

"No, you did not. I merely assumed that—"

"He's gone, that's all. Just plain gone. Walked out, good-bye." She throws the towel on the counter. "So you see, there's no reason to rush away. Here, have some more tea."

She is feeling brave all of a sudden, brave and resigned. It's no business of Haskell Reed's what Vinnie has done. He is a stranger and could not possibly have any interest, and yet here she is, showing off how well she can carry on despite her misfortune.

"I sympathize," he says. All this time he has been wearing his coat, and now he takes it off and folds it over the back of a chair. Underneath he has on a turtleneck shirt, a flannel shirt, and a crew neck sweater with an ink stain on the left sleeve. His coloring is the kind that reminds her of old tinted photographs: reddish-brown hair with pale skin and faded freckles. His age could be anything from thirty to fifty. Behind the glasses lurks either an aging boy or a youthful middle-aged man, and he is regarding her with true compassion, as if she were indeed bereaved. "My wife—my ex-wife, that is—handed me my walking papers several months ago. Divorce is difficult."

"Marriage is difficult," she counters, "especially with someone like Vinnie. He has one of those Mediterranean temperaments. You never know what his mood is going to be. And he seems to feel he can do whatever he wants, without even stopping to take my needs into consideration."

"Elizabeth was also extremely self-centered—"

"For instance," she continues, "the spare room downstairs. He knew how badly I wanted to get it fixed up, and yet he went off fishing on the very weekend we were supposed to paint the walls and pick out linoleum. And not only that, he pretended not to know what I was so angry about. When he came back from his fishing trip, he didn't even bother to ask why I wasn't speaking to him—"

"Excuse me. Did I hear you correctly? Did you say you had a spare room?"

"Yes. For now it seems to be just a repository for junk."

He pauses, considering something. "By any chance," he says slowly, putting a forefinger to his lip, "would that room be available for rent?"

Myra blinks. "No, of course not. Who'd want to live in such a hole in the wall?"

"Well," he says, tilting his head, "I'm thinking that I would."

She stares at him, but before she can give voice to her disbelief, he rushes on to explain how it has been since his divorce, how in the settlement the ex-wife was awarded their condominium, which forced him to try and find housing on his erratic income as a freelance writer.

"Let me tell you, it is virtually impossible to locate anything that's both affordable and decent. As a result I've been forced to reside in my office, a single room in an old building on Adams Street, west of the river. Fortunately, there is a janitor's closet nearby, so I have access to running water, and I also have an electric immersion heater for instant soup and coffee. I was actually making out fairly well until this recent turn in the weather. On weekends, you see, the building is unheated. As a consequence I've caught this miserable cold—" He coughs and blows his nose. "When winter comes, I don't know what I am going to do."

She's not quite sure how to respond: whether to laugh at the absurdity of his situation or weep with pity. She wonders if he qualifies as a homeless person. "I'm sure something will turn up," she says, taking his coat off the chair and handing it to him. "Have you checked out the YMCA?"

Before he has the chance to reply, they are distracted by a noisy scuffle overhead. She hears yelling, then Howie's horror-movie scream, which her son uses only when he has provoked his sister to the point of outright murder.

"Mom...? *Mo-o-om!*"

"*What?*" Myra shouts, rushing out of the room.

Jennifer has the orange cat in her arms, and Howie is trailing her down the stairway. "Tell her she can't call him Creamsicle," he wails, his face hot with tears. "He's *my* cat."

"He is such a dope. What kind of a stupid name is Poor Boy?"

The cat again. Myra is so frustrated with these children she would like to knock their heads together and send them to bed. "I absolutely do *not* want to hear any more about this. I thought I explained why we can't keep him, so put him—"

"It's my turn to hold him."

"—in the laundry room—"

"No, it's not!"

"—for tonight... Jen? Howie?" They're not listening to her. Lately, it seems, they never listen. Sometimes she feels like a radio that's been left playing in a room where people come and go.

"I wonder if I might intervene," Haskell Reed says, "as a disinterested third party." He has come into the living room (as if anyone asked him) with an expression of benign intent on his face. She expects the children to ignore him and continue squabbling, but they become suddenly shy and angelic.

"Howie found this cat," Jennifer tells him.

"Is that right?"

Howie nods.

"And the two of you are unable to agree on a name. Is that the problem?"

"I wanted to call him Creamsicle because he's orange and his tummy's white."

"Perhaps there is a name that reflects both his coloring and his origins." Haskell Reed puts two fingers to his temple and thinks a moment.

"Jennifer, stop kissing that animal!"

"Ah, I have it. Have you children ever heard of David Copperfield?"

"He vanished the Statue of Liberty," Jennifer says.

Haskell looks confused. Myra explains, "An illusionist they saw on television."

"Well, young sir, young miss, this is a different David Copperfield, an orphan boy cast out into the cold, cruel world at a tender age to make his way as best he could. It's a long, sad story but it ends happily. Would you like to hear it?"

"Uh-huh."

"There isn't time," Myra says. "Mr. Reed has to leave."

"I wanna hear the story."

"All right, Howie. And a story you shall have." He lays his coat over the arm of the wing-back chair and takes a seat on the couch. The children sit down next to him, nestling the orange cat between them. "I am very good with children," he whispers to Myra. "When I was in college, I spent an entire summer working at a day care center."

She's never really approved of day care centers, but that is hardly the issue. "I'm sure what you say is true, however—"

"Shhh, Mom, you're interrupting."

Haskell Reed sits back and begins the story. "Now, David Copperfield was a good little boy, but he had many misfortunes. His father died before he was born, and his mother married a horrible man named Murdstone…"

The children listen quietly, mesmerized by the steady drip-drip of his voice. Brownie wanders in and lies down beside the couch. The orange cat, eyes slitted with contentment, is purring audibly.

There is peace in the valley once again.

"So what's its name going to be?" Jennifer asks after Haskell Reed has finished telling his story. "David?"

He smiles. "No, not David. *Copperfield!*"

"Cool," Howie says.

Jennifer tickles the cat under his chin. "We'll call him Coppy for short."

Haskell Reed leans toward Myra. "I assure you, I am a person of modest and regular habits. I would not interfere at all in your family life."

Oh, no? Just his being here changes things. She considers the scene before her: the happy children, the tranquil pets, two adult figures in charge—but any resemblance to family is pure coincidence.

"But I don't know the least thing about you," she says.

"I have references." He pulls scraps of paper from several pockets and shuffles through them. "Here is Elizabeth's business card. Call her. She'll tell you whatever you want to know, and the worst she can say is that I failed to measure up to her impossibly high expectations."

Myra runs a finger across the raised print on the card and stares at the name: Elizabeth Baxter-Reed, Investment Analyst. "Gee, I'm not sure. This is so weird. I wouldn't even know what to charge you—"

"I can pay you seventy dollars a week for rent plus half of whatever you spend for groceries. I will give you a check right now."

"But if Vinnie comes back—I mean, *when* Vinnie comes back—"

"I'll simply disappear. Right now, all I need is a little time to regroup."

While Myra chews at her lip, he digs in his pockets again, pulls out a wallet and a fountain pen, writes a check and hands it to her: one hundred dollars made payable to Cash.

"Well..." she says, staring at the check and beginning to weigh the pros and cons, "I suppose we could try it for a week. What kind of car do you have?"

"An aging but dependable Ford Escort."

"And would I be able to use it?"

"Yes, certainly. Anytime you like. And let me assure you, Myra Calderelli, you will not—will *not*—regret this. You know, I had a premonition that something extraordinary would happen tonight. It came to me as I was sitting there in all of that terrible traffic. I was just about to turn around and go back to that inhospitable little room I have been forced to call home, but then something told me that I should pursue this heater, an inner voice, if you will..."

Myra offers a few nods and *mm-hmms* while she pulls his overcoat off the chair and shakes out the wrinkles. Then, resigning herself to another new—and, hopefully, temporary— reality, she drapes the coat around a wooden hanger and wedges it into the hall closet with all the others. ✺

## *FIVE*

On his way into the kitchen the next morning, Howie stops to stare at the sleeping figure on the living room couch. "How come he's still here?" he says to Myra, who is busy assembling breakfast from the bits and pieces she has on hand.

"Mr. Reed will be staying with us for a little while," she replies, pouring apple juice over his Frosted Flakes.

"Does Dad know him?"

"No, he does not."

He frowns at his cereal. Myra picks up a pencil and writes *milk* on her shopping list. She awoke at dawn, brimming with purpose. First, she is going to make the spare room ready for human habitation. Then, with a car at her disposal, she'll go grocery shopping, picking up everything she will need for a week's worth of meals and laying in a good supply of non-perishables as long as she's at it. She is determined to get back to running an efficient household, just like she used to.

Jennifer comes in to announce that she doesn't want any breakfast. Myra puts a finger to her lips. "Mr. Reed is sleeping," she whispers.

"So?"

"Have a little consideration." She turns the jar of jelly upside down and scrapes the last drops over a heel of toasted white bread. "Should I buy grape again, or do you want strawberry?"

"Are you going to marry him?"

"Who? Mr. Reed? Don't be silly. I am already married, to your Dad."

Jennifer says, "But, I thought—" and then falls silent. Myra understands there is a question behind that question, but really, this is hardly the time to sit them down for a discussion. Besides, what's there to discuss? She can still barely believe the events of last evening.

After hurrying Howie through his cereal and forcing the toast into Jennifer, she helps them into their coats, kisses them absently on top of their heads, and says, "Have a nice day."

"Bye, Mom."

"Yes," she says, "I will." Her thoughts have already turned to the tasks at hand. She will need to reorganize the pantry, too, but Cara is coming today to do her family's laundry. Perfect. Myra can take care of the pantry while Cara folds clothes.

Armed with her cleaning supplies, she descends the basement stairs, but on the threshold of the spare room she stops short, nearly losing her nerve. How have things gotten so terribly out of hand? There are boxes and cartons and stacks of papers everywhere she looks. The room resembles one of those cramped, dusty shops where collectors go to browse for old postcards and tobacco tins.

She sets down her pail. Before she can begin cleaning, she will have to decide what stays and what goes. Somewhere—in one of those helpful household hints columns, probably—she read that you should never try to clear out closets or storage areas unless you were angry and in the throwing-away frame of mind. Good advice, she supposes, but she wonders what on earth could get her angry enough to sort out this mess?

She begins with the table, an old white-painted metal kitchen table that once belonged to Vinnie's mother, Lena. Leafing through a stack of expired grocery coupons, school papers, brochures from various home improvement businesses, and bulletins from the utility companies, she comes across a street map of Milwaukee, and after puzzling over it for half a minute, she remembers: she had bought the map a few years ago in preparation for a little Sunday trip that she and Loretta had planned to take. At the last minute, someone came down with an ear infection, or maybe it was Vinnie having to work—whatever. She recalls her disappointment, how she slammed around for days afterward in a stew of self-pity.

Setting the map aside, she gathers the rest of the papers, slides them into the trash bag and turns to the next stack, wondering what else she will uncover. (Truthfully, this is not such a chore after all; she feels a little like an archeologist digging for clues to a lost civilization.) On top of the stack is an ancient issue of Woman's Day magazine with a photo display of Halloween cookies on the cover. When she picks it up she is surprised to see a square of toilet paper flutter to the floor.

The message printed there in red crayon—*Mom is in the shower*—gives her pause, and she spends a few moments pondering it. But all at once the whole scene comes flooding back. She was in the bathroom with Howie, trying to toilet train him according to a method that let you get it over with in a single day. After a solid hour, he was still dangling his feet and doodling with his crayons and refusing to let go. The telephone rang, and Jennifer came upstairs to tell her it was Nettie. Myra wrote the note so Jennifer would not forget what to say when she got back to the phone.

She smiles at the memory. What a different person she was back then. Motherhood was not sunny summer picnics by the lake, snowmen and hot chocolate, nursery rhymes, long naps and lazy afternoons, as she had pictured it. That was before she had any children, of course. The reality she hadn't counted on was daily tantrums and dried food everywhere, and she could not believe the number of diapers she changed, especially when you considered how little went in, in the first place.

Now she can look back and laugh at the harried young woman she used to be (though at the time she found almost nothing about it amusing). But look at these adorable cards the children made her for Mother's Day. Jennifer painted flowers and birds all over her card; Howie drew spiders in brown marker on his and printed his name with all the letters facing in the right direction. And here is another card: *To my loving wife*…. The words are written on a heart covered in dark pink satin and trimmed with white lace.

She opens the card and winces at the scrawl of Vinnie's name. He'd taped a crisp fifty dollar bill inside, and she used the money—most of it, anyway—for a new shower curtain, bathmat, towels and tooth brushes.

Had he been planning to leave even then? And how could she not have suspected? Better to have blown the whole fifty on a bottle of perfume, but she has always been too damn practical.

And now she feels the anger. There it is: rising in her chest like suds, foaming like hot butter. Slowly, carefully, she rips Vinnie's card into tiny pieces. She saves the children's cards but sweeps everything else into the trash. In minutes, the table is cleared, its chipped surface visible for the first time in years.

She goes on to the cartons stacked by the sofa-bed: Howie's baby clothes, Jennifer's party dresses, Myra's skirts from high school—why has she been saving them? Brownie watches warily from the safety of the laundry room while she hauls the cartons up the stairs, grunting and gasping with the effort. "Out!" she snarls as she trashes Vinnie's collection of bottles and souvenir ashtrays, and his prized team jerseys. "Out, out!" as she throws away the puzzles and the board games no one can find the missing pieces for.

The dog sighs and lays her head on her paws.

By now, sweat is running down Myra's face. She has not felt such determination since she pushed Howie out on the delivery room table nearly eight years ago. She wipes her wrist against her forehead and turns to the closet. Magazines, more baby clothes, a bridesmaid's dress she never liked even when it was new; and in the corner, hanging from a hook, Vinnie's Navy pea coat. She attacks it as if it were alive, punches it into a ball and flings it through the doorway.

"Bastard!" she growls. And the dog, with a snuffling moan, heaves herself onto her feet and slinks out of sight.

☙☙☙

Finally, she's ready to go grocery shopping, but Haskell Reed is gone, the bedding clumsily folded and piled on the couch with a note saying—as nearly as she can figure—that he went to get his things and will return either *soon* or at *noon*. She drums her fingers on her arm. Cara will be here for lunch, and she cannot wait. She revises her list, paring it down to the essentials she can carry in two hands, and sets off for the supermarket on foot. On the way home, she stops at the hardware store to have an extra key made.

He is there in front of the house when she gets back, unloading things from the trunk of a beige-colored Ford. A neighbor, Mrs. Spinka, is watching from her living room window. Myra wiggles her fingers in Mrs. Spinka's direction and calls to Haskell, who is trying to close the trunk lid and balance a wooden crate filled with books on his knee. The crate slips from his grasp and the books tumble into the gutter.

She sets her grocery bags down and goes to help him. "Sorry," he says, and then, "Thanks." In broad daylight, he looks different, less needy and almost handsome in a mild, non-threatening sort of way. He reminds her a little of Byron Levine, in fact, though that may have more to do with his attire—a sports jacket and chinos—than anything else. Together they bring his various boxes and bags into the house, Myra sending messages by telepathy to Mrs. Spinka and anyone else who might be watching from behind their curtains: *No, truly, this is not at all what you think.*

"You didn't bring much," she says, standing in the middle of the spare room and surveying his belongings, which seem to consist mostly of books and phonograph records, a portable record player, an ancient typewriter, and an umbrella. "Is this all you have?"

"I have what I need." He puts a suitcase in the closet and hooks the umbrella over the clothes rod. "It was Elizabeth who took care of the acquisitions during our marriage. The lithographs, the carpets, the tableware. They meant a great deal to her, so I told her to keep them."

His words leave behind a slight echo in the room, nearly empty with only the chipped kitchen table, a rickety wooden chair, and a lumpy sofa-bed that used to be in Grandma Rose's apartment before she went to live at the DallyGlen old people's home.

Actually, the room now reminds Myra of a painting she always stopped to see whenever she'd visit the Art Institute—Van Gogh's bedroom at Arles: tidy and spare, and with the same skewed perspective. That skewed perspective might have something to do with the single window, high on the basement wall, apparently set incorrectly when the house was built. Copperfield rests on the sill, gazing at the side yard. Myra cranks the window open and says, "Out, boy?"

The cat sniffs the air and gives her a glance filled with disdain: *Who, me?* Apparently, he has settled himself in, but good; no way she'll get rid of him now. She may as well call Dr. Thornberry and make arrangements to bring him in. "I'll take the cat out of your way," she says, pulling Copperfield down off the windowsill and tucking him under her arm. "Oh, and here, I've made you an extra key to the back door."

He takes the key and rests it in the palm of his hand. "You are very thoughtful, Myra. And I do appreciate your letting me stay the night."

"Well, I didn't see the point of having you go back to that cold office."

"No, and it wasn't only the cold, but the silence, too. Some nights I felt as if I were in a giant tomb. I would lie on my cot and listen to my heart beat, my socks dripping dry over the back of the chair…"

She nearly laughs out loud at the thought of this, but then she sees how serious he is, his eyebrows knitted in consternation.

"The janitor would keep the utility closet unlocked for me if I bribed him with few dollars. And the cleaning lady who came at night must have thought I owned the building, because she would give me a little bow every time she saw me. She spoke no English, so there was no way I could explain myself." He shakes his head. "Anyway, I am distilling the entire experience and putting it into my new play."

"Oh? You write plays?"

"Among other things."

She would like to find out more, but the cat is beginning to squirm, and she excuses herself and carries him out of the room. Halfway up the stairs, Brownie breaks into a fit of barking—Cara has arrived, no doubt—and Copperfield digs his nails into Myra's side. She tries to set him on the kitchen floor, but the barking has unnerved him. He springs from her arms onto the counter, and from there to the top of the refrigerator, where he glares at her as if she had purposely put him in danger.

Cara struggles through the door with two bulging pillowcases and a large wicker basket. "Got any powder, Aunt Myra? I forgot to stop for some on the way over." She pauses at the top of the stairs to kick the pillowcases into the basement before clomping down after them with the basket on her hip.

Myra calls after her, "Try that yellow bottle on top of the machine. It's one of those new liquid concentrates. You can measure with the cap."

She pulls deli chicken and tomatoes from one of the grocery bags and goes about preparing their lunch. Ever since some teenage punks vandalized the coin-op in their neighborhood, Cara has been doing her family's laundry at Myra's house on Fridays. It's the only weekday when she has no classes, and on Saturdays and Sundays she is busy with her job at Toys 'R' Us.

Last week, Cara brought cheese biscuits from the bakery. Myra heated up a can of Progresso vegetable soup to go with the biscuits, and they had tea and lemon cookies for dessert. These visits from her niece are something Myra truly looks forward to. No matter what happens the rest of the week, on Friday afternoons they can sit in her little kitchen and stir sugar into their cups: two happy, daffy housewives—never mind that Myra is not very happy these days and Cara is not, technically speaking, a housewife.

Today she is wearing a pair of black combat boots, a frilly off-the-shoulder white blouse and high-waisted jeans held up with suspenders. In the past, Myra has tried to counsel her on matters of fashion, but the girl has always had her own stubborn sense of style. "Do you realize there's a strange man downstairs?" she says, clomping back into the kitchen. "He's moving the furniture around in the little room that used to have all the boxes in it."

"Yes. I met him yesterday." Myra keeps her voice matter-of-fact. "He was desperate for someplace to stay—purely on a temporary basis, you understand—and I'm renting out the spare room to him."

"You're...what?"

"This was not something I had planned, but I think it's going to work out quite well."

"Trying to make Uncle Vinnie jealous?"

Though Myra denies it, the thought has crossed her mind. "This is purely a business arrangement," she says, spreading mayonnaise on whole wheat bread. "He's paying me rent and letting me use his car, and when I have to work, he'll be here to make sure your cousins don't set fire to the house."

Cara sits down at the table and rests her chin in her hand. "He's not bad looking, is he?"

"I haven't really thought about it. He is a little pale for my taste, though. I've always preferred men with stronger features."

"Like Uncle Vinnie?"

"I suppose. But people's tastes change as they get older. Maybe mine will, too."

Cara looks at her wide-eyed. "Really? You're going to look for someone else?"

"I'm kidding you." She brings their plates to the table. Honestly, the girl could sometimes be terribly gullible, and other times she bowls Myra over with her fierce idealism and determination. Lately, she's been on a save-the-environment kick. She won't let Myra use Styrofoam cups or aerosol sprays, and she insists upon going through her garbage for the recyclables.

"How come you bought laundry detergent in that plastic bottle?" Cara says, picking up her chicken sandwich. "It's not your usual brand."

"It was on sale. Plus I had a coupon. It was too good a deal to pass up."

"That's right, inflict another plastic bottle on the planet! Do you realize that in less than ten years—"

"Look, I'll ask Howie to make a bird feeder out of it. Would that be okay?"

Cara shrugs and goes back to her sandwich. "Do I get to meet him?" she says, gesturing toward the basement.

"I don't see why not." Myra brings a tomato wedge halfway to her mouth. "But you're not going to ask him any embarrassing questions, are you?"

"Would I do that? Besides, your idea of embarrassing and mine are two different things."

"Just go easy on him. He's getting over a bad marriage."

"Hmmm," she says, lifting her eyebrows but offering no further comment. They finish their sandwiches, and while Cara goes downstairs to put in the second load, Myra clears the table. She is already thinking about supper, whether Haskell Reed has particular ideas about food, when she hears a commotion on the basement stairs.

"I'm terribly sorry! Are you all right?"

"Yeah, fine. No big deal." Cara comes into the room, re-clipping her barrettes. Haskell follows.

Myra introduces them to each other. "But I see you've already met."

"We ran into each other," he says. "Literally." He smiles sheepishly, like a boy who has taken a wrong turn and ended up in the teachers' lounge. "I was looking for the bathroom."

"Up another flight. And I'm making coffee, if you want any." She turns to Cara, whose face is busy recomposing itself, and asks her to grab the bag of cookies on the top shelf in the pantry. She gets the Mister Coffee machine going and lays out three mugs, three spoons, the sugar and milk, and a plate of Mint Milanos.

They hear the toilet flush, and then the coffeemaker gives a final grunt and a long hissing sigh. Haskell returns and takes a seat at the table. He looks from Cara to Myra and back. "So, you two must be sisters," he says.

Cara laughs out loud. Myra says, "She's my niece, my husband's sister's daughter."

"And yet, there seems to be a resemblance."

Myra doesn't see how. She has dark hair; Cara's is honey blonde, and she is at least three inches shorter and several dress sizes smaller than Myra. They are about as different as two people can be. But not wanting to offend him, she says, "I'll take that as a compliment."

"Well, what about me?" Cara pretends to pout.

"No offense intended." He offers her a quick smile.

"Of course not." Myra senses the conversation has gotten off to a bad start. She fills their mugs with coffee and tries another tack. "Haskell is a writer," she says to Cara. "Isn't that interesting?" To him she says, "You're working on a play, isn't that what you told me?"

"Yes, though I actually make my living writing other things. "Promotional literature, public relations articles, an editing project here and there. But theater is where I exercise my true talents."

"What's the play about?" Cara asks, her voice a few degrees warmer now.

"What is it about? Well..." A vague look comes into his eyes. He presses the tips of his fingers together. "I guess you could say it's about love. Or more specifically, the failure of love and all related institutions. It's a comedy."

"I don't know," Cara says skeptically, "it sounds pretty depressing to me."

"A *dark* comedy," he says, backpedalling. "In fact, it borders on the satirical. I have had to place myself at an ironic distance from the material, since most of it comes from my own recent and painful experience."

"Aunt Myra said you were divorced. What happened?"

Myra scowls at her. Really, the girl could be supremely tactless. But to be fair, it's probably not her fault. More likely, Loretta's bad influence.

"What happened?" He gets the vague look again. "Many things. But what it boiled down to, I suppose, is that she was not the woman I thought she was."

"So, who was she?"

Cara seems to be angling for a debate. Sensing trouble again, Myra interjects. "Did I mention that my niece is a student at Loyola University? She's won a full academic scholarship."

Haskell leans forward and regards her with interest. "And what is your field of study, if I may ask?"

"I haven't declared a major yet. All I know is, I want to make gobs of money."

"There is certainly something to be said for that."

"If you want my opinion," Myra says, "the most important thing should be doing what makes you happy and fulfilled. When I was going to college, no one talked about money. Money was beside the point. You went to college so you could go out and save the world."

Cara laughs. "This from the woman who is eco-unconscious."

"At the time, saving the earth was not an issue. We were thinking in terms of suffering humanity." Myra bites into a Mint Milano and recalls the days when she and Byron Levine had talked about opening a clinic to guide the morally depraved onto the path of righteousness. He was going to be a doctor of psychology, catering to the underprivileged; she was going to run the business side of his clinic. They would live simply and frugally on government stipends, their happy, healed clients being their true reward.

Once she started running around with Vinnie, though, her aspirations seemed to vanish altogether, and with that Evelyn Delgado ID in her purse, she was fast becoming one of the morally depraved people she had recently been so bent on saving. That spring day in the Grant Park gardens, when he brought out the silver band with the reddish-purple stone, slipped it on her finger and said, "So, you wanna get married?" she guessed she would not be returning to school. Now she and Vinnie had to work in earnest and put aside enough money so they could begin their new life together.

Without bothering to finish out the semester, she took a full-time job as a sales clerk at Marshall Field's. They put her in the book department on the second floor, which made her feel a little less guilty about abandoning her college career. She began wearing blouses and skirts and cardigan sweaters to work, and when she looked in the mirror, she saw how much she resembled Miss Gustafson, her high school English teacher.

There was plenty of time to read the books she sold. At first, she would page through them idly, but then she'd find ones she liked, and these she devoured in frantic snatches. Customers asked her advice.

Which was the best book on home decorating? What could you get for a ten-year-old girl besides Nancy Drew? What would she suggest to cheer up a friend who was recovering from a hysterectomy?

Myra bought herself a pair of horn-rimmed glasses and wore them on a chain around her neck. They inspired confidence, she felt, and before long she was building a regular clientele of the sort her mother and father had. Certain people would buy their dresses from no one but Nettie Greenburg, others would let no one but Jack Greenburg fit them with shoes. And there was Myra Greenburg in her schoolteacher disguise, selling books and dispensing opinion as if she knew anything, as if she'd had more than her measly year and a half of junior college.

But now Cara is going to be the first woman in the Calderelli family to earn a degree, and Myra has to take some of the credit. Let Loretta lead her free-wheeling existence; Myra's always been there to guide her niece, to emphasize the importance of education and the consequences of not following the rules. If Loretta couldn't serve as a role model, she could serve as the bad example. *Learn from her mistakes.* That is the message Myra has been imparting, and so far, it seems, Cara has been listening. Myra is suddenly compelled to give the girl's earlobe an affectionate, proprietary tug.

"What?" Cara says, annoyed.

"Nothing."

Copperfield chooses that moment to leap from the refrigerator, knocking over a cereal box on his way down. "Ah, Copperfield!" Haskell says, as if he were seeing the cat for the first time today.

"Is he yours?" Cara asks.

"Howie found him yesterday," Myra explains, lifting the cat off the countertop and setting him on the floor. "I've decided to adopt him."

Cara chuckles. "Oh, Aunt Myra, you are too much!" She leans back and shakes her head in amazement. "I know just what I'm going to get you for Christmas. A big sign for the front lawn. And it's going to read:"—she holds out her palm and writes imaginary words across it with her forefinger—"Myra Calderelli. Rescuer. Stray Animals and People."

Haskell offers a thin, apologetic smile. Myra can feel her face getting hot with embarrassment. "Honestly," she mutters, gathering spilled cereal off the countertop with the side of her hand. One of these days, she is going to have a serious talk with that girl about the folly of blurting out a thought merely because it happens to be passing through your honey blonde head.

※※※

On Sunday, as expected, Vinnie brings the children home early, and she is ready for him. Yesterday, she went to Famous Footwear and bought a pair of high-fashion boots that she found on the store's close-out table; then she stopped by Loretta's to borrow a few large pieces of jewelry. And this morning she styled her hair in a new way so that it dips dramatically over one eye. She is busy pouring red wine into a large glass when Howie dashes into the kitchen, waving a new action figure in his fist.

"I'm surprised your father bought you that," she says. "You already have every one ever made."

"Not the Monster-King Devil-Dog." He gives out a few war whoops and wrestles the action figure to the floor.

"Next time, perhaps your father will help you choose something a little more educational." She addresses the remark to her son, though she is fully aware of Vinnie slouching in the doorway, hands in his pockets.

He shoulders his way into the room and taps Howie on the arm. "How's about you take that somewhere else, okay?" When their son is out of earshot, he turns to Myra, the muscle near his left eye twitching. "What's this the kids tell me, you got some guy living with you?"

She takes a sip of wine and lets it roll around on her tongue. She has been sketching this scene in her head all day. As expected, he's gotten right to the point: no preliminaries for Vinnie. She swallows and says coyly, "I don't know what you are implying. He is merely renting the spare room."

"Since when do we got a spare room?"

"Surely you remember the one in the *basement*? The one we were *supposed* to fix up?" She doesn't mention the fishing episode, but she is certain he knows what she's referring to. "I cleared it out, and now this certain person is paying me to stay there."

"Where is he?" Vinnie says, looking around.

"Out." She totters toward him in her spike heel boots and looks down into his eyes. "However, you are welcome to wait and meet him. He's an extremely interesting person, a writer. I think he'll be famous some day."

"Oh, yeah?"

"Count on it." She reaches around him to open the refrigerator and pulls out a plate arranged with slices of cheddar and a bunch of purple grapes."

"I ate already, thanks."

"This isn't for you." Clicking back and forth across the floor, she lays the table for two with placemats and napkins. "You know," she says, cradling a basket of breadsticks, "there is something incredible about living under the same roof with a creative person. I mean, this whole entire house simply vibrates with artistic energy."

"This guy got a name?"

"Haskell Reed."

Vinnie snorts. "Yeah, I bet."

"Tall, educated. He's the most delightful man, and he gets along well with the children."

"Where'd you meet him, the library?"

Myra offers a calculated grin. "Not exactly." She puts down the basket and takes another sip of wine. "Actually, I met him at Billy Halligan's. He's a friend of a friend of Loretta—"

"Hold it!" He puts up a hand. "Since when you been hanging out in bars?"

She ignores the insinuation. The wine is giving her a feeling of rosy well-being, though she realizes she must be careful: with her and alcohol, there is a fine line between rosy and tipsy. "Anyway," she continues, "there we all were, gathered around a table, talking about life and love and so forth. Haskell had just been through this tragic affair—the woman was an airplane pilot, and one day she took off and he never heard from her again. Someone said they saw her in New Mexico, or somewhere out that way…" She gestures with the hand that is not holding the wine, the bracelets clinking like tiny cymbals, a musical accompaniment to her story. "I could tell how broken-hearted he was—"

"Wait a minute. How come he winds up living here?"

"I'm getting to that. You see, he and this woman had a fabulous apartment in Lincoln Park. He said he was happy there, but now that he was alone, everything reminded him of her, and it was driving him crazy. He'd been looking for a place to go to recover from his broken heart, and we started to talk, and…"

She brings the hand to rest, palm open.

Let him fill in the missing details.

Vinnie's face is a screen of shifting emotions: confusion, doubt, disapproval, and a faint wrinkle of jealousy that Myra is hoping to deepen. He says, "How come he didn't go look for another apartment, like a normal person?"

"Try to understand," she says in a voice dripping with patience. "Someone as sensitive as he is needs to be supported emotionally through this kind of a crisis. Creative people are not like you and me—"

"He plan on staying long?"

She lifts a shoulder. "How long does it take to heal a broken heart?"

He starts to say something and then changes his mind. She looks at the clock. Haskell should be making an entrance any minute now.

Vinnie drums his fingers on the countertop. She reaches past him and turns on the radio, dialing around until she hits a classical music station. She almost expects him to grab her and demand she put an end to this charade, but he begins to whistle lightly along with the music, something from an opera: hysterical sopranos in dire straits. Vinnie only listens to opera, or else the Rolling Stones: from one extreme to another, but what could you expect from a man who thinks Paul McCartney is a wimp?

Finally—finally!—she hears Haskell's key in the back door lock, and then several moments of fumbling before the door swings open. He stands on the threshold with a stack of books balanced on his forearms, a gooseneck lamp in one hand, a small sailboat painting wedged under one arm. His face is wan, and his glasses are smudged.

"Haskell!" Her voice rings with false heartiness. God, how she wishes he'd worn the sports jacket. That black coat makes him look like a refugee.

He nudges the door shut with his foot. "Sorry to intrude. I see you have company."

"Don't be silly. This is only Vinnie." She lights two candles and brings them to the table.

"I'm the husband." Vinnie shoots out his hand.

Haskell has to hold the key in his teeth to take it. "Pleased to meet you," he says, speaking around the metal. Myra sees pain register briefly in his eyes. Vinnie's handshake has always been a bone-crusher.

"So you're the guy with the broken heart, huh?"

"Yes, sir. I guess I am." He drops the picture. Myra picks it up for him. Then he drops one of the books, and she feels like hitting him.

"I see that you've been shopping," she says, forcing a smile.

"Yes, I have. The White Elephant thrift shop, next to the Methodist church."

She scans the spines on the books. "Love In The Ruins. Welcome To Hard Times. I've never heard of these. Do you think I could borrow them some time?"

"Of course." He keeps shifting his eyes toward Vinnie. "I'd, uh, best be going."

"Wait. I've fixed a light supper for us. He was just leaving."

"I was?"

"Thank you, but I'm afraid I'm not very hungry." He edges toward the basement door.

"Some wine, then? The consultant at the Cheese Chalet said this was an excellent choice." She pours the wine, and in the few moments she takes to admire the sparkle of red in the glass, he disappears. She hears him on the stairs, dropping something else.

Vinnie snickers. "Seems to be a nervous kind of guy."

"I think you were extremely rude."

"Me? What'd I do?" He holds his hands away from himself. *Not guilty, Ma'am, not me!* She can imagine him as a boy, bullying the other boys, and it makes her angry to see he is still getting away with it.

She breaks a breadstick in half. "Isn't there someplace you have to be?"

"I guess." He pulls a few grapes off the bunch on the plate. "Listen, I bought Jen a bottle of nail polish. Blue."

"Blue nail polish!"

"She said you'd let her wear it, so if it's not okay, don't blame me. And listen..."—he puts a hand on the doorknob and cocks a finger in her direction—"...stay outta them bars."

She throws a breadstick half at the closed door. The soprano voice on the radio is now hiccupping endlessly through the final notes of an aria. Myra clicks it off, huffs out the candles and sits down heavily in a chair. "Rats," she mutters, noticing the trail of pockmarks her new boots have left in the linoleum. The wine is giving her the beginning of a royal headache, and her feet are killing her. ❧

## SIX

"Her name was Vanstrassen. Sally Vanstrassen. Remember her, Myra? The two-flat across the street when we lived on Harding Avenue?"

"I was in grammar school then, Ma. How am I supposed to remember so far back?"

"Red hair, skinny."

"Nope."

"Always dressed like she was going to a party. Ah, well, what else could you expect? She was divorced, you know."

Nettie wets a thumb and begins dealing cards around the table. The four of them—Nettie, Myra, Cara and Loretta—are playing kalukey, a game similar to gin rummy but requiring two decks of cards and all the jokers.

"I don't get it," Cara says. "What was the big deal with being divorced?"

"Once upon a time, my darling, you stayed married no matter what. If a woman did happen to get divorced, everyone knew what she had on her mind. Getting married again. Stealing someone else's husband."

Loretta clears her throat. "Excuse me, but speaking as a divorced woman myself, let me point out that is a total load of crap. Most of the married men I know are creeps. They should of done their wives a favor and stayed single."

"Back then it was different. Any husband was better than no husband, because who were you if you didn't have a man? An old maid, a leftover." Nettie deals the final card and stacks the rest at the center of the table, and they each drop a quarter into the "pot," a small brown bowl Myra made in a high school ceramics class.

"Are you telling me this Sally had you worried about Dad?"

"Divorced women weren't innocent girls anymore, and as they say, boys will be boys. A smart wife kept her eyes peeled." Nettie fans the cards in her hand, studies them a moment, and then plucks them into shape.

Myra looks at hers and groans softly. She has nothing but a couple of tens and a four and six of diamonds. Fifteen cards and not a single run. Well, she has never believed in luck the way some people do, but it's going to take work to turn this into any kind of winning hand.

"Of course, nowadays you have to watch out for other kinds of women," Nettie goes on. "Your sex-crazed secretaries, your bored trophy wives, your sweet young things. And apparently no one believes in the doctrine of damaged goods anymore." She raises her eyebrows in resignation. "Ah, give me the good old days."

"What's 'damaged goods,' Grandma?" Jennifer asks, coming in from the kitchen and reaching over Myra's shoulder for the basket of Fritos.

Nettie folds down her cards. "Way back before you were born, my dear, any girl who had sexual relations before marriage was considered.... Well, let me put it this way: you wouldn't buy a package of Lorna Doones that'd already been opened."

"Ugh, sex. Gross!"

Cara says, "I can't believe you were expected to wait until after the wedding. I mean, talk about Dark Ages."

"The good ones waited. I did." Nettie picks up a card, flicks it with her middle finger, and tosses it onto the discard pile. "I was as innocent as a lamb."

"Is this the part, Ma, where you get the standing ovation?"

"Wait! Let me tell you about your great aunt Gert. Engaged to a man for over thirty years and never married him. Went to her grave without suspecting how babies were made, or born."

"Impossible."

"True!" She pledges with her right hand. "Thought the doctor unscrewed your belly button and pulled them out, like rabbits."

"Didn't they teach her about babies in school?" Jennifer asks.

"There was no such thing as sex education back then," Myra explains. "Come to think of it, Loretta, we never got much more than a few hygiene lectures from our gym teacher, did we?"

"Then how'd you guys learn about…mating, and stuff?"

Loretta offers Jennifer a grin and a wink. "I had this private tutor. Big juicy hunk name of Tony Delvecchio…"

"God, Mother," Cara says, drawing a card, "you're not going to go into the gruesome details, are you?"

Myra pours three fingers of Pepsi into her glass and thinks about her own virginity, lost at the age of nineteen in the earnest embraces of Byron Levine as he grunted and mumbled endearments—in French!—into her ear and the record player played Michael, Row Your Boat Ashore.

She never understood what the fuss over sex was all about until she started going out with Vinnie, and then she could hardly get enough of it. They made love every chance they got: wild, crazy love in the back seat of his Chevy Impala, in the drafty back bedroom of the apartment he shared with two friends, behind the sofa in her living room, dark except for the light shining from the kitchen where her parents read the newspapers at the kitchen table. Myra had to bite her lip to keep from yelping out with joy, and meanwhile her father rattled a page of newsprint and said to her mother, "So, what do you suppose this guy Nixon's up to now?"

"You can wipe that smirk off your face, Myra," Nettie declares. She picks up the nine of clubs Cara has discarded and slaps a run of nines and a combination ten-jack-queen on the table. "You won't catch me with a mess of points in my hand."

"Good move, Ma." Myra picks up a queen of hearts on her next turn and curses silently for having gotten rid of its sister on the previous go-around. She bites into a corn chip and vows to concentrate harder.

It has been raining all evening, a steady November drizzle punctuated now and then by a brief cloudburst. Everything feels damp and chilly, even the playing cards. Myra yawns and rubs at a stiff spot in her shoulder, and hopes she isn't coming down with something.

"Where's that boarder of yours tonight?" Nettie asks. "Harold?"

"Haskell. He's out somewhere, I guess." She says this with elaborate disinterest. "He doesn't have to check in with me."

"So excuse me for asking."

"Awww. I'm disappointed," Loretta says. "I thought I'd get a chance to meet him. What's he like?"

"He wears glasses," Jennifer says, "and he talks like that man in our science class movies who explains about stuff like earthquakes."

"In other words, Mother, he isn't your type."

"You know who used to take in boarders, Myra? Your Grandma Esther, my mother. During the Depression, we always had one or two to help pay the rent. A violin teacher, a postal worker, a lady who made hats—all down on their luck, pour souls." Nettie chuckles. "What a collection of characters. Funny how you're doing the same thing now."

"It is not the same thing, not at all."

"At least there's a man in the house again. It's not safe for a woman alone nowadays."

"Please, Ma, I can take care of myself."

"Maybe you should get yourself a dog."

"I have a dog."

"I mean a real dog, a watchdog. One that doesn't hide under the bed every time there's a storm."

"Don't make fun of Brownie, Grandma. She's had a hard life."

"Haven't we all, my dear, haven't we all." Nettie studies her cards and on her next turn lays another run on the table. "Well, girls, are you playing cards, or waiting around for the bus?"

"I'm trying to get enough points together," Cara says.

Loretta chews a knuckle. She draws a card and quickly tosses it, and Myra understands at once that she's taking the gamble: going for the big one, kalukey, and the whole pot of coins. Loretta turns to her and asks, "So how old do you think he is?"

"Haskell? I'm not sure. What do you think, Cara?"

"He talks like he knows a lot, so he can't be very young. On the other hand, he can be a little spacey."

"Yes, but I suppose that's just the way writers are."

Myra is growing used to the clackety-clack of his Smith-Corona, as well as his phonograph, which sometimes plays in wavy counterpoint. He seems to favor jazz that features weeping horns and wailing clarinets. She has also grown used to his habit of walking into the kitchen for an apple or a handful of peanuts and looking right through her, not saying a word.

At first, this infuriated her. What did he think she was, a piece of furniture? But then she realized that it had nothing to do with her, that his preoccupation must be part of the mysterious creative process. She would like to ask him about it, but for fear of sounding ignorant, she hasn't. "If I had to guess his age," she tells Loretta, "I would say that he's probably still in his thirties."

"Too old for me! Give me a young stud any day. Oh, those muscles...those buns!"

"Loretta, please!" Nettie cries. "There's a child in the room."

"I'm not a child, Grandma. I'm almost eleven and a half."

"Don't be in such a rush to grow up. It's a party out there, maybe? Struggle, struggle all day long, and one day you wake up dead."

"What an encouraging little speech," Myra says.

"You know me, Toots, I never mince words."

Loretta lights a cigarette and blows smoke. "I can't look at life like that. You never know what a day's gonna bring, so why not expect the best?"

"You can talk like that, with everything that's happened to you?"

"Sure. It all worked out okay. I couldn't get an abortion, so I got married and had this terrific kid here." She punches Cara lightly on the chin.

"You're skipping over a lot, aren't you?"

"Yeah, but what's past is past."

"If I was in your place, Mother, I'd have gotten rid of me."

"Cara!"

"Who knows how your life might have turned out if you didn't have a kid so early on."

"Well, I wasn't exactly college material. I had enough trouble getting my GED. Nah, I believe what was meant to be was meant to be."

"Trust in fate?" Myra says. "That's ridiculous. In this world, you have to make your own luck."

"Right on, Aunt Myra. Women have always taken responsibility. Now we have to take control."

"Seize our opportunities and stay away from trouble."

"I'm never getting married," says Jennifer. "And I'm never having babies. It's too gross."

Nettie turns to Myra. "Where does she get these ideas?" To Jennifer she says, "You'll change your mind. Once you find a boy and fall in love—"

"Ugh, boys!"

"Boys turn into young men."

"Some of them do." Cara sighs. "And some just turn into older boys."

"I'm surprised you haven't found at least one young man at your school that interests you," Nettie says. "Everyone knows college men are your best bet."

"They're all so immature. Sports, sex, drinking, that's all they care about." Cara draws a card and counts on her fingers. "Fifty-one points on the nose." She sets down three runs. "And I can lay my king on top of Mrs. Greenburg's queen."

"Please!" Loretta cries. "There's a child in the room!"

Nettie twists her lips into a grin. "Very funny." She picks up Cara's discard and lays down another run.

Myra's stomach tightens. On her past two turns, she's picked up a five of diamonds and another ten, giving her two runs but still not enough points to get rid of any of her cards. All she needs is for a few more cards—or a joker—to come her way. Then, even if she can't pull off a win, at least the defeat will be a little less painful.

From the perch on top of his cage, Angelo stares down at the game, where suddenly no one is speaking.

Cara twirls a lock of hair.

Jennifer sips from Myra's glass.

And then Loretta flashes an ace of clubs. "What's the name of this game?" she says and lays out her hand for everyone to see. Myra studies the beautiful runs of sixes and eights, the ace-deuce-three and two royal trios. All the cards she needed are there.

"Luck of the Irish?" Nettie says with a wink, spilling the bowl of coins into Loretta's hand. "All right, ladies, let's count up the points."

"Can I make a small loan, Mother?"

"Pass the chips, please."

The skies open. On the roof, the hammering rain sounds like a round of applause. The commotion has stirred up the parrot, who begins to pace along the top of his cage, shrieking *woof-woof!* and *merde-merde-merde!*

And then an image of another parrot pops into Myra's head.

Or—no, not a parrot, a blue parakeet, clucking softly to the image in the mirror attached to the bars of its cage. She sees the cage, suspended in a corner of someone's dining room, the thin shoulders of a woman bending to sweep up the little mess on the floor beneath.

"Ma, I remember! Mrs. Vanstrassen, the lady who lived across the street from us. She had a bird named Schultzie."

"Bird?"

It comes back to her in a rush: those afternoons when Nettie had to work and Myra went up to Sally's apartment after school. Sally served her juice and coffee cake and let her hold Schultzie on her wrist. *Mama loves you*, the bird would chant. He'd peck cake crumbs from her palm and allow her to run a finger gently over his tiny head.

Of course Myra remembers Sally Vanstrassen. How could she have forgotten?

"She wasn't there long," Nettie says. "Moved away the year after she came, to a fancy apartment on Lake Shore Drive. There was a lot of talk in the neighborhood about where she got the money. Maybe she found herself a rich boyfriend. Women like that, who knows?"

"Are we talking about the same person, Ma? She was a nice lady with a pretty smile, that's all. You make it sound like she was a hooker or something."

"What's a hooker?"

"Never mind, Jennifer."

"I remember thinking how lonely she must have been, with just that little bird for company."

"She did all right. Drove her own car—which was a big thing in those days. Always dressed to kill."

"She sounds like a woman ahead of her time," Cara says.

"I suppose she was, poor soul, but it wasn't any help to her in the end."

"What do you mean, Ma?"

"You didn't hear?" Nettie shakes her head sadly and gathers the playing cards in a single sweep of her arm. "Breast cancer. She died. I saw the obituary in the paper yesterday."

Myra claps a hand to her heart. She feels genuine grief, close to this tragedy, somehow, without knowing exactly why. "But this is so unfair," she says, her voice cracking.

"What has fair got to do with anything?" Nettie says. "Life is life."

"And no one here's gonna get out of it alive." Loretta stacks her quarters. "That's why you gotta live it up while you can. Take a few chances. All in all, what d'ya have to lose?"

"I think you have to be to be sensible," Cara says. "You need to have a plan for the future. Otherwise, how do you expect to get from here to there?"

"Your Grandma Esther had a saying: 'Man plans, God laughs.' Well, it loses something in translation." Nettie shuffles the cards and asks Cara to cut the deck. "New deal, girls. Are you ready?"

"I suppose," Myra says, but already she has lost interest in the game. The news about Sally Vanstrassen has really rattled her. She has an urge to flee, to dash out of the house and run through the streets, not caring if she gets drenched in the pouring rain, not caring what anyone will think of her.

But does she do that?

Of course not, and how could she even think of it? After all, she is the hostess of this little gathering, and like a good hostess she simply grits her teeth, rises from her chair and asks who would like more soda, more snacks, maybe a piece of fruit?

Before heading to the kitchen she tosses another quarter into the bowl, and in her current state of mind what she hears is not the friendly chink of the coin—metal against ceramic—but something else.

What she hears is a cemetery sound, cold and menacing: the scrape of a shovel hitting rock. ✧

# SEVEN

These are the few things Myra knows for sure about Haskell Reed: he is forty-one years old (she happened to get a look at his driver's license when he handed her the second week's rent), he wears boxer shorts and sleeveless tee shirts (they happened to be in the dryer when she opened the door to put her own load inside), and he does not at all care for cooked squash.

And it's not as if she hasn't tried to draw him out. Every night at supper, along with the salad, or the broccoli, or the mashed potatoes, she passes him some random tidbit from her life. She's mentioned the ballet lessons she quit taking after Madame Gabriella scolded her for not paying attention in class, the habit Nettie has of drawing in her lower lip before giving someone a piece of her mind, and the family scandal involving her father's aunt Sophie and Mendel the Iceman. She brings up whatever morsel she can think of, casually dropping it into the conversation and hoping for a similar offering on his part.

And it's not that he doesn't talk to her. He talks plenty. Give him a topic and he will go on for twenty minutes. After she told him the Sophie story, he got onto the subject of refrigeration, and before she knew it, they were discussing the Industrial Revolution. Howie became bored and tried to tell one of his knock-knock jokes, and Haskell paused with his butter knife over his bread to ask if anything was wrong.

"You're supposta say, Who's there?"

Haskell put down the knife and said, "All right, Howie. Who's there?"

Jennifer grumbled. "I hate these dumb jokes."

"Boo!" Howie waited. "You're supposta say, Boo who?"

Haskell smiled good naturedly and said, "Boo who?" Whereupon Jennifer opened her mouth, all set to steal the punch line. Myra saw it coming. She *ahem-d* noisily and sliced a forefinger menacingly across her throat. Not wanting to yell at the children in his presence, she has been resorting to elaborate gestures and facial expressions to keep them in line. (Really, she's had to turn herself into the Marcel Marceau of mothers.) Jennifer got the message and slumped back in her chair, and Howie announced, "If you're gonna cry, I'm not gonna tell you!"

Haskell chuckled and Jennifer gave a grudging snicker. "So," Myra said, breathing out again. She was happy to have averted another squabble and comforted by the presence of a second adult at the supper table. It was almost as if the four of them were a family unit. If only Haskell would open up to her, tell her of his dreams and disappointments. How can she help him get his life back together if he won't come clean?

She thinks that maybe his reluctance to confide in her has something to do with his fear of adding to her burdens. Whenever it appears she may have to do anything out of the ordinary—make an extra trip to the grocery, say, or relay a telephone message—he shakes his head with regret and says, "As if you didn't already have enough to worry about."

Meaning, she supposes, Vinnie. She cannot seem to convince him that things with Vinnie have settled into a manageable status quo. They have brief but polite telephone conversations, and when he comes for the children they exchange cousinly-type kisses. He's taking his time, and she is giving him the space he asked for. And maybe, when she sees him at his mother's on Thanksgiving, he'll be ready to admit his mistake and come home.

Meanwhile, there is Haskell, and most of the time she hardly knows he's around. She tells this to her mother on the phone one day, and Nettie says, "But he *is* around," her voice crackling over the wire. "Just make sure you don't get yourself involved. Don't ask for trouble."

"What do you mean, involved?"

"Right now, you've got a nice business relationship. So keep it that way."

Myra studies the label on a can of tomato sauce. For the sake of privacy, she has been conducting her telephone conversations from the pantry. "I cannot believe this. My own mother thinking that I'd be capable of having an affair."

"A word to the wise. I'll say no more."

"If I was going to have an affair, Ma, I would choose someone rich and handsome. Robert Redford, maybe."

"You can joke if you want, but listen to me, Myra. You're a woman alone, and a woman alone is vulnerable."

At the moment, Brownie is also in the pantry, sitting on her foot. On the other side of the door, Howie and his friend Jeremy are teaching each other to juggle lemons. Myra can hear Jennifer's hair dryer whining away upstairs, and Angelo shrilling his parrot version of Born Free in the next room.

"Alone? In this house?"

"You know very well what I mean."

"Put your worries aside, Ma. This is only a temporary situation that happens to be mutually convenient. Once I help him get his life straightened out, he'll be gone."

"So what's wrong with his life?"

"Well," she says, tracing her initials in the dust on top of a can of crushed pineapple, "I'm not exactly sure. I don't know too much about him."

"And he's asked you for help, I suppose."

"We haven't discussed it."

"See? This is what I mean by 'involved.'" Nettie pauses. Myra can picture her drawing in her lower lip, ready to launch an assault. "Did you forget what happened to Aunt Sophie? Threw away her happiness, sacrificed her husband and her children, and for what? I was only a little girl, but I remember what a commotion there was. Such a disgrace—"

"Did you know Daddy when you were little?"

"I met your father when I was twenty-two. Why?"

"I thought Sophie was *his* aunt."

"She was my mother's younger sister. Mendel lived in my mother's house, one of her boarders. Sophie used to come around all the time, sit in the parlor and play the piano and wait for him to come home from work. What a flirt she was, with those blue eyes and a voice that could charm birds out of trees. Asking for trouble, and everyone knew it. One day we wake up: no Mendel. And the next day: no Sophie."

Myra waits. "And...?"

"And what?"

"Didn't Sophie's husband hire a private detective to find them? I heard he tracked them down to a seedy hotel in Crown Point, Indiana. Or was it somewhere in New Jersey? And didn't someone threaten someone with a knife? Or was it a gun? Daddy said—"

"Your father! He makes everything into a Hollywood production. And it wasn't even his family. No, Sophie came home eventually, but her marriage was ruined and her children barely spoke to her. She paid a big price for a little romance."

The story Myra heard was that Sophie and Mendel eventually made their way to the Holy Land to work on a kibbutz and died in each other's arms during the first Arab uprising. She prefers that version to Nettie's, true or not, but already her image of Aunt Sophie has diminished. Myra sees her not in silk stockings and flapper's dress, as she had imagined, but in an apron and kerchief, a broken woman, forever sweeping up the pieces of her shattered life.

But what she really cannot stomach is her mother's puffed up self-righteousness. Hoping to deflate some of it, she says, "I'll bet Sophie had the time of her life on that little fling. I'll bet she never regretted it for a minute."

"You'd be wrong. She regretted plenty."

"She found love."

"Hah! She gave up more than she got, believe me."

She's losing heart for the argument but is still unwilling to yield. "I'm only sorry that I didn't know her," Myra says, defiant. "I would love to have known her. I'll bet we had a lot in common."

"Myra!" Nettie sounds hurt, disappointed. "You've always been such a *good* girl. Don't talk that way."

"Anyhow," she says, unable to resist one last dig, "it's nice to know I have a relative who is famous for something more interesting than keeping a tidy house."

∽∽∽

On Friday, Cara brings a bottle of wine. Myra is timing a macaroni and cheese casserole and trying to lure Copperfield down from the refrigerator by shaking a box of Crunchy Meals at him. "White zinfandel," she says, eying the label on the bottle. "What's the occasion?"

"I've decided to relax more, and besides, I don't have to do any real thinking until Monday." Cara holds the basement door open with her elbow as she maneuvers the laundry basket through. "Is Haskell home?"

"He went downtown to see a client. Something about an insurance brochure on accidental death and dismemberment."

Cara grimaces. "Ugh." She carries the basket downstairs and returns a few minutes later just as Myra is giving up on the cat. She sets the box of Crunchy Meals on the counter and peeks at the casserole in the oven. Cara says, "Is he settling in all right?"

"Well, you know how it is. There's always a period of adjustment."

"But he seems more…together…wouldn't you say?"

"A warm bed, plenty of food—they all respond to that. He just needs a little time to get his bearings."

"What about Howie and Jennifer? I mean, what do they think of him?"

Myra shakes her head. "It has given them something else to squabble about. Every night they argue over who's going to sleep with him, even though I made it plain he is to stay in the basement. He terrifies the dog, and there's the problem of the extra litter pan—"

The timer bell dings. Myra brings out the casserole, perfectly brown and bubbling. Cara says, "Aunt Myra?"

"Hmmm?"

"I was talking about Haskell."

"Oh." Myra ducks her head. "I thought you meant—" She gestures toward the cat, who has become suddenly alert to the aroma of hot cheese wafting his way.

Cara unscrews the cap on the wine. "Apparently, you need lots of this stuff," she says, pouring.

They clink their glasses.

"Not bad," Myra croaks. The second sip goes down more easily. "Did you want to see Haskell about something?"

"I've been kind of thinking of taking a course in modern drama next term, and I wanted to discuss it with him."

"Drama? You? I thought you were interested in more serious subjects."

"That *is* a serious subject. I'm also considering the history of film, or Renaissance literature. You know, Aunt Myra, I never realized there are whole areas of culture I've never even been exposed to."

"Are you surprised? Ours is not exactly a family of highbrows." She hands Cara a plate. "Does your advisor think there's room for these extra classes?"

"My advisor? She doesn't know anything. At least, nothing about real life. Haskell says I should get a truly liberal education because you can never predict what the future might hold. Did you know he graduated from the University of Michigan with a degree in anthropology? Then he joined the Peace Corps and got sent to Africa, only he developed this rash and had to come home. After that, he took a job with a printing company."

"When did you find out all this?"

Cara narrows her eyes. "I haff my veys. Actually, I came by last Tuesday to look for one of my brother's shirts. I thought it might have fallen behind the sink. You were out, and Haskell asked me to stay and have a drink."

"Drink?"

"Orange juice. Okay? Anyway, we had an interesting conversation. Did you know his mother used to be a nightclub singer?"

"No."

"And his father had some kind of secret job with the government, the CIA maybe."

"Did he say anything about his ex-wife?"

"Nope, not a word."

"He probably thinks you're too young to confide in." Myra taps a finger against her glass. "I wonder if he had an unhappy childhood. His parents don't sound like ordinary people, do they?"

"I wouldn't know anything about ordinary parents."

Myra smiles at her. Cara's story about her brother's lost shirt doesn't ring true—she is not that conscientious—but she's not surprised that Cara would come looking for an excuse to talk to Haskell. A girl like her, growing up pretty much fatherless, would be inclined to seek the advice of a worldly and experienced older man. That's not exactly how Myra views him, of course, but she would never admit that to her niece.

"What have you told him about our family?" she asks.

"I said that I thought Loretta's life would make an interesting movie. Lots of sex and violence—"

"You didn't!"

"—and I mentioned that Uncle Vinnie was almost killed in Viet Nam."

"He never left the ship his whole tour."

"Ship? I thought he flew a helicopter."

"Who told you that?" Myra is vaguely irritated that such an obvious fabrication should pass for truth. "Never mind, it doesn't matter. Did Haskell want to know anything about me?"

Cara pauses to consider the question. "Well, he did wonder where you get your energy. He thinks it's amazing the way you take care of everyone all day and then go out to work at night. He went on and on about it." She shoots Myra an ironic look. "Pretty sickening, if you ask me."

Myra feigns annoyance. "You!" Every so often, she still gets the urge to pinch Cara's round, rosy cheeks.

Copperfield has come down from the refrigerator and is investigating something on the counter. Myra can see his long orange tail swaying contentedly. She rises slightly from her chair, then rushes for the cat, who has been licking at the macaroni casserole. "I swear," she says, grabbing him by the scruff of the neck, "I'm going to drop this guy at the pound. I am going to gas him myself."

"You'd never do that, Aunt Myra. You're too soft hearted, and besides, it would ruin your sterling reputation."

She has no comeback for that remark, which she finds flattering despite Cara's snarky tone of voice. So Haskell admires the things she does; practically stands in awe, if her niece is to be believed. Myra scrubs at the cheese prints on the counter with a dish rag, thinking that at least someone recognizes the kind of non-stop effort it takes to run a household and raise children and build a small business, facing with diligence—and, often, cheerfulness— the various and sundry demands on her time without buckling under the pressure.

That thought keeps her spirits up for the next several days while she tackles a few chores she has been putting off for too long. She spends Saturday washing windows; Saturday evening, with an old Judy Holliday movie on TV for company, she pays a few bills and eventually balances her checkbook. Then on Sunday morning, as she is removing the glass globe from the light fixture in the hallway, a scene from the past comes rushing back, and it nearly knocks her off the stepladder.

She remembers the afternoon the four of them went out to buy the fixture, a horrible rainy Sunday afternoon in the middle of September.

It was a family outing destined from the beginning to fail. The children were cranky—Howie cutting a tooth and Jennifer getting over a chest cold. Vinnie had been in a bad mood all week, ever since he flipped on the wall switch and the old ceiling fixture blew out and crashed to the floor, the latest in a series of minor household disasters. At the appliance store, they trudged through the aisles for over an hour, Vinnie grumbling that everything was too expensive. They compromised finally on a white globe with gold trim, Myra giving in because Jennifer was falling apart and she herself had a pain from carrying Howie around on her hip.

They should have just gone home, but she had promised the children burgers and fries for lunch. Vinnie rolled his eyes at her when she asked him to stop at McDonald's, and it surprised her to realize how the casual surliness she had once found so appealing in him could look so much like plain old grouchiness when you ran into it on a daily basis.

Howie's hamburger had to be broken into tiny pieces. Jennifer insisted on a quarter pounder and a milkshake, and then refused to eat. Vinnie threatened; Jennifer cried. Still angry about the light fixture she would now be forced to live with for at least another decade or more, Myra remained silent.

It was stupid, and she knew it, even as she made a big show of comforting Jennifer and wiping ketchup tenderly from Howie's forehead. Vinnie she ignored, treating him as if he were a stranger who could not possibly know the right thing to do. And then she looked up and noticed the way he was staring at the three of them: ice in his eyes, as if they were no relation to him at all.

Slowly he rose and threw his napkin on the table, where it landed in a puddle of milkshake leaking from a straw. The three of them watched as he walked out of the restaurant and climbed wearily into the car.

Jennifer said, "Mommy?" Howie sucked at a French fry and kept his eyes on his father.

Oh, she knew how he felt, and she couldn't honestly say she blamed him. For love of her, he had entangled himself in the sticky web of family obligations, and what had it gotten him? She would not have been a bit surprised if he drove away and left them there.

But he didn't drive away. He waited behind the rain-spattered windshield while she fed Howie the rest of his Happy Meal and finished Jennifer's herself.

On the way home, nobody spoke. Myra kept looking for opportunities to break the silence, to let him know she was sorry without actually coming out and saying so. (After all, she was not entirely at fault; his moodiness hadn't helped matters one bit.) Only blocks from their house, she mentioned that maybe they should stop for gas, and that's when he blew up.

"I could read a fuel gauge," he bristled, glaring at her. "I could do that right!" He took a corner too fast and zoomed up their street, veered into a parking space and killed the engine. He pulled the ceiling fixture box from the trunk of the car and stomped off into the house, and spent the rest of the afternoon hammering and drilling and knocking it into place.

And this is what Myra is remembering, loosening the last of the screws, when Haskell walks in and says, "May I help you with that?" His voice startles her enough that she fumbles and drops the metal cap. He rescues the glass globe, taking it from her hands and setting it on the hall table. Then he helps her down from the stepladder.

"Thanks," she says, sniffling.

"I was wondering if you'd do me a favor—oh, have you caught a cold?"

"Dust," she says. "Did you want something?"

He appears rumpled today. His hair sticks up, as if he's been pushing his fingers through it, and there are ink stains all over his hands. He holds out a sheaf of papers. "I was hoping you would have a few minutes to read through this with me."

"What is it?" she asks, taking the papers. "Your new play?"

"Act two, scene one. Something is wrong with it, and I thought that being able to hear the voices of the two characters out loud might help me locate the problem."

"I'd be happy to read," she says, remembering how lavishly he complimented her to Cara. "Did I ever mention that I was involved in my high school dramatic arts department? I was the understudy for the female lead in The Man Who Came to Dinner."

"Excellent."

"Though I haven't been to a play since…" Since she met Vinnie, she was going to say. "But my father used to act in amateur productions before he married my mother. I think I may have inherited a little bit of the acting bug."

"Do you still have an interest?"

"Maybe a little," she says, smiling. There are days when it does seem like she's walking through someone else's life, reading lines. She pages through the script, trying to make out the text between the scratched-over passages.

"Perhaps you have some familiarity with Theater of the Absurd."

"The name rings a bell." She recalls dimly something Byron Levine once took her to see, six actors wandering around an empty stage, spouting nonsense. "Theater of the Absurd," she repeats and remembers how, to Byron's infinite annoyance, she had dozed off before the final curtain.

"Beckett? Pinter? Ionesco?"

She gestures noncommittally. "It's been a while."

"No matter. I merely wanted to point out that my plays fall into that general category." He is standing very close to her, and she can smell his stale aftershave, a mild tang of sweat, and the musk of unwashed clothes. His breath whistles through his nose as he studies the pages over her shoulder, and it's making her a little uncomfortable, especially since no one else is home.

"Could you tell me a little about the play?" she asks, sidestepping away.

"I can tell you in three words. Man. Woman. Lifeboat." He follows her into the living room and takes a seat on the couch.

Removing a cat, Myra sits down beside him. "How did they get into the lifeboat?"

"*How* is not important. The point is, they are trapped. To leave is to risk death."

"But if they'd just been through something horrible, like a shipwreck, wouldn't that have an effect on their motivations?"

She believes she has asked an intelligent question, but he frowns with impatience. "These characters *have* no motivations. In fact, it's a mistake to think of them as characters in the traditional sense. They are, simply and tragically, man and woman dehumanized to the point where their thoughts and actions are little more than a series of nervous impulses."

Myra hesitates before she asks, "Are they married?"

"Perhaps, if you view the lifeboat as a symbol of matrimony. Perhaps not. But you may think of them as married, if you wish."

She does. Haskell and—what was her name?—Elizabeth. "So, what happens during the play?"

"Nothing, really. That is the point of it. But they wait, and they engage in philosophical debate. And they fish, of course."

This doesn't sound to her like much of a play. In The Man Who Came to Dinner there were lots of interesting characters coming and going in great sweeps of emotion. Myra never actually had the chance to perform on stage—Natalie Rosenthal had been irritatingly healthy throughout the run—but she'd gotten so wrapped up in the role of Miss Maggie Cutler, secretary to the acerbic and dictatorial Sheridan Whiteside, that it took her weeks after the play was over to return fully to herself and her real life.

"In this scene," Haskell goes on, "the man and the woman are discussing the notion of identity. The woman claims it is a fixed quantity, and the man argues that identity is dependent upon circumstance."

"Identity." She nods solemnly.

"You can start reading here." He points at a spot halfway down the top page.

She clears her throat and begins. "'I am I. I am what I am. I think, therefore I am—'"

He rushes in with the next line. "'I am the great I am. That's what you were going to say next.'"

"'You don't know everything.'"

"'I know enough to predict the future. I say we will have fish for lunch.'"

"'This is hopeless.'"

"'Hopeless, yes, but not serious. Who are you today?'"

"'The same person I was yesterday.'"

"'Ah, but yesterday, you were less thirsty than today. Yesterday, all things considered, you were a happy woman.'"

The scene goes on like this for eleven long pages. Myra cannot make sense of it or see what it has to do with him and his ex-wife. It's obvious that he's put all his pain and disappointment and failure into these lines—she can hear it in his voice. But it's all in code. What were the issues? And who was to blame?

They finish the scene, and then Haskell folds his hands behind his head and stretches his long legs under the coffee table. He sighs deeply and stares off into space "I don't know…" he begins, but does not continue.

After a moment, to break the silence, Myra says, "It sounds very…deep."

He nods absently.

"Profound, I mean. And the characters—the man and the woman, that is—certainly have a lot to say to one another."

"There is a great deal of talking, yes. But you'll notice there is no real communication."

"Then they must be married after all," she says, joking; probing. "They must have been in that lifeboat for a long time."

"Long enough." He does not elaborate.

She tries another tack. "Actually, with Vinnie and me, it was always the things we didn't say that caused the trouble."

"Angry silences?" He grunts. "Yes, I know exactly how that goes."

"Sometimes, though, it's just hard for people to come out and say what they're thinking and feeling."

"The issues get confused, the truth gets lost."

"Right." Myra turns to him, tucking her legs under her. She feels he is on the verge of revealing something to her, some clue that will unlock the mystery of him.

"What did you think of the discussion over the missing necklace?" he asks.

"Where he accuses her of losing it and she accuses him of using it for bait?"

"Whom did you believe?"

"Actually, I didn't think too much about it."

"It didn't seem important?"

"Not really. That's the kind of quarrel people have all the time."

"Exactly. That is why you must consider the *subtext*."

"Oh, well. Sure." Suddenly, she's in over her head.

"You have to search through the banality of ordinary conversation, dig deep and arrive at the core of veracity. After all, it's only logical that if one character is telling the truth, the other must be lying. Right?"

"Y-yes," she ventures.

"Wrong!" He folds himself forward and grips his knees. "Don't you see? The objective truth has absolutely no relevance here! *What* does a character *need* to believe, and *why*? *Those* are the pertinent issues, and the *only* ones worth considering."

"It seems to me," Myra says, feeling her face redden, "that when you ask a person to do you a favor, it's rude to jump down her throat just because she isn't an expert on every little thing." She taps the pages into an orderly pile and hands them back to him, excuses herself and leaves the room. On her way into the kitchen, she picks up the glass globe and carries it to the sink.

He follows, muttering an apology, something about lack of sleep and creative tension. "If you're interested, I could recommend a few books on this particular genre of theater."

"Thank you. I will try to find the time." She sets the globe under the tap and turns on the water, and the powdery corpse of a large moth floats to the surface.

"That's the trouble with the world nowadays. No one has time for culture. No one has time for art."

"Some of us have busy lives," she sniffs. "Some of us have houses to tend to and children to raise, not to mention business obligations and extended family—"

She turns away from the sink, but he is already gone. She can hear the scrape of his shoes on the stairs and then his door shutting, deliberately, with the force of a final rebuke.

## EIGHT

At Lena's house, Thanksgiving dinner begins with bowls of rigatoni in an avalanche of homemade tomato sauce. The fennel and mushroom salad comes next. Myra has never quite gotten used to the licorice taste of the fennel, though she's managed to eat most of the salad and dutifully nibbled an olive and half a garlic roll. Now, as they are waiting for the turkey, she is sure she won't be able to swallow another bite. With Vinnie sitting only a table's width away, it's been hard enough getting this far.

He's looking awfully good in a new tan and red striped sweater, a white shirt setting off his skin, but the expression on his face is pure misery. He looks like someone sitting in a dentist's chair, waiting to have a tooth extracted.

As soon as Lena emerges from the kitchen with the big oval platter, Nettie comes alert. "Wait, Lena dear," she says, rising and pushing back her chair, "let me help." She reaches past Myra's father and clears a space at the head of the table in front of Uncle Aldo. With a small groan Lena sets the platter down, and Nettie clucks her approval at the huge browned bird resting in its parsley nest. "Beautiful, beautiful! Will you look at that!"

Stifling a belch, Myra takes a sip of water.

Her father has been telling a joke, and now he straightens his tie and tries to pick up the thread of his story. "So Becky says to Morris, 'Listen, Mister Smartypants, I ain't no dummy. I got just as much culture as anyone. I know who Wolfgang Amadeus Mozart is—'"

"Jack, let it alone already!" Nettie takes a friendly swipe at his shoulder. "That joke's so old, it has whiskers. Everyone's heard it already."

"Not me, Mr. Greenburg."

"Don't encourage him, Cara."

In the next room, Jennifer and Howie are sitting around a card table that has been set up for them and their cousins, Joey and Tim. Myra can hear them giggling, making farting sounds with fists in armpits, not eating. Vinnie gets up to see what's going on. His voice rumbles, and the children fall silent. Then another giggle, then a whole round of them. Vinnie's voice comes again, higher pitched. "Okay, Wiseguy…"

"Tell them no one gets turkey until they finish their salads," Nettie hollers.

"Tell Joey I'll bust his butt if he even thinks of spitting food at anyone." Loretta reaches for the wine; her third glass, Myra notes.

Vinnie returns to the table, lips puckered in irritation. "Think those rug rats appreciate good food? Ma's been at it since five this morning, but they don't care. I say, give 'em hot dogs and the hell with it."

Myra smiles. Tough guy, hard as nails; but she's seen him melt over stray kittens, school pageants, Bette Davis movies. She asks him, "Is Howie eating?"

"Got as much food on him as in him." He picks up a spoon and taps it against the tablecloth, waiting for Uncle Aldo to finish carving the turkey. Either he cannot look at her, or he will not.

Lena wipes her forehead on her apron and backs into the kitchen, returning moments later with bowls of sweet potatoes, Brussels sprouts and green beans balanced on her sturdy arms.

Uncle Aldo says, "Hey, Vin, how 'bout a drumstick?"

"Sure."

Nettie asks for white meat. "Just a slice." She adjusts her pearls and pats her hair, which has been freshly colored and set; her nails are painted an appropriate shade of cranberry. "Everything looks so good, Lena," she remarks.

Lena laughs. "Sure it's good. It's made with love." She watches as Myra shakes a dollop of potatoes onto her plate. "Whatsa matter?" she says. "You on a diet?"

"N-no."

"Take some more." She scoops out a hefty portion and then hands the bowl to Cara.

"Thank you," Myra says, amazed that she can still be so intimidated by a woman barely five feet tall.

The first time Vinnie took her to meet his family, it was Easter. Cara was just a little girl then, and his grandparents were still alive, though his father had already been dead for several years. His portrait in a heavy oval frame on the wall above the buffet showed an older, jowlier version of Vinnie with the same smoldering eyes. Myra tried not to stare at it. She tried to pretend she wasn't terrified of this strange, dark house and the somber-looking family who lived in it.

Nettie had counseled her before she left. "If they pray," she said, "just sit and be quiet. Be respectful. If they ask why you're not praying, tell them you're Jewish. You have your own God. Don't be ashamed to speak up." Then she sighed and straightened the collar of the plain wool dress Myra had bought especially for the occasion. "I don't suppose I can talk you out of this," she said, and as an afterthought added, "They'll probably serve ham."

Ham, yes. And chicken cacciatore, linguini with white clam sauce, stuffed artichokes, risotto, zabaglione. Myra had never seen so much food at one meal. No one prayed, though they treated the food with reverence, endlessly passing the platters and bowls, tasting, smacking their lips and murmuring approvals. Myra thought of meals in her own home: hurried affairs, sandwiches washed down with soda or instant iced tea. She never knew it was possible to spend more than ten minutes over a meal.

The grandparents spoke no English, so everyone spoke Italian to them, and sometimes to each other. Myra heard the grandfather say, "Bella, bella," though she could not tell if he was referring to her or to the platter of ham. No one seemed interested in bringing her into the conversation.

Vinnie ate and otherwise kept his mouth shut. Myra felt their eyes on her. She wasn't fooling anyone. Never mind her plain dress and pink lipstick, they knew she was no virgin.

"The trouble with my family," he told her later, stroking her shoulder while she wept into her white gloves, "is they're all nuts."

"They don't li-ike me," she hiccupped.

"They don't know you yet."

"I'm too sk-inny, too tall —"

"Give 'em a little time."

"I'm not Italian. They'll never ac-cept me—"

He drew her into his arms and rocked her gently. "Don't worry, My-ra. They'll come around."

And to her amazement, they did. Loretta called the next day to apologize for thinking Myra was like the girls who used to snub her in high school. That summer, Uncle Aldo sent her a postcard greeting from Atlantic City, and at Christmas the grandparents presented her with a bottle of their homemade wine.

Lena was the only holdout. She kept a cool distance, continuing to treat Myra as if she were some schemer, tempting the prince away from his home and family, and it was not until years later, when Myra had miscarried their first baby, that she saw fit to give in. She came to see her in the hospital, bringing a clay pot filled with herbs. Having no faith in doctors, Lena preferred to treat illness with her own homemade remedies: rosemary tea, garlic soup. She gave specific instructions for making a brew from the leaves and said that Myra must drink it three times a day, and Myra promised that she would.

"You'll see," Lena said, putting the clay pot aside, "you'll be better soon. Have lotsa babies." Then she held out her arms and Myra sank into them, resting her head between Lena's soft breasts. So this is what it means to be drawn into the bosom of the family, she thought. She might have laughed then, if she had not been so busy sobbing for her little lost daughter or son.

Now she holds out her plate to Uncle Aldo for a serving of turkey, while her father tries to go on with his story. "So, anyway, Becky says, 'Why, I saw Mister Wolfgang Amadeus Mozart himself just yesterday. He was getting off the number one-thirty-one bus at Oak Street Beach'—"

"My-ra."

"Mm?"

"Are you—"

"Yes, Vinnie? What is it?"

"—finished with the salt?"

She passes the shaker across the table. "Pepper?" she says, trying to catch his eye.

"No, thanks." He goes back to his food, chewing sullenly. It's more than obvious he would rather be anywhere else, but an invitation from Lena is like a jury summons. You don't even consider not going.

Years ago, it would have been unthinkable for them to sit through a long family dinner like this. Halfway into the veal marsala, she might suddenly feel his fingers slip around her upper arm, his breath in her ear. "Let's split," he'd whisper, sending shivers of anticipation rolling through her. She let him muscle her outside, to the back porch or the front hallway, and they would grind against one another, their tongues searching like desperate squirrels.

Has he forgotten how it used to be?

Things seemed to change after they decided to get married. He traded in the Chevy for a VW with reliable brakes and went out to find a job with a future. They opened a joint savings account at Talman Federal and stopped going to the Tip Tap Lounge. It was wonderful, of course—marriage to Vinnie was what she'd wanted—but sad, too, in a way she could not explain: like opening your hands to grab a floating dollar bill and dropping all your shiny new pennies.

Now she steers her fork around her plate and wonders what she can say to him to get a conversation going. Idly, she forms an L with two green beans, cutting one in half with her knife to get the short part of the letter. One long bean and three short pieces for the E. The T is easy, and she uses a little curved bean end piece for the apostrophe. Smiling, she imagines Vinnie reading the message on her plate, giving her a wink, slipping away and waiting for her on the back porch...

Or might he get the wrong idea altogether? Would he think she was asking for a divorce? A division of property and children?

LET'S SPLIT.

These days, that could mean anything.

Horrified, she stabs her fork at the beans and eats up every one of them. Nettie leans over and says, "I never knew you cared so much for vegetables."

"Vegetables got vitamins," Lena says. "More stuffing, Nettie?"

"No, thank you. But it's delicious. Really, delicious." She has been using her knife and fork to remove the pork sausage from the bread stuffing and transfer it to the side of her plate. Last year, Lena hid the sausage in the pasta sauce, and Nettie finished half the serving before realizing it was there. Myra does not understand the fuss; she happens to know that her mother's favorite sandwich is a BLT. Only at Lena's house do Jewish dietary laws become an issue.

"I just love Thanksgiving," Nettie says, patting her lips with a napkin. "It's such a democratic holiday."

"I'm crazy for Christmas," Lena counters. "Trees and presents. Midnight mass."

"Chanukah." Nettie hawks the ch. "The Festival of Lights."

Myra is expecting Lena to come back with something about Santa and the reindeer, when her father's voice edges in. "So Morris is looking at his idiot wife telling everyone she saw Wolfgang Amadeus Mozart getting off the number one-thirty-one bus at Oak Street beach—"

"Jack, for God's sake…"

And suddenly the whole room is alive with voices.

"I got a nice piece a dark meat here. Who wants seconds?"

"I do, Uncle Aldo."

"…gravy?"

"What's for dessert?"

"Spumoni and fruit. Two kindsa pie. Biscotti. Cannoli. Coffee or milk."

"S'matter, Ma? You didn't have time to bake a chocolate layer cake?"

"Anyone out there wants dessert better clean off their plate!"

"—so wait. Then Morris says, he says, 'What are you talking? Wolfgang Amadeus Mozart getting off the one-thirty-one bus at Oak Street beach? Becky, sweetheart, everybody knows—'"

"…pass the butter, please…."

"—the one-thirty-one bus, it don't stop there.'"

❦❦❦

On her feet now and helping to clear the table, she is feeling a little less stuffed; but Nettie is giving her a headache, chattering about a doll she once bought for her as a Chanukah present. "It had a little wrinkled face, just like a crying baby," she says. "It was the Blessed Event doll, but you called it Blessedy. You thought its last name was Vent."

"Didn't you always give me those greasy chocolate coins wrapped in gold foil?"

"You don't remember the doll?" Nettie presses a hand to her heart, wounded. She has been attempting to convince Myra of her happy childhood. "You took that doll to bed with you every night. She was the guest of honor at your tea parties."

Dolls? Parties? All Myra can remember of her childhood is a lonely country without a brother or a sister, without so much as a cat or bird or turtle. "Once I had a make-believe friend," she says, trying to be helpful, "but I don't remember the doll. Why bring that up now?"

Nettie frowns. "I didn't want you to forget that the Greenburg family also used to get together on the holidays. Remember your Grandpa Max, how he used to make you laugh by swallowing a whole boiled egg? You'd want him do it again and again."

"He died of a stroke, didn't he?"

"I can see you're in a wonderful mood tonight." Nettie stacks cups and follows Myra into the kitchen, where Cara is busy scooping leftovers into empty cottage cheese containers. Lena and Loretta are rolling the portable dishwasher in from the back porch. As usual, the men and the children have escaped to the living room.

"It's a little obscene for us to gorge ourselves on all this food when half the world is starving," Cara declares. "And look at all this garbage."

"Wrap some turkey for that boarder of yours, whatshisname. Henry."

"I've got sweet potatoes for him, too." Cara slides a container along the counter in Myra's direction.

Myra opens the refrigerator and puts away the butter and milk. She feels weighted—like one of those clown toys that bobs up each time you knock it down—tired and discouraged. She had hoped that tonight would be the beginning of something good between her and Vinnie, had even rehearsed several possible scenarios. Riding to Lena's in the back seat of her parents' car, she pictured Vinnie bringing her home, falling asleep on her couch; or Vinnie putting Howie to bed, coming into her bedroom to say goodnight, not leaving; or Lena inviting the children to stay the night, Myra and Vinnie driving away alone...

She closes the refrigerator door and stares into the living room. Her father and Uncle Aldo are trying to teach Howie to play gin rummy. ("It's called a *suit* of cards, Howie," one of them says, "not a *jacket*.") Loretta's boys are slugging each other with sofa pillows. Myra can smell the smoke from Aldo's cigar and make out some of the dialogue from the M*A*S*H rerun on TV; and if she cranes her neck a little to the left, she can see Vinnie's profile over the arm of the sofa, the top of Jennifer's head next to him.

*Awww, Margaret,* Frank Burns whines from the television set, *you don't mean that!* Vinnie's profile jiggles with laughter.

"Have you noticed how much he's been drinking?" Nettie whispers, passing behind Myra on her way to the stove. "I'm telling you, the man is on a downward slide."

"A few glasses of wine. No big deal."

"And brandy, or whatever they're pouring down their throats out there. And did you notice? He hasn't spoken a word to me or Daddy all night."

"He's depressed. Being here makes him think of his father."

"I don't know how you can continue to defend him."

"What?" Lena says, reaching around the dishwasher to attach the hose to the faucet on the kitchen sink.

"Myra and I were just discussing how much work it must be to prepare such a lavish dinner."

"Sure it's a lotta work, but better a happy occasion than a sad one."

"You're absolutely right, Lena. Like I tell my customers, better to pay the tailor than the doctor. Am I talking?"

"Sure. Better the grocer than the pharmacist. Better the accordion player than the—"

"What should I do with all this pasta?" Myra says, feeling her store of patience draining rapidly.

"Take some home."

"There's enough here to feed an army," Nettie mutters, tearing off a sheet of tin foil.

The kitchen is still warm and fragrant with the lingering aromas of tomato sauce and roasted meat, pumpkin and almond. Exhausted, Myra sits down at the table, resting her head on her hand while the women bustle around her: Loretta loading the dishwasher, Nettie and Cara stowing food in the refrigerator, Lena making another pot of coffee.

She closes her eyes. Last night she dreamed she and Vinnie were in a small rowboat, peacefully drifting along the Lincoln Park Lagoon. The dream was so vivid she could feel the warm sun on her skin and the cool breeze in her hair. As they passed into the darkness under a bridge, he suddenly lifted her dress and made love to her right then and there. It was a moment charged with lust and danger—broad daylight and crowds of people everywhere—and when she awoke, she realized that she'd had an orgasm in her sleep, the tingly dampness between her legs just beginning to subside.

Lena comes over with a plate of cookies and sits down next to Myra. "You okay?"

Taking one, she nods.

Lena puts a hand over her arm and leans close. She smells faintly of sweat and cinnamon; her jet black hair is streaked with silver. "Italian men," she says. "You gotta understand…"

"But he won't even talk to me."

"He'll be back, you'll see."

That's what Myra has believed all along, but now, hearing the words, she is not so sure. They sound hollow, like a promise no one has the power to enforce. "What am I going to do?" she almost wails, disheartened to hear the panic in her voice.

"Wait. Be strong." Lena emphasizes the words with a firm squeeze.

Myra bites into a biscotti, letting the flavor of toasted hazelnuts crumble on her tongue. What she'd really like to ask her mother-in-law is this: If the worst should happen, if he is really gone for good, then what about her? Would an ex-daughter-in-law still be welcome at Lena's table for the holidays?

❧❧❧

Her parents drive them home. Jack toots the horn playfully as he pulls away, leaving Myra at the curb with a bulging grocery bag and two cranky children: Jennifer complaining because they couldn't stay later at Lena's, Howie wanting to know when his dad is going to live with them again.

Myra pinches the bridge of her nose. "Have you asked him?" she says, trying not to let her exasperation show.

He stares at his shoes. "Dad gets mad when you ask him too many questions."

"That's cause Howie always wants to know dumb things like where the sun goes at night."

"That is not a dumb question, Jennifer."

"And why cats can't have puppies."

"That's not what I said, stupid. I asked him why dogs can't have kittens."

"Howie," Myra says, "is that a cranberry stain on your shirt?" She makes him take it off and then she shoos them both up to bed, reminding them to brush their teeth and put the cap back on the toothpaste. Tomorrow she will sit her son down and go over the facts of life with him one more time, but right now, all she wants is to crawl under the covers and wait for the merciful oblivion of sleep.

She carries the grocery bag into the kitchen and whistles for the dog. The stove light is on, but she doesn't notice Haskell sitting at the table until he says, "Did you have an enjoyable get-together?" His voice sounds rusty, and she realizes he has spent the entire evening here alone. She doesn't know what made her assume he would have someplace to go.

"It was a typical family dinner," she says, filling a bowl with cold water and dipping Howie's shirt into it. "Noisy and fattening." She whistles again for the dog, who stumbles in bleary-eyed.

"I've already walked her. I hope you don't mind." He brings a mug to his lips and drinks. "There is more hot water for tea, if you'd care for some."

"I don't think I can get another thing down. But here—" She takes the containers out of the bag and sets them on the table. "Help yourself."

He pops off the lids, and soon a version of Lena's feast in miniature is spread before him. "Are you sure you won't join me?" he says. "This looks quite good."

"I really ought to get to bed." She pulls out a chair and sits down. "Tomorrow I'm taking the children to see the Christmas windows on State Street."

"The crowds will be terrible, and the forecast is for drizzle." He sounds almost cheerful. He breaks a cannoli in half and delivers the pastry carefully to his lips.

Myra dips a finger into the tub of sweet potatoes. "We've always gone as a family, the four of us. The children look forward to it, and I would hate to disappoint them." She licks off the potatoes. "Anyway, I think it's important to provide them with as much continuity as possible. This is a difficult time for them."

"Yes, I very much suppose it would be." He holds out a sheet of tin foil with a little heap of turkey on it. "I was reading an article on the subject only the other day. One of a continuing series on families in crisis…"

She takes a slice of turkey and eats it slowly, by shreds, while he drones on about some new psycho-social theory. She's too tired to take in most of what he is saying, but it doesn't really matter. The kitchen is peaceful, and this is the first time today she's had any appetite at all. ❧

## NINE

"Because it happens to be a tradition, that's why," Myra says, stepping into her good wool slacks. "We've been going downtown to look at the Christmas displays every year since you were a baby."

"But Heather said I could come over and see her new boots."

"You can see them some other time."

Jennifer slouches against the wall in Myra's bedroom, frowning as usual. Howie stands in front of her full length mirror, sliding his palms up the sides of his head. "If you keep doing that to your hair," Myra tells him, "you're going to end up looking like Groucho Marx."

"Was he a cool dude, too?"

"Well, if I go," Jennifer says, "can I get new earrings?"

Howie demands a double chocolate mint sundae with nuts and whipped cream. "And a cherry," he adds.

There was a time when a few pieces of candy would have been enough of a bribe, but Myra says, "All right," giving in too easily because she wants this to be a good day, one Jennifer and Howie will look back on and remember fondly.

She buttons the sleeves of her blouse and dabs Youth Dew behind her ears. She loves this perfume, which she has worn on all the major and minor occasions of her life. At the hospital when the children were born, she'd gone a little heavy with it (behind his blue mask, Dr. Gurvitz remarked that she smelled as if she'd been stewed in flower petals), but it was not her fault. Both times, during her eighth month of pregnancy, she had almost totally lost her sense of smell.

She remembers those delivery room scenes as if they happened yesterday, but look at Jennifer, already sprouting breasts. And Howie—willing now, apparently, to let go of his babyish ways—is finally on the road to becoming a young man. He fools with his hair a moment longer; then, satisfied, steps back from the mirror and sneers at his reflection, draws an imaginary pistol from an imaginary holster, and aims.

"Pow-w-w!" He tilts up his shooting finger, blows on the tip, and saunters out of the room, his pajama bottoms dipping down his skinny behind.

"Pathetic." Jennifer peels herself off the wall. From the bathroom, she calls, "Can I wear your white sweater?"

"Okay, but you'll have to be careful with it."

"Gee, Mom. Like, I promise not to drip my strained carrots down the front."

Myra lets the remark pass. The children are still wired from last night at Lena's, and this morning, before she could do a thing about it, they finished off the rest of the leftovers, including the desserts. On the positive side, however, she won't have to bother about lunch, though she does toss a few granola bars into her purse, just in case.

On his way to the post office Haskell drops them off at the Morse Avenue El station, where they climb a long flight of stairs and board a Loop-bound train. Myra takes a double seat for herself and Howie and motions Jennifer toward one directly across the aisle.

"I wanted to sit by the window," Jennifer says. Her lips are smeared with coral-colored gloss, making her look very grown up. But the pout gives her age away.

Myra tries to explain the logistics of the situation. Howie is too little to sit by himself, especially since the train is filling up fast and people will be standing in the aisles, blocking him from view. She doesn't mention the possibility of child-snatching or deviate behavior, or the probability that if she let the children sit together, they'd end up duking it out in public.

"You can have a window seat on the way home," she says, but Jennifer has already turned away, miffed. Lately, Myra has had to work harder and harder to stay on her daughter's good side. She wonders how much of Jennifer's moodiness has to do with adolescence and how much has to do with Vinnie. Well, maybe this outing will help. Who wouldn't be cheered by a big city all decked out for Christmas?

With a sigh of almost contentment, she settles back to watch the passing scenery: back porches looming into view and disappearing, bundled figures moving along the streets under a low, gray sky. A sprinkling of snow would be welcome—just the thing for the season— but it is not quite cold enough for snow.

Once they pull away from the Fullerton Avenue station, the lights go on and the train plunges into the subway. Now the window gives back Myra's own face, just as it did on those long-ago Saturdays when she rode downtown for her lessons at the Lilly Lasser School of Singing and Dramatics. The lessons were Jack's idea (Myra could have lived without them), and since Nettie worked on Saturdays, he was elected to accompany her. "Believe me," he'd say each week as they left the subway and headed up the stairs to Randolph Street, "these classes won't be wasted. You'll learn from them. Poise, confidence. You'll see. Years from now, you'll be glad."

Always the same pep talk. Jack loved show business and anything to do with it. He sat with his hat on his knee, the only father in the audience, and watched as Myra struggled through her monologue. "Big smile," Lilly Lasser told her, drawing back her lips to reveal yellowed teeth and a serious overbite. It was rumored she had worked as a showgirl on Broadway long ago, though Myra found that hard to believe.

"'Why worry?'" Myra recited. "'*The way I figure, there are only two things to worry about: either you're sick, or you're healthy. If you're healthy, you have nothing to worry about. If you're sick, there are only two things to worry about…*'"

Her discomfort must have showed. Though she'd practice in front of her mirror each night for a week, she was never sure what to do with her hands. Later, she had to sing. It was lucky that Niles Lasser, Lilly's son, always went before her. Born with some kind of palsy that made his feet turn inward and his head wobble, he was the only boy in the class and the only student with a worse singing voice than hers.

When it was over, Jack heaped her with praise, called her his little trouper, a real talent. A wild exaggeration, she knew, but it didn't matter. Now the rest of the day was theirs to spend. They ate lunch at the Kopper Kettle—hamburgers, fries, banana cream pie—and then took their customary stroll through the Loop. Up State Street, down Wabash, across Madison and Monroe. People passing by might stop to stare. Like someone in a movie, Jack had a habit of breaking into song at the slightest provocation, and before she knew it, he'd be crooning, "*Chicago, Chicago…*" and urging her to join in.

"Oh, Daddy," she'd say, but then she would begin. Her voice, with his behind it, was steadier, less fragile, and soon they were singing about other cities, rivers and highways, uptown and downtown and hometown blues. Tripping lightly on the pavement arm in arm, skipping over curbs, Myra guessed this was as close to show business as Jack could hope to get anymore, and closer than she wanted to be right then.

"Mom…?" She feels Howie tugging at her coat. "How many more stops?"

She looks around: the aisles are packed. Unable to see Jennifer, she feels a momentary panic; but then the train pulls in to the first downtown station, the aisles empty a little, and there is her daughter, in her seat, staring at a woman with a purple bruise under one eye. "The next stop is ours," she says, pulling Howie to his feet. She holds his hand tightly and grasps Jennifer's arm, directing them through the doors when they open again with the familiar hiss Myra remembers anew each time she hears it.

The subway air smells of stale popcorn and cinders. An escalator carries them to street level, where Salvation Army workers are clanging their bells. "Where do you want to go first?" she asks.

"I wanna eat," Howie says.

Jennifer wants to know if they have earrings at Marshall Field's.

"Expensive ones, yes." Myra stops to search her purse for a granola bar. She feels the children are missing something important here. "Do you remember when you were little, Jen?" she says, trying to impart some small sense of continuity. "Dad used to carry you up and down the streets on his shoulders."

"I bet Dad would buy me earrings at Marshall Field's."

Myra hands the granola bar to Howie and starts walking, pretending she didn't hear. She is going to hold her temper if it kills her. "Oh, look at that!" She points to a window where oversized dolls are stirring pots of cookie dough.

"We saw that last year."

Myra remembers last year. Vinnie was angry about something, so she had to be twice as cheerful. On the sidewalk in front of C.D. Peacock, he bent over and pressed a hand to his lower back. "Oh, hell," he groaned, "all this walking is tough."

"What are you," she joked, "an old man?"

He turned and gave her a look that made her want to sink into the pavement. Then he told her to shut up.

In all the years she'd known him, he had never said that to her, but if that was what he wanted, she would shut up—but good. She spent the rest of the afternoon not speaking to him, even though she could tell he was sorry.

And now he's not here. So it's up to her to keep the tradition going. Surely he will be back by Christmas. All Myra has to do is hold things together for just a little longer.

She stops in front of another window where elves are hammering toys in Santa's workshop. A little girl in her mother's arms presses a mittened fist into the windowpane and says, "Aaga-buh!"

Myra smiles at the baby. Jennifer says, "Don't they have any rides around here?"

"Rides?"

"Like a roller coaster, or a tilt-a-whirl?"

Myra draws in a deep breath, summoning all her patience. "Are you aware that this is one of the most exciting cities in the whole world? It has wonderful museums and a big, beautiful lakefront, and loads of restaurants with every kind of food—"

"Someday I'm going to ride on the Eagle at Great America."

"Is Great America in Chicago?" Howie wants to know.

"—Greektown, Chinatown, Old Town—"

"No, dummy. It's the other way, toward Wisconsin."

"—not to mention all the stores—"

"I'll bet Dad would take us to Great America if we ask him."

Myra stops in her tracks and whirls around. "*Some* children would be tickled pink to be where you are right now," she fumes. "Some children would be *grateful*!"

The three of them are suddenly an island in the middle of the sidewalk, the crowd eddying carefully around them. A man with a large red shopping bag slows down to assess the situation. With a wink, he says, "Merry Christmas, y'all."

"And Merry Christmas to you, Sir, and ho, ho, ho!" Myra manages a defiant smile. The children turn away, humiliated. They shuffle along beside her like prisoners on a chain gang. After a while, when she is calmer, she says, "Maybe later, if there is time, we can walk over to the Sears Tower. They have an elevator you can ride all the way to the top."

৵৵৵

"A double chocolate mint sundae," Howie says to the waitress, "with nuts and whipped cream. And a cherry." He is usually shy talking to strangers, unless ice cream is involved.

Jennifer orders a banana split, and Myra asks for coffee and a slice of pound cake. They are seated around a marble-top table not much larger than a sunbonnet in the Crystal Parlor, a sweets emporium located on the third floor of Marshall Field & Company. After an hour of fighting the crowds up and down State Street and then another forty minutes waiting in line here—telling each other riddles and trying to repeat tongue twisters—Myra feels as if she's completed some sort of marathon. The children, cowed by hunger and fatigue, have stopped asking about the Sears Tower.

She looks around her at the pink and green stained glass windows, the little white chairs and tables, and says, "Can you believe this used to be a dumpy old waiting room?"

"What's a wading room?" Howie asks, apparently picturing something with a pool.

"Wai-*ting*." She describes the place she remembers: scuffed leather chairs and wooden tables, dim lighting, gray-haired ladies dozing over their purses in a limbo halfway between shopping and death. "And now look at how beautiful they've made it....Uh, Howie?"

He has stopped listening to her. A young couple at a nearby table, signing to each other in the language of the deaf, have caught his eye. Jennifer shoves her elbow into her brother. "You're not supposed to stare."

But Myra also finds it hard to turn away from the two sets of rapidly moving fingers. She is torn between pity for them and envy at their total absorption in one another. The girl scratches the air with two fingers; the boy chuckles and replies, tapping one fist lightly against the other. When the waitress sets down their dishes, they seem not to notice.

"What are they saying?" Howie asks. He knows a little about sign language from watching Sesame Street.

Myra sees a perfect opportunity to challenge his imagination. (She had to agree with that guest expert on Phil Donahue's program the other day that children were becoming entirely too dependent on television and Pac Man video games for entertainment and were in danger of losing their creative abilities.) "What do you think they might be saying?"

Howie looks at her as if she'd asked him how many miles to the moon. He shrugs unhappily. Jennifer jumps in. "They're probably wondering who's the little dork who keeps staring at them."

"I'm not the dork, you are!"

"Am not!"

Myra is saved from having to intervene by the appearance of their waitress, and for the next several minutes there is blissful silence as the children contentedly slurp their ice cream. Halfway through his sundae, Howie puts down his spoon and asks if there's a bathroom.

"Of course there is," Myra says. "All restaurants have bathrooms. It's the law—oh…I suppose you have to go?"

"Uh-huh."

She takes a sip of her coffee, which is absolutely delicious and just the right temperature. Reluctantly, she stands. No way she'd let Howie go by himself, especially not in this crowd. On the other hand, she doesn't like the idea of leaving Jennifer on her own, either. "I'll be right back," she tells her. "Don't talk to anyone."

"But Mom—"

"I mean it." She aims a stern gaze at her daughter's face. Then she takes Howie's hand and maneuvers him between the tables and through the doorway, around a corner and down a short corridor. When she gets to the ladies' restroom, he pulls his hand away and says, "I'm not going in there with you."

"Oh, for heaven's sake." She grabs for his hand again, but he steps away, defiant and on the verge of tears. "Have it your own way, then," she says, "but make it quick." Positioning herself at the door of the men's room, she watches as Howie walks through, scanning the faces of the men entering and leaving, alert for anyone who looks the least bit suspicious.

She hears someone calling. "Ma'am? Ma'am!"

She looks around: no one there. But then she turns and nearly falls over a young man sitting in a wheelchair. "Ma'am?" he says again. "Want to see…something?"

"See what?" she says, recovering her balance.

He flashes her a quick grin, grabs the wheels of the chair and spins them backwards. Abruptly, the front end of the chair rises, sending him tilting back at a precarious angle.

Myra sucks in a breath. Just as she is ready to reach out for him, he spins the wheels forward and the front end of the chair bumps toward the floor.

"Thought I was…gonna fall…didn't you?"

She takes a step back. "I didn't realize it was possible to do stunts in that."

"Been five years in…this thing. Dystrophy…you know?" He looks to be in his early twenties. He wears a flannel shirt and high-top athletic shoes, and he speaks in gasps, as if he'd been running, though clearly that's impossible. Beneath his jeans, his legs are sticks.

Myra nods and *tches* sympathetically.

"Supposed to be…bedridden…by now… Dead…in a year." He touches a button on the armrest and sets the chair in motion, moving it back a few feet and forward the same distance, as if he were trying to do the samba. Myra is all set to recite a short speech about advancements in medical science and the need to keep up one's hopes, when he says, "Ain't dead…yet!" He makes a sound somewhere between a laugh and a snort and pushes another button on the armrest. Now the chair is making circles around her legs. "Amazing…what they can do…with machines, right?"

"Y-yes," she agrees.

What does he want from her? Money? Admiration? A few Praise the Lords? She taps her foot impatiently, still keeping an eye out for Howie.

"Bet you're…wondering…how I keep from…going crazy. Losing little…bits of myself…like this. I'm not…what I used to be."

Casually, she turns her hand upward and says, "Oh, well, who is?" and then she winces. How can she make jokes at someone who is dying by degrees?

"I could do…another…wheelie—"

"N-no!" She wants to stop him, but he is too quick. In an instant, he's tilting the chair back again, head close to the floor, grinning his fool's grin at her startled face.

This time, she folds her arms across her chest. "Aren't you afraid you are going to hurt yourself?" she says in the cold, starchy voice she recognizes as Mrs. Nelson's, her high school biology teacher.

"H-hurt myself? Me?" The young man opens his mouth in astonishment and lets out a howl of derision. "Hoo-hah!" He rights the wheelchair again, looks at her and laughs some more. Though people are continually passing by, no one stops. No one comes to wheel the annoying young man away.

Myra tries to resist the feeling that she has made herself the butt of some huge joke. She pivots on her heel and calls into the men's room, "Howard Justin Calderelli! Come out this instant!"

After an agonizing half minute, Howie shuffles through the door, his cheeks burning. He has done something to his hair, plastered it down with water, and his fly is half-zipped. "Aw, Mom. Did you hafta say my name out loud?"

She grabs his hand and hustles him back to their table where, sure enough, Jennifer is deep in conversation with a stringy, hippie-type boy wearing a kerchief on his head and a hoop in one ear.

"Mom?" Howie whispers. "Is that man a pirate?"

"...never stops ragging on me..." Jennifer turns as Myra taps her on the shoulder.

"I thought I told you specifically not to talk to anyone."

"Like, what, he's gonna kidnap me?"

"When I tell you something, young lady, I expect you to listen. And you, young man, it's going to take an hour for your hair to dry." She wipes at Howie's head with a paper napkin, muttering and grumbling while both children slump down into their chairs; humiliated again, twice in the same day.

But she cannot seem to stop. Having gotten up a full head of steam, there is nothing for her to do but let it run its course. She is angry at them, yes, but also she's angry at the young man in the wheelchair. And at Vinnie. He ought to be here with them, enjoying their family holiday outing or at least pretending to. She waits a moment after she's done chewing them out, and then she says, "I'm sorry." She takes a sip of her cold coffee and puts down the cup. "It's not easy being a parent. Some day you will realize that."

Jennifer chops at her banana split with her spoon. Howie stares at his sundae, which is now a sugary brown puddle. It's going to take more than an apology, she sees.

"Maybe on our way out of the store," she says to Jennifer, "we can find you some new earrings. Okay?"

Jennifer nods, her face still serious.

"I want a comic book," Howie says. "And a candy bar."

❧❧❧

On the train going home, she claims a double seat and squeezes in beside the children. All the other seats are taken, and soon even the aisles are jammed from end to end. With every lurch of the train, the teenage girl standing next to Myra nearly falls into her lap.

Howie dozes against her chest. Jennifer gazes out the window, her chin resting in her hand, her new earrings swaying gently with the rocking of the wheels. The earrings look like miniature chandeliers, like something you'd wear to a wedding or a prom. Myra thinks about a prom she went to once—or, no, it was a benefit dance for some cancer charity. She cannot remember the name of the boy who took her, but she recalls exactly the shoes she wore. They were bone-colored pumps with a thin strap that snaked across each arch and made her size eights appear almost dainty.

She bought the shoes at the store where her father worked, had gone down there after school, and Jack himself had waited on her. He knelt before her to slip them on, then sprang away, nimble as a dancer. (Oh, wasn't he the Nureyev, the Barishnikov of shoe salesmen!) Afterward, for old times' sake, they went to the Kopper Kettle for supper, but Myra was on a diet and wouldn't touch the fries or the pie. Later, walking to the subway, her father started to sing—"*...show me the way to go home...*"—and though Myra resisted his entreaties to sing along, she did manage to hold a grin on her face.

The dance was held in memory of Robby Beeman, a classmate who had died of leukemia. He was the kind of boy no one ever paid much attention to. A life-size cardboard cutout of Robby Beeman stood near the reception table, and except for the dark eyes staring out from the thin, doomed face, he looked like any other boy in the room. Myra tried to recall if she'd ever spoken to him, ever said anything unkind. She danced every dance and wondered if it would be considered disrespectful to be having too good a time.

And then, midway through the song Travelin' Rosie, a thought struck her: if such a terrible thing could happen to Robby Beeman, it could happen to any one of them.

It could happen to her.

The thought left her so breathless, she had to stop dancing and sit down. So life was not the long and winding road she used to picture. It was more like a series of blind curves. She'd always been so careful, attentive, obedient, but what good was that if fate ultimately had it in for her?

For days after the dance, she walked around in a funk of despair. In class, she let her mind wander, and crossing the street she sometimes neglected to look both ways. She cried at the slightest thing. "What's the point?" she often murmured. It went on for more than a week until, looking at herself in the bathroom mirror one night as she was brushing her hair, she realized there was no cause for surrendering blindly to fate. That would be silly; that would be stupid; ridiculous; insane. Maybe she couldn't control everything—no one could, obviously—but she wasn't helpless. She had the power to improve the odds.

And that would require vigilance: lots of vigilance. And so she became doubly cautious, doubly attentive, and she has never lost the habit, not to this day. Oh, she gets on people's nerves; she realizes that. She's a nagger and a worrier, and she sometimes envies people who can plunge recklessly forward, who can leap without looking first. But then she remembers the cardboard cutout of Robby Beeman, the eyes that followed her around the dance floor all night, and she knows she isn't wrong.

Now, remembering him, she is swept by a wave of guilt for not having acted nicer to the young man in the wheelchair. It wouldn't have killed her, and anyway, she did have the benefit of all those lessons from Lilly Lasser's School of Singing and Dramatics.

Outside, in the darkening afternoon, the houses and cars appear to be dissolving in a misty haze. The train has emptied considerably. Myra kisses Howie on the forehead and nudges him awake. "Next stop is ours, Jen," she whispers. She helps them up and leads them down the aisle toward the door, buttoning her coat and wondering if the chicken drumsticks she planned to cook for dinner have sufficiently defrosted, when she notices the man in the tasseled cap sitting near the door. His arms are pumping wildly and his face is a mask of ecstasy. It takes her a moment to realize that he is masturbating, his penis so engorged it looks as if he is holding Mister Wriggle in his lap.

She stops in her tracks and the children bump into her from behind. "Wrong way," she says, wheeling herself in the opposite direction.

"But that door's closer," Howie says.

"Mom?" Jennifer says. "What is that man doing?"

Howie jumps to peek over her shoulder. "What man? Where?"

"It's nothing, Howie, nothing at all." She holds out her arms to block their view and shepherds them quickly to the rear of the car. ✥

## *TEN*

Speeding east on Pratt Avenue Saturday night after the movie, they are almost at the Sheridan Road intersection when the traffic light blinks red. Loretta slams on the brakes and the car screeches to a halt. "Aw, shit," she mutters, punching the steering wheel with the side of her fist. "Now we're gonna have to sit here for a day and a half."

Myra eases her foot off the imaginary brake on the passenger side of the car, and Cara says, "Would you like me to drive for a while, Mother?"

"No, thanks, kiddo. Lean back and enjoy the ride."

"There's no room to lean back, back here." She is folded nearly in half, the long way, like a greeting card.

"Well, *excu-u-use* me, Miss Priss. Next time I'll buy me a big limousine." Loretta shifts the car into neutral and digs in her purse for cigarettes. On the radio, the Righteous Brothers are singing Bring Back That Lovin' Feeling, just finishing up. "Boy, that song brings back a lot of memories," she says as the last notes drift off through her half-open window and out into the night. "Slow dancing on my back porch with

Benny—whatshisname—Fortini... I wonder whatever happened to him."

The song reminds Myra of Vinnie, but then, in one way or another, every song does.

She turns up the collar of her coat against the chill from the open window. Loretta and Cara have taken her out for her birthday, treated her to supper at Kelly's Deli and then a first-run movie, a science fiction-horror-romance starring a bunch of ridiculously young actors with unlikely names and impossible good looks. The movie has given her a mild headache, and she is still tasting garlic from the "mile high" corned beef sandwich she was certain she could never eat all of, but did. When Cara tears open a package of spearmint Lifesavers and offers her one, she takes it gratefully, slipping the tip of her tongue through the center hole, the way she's always done.

The stoplight for traffic going east and west, across Sheridan, is several minutes longer than the one for traffic going the other way, parallel to the lake. Myra understands Loretta's impatience at having to wait, but still, you'd think she was going to a fire the way she drives. Loretta fiddles with the dials on the radio until they hear the voice of Dick Biondi, deejay to the generations, saying, "...and Donna in Bensenville, this one's for you from Roy in Darien."

*Jes-lemme-hear-some-uh-thet-rock-en-roll-music...*

Loretta turns up the volume. "Oh, boy, I love this song!" she cries, snapping her fingers and jiggling her shoulders.

Cara says, "Is this the Beatles?"

"No, it is not the Beatles. Any dope knows that."

"But I heard this song the other day, and I'm sure the announcer said it was the—"

"What you probably heard was the Beatles version of this song. But what you are listening to right now is the gen-u-ine, the o-riginal, the one-and-only..."

Myra is still trying to figure out where Darien could be, when an ancient Riviera convertible with the top down slides up next to them. There are three men in the front seat, and Chuck Berry's voice is also blaring from their radio.

…*gotta-back-beat-you-cain-lose-it*…

"What d'ya know. More oldies fans." Loretta smiles at the men. By now, she is wriggling like a snake in heat, and before Myra can think to stop her she flings open her door and jumps into the street.

"Mother?" Cara's voice wobbles with disbelief.

In the spotlight formed by the headlights of the two cars, Loretta begins an impromptu jitterbug, pounding her feet against the pavement, throwing her head back and forth. "Your mother is making a total fool of herself," Myra observes, certain that the men are getting a good laugh out of this. Then, to her amazement, one of them hops out of the convertible and joins in the dance.

From where she is sitting, Myra cannot see his face. He's wearing jeans and a short jacket that barely covers a beer-bloated belly. "Hey, little girl!" he shouts, grabbing Loretta's hand. He pulls her close and then spins her away.

Myra's got her eye on the red light. Any second now it will turn green, and then what is she supposed to do?

"This is ludicrous," Cara sniffs. "A grown woman acting like that. It'd serve her right if we drove away and left her."

"And she's not even wearing her coat!"

The traffic light is still red, but now another car has pulled up behind them, the driver a large, dark shape behind the wheel. Myra's stomach tightens. Loretta and her dancing partner show no signs of quitting, and now his two buddies are beating time on their dashboard and singing backup.

It's a party, that's what.

Parties are something Myra has never been particularly good at. She leans over and calls out the driver's side window, "Let's go,

Loretta," and on that last syllable she inadvertently swallows her Lifesaver. It's sticking in her throat. For a panicky half-minute, she wonders if anyone will notice her choking to death; but then she swallows—hard—and the candy goes down.

Without warning, the traffic signal blinks green. The driver of the car behind them sounds two little taps of his horn. Loretta shimmies and jumps her way back to the car, gets in and tears off, laying rubber on a sharp right turn. "Bye, you guys!" she calls to the men in the Riviera, who wave back as they shoot across the intersection. "Ooh, that was fun."

"Fun?" Cara says. "More like an extremely silly stunt. Who knows who those men could be? Gang bangers, dopers—"

"Aw, kid, lighten up." She flips a cigarette out of the pack and pushes in the lighter.

"This probably qualifies as disturbing the peace. I'll bet someone has already called the police. They're probably looking for this car right now."

"Give it a rest, will ya?" She lights the cigarette and then says to Myra, "Well, birthday girl, where to now?"

Myra feels Cara's knee bumping against the back of her seat. She belches—garlic again. "Maybe we'd better just call it a night," she says.

"No! It's early! How 'bout stopping at Halligan's? I could really go for a cold beer."

"I don't know..."

"C'mon, just one drink."

"Well..." She is almost ready to capitulate, but then she pictures the bar: the noise and smoke, the free-ranging men scouting around for a good lay. She doesn't think she has the energy to fight her way through that.

But look at Loretta, breathless and flushed, still bouncing to the music. She makes Myra feel old, older than her birthday years, like someone's grandmother or one of those Spanish chaperons who sits in the shadows, making sure that the young folks aren't having too good a time.

And it does not help at all to realize that, once again, Loretta has done something outrageous, and survived.

And that she was stone cold sober, to boot. ᪄

## *ELEVEN*

December.

Attacking a cobweb hanging in the corner of the living room one morning, she notices that the ceiling has developed a worrisome crack. A few days later, Howie comes home from his little friend Jeremy's house with a bloody nose. And then, for no reason she can think of—because she'd just given the damn thing its weekly dose of water—the umbrella tree slumps over dead in its pot.

So when the school nurse calls to say that Jennifer has caught head lice and would someone please come get her, Myra is not at all surprised. An astrologer she once consulted told her that December is typically a bad month for Sagittarius.

The Escort would have to be in the repair shop, of course, waiting for a new fuel pump. She walks the five blocks to school in the bitter cold (the weather has been none too good, either), retrieves Jennifer from her solitary chair in the nurse's office, then walks seven blocks the other way to the drug store, where she picks up a fine tooth comb and a bottle of insecticidal shampoo. They all have to use the shampoo, and afterward Myra has to pull the comb through Jennifer's hair strand by strand while she hangs over the bathtub.

"This would be a lot easier if you didn't have a perm," she says, tugging at a snag.

"Oh, right, like I really expected to get head lice." Jennifer moans. "Why does everything happen to me?"

"It's no disgrace. That's what the school nurse told me. It can happen in the best of families." Myra has done everything she was supposed to—washed all the bedding and vacuumed the carpets twice and worked the nozzle attachment into the crevices of the upholstery—but she still feels a little contaminated. She decides to powder the cats, dip the dog, and spray the crawl space thoroughly with Raid.

"That ought to do it," she says, shutting the crawl space door. "You can come out now."

Haskell speaks through his closed door. "I think I'm going to wait awhile. I have an annoying sensitivity to chemicals."

"Whatever." She recalls how he almost passed out from the shampoo. And then he broke out in hives all over his head. She goes upstairs and pulls the curtains off their rods (no telling what could be hiding there); she also washes the scatter rugs and whatever else she can get into the machine.

By this time, the clothes dryer has developed a cough. Normally, she'd have Vinnie look at it, but that would require an actual conversation, something she has not attempted since Thanksgiving. Two could play his game, she figured. They have been speaking through the children, which is how she learned about his plans for Christmas. Howie, bouncing in his shoes and delirious with excitement, told her they were going to Lena's house on Christmas Eve and sleeping over for Christmas Day.

Well, that seemed to leave her out, but she should have expected as much. What did anyone care if she spent the holiday alone, dining on cottage cheese straight from the carton while they stuffed themselves on roast goose? She is beginning to feel enormously put upon and sorry for herself, and she doesn't care who knows it.

She picks up the phone and dials her mother, but her father answers and he sounds as happy as an elf. "Myra, Myra, how's it going? Got your tree up?"

"No, not yet."

"Christmas will be here before you know it," he sings, admonishing her in his cheerful salesman's voice. December is Jack's favorite month, the one selling season of the year when he and Nettie can depend upon raking in commissions hand over fist. "Of course, it's not *our* holiday," he goes on, "but you should make an effort for Howie and Jen."

"Come down to the store," Nettie says on the extension telephone. "We're having forty percent off better dresses."

"I don't need a dress," Myra whines. "I never go anyplace. I'm going to be alone on Christmas."

"Oh, darling. Don't be sad. You can come out with Daddy and me and help us celebrate our anniversary."

Myra knows the reason why her parents got married on Christmas Eve, and it had nothing at all to do with the festivity and romance of the season. Practical to a fault, Nettie set the wedding date so that she and Jack could take the next day off for a honeymoon without having to sacrifice a day's pay.

"We're going to Tio Mio's," her father says. "Very classy place, with big steaks and crab claws, cocktails and dancing, And if you come along, I'll have the pleasure of escorting the two loveliest ladies in town."

"Remember when you were a little girl, Myra, how you used to dance with Daddy?"

"When was this?"

"Fiddleman's Resort? Hot summer nights? The band played waltzes and mambos and the cha-cha-cha. You'd stand on Daddy's shoes, and he'd glide you across the floor. You two looked like a regular dance team."

"Ma, I'm a grown woman! I am not going out with you and Dad on your anniversary and dance on his shoes!"

"You don't have to bite my head off. I was only suggesting." Nettie sounds so hurt that Myra apologizes immediately and gets off the phone.

She can hear Haskell's typewriter clackety-clack-clacking away. He's been working non-stop for days, and all she's seen of him is his shadow slipping occasionally into the bathroom. Her business is lousy, but is it any wonder? With all those Christmas displays everywhere you look—with all the carols and bells and holiness clogging the air—she can't blame anyone for not wanting to host a Let's Be Lovers party. She has already paid her weekly visit to Grandma Rose at the DallyGlen Home, and did the grocery shopping on her way back.

For a while, she sits and watches dust settle over the furniture. Then she turns on the television and channel surfs with the remote. There is a game show, a commercial for soy sauce, a woman explaining something in Spanish about a plate of pastries; there is a scene with two people clutching each other nervously and whispering about a man named Philadelphia Sal. Myra watches the daytime drama for a few minutes and then flips to another channel.

*…stamped and numbered. And hello, there. You're on the air. What's your name?*

*Oh, my goodness! I'm really on? I'm Judy from Sandusky. Ohio?*

*Yes. Welcome to the home shopping club.*

On the screen a camera closes in on a tiny porcelain figurine, a flying horse. A woman's finger traces the arch of the horse's neck and then lovingly glides along one wing.

*Look at this beautiful thing. Can you believe the detail? Wouldn't this be the perfect Christmas gift?* The woman's voice is husky and seductive, with a faint Southern drawl.

The other voice, Judy from Sandusky's, has a definite twang. *I'm tempted. I can't say I'm not tempted. Yesterday? I bought that Marian Yu doll, and the bracelet with the unicorn charm.*

*They're going fast, as you can see. I hope you can get through before they're all gone.*

Myra watches the box in the lower right corner of the screen. *131 sold…132…* She finds herself rooting for Judy from Sandusky. Hurry, she's thinking when, suddenly, Judy is gone and there is another voice.

*Yep, did all my Christmas shopping in the summertime. Now I'm buying for just me.*

Myra snaps off the set. All this talk about Christmas is making her feel edgy. Every year, it's always Vinnie who picks out their tree and hangs the wreaths and mistletoe and buys the presents. Their first Christmas together, he gave her a watch on a long gold chain. He must have bought it at a real jewelry store because engraved on the back of the watch was a heart enclosing both of their initials, like something you might see carved into a tree.

The watch stopped working soon after the warranty expired, the hands frozen in a gesture of surrender at five past eleven. She never had it repaired. It would have cost less to replace it, but she couldn't do that either. Instead, she has kept it curled in a corner of her jewelry box, where it reminds her of those early days, which seem to her now like a lifetime and a half ago.

Thinking about Vinnie has given her the urge to clean closets again, and before long she is hauling another box out the back door: the children's school papers, Vinnie's sweat pants, his autographed portrait of Mike Ditka. Howie intercepts her on the stairs. "Hey, that's mine!" he cries, grabbing a poster of zoo animals he made in kindergarten.

"All these papers lying around can create a serious fire hazard," she says. "Hasn't Officer Friendly explained that to you?"

"Officer Friendly doesn't do fires," Howie informs her. Myra notices the sad slope of his little shoulders, which seems to have become a permanent feature of his appearance. Maybe her father is right about making a holiday effort for the children's sake.

That thought sends her out on a windy Thursday evening a few days before Christmas Eve. She drives to the Toys "R" Us store on Western Avenue where Cara works, hoping her niece can make a few suggestions about what an eleven year old girl and a seven-and-a-half year old boy might like that their father has not already bought for them.

But Cara isn't here, the manager tells her. Myra stands in the middle of an aisle, bewildered, trying to decide whether Howie would be too young for a book of Little Genius science projects, trying to remember if Jennifer still collects Cabbage Patch dolls. She wanders through the store in a kind of trance, picking up and then replacing bubble packs and boxes while shopping carts full of fretful children zoom around her. A little boy lunges for a plastic candy cane. "Wan dat!" he cries, as his mother mashes him back into his seat. A young couple in black leather jackets pass by, deep in discussion over a Bert and Ernie paint-by-numbers kit.

It seems that hours have elapsed before she finally arrives at the checkout counter with two books on bugs and a magnifying glass for her son, a "Guess Who?" board game and a jewelry craft kit for her daughter, and a small plastic tree.

Cara helps her put it together the next day. "This looks simple enough," she says, reading from the assembly instruction sheet. "You fit Branch A into Slot A, and so on."

"Branch A doesn't seem to want to go into Slot A." Myra drops the pieces in disgust. "This is a stupid tree. I wish you had been at work last night."

"I was all set to go, but then Uncle Vinnie came by and got into an argument with my mother, and I thought I'd better hang around in case they came to blows."

"Vinnie? What did he want?"

"I guess he wanted to make sure everything would go smoothly at Christmas. He told Loretta she'd better not bring any of her slimeball boyfriends over to Granny's. He said that this year it was just going to be family."

"Oh," Myra says in a very small voice. Wasn't she considered family anymore?

"And then he started in on me. What kind of grades was I getting? Who were my friends? A bunch of other garbage." She bristles. "I mean, who does he think he is?"

"Isn't it nice he's taking such an interest?"

"You don't have to defend him to me, Aunt Myra. I know how hard it is to admit a mistake."

"What mistake?"

"That you ever married him in the first place." She picks up the pieces of the tree and begins assembling it.

Myra winces at the barb, gets up and limps into the kitchen, shaking out her foot, which has fallen asleep. She doesn't expect Cara to understand how she can still cling to the hope that Vinnie has not left her forever, or why she would even want to. "Salami or tuna for lunch?" she calls, opening the refrigerator.

Cara's answer is lost in the snarling storm of brown fur racing to the front door. The mailman has arrived. They wait for him to leave, for Brownie to quiet down and lumber off to her spot in the middle of the living room, and then she says, "Salami."

Myra takes what she needs and nudges the refrigerator door shut with her heel. Cara comes in with the mail. "Bill from the phone company," she says, sorting through. "And something…looks like a Christmas card…from Dr. Thornberry?"

"The vet."

"A couple of advertising circulars. And the rest is for Howie."

"Give those to me," Myra opens two envelopes, one of which contains a newsletter from an organization that wants to save the wild burros. In the other is a brochure from someplace called Out In The Open Vacations, Unlimited.

"It's illegal to open someone else's mail," Cara points out in all seriousness.

"He keeps getting appeals from animal welfare groups and conservation lobbies. They must have gotten his name from his Ranger Rick subscription. I just don't want him looking at pictures of baby seals with their heads bashed in." She tosses the mail on the table and resumes making their lunch. "Mustard or mayo on your sandwich?"

"Mustard." Cara pulls the brochure from the envelope. "'Be there this spring to see the eagles at Cedar Point.'"

"Whole wheat or white?"

"White."

"What in the world is Cedar Point?"

Cara scans the brochure. "Looks like someplace in Iowa by the Mississippi River. It says that eagles stop there every year on their journey north. Every year without fail." She reads silently for a moment, then says, "Ooh, this sounds like fun…"

"Tea or coffee?"

"…you ride a rickety bus for half a day and then spend the night in some rustic—they probably mean 'unheated'—cabin, and then you get up at dawn and go out to crouch in a wet field with your binoculars. Hey, Aunt Myra, why don't we go?"

She lays down her knife and sets her fists on her hips. "Cara! Do you honestly think that I can just pick up and run off to see a bunch of eagles? I have responsibilities!"

"Really? You can't tell I was only joking? This doesn't exactly sound like a Club Med Caribbean holiday."

Myra picks up the knife and saws their sandwiches neatly in half. "No, it does not," she admits, though when she thinks about family vacations they've taken—most of which involve standing in long lines in the hot sun with two cranky children and several dollars' worth of junk food spoiling in her purse—crouching in a wet field at dawn doesn't sound like such a terrible alternative. "Was that tea or coffee?" she asks again, carrying their plates to the table.

"Tea. No, coffee. No, wait a minute. Do you have any diet pop?"

"Look in the pantry." Myra bites into her sandwich and chews without appetite. This is going to be her worst Christmas ever, worse even than the Christmases she spent as a child, playing dreidel with the babysitter and waiting for her parents to come home with a doggie bag of leftovers from their anniversary dinner. She pushes her plate aside and pours herself glass of water.

"You know what I think?" Cara says. "I think you ought to call Uncle Vinnie and tell him you're going away for a couple of days. Then he'd be forced to come home to take care of the kids, right?"

"It's not that simple."

"Why not?"

"Because you can never predict what he'll do. He might come home, yes. But then again, he might claim I was deserting the family."

"And, what? You're afraid to find out?"

"I am not a gambler. I'm not the kind of person who'd take a risk like that."

"I'll say you're not." Cara examines her sandwich, pulls out a piece of salami and takes a bite. "Tell me, though, where has playing it safe gotten you? Don't you ever get the urge to stand up for yourself, and damn the consequences?"

It's not the question so much as the look in Cara's eyes that gets to her. The look is one of amused pity, the kind you'd give to a child who has tied its shoes together.

"Honestly—" Myra huffs, feigning annoyance to divert her chagrin as she grabs the salami from Cara's fingers and shoves it back between the slices of bread, "hasn't anyone ever taught you the proper way to eat!"

❧❧❧

On Christmas Eve, Vinnie comes by and hands her an envelope, mumbles something about buying herself a gift, and leads the children away. She wants to cry, *Stop! Keep the money and give my babies back!* But it is only a momentary hysteria. They'll be home in twenty-four hours. Meanwhile, she consoles herself with the cards they made for her. Jennifer drew little green hearts all over hers; Howie's features a skinny Santa and a piece of candy taped to the inside. Both cards claim "love-4-ever."

Ah, but if they truly loved her, she thinks, unwrapping the grape sourball, they would have refused to go away.

She curls up on the couch next to Lucy and opens the morning paper. Her horoscope says she is in danger of becoming obsessed with matters over which she has no control. Vinnie's horoscope warns him to be careful regarding finances. Well, that's for sure. Inside the envelope he gave her was a crisp new hundred dollar bill.

Payment for what?

Staying out of his way, no doubt. Sucking thoughtfully at the candy, she pages through the paper from back to front, and by the time she gets to the front page headlines (some flap over President Reagan's latest diplomatic boo-boo, this one with a Middle Eastern leader; more speculation about Princess Diana and Prince Charles), they seem a little less alarming, the world still, basically, intact.

Haskell comes into the room then, though it's a while before she notices him. "I'm not disturbing you, am I?" he asks. He has taken the wing-back chair, and a fat book is open in his lap.

"No, not at all." She tries not to sound annoyed, but she had intended to spend the evening alone, wallowing in self-pity. She finishes the story about Charles and Diana and refolds the newspaper, laying it on the coffee table with a small, unhappy sigh.

Haskell looks up from his book, apparently unaware of Copperfield draped across the top of his chair: the cat's tail hangs like half a parenthesis next to his ear. "Do you suppose there would be any music worth listening to on the radio tonight?" he asks.

She reaches across the arm of the couch to snap the radio on and dials around until she finds a classical music station. "How's this?"

"Ah, Mahler. Perfect." He smiles at her. His face looks scrubbed, his hair freshly combed, and he is wearing a shirt with no visible stains on it. She is touched. This is the first time in months that a man has made any kind of effort on her behalf.

"I have some sherry in the kitchen," she says, rising.

"Please, don't trouble on my account—"

"No trouble." She goes into the kitchen and returns with a bottle of Harvey's Bristol Cream and two glasses. The sherry had been a present from Jack and Nettie, who had themselves received it as a gift from a neighbor in their apartment building. For all Myra knows, the bottle has been traveling around like this for years. "I suppose eggnog would be more traditional," she says, pouring, "but cheers, anyway."

"To Christmas," he says, raising his glass, "the most enduring—and endearing—pagan ritual of them all."

"Pagan…?"

"Ritual. This late December holiday dates back to the Roman festival of Saturnalia, and probably well before that to the ancients celebrating the return of the sun after the winter solstice. Christmas is quite simply a modern version of an old sport."

"I never realized that." Myra's opinion of herself always slips a notch when she is in Haskell's presence. "I guess you aren't a very religious person, then?"

"Not in the churchgoing sense, but I am cognizant of the holiday. I see you are, too. That is a lovely tree you've put up."

"Cara did the decorations," she says. Overdid, she thinks: the little tree droops under the weight of the ornaments. "I'm glad you like it."

"Did you happen to notice? There is something under the tree for you."

"For me?" She lifts Lucy out of the way and scoots to the other side of the couch. The little fake tree stands on the end table, and peeking out from a bottom branch is a single small package wrapped in blue paper.

"It's a book," he says, coming over to sit beside her.

She tears off the paper. "An Herbal Companion." She tries to sound elated.

"This was a real find. Look at the copyright date."

"Nineteen twenty four."

"And the illustrations!"

She has never seen him so animated. He helps her leaf through the musty pages, pointing out hyssop, sage, lavender, chamomile, calendula. He reads lines from a few of the poems that face each watercolor picture. "The minute I saw this," he says, "I knew it would be perfect for you."

"You did?" Myra has never cared anything about herbs, and the only poem she knows is I Have a Little Shadow. But she arranges her features into a smile, and aiming for a note of sincerity she says, "Thank you, Haskell. I am touched, really."

"You are quite, quite welcome."

"But I didn't buy a Christmas present for you."

"Actually, Myra," he says, reaching for her hand and looking directly into her eyes, "you have already given me a gift. You have given me your friendship, and I cannot tell you how much that has meant to me. I think you are, without doubt, the most incredibly sensitive woman I've ever met. You have a compassionate nature, and a wonderful generosity..."

He's beginning to sound as sappy as a Hallmark sentiment. She tries to brush away the compliments and retrieve her hand, but he goes on. "Truly, these past few months have been unbelievably difficult for me. Your kindness has helped enormously."

"Well, thank you again. For the book and for the nice words."

"My pleasure entirely." He gives her hand a gentle squeeze and lets it go, and for a few moments there is only the music from the radio and an awkward silence between them. To break it—and to change the subject—she says, "I was wondering, how is your play coming along?"

"Ah!" A syllable of despair. "I cannot talk about it."

"Oh, I'm sorry—"

"Please, you don't have to apologize. It was good of you to ask. But perhaps I'm deluding myself into thinking I can actually write this thing. Sometimes I wonder if I shouldn't just stick to composing brochures for insurance products, something I believe I am reasonably competent at."

"No, no. You should *not* give up." She puts a hand on his shoulder and then hastily removes it. "I mean, you have talent. I'm sure you'll get over this little rough spot and the play will be a great success."

She is not at all certain she believes this, but he seems to perk up at her words. He says, "Thank you for your vote of confidence," and a shaggy smile creeps across his face. He is beginning to remind Myra of one of those wild burros the animal welfare people are trying to rescue.

She picks up her glass of sherry, lifts a cat hair off the rim and takes a sip. She cannot bear this—the mournful sawing of violins on the radio, the dispirited little Christmas tree—and she can't think of a thing to say that would not make the moment even more depressing.

In the meantime, Copperfield has leapt off the wing-back chair. He sidles up to the couch and rubs his flank lavishly against Haskell's leg.

Lucy comes alert. Backing into Myra's lap, she hisses sharply and yowls a warning, and Myra uses the opportunity to grab the cat, mutter an apology, and make her escape from the room. ~

## TWELVE

If it had been up to Myra, they never would have sent Rose Greenburg to the DallyGlen Home for the Aged. She made it plain that Grandma Rose was perfectly welcome to move in with them. Vinnie wouldn't have objected; he got along pretty well with her. Grandma Rose was harmless and easily overlooked, and she would have caused no problems in the Calderelli household.

But everyone said how Myra already had enough on her hands. At the time, Howie was only a toddler and Jennifer was still throwing the occasional tantrum. How would she cope with an old lady who sometimes had trouble finding her way home from the grocery store?

Well, she'd have found a way to manage. It would be like Little House on the Prairie: three generations under one roof and everybody helping out.

Now, each time she visits, it tears her apart. She can hardly believe that her grandmother's tidy two-bedroom apartment on Lawndale Avenue is gone forever. If pressed, though, she would have to admit that DallyGlen is not really so bad. With its tastefully furnished lobby, pastel-colored hallways, and the paper cut-outs of birds and flowers taped to the walls, the place reminds Myra of something halfway between a hotel and a grammar school.

In the lobby, she picks up the pen on the writing desk. Haskell watches over her shoulder as she signs the guest register *Mr. & Mrs. V. J. Calderelli.*

"I feel exceedingly awkward about this," he says. "I fail to see how I can possibly pass myself off as your husband."

Myra sets the pen down. "I've told you. My grandmother will not know the difference. She only recognizes people she sees all the time, and she hasn't seen Vinnie in months."

"But I look nothing like him. I'm so much taller."

"Can't you just act the part? Stoop a little. Mumble. And will you please stop fretting?" She would not have dreamed of imposing on him this way, except that on her last two visits Grandma Rose kept asking about "that cute fella" of hers, and Myra hadn't the heart to let on to what has happened.

She pushes through the lobby doors and rings for the elevator. Haskell removes his gloves and unwinds his scarf. "Awful warm in here," he says, mumbling.

"What?"

"*Warm.*"

"Yes, it is. Like Miami in August." She unbuttons her coat. When the elevator comes and the doors open, there is an old woman standing inside, bent almost double over an aluminum walker. "Hello," Myra says.

"Looks like some-one is having vis-i-tors," the old woman warbles. She tilts her head to get a better look at them but makes no move to leave the elevator. "Which person are you coming to see?"

Myra smiles and says, as politely as she can, "Rose Greenburg. She's my grandmother."

The old woman turns her eyes toward the ceiling and taps her cheek with a yellowed nail. "I'm wondering if I know her."

"S'cuse me, lady," Haskell says. "This your floor?"

"I have to get off on the third floor. What's this?"

Myra steps into the elevator and presses the buttons marked two and three. "I guess we're all going the same way."

The elevator door creaks shut. The old woman says, "A nice day today, yes?"

"Yes, it is a nice day," Myra replies amicably.

"Kinda cold. But we're gonna get some sun later, maybe snow by Sunday."

Haskell sounds like Vinnie giving a weather report. Myra wonders if he plans to do the news and sports as well. But he is right about the weather. It's too cold to take Grandma Rose outdoors. Now they'll be stuck here in the heat and the suffocating smells of boiled beef and pine disinfectant.

At the second floor, the elevator wheezes to a stop and the doors open again. A nurse in a powder blue uniform waves from her station. "How y'all doin' today, Mrs. Stein honey?"

"What floor is this?"

"Do you think she'll be all right?" Haskell asks.

"Come on." Myra takes his arm. She hasn't got time to worry about everyone else's grandmother, and they are late as it is. She hurries down a hallway littered with wheelchairs and people walking along in slow motion.

Grandma Rose rises from her chair by the door as soon as they turn into her room. She smooths her apron over her dress, the same purple and white flowered housedress she always wears when she has company. Myra wraps her arms carefully around the tiny woman and plants a kiss on her cheek. Bare of the powder and the rouge she used to wear, her skin is remarkably smooth for a woman nearly ninety.

"So how's by you?" she says. "It's been such a long time since I didn't see you."

"I was here last week."

"You could call once in a while."

"I called yesterday. Don't you remember?"

Grandma Rose puts a shaky finger to her lip, thinking. Instantly, Myra is sorry. She should not have said anything about remembering. It was like saying the word "see" to a blind person.

"Look what we brought," she says brightly, holding out the bag of cookies they picked up at the bakery on the way over.

Grandma Rose takes the bag and peers around Myra at Haskell, who is crouching behind her. "Hi," he says, rolling forward a step and waving his fingers.

Grandma Rose gives him an uncertain smile. She puts the bag on top of the dresser, among the rows of pictures standing there. "Thanks you very much," she says to him. To Myra she whispers, "He lost a little weight?"

Figuring she'd better change the subject quickly, Myra asks about Mrs. Olefsky, her grandmother's roommate.

"Oy." Grandma Rose shakes her head and points upward with a crooked finger. "Gone."

"She died and went to heaven?"

"Worse than that!" says a sharp voice from the doorway. Myra turns to see an ancient woman in skinny white braids, and she is holding on with both hands to an enormous black cane. "They took Olefsky to the fourth floor, with the rest of the nut cases." The woman hobbles over to Myra and extends her hand. "I'm the new roommate. Matilda Applefeld Drebbenweiss. But you can call me Tillie."

Grandma Rose pulls Haskell by the arm. "You like a nice brisket, huh? Potatoes and carrots?"

"Yeah. Sounds real good."

"Come, siddown. I'll put on the stove."

"What stove, Grandma?" Myra says gently.

Tillie thunks her cane against the floor. "So, Rose? Am I going to drop dead before you introduce me to your family?"

Reluctantly, like a child unwilling to share, Grandma Rose says, "Mine granddaughter."

"And you're the husband, right?"

"Yep," Haskell says.

Tillie removes a picture from her side of the dresser and shows it to them. "This was my husband, may he rest in peace. And this was my father, a great scholar. My sister...my mother—"

"And who is this?" Myra asks, picking up a portrait in a tarnished silver frame. It shows a young woman with sparkling eyes and hair like black lace.

"That used to be me." Tillie considers the picture without emotion and replaces it among the others.

Myra feels a tug at her arm. "The children?" Grandma Rose says. "Janey and Herbie?"

"Jen and Howie are just fine, Grandma. Jennifer and Howard. They send their love."

Grandma Rose lifts their pictures from her side of the dresser. They are the school pictures from last year. Howie's cowlick is sticking straight up, and Jennifer looks as if she is holding ice cubes in her mouth. "Such gorgeous children," Grandma Rose murmurs.

"I never had time for children," Tillie says. "Forty-nine years I was in business. An office on Clark Street. Three people I employed."

"How interesting," Myra says. "What sort of business did you have?"

"Tickets. Any kind of tickets. The opera, the ball game, Kiss Me Kate. I sold them all, every one. Three people worked for me in the office, did I tell you? Three people and their families had what to eat because I gave them a job." Tillie clicks her dentures with satisfaction and pats the collar of her housecoat.

"So clever, these children...," Grandma Rose murmurs, leaving more words of praise trembling on her lips, unspoken.

Myra hopes she is not going to break down in tears. On her last visit, her grandmother wept over the indignity of having to drink her tea lukewarm from a plastic cup instead of the right way: piping hot from a glass, with a cube of sugar held between her teeth. If Myra were visiting at the apartment on Lawndale, she'd be sitting in the parlor, eating little cakes—or else those delicate egg cookies crusted with sugar—and Grandma Rose would be bustling in and out of the kitchen, stopping to polish a smudge off a tabletop, pouring out the latest neighborhood gossip along with the coffee.

But here she stands, plucking uselessly at the hem of her apron.

It's enough to break your heart.

The conversation seems to have come to a halt. Tillie and Grandma Rose are busily re-arranging their pictures on opposite sides of the dresser, an angry silence hovering in the air between them.

"I have an idea!" Myra says, clapping her hands together. "Why don't we all go for a little walk? Wouldn't that be nice?"

Grandma Rose's eyes fill with fear. "Far?"

"No, not far. Just to the end of the hall."

"Wait," Grandma Rose says. She has to check her lipstick and take off her apron, and meanwhile, Tillie decides to come along. She slides her hand through Haskell's arm. "You mind?"

"Nope."

Myra thinks he is carrying the charade a little too far. He has not spoken a complete sentence since they got here.

Moving out of the room and along the hallway, the four of them constitute a small, shuffling parade. Grandma Rose holds onto Myra's hand; Tillie waves at people she knows. "Hello, Irwin," she says to a man with gray sideburns who apparently has Down Syndrome. He stares at her, then spreads his lips into a porpoise-like grin.

At the end of the hallway is the dayroom, where a number of people have gathered to play cards or watch TV. Myra helps her grandmother to a seat along the wall. She positions herself between her grandmother and Tillie, with Haskell sitting as far from Grandma Rose as possible. "Could you get some pop?" she says to him, pointing toward the vending machine in the corner.

"Sure."

"They got a Doctor Pepper?" Tillie asks.

Haskell reads the selections. "Seven-Up, Coca-Cola, Root Beer, Orange Crush."

"What?" Tillie says.

He reads the selections again, enunciating.

"No Doctor Pepper?"

"Get Tillie a root beer," Myra says, "and a Seven-Up for my grandmother."

"I used to like a nice cold seltzer, plain, no ice," Grandma Rose says, and her eyes grow shiny with the memory.

Myra also remembers: tall blue tumblers on her grandmother's white tablecloth, both glasses filled with sparkling seltzer. But then Grandma Rose would stir Hershey's syrup into Myra's glass, turning her drink—presto!—into a chocolate phosphate, and it was better than any you could buy at the soda fountain. Those chocolate bubbles breaking under her nose…the sweet fizz tickling her throat…

How wonderful it would be, she thinks dreamily, if the vending machines in the DallyGlen Home dispensed chocolate phosphates and hot tea in glasses and maybe even little packages of sugar-crusted egg cookies.

Haskell brings the old women their drinks. "Want anything?" he asks Myra.

"Yes, I do," she whispers, leaning forward. "I want you to stop slouching so much. You look like a gorilla. And stop talking like that. Vinnie *is* a high school graduate, you know."

She is aware that others in the room are watching them. At one of the tables, four old people are playing cards; well, three of them, anyway. The fourth has his head on the table, napping. Two ladies in velour bathrobes sit side by side, watching television. On the screen, Humphrey Bogart, in tinted skin, sneers into the room.

"Look, Grandma, your favorite actor!"

"The doctor? The doctor came yesterday."

"Not the doctor. Bogart. The actor. On television."

Grandma Rose peers at the screen, and then her eyes soften in recognition.

"I think she saw every movie he ever made," Myra tells Tillie. "I think she had a kind of crush on him."

"That bum? That no-goodnick!" Tillie bristles with disgust. "He drank like a fish. He beat up his wives."

Grandma Rose whispers in Myra's ear. "That one, such an expert. Just ask."

"Don't worry, Grandma. You have my permission to be a little in love with Humphrey Bogart."

Grandma Rose pushes at Myra's arm. "*Pisher*," she says lovingly, and Myra is given a glimpse of her grandmother the way she used to be. She thinks of the afternoon she brought Vinnie to meet her, the way he slouched in her chintz-covered chair, one leg thrown carelessly over the arm. Grandma Rose brought him a bowl of ripe pears, looked him up and down. "A ban*dit*," she pronounced privately to Myra, and then she nudged her with her elbow and laughed. She understood Myra's attraction to this bad boy. Before she married Grandpa Max, the costume jewelry salesman, she had taken up with a fiery young union organizer who spent his nights composing long letters to President Roosevelt. She knew what it was to be helplessly in love with someone your parents despised.

She squeezes her grandmother's hand and blinks back tears. Haskell leans across Tillie and asks Myra if she knows the name of the movie they are watching. "It's on the tip of my tongue," he says, snapping his fingers as if to spark his memory.

"Isn't this the one with the statue of the bird?"

"The Maltese Falcon?" He considers. "No, that was with Mary what's-her-name."

Myra finds herself wondering if there is something about the DallyGlen Home that induces memory loss.

"When I was a girl," Tillie says, "my father wouldn't let us go to the pictures. He was old-fashioned. Didn't think pictures was respectable."

Myra clucks with sympathy. "What a shame you had to miss out."

Tillie chuckles. "Who missed out? My sister told him she was taking me to the park, and off we'd go. We saw Keaton, we saw Jolson, we saw them all." Her shoulders shake with mirth, and her root beer sloshes in the can. "Oy, we were a couple of devils, me and my sister, may she rest in peace."

While they are musing over Tillie's story, an old man lurches into the dayroom. His chest is as flat as an ironing board, and his arms and legs flail stiffly, as if they'd somehow been starched. "*Ehrrrt?*" he sputters, reaching for Tillie, who draws back in alarm. A gray-haired woman with a frizzy perm grabs him from behind. "Pa, come here!" she cries and pulls him back through the doorway.

The card players halt their game. The women in the robes lift their eyebrows at each other. Grandma Rose sips her Seven Up. "Your boyfriend?" she says to Tillie in a frosty voice.

Tillie gives a small shrug. "Not him. But I'd like to have someone." She watches Bogart slipping his arm around the waist of a slender woman.

"Do you still like the movies?" Myra asks.

"Sometimes. I like boyfriends better."

"But if you can't have a boyfriend…"

"Ah, well." Tillie gets a faraway look in her pale eyes. "Sometimes, you just need a good tickle." She flashes Myra a grin; then she giggles and puts her fingers to her lips. "Oooh!" she squeals. "Don't tell anyone."

"What?" Grandma Rose bends around Myra. "Who is she talking about?"

"Nothing, Grandma." Myra is a little appalled. She cannot imagine how a woman Tillie's age can still be thinking about sex. It seemed indecent. Wasn't there a point where you put it all behind you?

Grandma Rose gets up and brings her can of soda to the wastebasket. "I should maybe check on the roast," she says.

Myra lets out a grunt of impatience. Haskell springs to his feet and holds out an arm for each of the old women. Stretched to his full height, he looks like himself again. Their heads come to the middle of his chest.

She makes their good-byes as brief as she can. "Don't forget the cookies," she reminds her grandmother.

"We'll have them for dessert. Too bad you couldn't stay. Your grandpa should be home from work soon." Grandma Rose accepts another kiss from Myra. Tillie says, "Take care of that husband of yours. He's a killer." She lets out another giggle and waves shyly at Haskell.

Outside, Myra gulps cold air. "It's getting worse," she says, searching her pockets for Kleenex. "I'll have to talk to her doctor. Maybe she's on the wrong dose of medication. Sometimes, side effects can do that to a person."

"Your grandmother seems fine to me—"

"Fine? She's in a dream world. My grandfather has been dead for close to twenty years." She finds a crumpled tissue and dabs at her nose. "But at least she has a better roommate now. That Mrs. Olefsky really was kind of screwy. She thought there were little men who came into the room while she slept and stole locks of her hair."

"If I were you, I would not make any bets on Tillie's sanity."

"At least she knows who's dead and who's not. Besides, didn't she mention she was in business for fifty years? I'll bet she still has a lot of good common sense."

"For your information," he says, guiding her toward the car, "Mathilda A. Drebbenweiss is under the impression she owns this building here, and that all the people who live in it are renting from her."

Myra stops in her tracks. "She told you that?"

"More than once. She spoke very highly of your grandmother. Said she wished all the tenants were like her."

She puts a hand to her head. "This is a nightmare."

"I fail to see what you're so upset about. What possible harm could there be in letting two old women believe whatever they want?"

"You wouldn't say that if you knew my grandmother when she was keeping a big apartment spic and span, and making strudel by the armload, and bossing my grandfather around like a drill sergeant."

"But she's a very old woman now. Why not let her live with her illusions? Anyway, what is so terrible about your grandmother having forgotten that her husband is dead. Wouldn't that mean she has also forgotten the pain of her loss? And don't you consider that a positive consequence of her mental state?"

She doesn't expect him to understand: Grandma Rose is not his grandmother. She stalks off toward the car. Haskell unlocks her door and they get in. He turns the key in the ignition and lets the engine warm, and while they are waiting he turns on the radio. The music sounds to Myra like a couple of mice chasing each other up and down piano keys. She looks at him, annoyed, and he turns the dial until he finds a soft rock station playing some forgettable song.

When she has calmed down a little, she says, "If you want to know why I'm so upset, I will tell you. I am afraid that someday I'm going to walk in there, and she will have forgotten who I am. She'll look right through me, as if I were a total stranger."

He nods. "I understand your concern."

Myra stuffs the tissue back into her pocket. "Thank you."

"You know," he says, backing out of the parking space, "it is a privilege to grow old. Many are not given that opportunity."

"Is that from some kind of Eastern philosophy?"

"Actually, I read it on a bumper sticker. But I think it might be a sensible perspective to adopt, all things considered. Don't you?"

She sighs with resignation and leans her head against the seat-back. "I suppose." The charade of passing Haskell off as Vinnie to Grandma Rose—of trying to keep the visit upbeat and avoid the skirmishes threatening to break out between her grandmother and Tillie—all of it has left her hollowed out and sad and very, very tired.

She watches Haskell's gloved hand on the wheel as he cruises to the end of the row of parked cars. Waiting to make a left turn from the parking lot onto the street, he taps his forehead and shouts, "Ah! I remember!"

"Remember what?"

"The name of the movie we were watching."

"With Bogart?"

"Yes. I am almost positive it was The Big Sleep." ❦

## *THIRTEEN*

It is now the last day of the year. The last day of what has turned out to be the very worst year of her life, and after a mostly sleepless night she rises early, takes a long shower, styles her hair, spends ten minutes with a cover stick and a bottle of Natural Wonder liquid makeup, and changes clothes twice. Today she is going to drive to Northbrook, to the store where Vinnie works.

Today is the day she will finally have it out with him, face to face.

She wishes there were another way, but she has not heard a word from him since Christmas Eve, when he gave her the envelope with the money. At first, she thought she'd blow it on something silly— a Cuisinart, maybe, or a designer blouse. But then, running through several possible scenarios in her head, it occurred to her she would need every cent. At best—and here she indulged herself once more in the fantasy of him crawling back to her and begging forgiveness—she would have to put the money toward marriage counseling. But if worse absolutely came to worst, she'd need a good lawyer, someone other than her father's cousin Sam. No way on earth would she lay her future in the hands of a man with dandruff and bad teeth.

She has been set on this course of action since the day before yesterday, when she overheard one of Jennifer's telephone conversations. "I suppose I'll hang around here for a while," she was saying, and Myra assumed she'd been talking about her plans for the afternoon. But then she went on: "Later, when I'm old enough to drive, I'll go and live with my dad. He has the car."

Myra was so startled, so hurt, she had to reach out and steady herself against the wall.

How could she have been such a fool, letting Thanksgiving go by, then Christmas? Had she really believed that everything would turn out all right if she just kept quiet and didn't cause a fuss?

A final check of her hair in the mirror, and then she tiptoes downstairs and quietly fixes her breakfast: eggs and toast and juice, a mug of coffee. She will need her strength. In the middle of buttering the toast, Howie pokes his head into the kitchen.

"Mom…?" He yawns and rubs his eyes, and asks for something to eat. She offers him one of her eggs, but he insists on oatmeal with cinnamon sugar. Apparently he has forgotten his declaration of yesterday, that he would rather die than eat oatmeal. He's been fighting her on every little thing, and she understands this is just acting out because he is angry at his father.

But sure, take it out on his mother.

Isn't that what mothers are for?

By the time Howie's cereal is ready, her own breakfast is cold. She scrapes the eggs into the dog's dish and offers the toast to the parrot. Gulping coffee, she tells Howie she has to go out.

"I wanna come with," he says, looking at her wide-eyed, alarmed, as if she had announced the plan for another parent to abandon him. He begins to wheedle and whine, and out of habit she nearly gives in. But she can't give in; not today of all days. She negotiates: a hamburger and fries in exchange for a half day of freedom. After a half minute's consideration, he takes the deal.

"Be good, Sweetie, and listen to Mr. Reed." She kisses the top of Howie's head and leaves him carving trenches in his oatmeal with a spoon while she searches through the front hall closet for her long woolen coat. With its smart tailoring and classic design, the coat gives her the look she's aiming for today: competent sophistication, a brave face to camouflage her withering fears.

Before leaving the house, she fingers the watch hanging on the chain around her neck, rubbing it for luck. The watch on her wrist tells her it is eight-twenty. Finally, she pulls on her gloves, loops her purse strap over her shoulder, sets her jaw and strides out the door.

At the Arco station on Touhy Avenue, she pulls into the full service lane and asks the young man inserting the gas nozzle into the Escort to also check the oil and the tire pressure and add windshield wiper fluid to the reservoir. With his dirty yellow hair, he reminds her a little of Loretta's second husband, the one who showed up at Myra's wedding with a black eye and one arm in a sling. The boy holds out a grease-stained palm while she counts nine dollars into it. "Have a nice trip, Lady," he says, eying the map on the passenger seat. "Looks like you're heading west."

"As a matter of fact, I am," she says crisply. She rolls up the window and, with the sun winking into her rearview mirror, travels along Touhy to the Edens Expressway ramp, holding her breath as she lurches into the swift, heavy stream of expressway traffic. Her heart does not stop thumping until she has glided safely into the center lane.

"And how have you been?" she says aloud, testing her voice. She takes a deep breath and repeats the question. Then she says, "Yes, you're looking well, too." The tone of her voice has to be right—not hysterical, not threatening. Vinnie gets his back up when he thinks he's being accused of anything.

A silver Volvo swings out in front of her, and she has time to read its vanity license plate—IM OK RU—before it veers into the left hand lane and speeds off.

"On the whole," she says to her rear view mirror, "I believe I am. I'm coping. I'm keeping it all together." She likes the sound of that: reasonable, detached. Last night, during a brief snatch of sleep, she dreamed a former classmate, Sherry Jo Jacobson, met her on the street and begged forgiveness for the shabby way she had treated Myra in high school. "You were always resplendent," Sherry Jo said. "We never understood."

Myra was uncertain about the choice of words, but the sentiment pleased her. Of course she was resplendent, Myra told her. She followed the rules, waited her turn. She wonders now whatever happened to Sherry Jo, whether she married the quarterback whose letter sweater she wore everywhere. If she did, he probably had to knock her up first.

At the sign for the Dundee Road exit, she clicks on her turn signal and edges into the right hand lane, emerging minutes later into a land of open fields, sprawling houses and acres of parking spaces. The Dominick's shopping center looms up suddenly on her left, and she has to turn around and double back. Though it's early, the lot is packed. She maneuvers the Escort into a space between a powder blue BMW and a lime green Jaguar.

The supermarket, like everything else in the land of Northbrook, is huge: aisle after aisle of oral gratification, most of it instant or, at least, microwaveable. Myra grabs a cart—she needs a little time to ease into this—and turning away from the produce department, she sets off toward the in-store bakery where the warm smell of fresh bread is wafting her way. Remembering her uneaten breakfast, she picks up a paper doily with a bite-size sample of coffee cake on it, but she hasn't enough appetite to put it into her mouth. Carefully, she replaces it on the tray. In the deli department a woman in a pink and white checkered apron offers her a sample of jalapeno-flavored cheese on a piece of cracker no bigger than Myra's fingernail. "No, thank you," she says. She also declines a microscopic mound of caviar and a thimbleful of champagne off the gourmet food cart.

A string version of a Stevie Wonder song plays over the PA system as she ambles up and down the aisles with the rest of the shoppers. A number of the women wear tennis skirts under their fur jackets. Others sport ski parkas with lift tags still hanging from the zippers. They all appear busy, preoccupied, tossing things into their carts without even pausing to compare prices. Myra's cart remains empty. At last she wheels it to the edge of the produce section and parks it beside a table displaying a holiday assortment of packaged nuts.

Now she is ready for Vinnie.

But where is he? She sees a man in a long apron stacking oranges, and a boy with raggedy black hair watering the lettuce. She walks over to the boy—his name tag reads *Chuck*—and says, "Excuse me."

Intent on the lettuce, Chuck doesn't notice her. Then a girl with a clipboard brushes past; she doesn't notice Myra either. She peeks through the double doors to the back. Vinnie isn't there.

Maybe she has the wrong store. Maybe he doesn't even work here anymore. For all she knows he could have moved to Canada since they last spoke. Under the bright lights the fruits and vegetables seem to be winking at her, as if they knew a secret. She stands there trying to decide whether to stay or go, when she feels a tap on her arm.

"My-ra?"

And suddenly she is seized by a flash of panic she has not experienced since her third grade stage debut in The Little Red Hen. She gropes for his name. Consulting at last the plastic badge on his apron, she hears herself say, in a small, strangled voice, "H-hello, Vinnie."

"Hey. What's wrong? Something with the kids?"

"No, they're okay. Really. The children are fine."

"Good. That's good." He folds his arms across his chest. He looks preoccupied, irritated, the lines on his forehead dipping into a familiar scowl. "So what're you doin' here?"

She swallows. Her throat is dry. (Oh, why hadn't she taken the champagne?) "I have to talk with you," she says. "Now."

He takes a step back and motions her to a spot behind a table heaped with Idaho potatoes, a khaki-colored mountain of them, ten pounds for two dollars. "Make this quick, will ya? It's crazy in here today."

Grabbing onto the strap of her purse and forcing herself to look into his eyes, she says, "I came here to ask you…when…you—" She falters and tries again. "Can't you just tell me…what…"

This is not working. Right before his eyes, she is dissolving like an aspirin in a glass of water.

He frowns with impatience. "What? You need something? Money? The furnace blew?"

"It is none of those things, and you know it." She is not going to let him bamboozle her this time. She pauses for breath; then she says brightly, "You're looking well."

He tugs at his nose. "You come all the way out here to tell me that?"

"I was just making an observation. I came here because…because I need to ask…" She takes another breath. "What is going on, Vinnie? With us, I mean. When are you coming home?"

She had not meant to be so blatant, to put it on the line like that. With Vinnie you had to give him room to maneuver. But there it was, and too late to take back the words.

"All right. You wanna talk about this? Okay." He steadies one hand against the table and passes the other across his face: a tired man, a beleaguered man, a man whose silly wife insists upon breaking into the middle of his business day to talk about their future. "So, it's like this. See, I'm kind of staying temporarily with this lady I know."

"Uh-huh." She nods dumbly. The information does not surprise her, not at all, but still, it's a blow to the heart.. "And…"

"And what? Like I told you before, I'm trying to work a few things out."

"You're having an affair with another woman, is that what you're trying to tell me?"

He puts up his hands. "Hey, shhh! I didn't say nothing about an affair. Did I say this was an affair?"

"No, but—"

"So don't put words in my mouth, okay?"

"Okay, but—"

"I need a little time, that's all." He puts his fists into the pocket of his apron and looks away.

"And in the meantime? I'm all by myself, with the children and the house and everything else. Jennifer came down with head lice, did you know that? And Howie has started wetting the bed again—"

"Sir?" A woman wearing heavy silver bracelets embedded with large turquoise stones comes by and asks him where to find the avocados.

"Right over there, Ma'am, next to the mushrooms. Got some that are just ripe for tonight, make a nice guacamole."

"Why, thank you." She bats long eyelashes clotted with mascara.

"No trouble."

"—I keep telling myself to hold on, to try and keep things together, but it's so hard!"

"What about that guy...Weed? Can't he help you out?"

"*Reed*. Haskell's just a boarder. He never gets involved with us."

"Oh, yeah?" He squints at her. "You sure 'bout that?"

Myra feels the blood rise in her face. "Exactly what are you implying?"

"Nothing, nothing." He puts up his hands again and backs away, but a knowing smirk is forming on his lips.

"I would *never*," she snarls, swinging her purse onto her other shoulder, "never even *think* of—"

She hears a thump.

Then another thump.

Then several more, coming one after the other. Somehow, a potato has gotten dislodged from the bottom of the heap on the table, and the resulting avalanche quickly transforms the thin smirk on Vinnie's lips into a gaping O of disbelief.

"Holy shit!" he cries. Arms open wide, he flings himself against the moving mountain of Idahoes, while Myra stands there, frozen to the floor.

All around her, shoppers are stopping to stare. Some pick up potatoes that are rolling in their direction. Chuck wanders over, the hose still in his hands. "Mister Calderelli?" he says. "Y' want me to get the broom?"

She edges away, turns and flees from the store. No one points a finger or tries to stop her. Once inside the car, she breaks down, the tears coming hot and profuse as her chest hut-huts sob after sob. She imagines this lady of Vinnie's. She'd be a fancy Northbrook woman, no doubt, with an athletic body and unusual jewelry. She'd be divorced and the owner of a big house with a kitchen so massive it would set any produce man's heart aflutter.

"Guacamole, my foot!" she cries, the words a cloud in the frosty air. He knows the way women look at him.

She grinds the key in the ignition and shoots out of the parking lot. She needs to go somewhere and pull herself together. Making a series of left-right-left turns, she winds up eventually at a giant shopping mall, the building a low, white palace in a shiny sea of automobiles. She races across the parking lot and pushes through the nearest set of revolving doors, landing with a gasp in in the accessories department of Lord & Taylor. A saleswoman with scarlet lips and extraordinarily white teeth points the way to the ladies' room, her silk-clad wrist giving off a scent of rare flowers.

Once inside, Myra collapses onto a leather couch. She closes her eyes and tries to bring Vinnie's face into focus. She sees the name on his badge, his apron, his eyebrows and hands, but his features refuse to come clear for her. Then she becomes aware of a conversation going on in the next room, hears a toilet flush, and a voice: "…and I'm just saying there is no way he can tell if you're faking it, Ilene." The voice is nasal, bored.

Another voice responds: "I hope you're right. Because if Darryl knew that I'm more turned on by what he has in the bank than what he has in his pants, he'd have a freaking stroke."

"And that would be such a tragedy?"

They laugh, and whatever else is said is drowned out by the whine of a hand dryer. Eventually they leave, and Myra is alone.

She sits up suddenly, muttering, "To hell with you, Vinnie." She should be figuring out what to do next. She stares at the wall, closes her eyes, stares at the wall some more.

But nothing comes.

❦❦❦

Clouds have gathered by the time she gets into the car to drive home. She feels as if it were the end of a long, dreadful day, though it is barely noon. The minute she opens the front door, Howie says, "Where's my hamburger?"

For a moment, she considers going out again, but then Haskell comes in, takes one look at her damaged face and asks if she's had an accident with the car.

She shakes her head and hands him the keys, turns and trudges upstairs, leaving Howie still whining about his lunch. In her bedroom, she steps out of her shoes and slips under the covers, and in minutes she is asleep, floating beneath the surface of wakefulness in a sea of peculiar dreams.

In one, her philosophy professor, Mr. Karimer, appears and asks for her advice. In another, their house burns down and she is forced to move to a mansion and wash all the floors on her hands and knees. In the middle of that dream she suddenly finds herself in another, and in this dream she is standing in the upright freezer case of a busy grocery store, taking a shower.

Vinnie walks by, and she expects him to say something, but he doesn't seem to notice her. Shoppers opening the freezer door to pick up fish sticks and microwave pizza snacks don't notice her either. She lathers her hair and rinses it in icy water. Naked and dripping wet, she steps out of the freezer and checks her shopping list. She needs hot dogs and peaches and several giant bags of pet food. In the jewelry aisle, she plucks a diamond bracelet off a display rack. A stock boy says, "Don't put that on until you pay for it, Missy." He squints at her through his monocle, a bent old man.

"You needn't worry about me," she tells him. "All my orgasms are genuine."

She has to wait a long time in the checkout line. Nettie is the cashier, and she insists the groceries be arranged alphabetically on the conveyor belt. "You never dress properly, Myra," she says, reaching overhead for her microphone to send a call out on the PA system. "A coat, please. Customer at register five needs a coat."

And then, in the distance, she sees Haskell galloping toward her, his black overcoat waving behind him like a flag.

She wakes suddenly and finds herself staring at the bedroom ceiling.

Now it is almost dark. She must have slept the afternoon away. Groggy, wondering why no one has tried to awaken her, she makes her way downstairs, turning on lights as she goes. She finds them in the kitchen, Jennifer stirring a pot on the stove, Howie and Haskell busy at the sink. "It's New Year's Eve, Mom," Howie says. "We're making a special supper."

Jennifer urges her back upstairs. "Put on something nice. We're all going to dress up."

Back in her bedroom, standing in front of the closet and swaying slightly, she puts all her effort into deciding what to wear. When she comes downstairs again in a corduroy jumpsuit and suede boots—a favorite outfit that went out of fashion ten years ago—they are waiting for her, seated around the kitchen table which has been set with a profusion of dishes and silverware and, as a centerpiece, a soup pot brimming with Cabbage Patch dolls.

"See?" Jennifer says. "I told you Mom could look pretty when she tries." Howie stands and pulls out her chair and bows from the waist. He is wearing a battered top hat and a wide tie patterned with big pumpkin-colored flowers.

"Where in the world did you get that hat?" she asks.

"At a garbage sale."

Jennifer corrects him. "*Garage* sale. Haskell took us after lunch. See what I bought?" She stands and twirls once, showing off a scraggly feather boa.

"Lovely," Myra says.

Now it's Haskell's turn. He reaches under his chair and produces a pair of Mickey Mouse Club ears, which he clamps onto his head. "I was coerced into buying this," he says, grinning.

They look so ridiculous, she laughs in spite of herself.

Howie scoots under the table and comes up on Myra's side with a brown paper bag. "We got this for you," he says, pulling out a filmy, lavender-colored shoulder cape. It's the kind of thing Grandma Rose might have worn when she was a young woman.

"Oh, this is beautiful." She forces the words past the lump in her throat. She takes a sip of the red wine Haskell has poured for her, and it goes right to her head.

For dinner there is spaghetti with butter, a bowl of black olives, a platter of Ore-Ida oven fries and a salad composed mainly of cucumbers, Howie's favorite vegetable. "We're having marshmallows with butterscotch syrup for dessert," Haskell tells her, passing a basket of Ritz crackers.

Myra smiles at him and straightens the Mickey Mouse ears on his head. What a nice man he's turned out to be.

The children insist on staying up until midnight. Myra tells them they can stay up until midnight in New York. Howie wants to know why it isn't midnight in Chicago then, too, and that launches Haskell into a complicated explanation of Greenwich Mean Time that no one can follow.

"Hey, I know a riddle," Howie says, his top hat falling over one eye. "What time is it when an elephant sits on your watch?"

Haskell grabs his chin and ponders the question as if there was money riding on the correct answer. Jennifer sucks up a strand of spaghetti. "That's easy," she says. "I heard it before."

"Well, then, let me guess." Myra adjusts her shoulder cape and takes another sip of wine.

"Give up?"

"No. The answer is on the tip of my tongue."

"Would this be an ordinary elephant?" Haskell asks.

Howie shrugs. "I suppose."

"C'mon, Mom, can't you guess?"

"Could you repeat the question?" Myra says.

"What *time* is it when an *elephant* sits on your *watch*!"

"Thank you." She notes with pleasure the exasperation on her children's faces. "Now, the answer wouldn't be 'time to go home,' would it?"

They laugh. "That's stupid."

"And it wouldn't be 'time to take out the trash.'"

"Mom, quit it!"

She smiles. Her eyes take in Howie's flowered tie, the silly black ears atop Haskell's head, the pot of Cabbage Patch dolls, the table littered with Ritz cracker crumbs. Apparently she has fallen through a rabbit hole and stumbled into the Mad Hatter's tea party.

"Okay," she says, obliging because Howie and Jennifer seem ready to explode, "I'll tell you what time it is when an elephant sits on your watch." And then, tipsy as a Dormouse, she giggles out the answer.

୶୶୶

Howie falls asleep on the floor in front of the television, watching the countdown from Times Square. They wake him so he can toss confetti, bang a pot and scream, "Happy New Year!" Haskell carries him off to bed, and a little while later, Myra tucks Jennifer in.

"I like Haskell," Jennifer says, "don't you?"

"Mm-hmm."

"Mom…?"

She waits for the rest of the question, but Jennifer has drifted off to sleep, her heart-shaped face framed by her ruffled white pillow. Myra wipes away the smear of butterscotch syrup on her chin, kisses her cheek and turns off the lamp.

Downstairs, Haskell is picking confetti off the carpet and dropping it into an empty saucepan. On the television screen, Bob Sirott is broadcasting from somewhere above the crowd on the Michigan Avenue bridge. Myra sinks into the couch. "Don't bother with that," she says wearily. "I can get it tomorrow with the vacuum."

He shakes off the few pieces of colored paper clinging to his fingers. "Old habits die hard, I guess. Elizabeth was particular about cleaning up as soon as the party was over. She couldn't stand having to deal with the mess in the morning."

After a moment, Myra asks, "Do you miss her?"

He considers the question. "She was a difficult person to live with," he says at last, "unusually demanding and highly critical. But I do miss being married. And I miss our home. Silly, isn't it."

His voice is heavy with regret, his face dark with sorrow, and Myra has the urge to put a comforting arm around his shoulders. But he gets up quickly, brushing confetti off his trousers, and goes into the kitchen, returning with the traveling bottle of sherry and two glasses.

"A toast," he says, filling her glass. "To the end of this year, and good riddance."

"Yes, good riddance." She slugs back the sherry and holds out the glass for more. "Another toast," she says. "To better times."

"Better times." He looks exhausted, which does not surprise her. He has spent the entire day dealing with children.

She says, "I have to thank you for all your help. I don't know how I would have managed without it."

He puts his glass down and turns to her. "Do you want to tell me what happened?"

She does, just to spill out the story and be done with it. But where would she begin? Already the day has become a little unreal to her, like a movie she saw years ago. "Maybe some other time," she tells him, "not right now."

She turns her attention to the antics of the crowd on the television screen. People are riding around on each other's shoulders, waving frantically at the camera, and Bob Sirott's blonde curls are being whipped around his face by the wind.

"It must be freezing out there," Haskell says.

"And there's a man with no shirt!"

"I guess some people feel obligated to go out and make fools of themselves just because it's New Year's Eve."

Myra agrees. "Some people."

The crowd begins to chant, *"Ten…nine…eight…"*

She wishes him a happy new year. He pecks her on the cheek, and she pecks him back. There is a bit of confusion when she bumps his eyeglasses and they fall into his lap. He interrupts her apology with a soft kiss right on the lips, and she does not resist. He pulls her close, strokes her hair, kisses her again, a deeper kiss this time, filled with tenderness and desire.

By now, Bob Sirott has screamed himself hoarse, and the crowd has gone wild.

Haskell turns off the set. Taking her by the hand, he leads her through the silent house, down the stairs and into his room. The dim glow from the stairwell light shows her how much the room has changed. The walls are filled with pictures hanging crookedly in their frames, groups of objects line the windowsill, papers sit in scattered piles next to the typewriter on the old kitchen table, and every corner is stacked with books. This is his place now, his home and refuge. In this room, she is the guest.

She helps him unfold the sofa bed, sheds her boots and jumpsuit, rubs the toe she has stubbed against the pot of plastic flowers on the floor next to the sofa bed, and scurries beneath the blanket.

He is there.

Groping tentatively, like the stunned survivors of a shipwreck, they move together. He murmurs her name, draws her into his arms, holding her close and nuzzling her neck. She feels the dryness of his lips, the astonishing warmth of his skin, and wonders if he might have a fever.

But, no. This is just not the body she's used to. There's not enough hair on his chest, and his legs are way too long.

No, no. This is all, all wrong.

She tries to stop him before he goes any further. "Ha-ahhh," she says, and her voice is barely a whisper. She presses her hands against his shoulders, but her arms seem to have surrendered their strength. And her body—with traitorous disregard for the gold band glaring at her from the third finger of her left hand—has already begun its sweet, witless throbbing. ∽

## *FOURTEEN*

She's dreaming again. She and Vinnie are sitting up at the bar of the Tip Tap Lounge, and a rabbi in black gabardine is behind the bar, handing out exam papers on which they have to fill in the missing words to old rock and roll songs.

*Met him on a M\_\_\_\_ and my heart stood still.*
*Keep away from Runaround S\_\_\_\_.*

This should be a cinch, but Myra finds it impossible to concentrate over the noise of the jukebox. Jennifer won't stop feeding it quarters, and Vinnie refuses to show her his answers. The rabbi calls "Time!" just as she's about to write something down.

She wakes up angry—how dare Vinnie be so selfish, how dare he invade her dreams!—and cold. Haskell has rolled to the far side of the sofa bed and taken most of the covers with him. He lies with his back to her, the knobby hump of his shoulder a great divide separating their two sets of dreams.

The minute she gets out of bed, Copperfield leaps up to claim her spot. Purring victoriously, he settles himself into the warmth of her pillow, the green glow of his eyes following her as she gathers her clothes and pads into the laundry room.

She throws the jumpsuit into the washing machine, hides the boots in the dryer, pulls on the two odd socks lying inside the dryer, and wraps herself in the ratty chenille robe hanging on the back of the laundry room door. No way would she risk running into Jennifer or Howie and having to explain why she is still dressed in last night's clothes.

Her head is muzzy: she may as well face the fact she'll never be able to drink red wine. She needs to sit down with paper, pen and a pot of coffee, and sort out her feelings about everything that has happened in the past twenty-four hours.

But Lucy jumps into her lap; she wants a rub behind the ears, and breakfast. The sound of the can opener brings Brownie into the kitchen. Then Ethel gets himself shut into one of the cabinets, and while she's coaxing him out she knocks over an open box of rice. By the time she finishes sweeping it up and putting the broom and dustpan away, the sun's come up and so has Haskell. She can hear the flap of his slippers on the basement stairs.

"I didn't think you would be awake this early," he says, shuffling toward the coffee pot. He is wearing a shirt and a pair of chinos, but no socks, and his eyes look pouchy. He brings his mug to the table.

Pushing her hair out of her eyes, she tucks the foot with the argyle sock beneath her and points the foot with the white crew sock at the floor. "I'm always up early," she says, trying to keep her voice steady. "I have a million things to do."

"Making out your shopping list?"

"Y-yes." Before she got busy with the animals, she had written *Good w/H &J* at the top of the page. She crosses that out.

"I believe we need canned tuna."

"Tuna." She prints the letters slowly and carefully.

This adultery business is all new to her. If her life were anything like the movies, they'd have awoken in each other's arms, relishing the rosy warmth of each other's naked flesh. They would be pleasantly, artfully disheveled and still ripe for passion. As it is, she can barely remember last night. Her dream about Vinnie and the rabbi seems more real.

"And for some reason, I have a taste for green olives. Can you purchase some of those?"

"Olives." She writes the word and then goes on to list the items she is always running out of: milk, bread, kitty litter. Maybe she'll pick up a rump roast on sale, or some chicken leg quarters. There is a recipe she cut out of the newspaper a few weeks ago that she's been meaning to try—

"Myra?" He reaches across the table and touches his fingertips lightly to her wrist, as if he were afraid of startling her. "I just wanted to tell you that I am—"

"You don't have to apologize." She draws her hand away. "I realize that last night was as much my fault as yours."

He smiles. "I hadn't planned to apologize." He takes her hand and lifts it to his lips, pressing a kiss into her palm. "Last night was an adventure, and a revelation. I cannot begin to describe how wonderful you were. For the first time in many, many months, I feel able to count myself among the living again."

She lowers her eyes, remembering the way he traced his fingers over her throat, between her breasts and across her ribcage, mapping her contours like a blind cartographer; the quiet rush of her breath as he drew her knees apart.

"Last night meant a lot to me, too," she admits. "I mean, it was really very nice." She places her other hand over his and offers him a smile in return.

*Among the living.*
Yes. Now, she is.

꿍꿍꿍

And now, for the first time since she met him, she can begin to consider a life without Vinnie. Who was he, anyway? A balding, overweight man approaching middle age who worked at a job where he had to wear an apron. And who was that girl who fell in love and said, yes, she would marry him? Another person altogether: an impulsive, silly young thing who did not have the good sense to pull that hot little ring off her finger and tell him, "Thanks, anyway, but—"

Well, you live and learn.

She will just have to put the past behind her; that should be simple enough. Put the past behind and move forward into her future, which she ponders later that day while they are standing in line in front of the Lincoln Village Theater. The temperature, according to the sign on the Lincoln Village Bank, is two degrees above zero. No mention of the fierce wind blowing off the lake, or the wind-chill that could probably flash-freeze molten steel. She and Haskell are shielding the children between their bodies, like two parent penguins at the South Pole.

Jennifer hops from foot to foot, while Howie whines into Myra's stomach. "Why, Mom? Why can't we go inside?"

"This is really dumb," Jennifer says. "We could've stayed home and rented a movie."

"It would not be the same, and you know it." Every New Year's Day, the four of them have gone out as a family, and Myra is not willing to give up the tradition, Vinnie or no Vinnie.

"What if there was a snow storm? Would we still go?"

"Yes."

"If there was a flood?"

"Yes."

"That's stupid. How could there be a flood in January?"

"Actually, Jennifer," Haskell says, tapping his gloved fists together, "if heavy snow was already on the ground, and the temperatures rose above freezing, and the weather patterns in the West—"

"Oh, look," Myra says, "the doors are opening."

Just in time. She hobbles forward on frozen feet. A blast of warm air greets them as she hands their tickets to a small, totally bald man in a maroon uniform. "Come in, folks," he says, offering Myra a grin of recognition. "The popcorn is fresh, the picture is terrific. Come in and enjoy."

"What a friendly old fellow," Haskell remarks.

"He owns the place. And see the lady over there selling candy? That's his wife." Myra indicates a woman somewhere in her seventies wearing her platinum blonde hair in a ponytail perched high on her head. She greets them as they step up to the candy counter, her false eyelashes fluttering like little wings, as if they might take off.

"Nachos and a coke, please," Jennifer says.

The woman winks at Myra. "That gorgeous daughter of yours, I bet she'll be breaking a few hearts when she grows up."

Myra stretches an arm proudly around Jennifer's shoulders. "Do you realize this lady has known you since you were a baby?"

"Yes, Mom. You say that every time we come here."

"Dad and I took you to see the first Rocky picture. You were just a tiny thing."

"And I threw up."

"You did not. You had perfect digestion."

What Jennifer had done, though, was begin to whimper and fuss barely ten minutes into the movie. By the time Myra got her out of the theater and into the restroom, she was purple with rage. The candy counter lady brought a chair so Myra could nurse comfortably, then came back with a complimentary glass of tropical punch and another chair. "I know how it is," she said, sitting down. "All my kids were screamers."

That dram of sympathy was exactly what Myra needed. She poured her heart out then, confessing all her shortcomings as a new mother—real and imagined—all her frustrations. "I never thought it would be this difficult. I spend practically my whole day nursing her or changing her or holding her so she won't cry." The little restroom was like the cabin of a plane (Myra imagined this; she had never been on an actual airplane), with the voice of Sylvester Stallone droning behind one wall.

The woman asked about the birth, and Myra told her what she could remember about the hazy, exhausting hours at the hospital and then the one glazed moment when Jennifer appeared, a beautiful, squalling mess. The doctor let Vinnie cut the umbilical cord.

"My, my. Husbands in the delivery room." She seemed to feel they had gotten away with something illegal.

"I didn't think he'd go through with it," Myra admitted. "But when Doctor Gurvitz practically dared him—well, you'd have to know Vinnie. He looked so handsome in his mask and gown, almost like a real doctor. He coached me right up to the very end."

"Coached?"

From there, they went on to talk about other things. Eventually, Jennifer fell asleep and Myra reluctantly returned to her seat to watch the last bloody minutes of the film. For some reason, she never has learned the candy counter lady's name, but over the years Myra has kept her abreast of certain major developments: Jennifer's first steps, Vinnie's promotion at work, her pregnancy with Howie. More recently, she handed her a Let's Be Lovers business card and told her to call if she and some of her girlfriends ever wanted to set up a fun evening.

Now Myra wonders if the woman happens to notice that she is here with another man. She has the urge to make another confession. But the woman only smiles as she hands them their refreshments and says, "Six-fifty, please." Haskell opens his wallet and gives her the money.

The theater is filling up fast. They take four seats in the center section, and as soon as they are settled, some boys come in and sit in the row behind.

"Hey, dorkface, hand over the Twizzlers."

"Buy your own, asswipe."

Myra gets up, and they change their seats. Then a woman with a noisy toddler turns up across the aisle, and they have to move again. She cannot remember having this much trouble when they went to the movies with Vinnie. One dark look from him—one scowl and cocked eyebrow—and any commotion stopped dead.

Now there she goes again, thinking about Vinnie.

This will have to stop.

"I don't recall reading any reviews about the film," Haskell says, offering her a Milk Dud. "Have you?"

"I think it's some kind of screwball family comedy. You know, where the kids get all the good lines and the parents come off looking like total idiots."

"Well, I'm sure it will be quite amusing, nonetheless."

They settle back in their seats as the house lights go down, but the picture doesn't start right away. A spotlight appears on the curtain, and then the husband and wife who own the Lincoln Village Theater walk onto the stage. He is still wearing the maroon uniform, but she has slipped a frilly black hostess coat over her candy counter outfit. "Ladies and gentlemen," she announces while the husband strolls to the end of the stage and takes a seat at an upright organ, "our holiday program is about to begin."

He plays two introductory chords. The curtains part, and there on the screen are the words to the song Joy to the World.

"Sing along, everyone," says the wife. She holds out her arms like a conductor, and the audience begins.

*Jeremiah was a bullfrog…was a good friend of mine…*

Jennifer disappears into her seat, embarrassed. Howie keeps looking around at the people in the audience. Haskell appears to be confused, so Myra has to make the effort for all of them. When the song ends, the audience cheers and applauds. Haskell shouts into her ear, "I thought Joy to the World had different words."

"Don't tell me you've never heard of Three Dog Night."

"Three long what?"

"Never mind."

Is she going to have to spell out every little thing to him? This morning, he offered to make breakfast and nearly drove her crazy. Where was the frying pan? The flour? He didn't know that Howie's pancakes had to be drizzled into animal shapes. He didn't realize there was no syrup because Jennifer had used it all in some kind of craft project. He couldn't think of what to substitute until Myra suggested powdered sugar.

With Vinnie there was never a need for tiresome explanations. Over the years, they had developed a kind of shorthand communication. If he asked *What did you do with the whatchamacallit*? she'd know what he meant. *That thingamabob you brought back from the hardware store? It's in the drawer.* And he would have no need to ask which drawer because there was only one it could possibly be in, the rest having been designated for other uses. The thought of starting over at this stage of her life with someone else makes her feel a little faint. When the words to Frosty the Snowman appear on the screen, she can barely summon the strength to sing them.

But Haskell knows this song. His voice is a baritone, rich and surprisingly strong, unlike Vinnie, who Myra has never heard sing anything except The Star Spangled Banner. For Vinnie, singing appeared to be an uncomfortable activity, like scraping a callus off your thumb.

The holiday program ends with several choruses of Jingle Bell Rock. The husband and wife take a bow, and the wife says, "Thank you, friends. Thank you, thank you." She wishes everyone a happy, healthy new year and blows them a lavish, Dinah Shore-style kiss. "*M-m-m-wah!*"

Hand in hand, they leave the stage and walk up the center aisle toward the lobby. "Aren't they are the sweetest couple imaginable," Myra says, dabbing at her eyes. She feels as if she's just been to a wedding.

Haskell pops another Milk Dud. "Do they do this sort of thing often?"

"Every year. They love to entertain in front of an audience. In fact, if I recall, they met in the chorus line of a traveling company. Whirlwind romance. He swept her off her feet."

"You seem to know a lot about them."

"I got to talking with the wife one night. You know how it is, you tell your life story, she tells hers…"

The woman told Myra how her family had tried to talk her out of the marriage, claiming it could never last. Myra listened eagerly. It was the same with her and Vinnie, everyone saying how she was just throwing her life away on him. But there she was with a new little baby, and they were saving to buy a house.

"You must listen to your heart, honey, that's what I believe."

At that moment, Myra wished she'd had that woman for a mother. How wise she had seemed, how understanding.

Now, of course, with perfect hindsight, she wishes she had heeded the warnings. But at the time, the future was a long, sunny road. She and Vinnie would grow old together, just like the old couple. They would be wrinkled and gray, yes, but still in love.

Well, that is not going to happen, and no sense dwelling on it.

She turns to Howie and asks if he wants to go to the bathroom before the picture begins. He doesn't answer. His eyes are riveted to the screen, where a half-naked woman is screaming in terror at a shadow with a knife in its hand. "These are only the coming attractions, Sweetie. It's okay to miss them."

"I don't hafta go."

"You never have to go until smack dab in the middle of the movie. And please stop chewing on those Jawbreakers. They can chip your teeth."

"Actually," Haskell says, "I wouldn't mind taking him to the men's room at the appropriate time." He reaches for Myra's hand and gives it a secret squeeze.

"Thanks," she says, and offers him some popcorn. Sometimes she wonders what would happen if she just let the children do whatever they wanted, left the spills and the messes and the hundred little details requiring her attention. Someday, she's going to do it: sit back and let everything go all to hell.

Finally the picture begins. People hurry back to their seats. A heavyset man balancing a tub of popcorn and several large drinks edges past Myra's knees. She shifts her legs sideways, but her feet get trampled on anyway. Howie's coat falls to the floor. She picks it up, shakes it out, and lays it across her lap.

The credits are rolling over a typical suburban street scene: squared off yards and boxy houses, flimsy young trees. A dog barks. A lawn mower starts up. Cut to the inside of a house. The family is going on a trip, it seems, and everything is chaos. The father keeps stumbling over the suitcases, and the mother is in a panic because she can't find her birth control pills. There are three or four children darting in and out, making wisecracks that keep the audience laughing and sniggering and shaking their heads.

"Cartoon characters," Myra mutters, feeling somehow offended. She tries to get interested in the story, but soon becomes aware of a commotion to her left. "What's the matter?" she whispers to Howie.

"Jen won't let me have any nachos."

"I already gave him one."

"I gave you all those Jawbreakers."

"Sshhh! Both of you!" Myra turns back to the screen. The audience laughs; she's missed something important. "What did he say?" she asks Haskell.

"'No one told me I would need it.'"

Myra cannot make sense of that. She must have missed more than she thought, and she vows to pay closer attention. But moments later, she is distracted again by a sudden flash of light from the lobby doors and a male voice shouting, "*What?*"

The lobby doors thud softly. A large man in a heavy coat comes toddling down the aisle, a tiny woman at his side. The audience turns in unison to stare at them. The man grumbles. "So damn dark…where am I?"

The woman tries to quiet him. "Sshhh! You're making too much noise," she whispers as they turn in at the row in front of Myra.

The man—a huge old man, with great stooped shoulders—sidesteps along the seats and stops right in front of Howie. "*What?*" he says again.

A loud series of shushes goes around the theater. Howie grips the armrests and lifts himself onto his knees. "Mom?" he says, craning left and right. "Can't you do something?"

Myra gives Haskell her purse and her popcorn box, and Howie's coat. She stands—why is it always up to her?—and places her hands firmly on the old man's shoulders. "Sir?" she says.

"*Who's this?*"

"Please, Ralph." The woman's voice betrays her desperation. She tugs at his sleeve and Myra pushes downward, and together they muscle him into his seat. He keeps wheezing and muttering until the woman opens a box of candy and rattles it at him. He takes one and then falls silent.

Howie still can't see, and Myra gets up and changes places with him. On the screen, the family is driving down the highway in their giant van, complete with television and wet bar, refrigerator and microwave. "Isn't this great?" the bumbling movie husband says. "All the comforts of home. Why, we could stay in here practically forever."

What is the point? Myra wonders. Wasn't travel supposed to be about exploration and adventure? She finds herself getting angry again.

Apparently, she is losing the patience that's required to deal with a film that should be an insult to the average person's intelligence.

In front of her, the tiny woman is helping the old man off with his coat. Myra watches as she unwinds his scarf and folds it into her lap, takes off his glasses, wipes them and puts them back over his ears. She offers more candy.

Myra decides they must be husband and wife. Who but a wife would put up with such a helpless mountain of a man? Once, long ago, that woman took a vow, but Myra would bet good money she never bargained for this. She would like to shake that old man by his sloppy shoulders and scream, *Look at your little wife! You're using her up! There is almost nothing left of her, can't you see?*

But of course he can't see. Wasn't that the problem?

Myra snickers to herself. Till death do us part?

Oh, that is rich!

❦❦❦

Pushing out the doors of the Lincoln Village Theater, they are amazed again at how cold it is. An icy blast hits Myra in the face and penetrates to her bones. Locked together arms over shoulders, the four of them make their way to the car and huddle inside until Haskell can get the engine started and then the heater. "What did you think of the film?" he asks.

Jennifer mumbles through her scarf. "It was okay."

"I liked the grandfather," Howie says. "He was funny."

Myra is silent, waiting for her teeth to stop chattering. She is surprised to hear Haskell say how much he enjoyed the movie. "It was marvelously satirical, and that last scene at the picnic made me hungry."

"Can we get corn dogs?" Howie says.

After all the junk they've eaten? Myra picks a kernel of popcorn out of a back molar. "We really ought to be getting home."

"But we always go out for supper after the movie," Jennifer says. "I want a milkshake."

"It's too cold for milkshakes."

"Okay, Chinese then. Egg rolls and apricot sauce."

"I have a taste for curry for some reason," Haskell says. "Something hot and spicy, and then one of those sweet cheese desserts."

"If you're all bent and determined on eating out, we can stop at that restaurant on Devon and Western. I'm sure we can each find something on the menu we like."

"That sounds like an excellent idea." He puts the car in reverse and backs out of the parking space.

"You can't get egg rolls there," Jennifer says.

"We'll go for Chinese some other time."

"Tomorrow?"

"Not tomorrow."

"Well, when?"

Myra sighs. Haskell says, "Next Friday evening. We will go to Chen's Cantonese Garden, my treat. Is that all right?"

"Yes," Myra says, "fine." She puts a hand on his knee, hoping to show her gratitude. He *is* good with the children. He's a good man, intelligent and gentle and kind, and she has decided that, if he asks her, she will go down to his room tonight once the children are asleep. It will be a relief to make love with someone she has not sworn to love and cherish through senility and beyond.

By now, the sun has dropped from the sky. A pinkish light glows behind the stores and apartment buildings, and the sidewalks are dusty with frost. But inside the car, the heat is making her drowsy. She feels as if she is in a submarine, cruising silently through the cold streets. They are traveling east on Devon Avenue, behind a red Mustang whose license plate reads: HI IM IDA.

"Care to guess who the driver of that car is?" he asks.

She thinks it might be someone's oversexed grandmother, or else the neighborhood busybody. Then the Mustang puts on its left turn signal, slows for oncoming traffic, and speeds away.

"I'd say those were pretty hot wheels for someone's grandmother." He pokes her arm and she playfully elbows his hand away. At Rockwell Street, he brakes for a red light behind a station wagon plastered with bumper stickers. They take turns reading.

"Jesus is coming…look busy"

"Humpty-Dumpty was pushed!"

"Do vegetarians eat animal crackers?"

The license plate on the car reads FAMILY.

Haskell peers through the windshield. "I can't seem to make out that decal on the rear window."

"Neither can I. Move a little closer." She leans forward until her nose is nearly touching the glass. She can feel Haskell's breath on her cheek. Then the letters jump into focus, and together they recite:

"Please keep your distance. We hardly know each other." ✥

## *FIFTEEN*

Howie wants a party for his birthday, and he wants all of his little friends to be there. "Nine boys and two girls, " Myra says, "on top of all this." She is upstairs in the bathroom with Haskell, searching through the linen cupboard for a bottle of cough syrup while he sits on the edge of the bathtub and fills her in on the past thirty-five or so years of his life.

For the past two weeks, off and on, he has been talking about his childhood, his adolescence, his first love, his college years, his married years, his ex-wife and his divorce. There are things she would really rather not know—who cared if Elizabeth Baxter-Reed bit her toenails?—but he insists it's good for him to open his heart to her like this. Therapy on the run, he calls it, trailing her all over the house.

"When I was a boy," he says, examining a yellow bath sponge shaped like a fish, "my mother gave a party in honor of my birthday every year. Cake, ice cream, pin the tail, musical chairs. I'd look forward to it for weeks, and then, on the big day, I would be absolutely sick with fear. One time I worked myself into an actual fever and she had to call it off."

"But why should having a birthday party cause you so much anxiety?"

"Why? Because, Myra, that is the kind of child I was. On the one hand, I feared being alone. On the other, I feared being the center of attention. In social situations, I was at a complete loss."

"But you must have grown out of that eventually, didn't you?"

"In some ways, yes. Though I never completely lost the feeling that I was..."—he pauses for recollection—"*'...still unborn and already compelled to walk around the streets and speak to people.'*"

"Really? You felt that way? It sounds so extreme."

"Actually," he says, "the words belong to Franz Kafka, famous writer and neurotic. But I shared the sentiment. I was a difficult, unhappy child."

She has located the cough syrup, stuck against a roll of toilet paper. "Speaking of difficult," she says, turning on the hot water and holding the bottle under it, "Howie has been terribly moody lately, even more than usual. I'm hoping this party will cheer him up a little."

"Cake and candy, games and presents—how can you go wrong?"

Jennifer calls from downstairs. "Mom? Mommy!"

"Coming!" She turns off the water and tries the cap, which comes loose this time. Then she sprints down the stairs, Haskell close on her heels.

Jennifer lies on the living room couch, surrounded by pillows, dirty dishes, little hills of used Kleenex and two of the cats, who are tucked into the folds of the faded quilt she has treasured since babyhood. "I think I need some tea," she says weakly, "with lots of honey."

While Haskell checks her forehead for fever, Myra spoons cough syrup into her mouth. "I was thinking that maybe I'd hold the party at one of those pizza places for kids. They have all kinds of entertainment. Video games... electronic puppets.... I wonder how much it would cost."

"Whatever happened to cake and ice cream and musical chairs?"

"Children seem to expect more nowadays."

He follows her into the kitchen and takes down the box of tea bags while she fills the kettle and sets it on the stove. "Expectations. Ah, yes. I know how difficult it can be to meet them. Elizabeth's, for example. She assumed that because I'm a writer, I would be capable of great wit or erudition at the drop of a hat. She expected me to be brilliant on command. And as for me, well, I was so blinded by her sophistication and self-confidence, I failed to detect the flaws in her character until much too late…"

Myra lets him rattle on about his ex-wife and all their problems while she waits for the water to boil. Howie will be home from school soon. He'll need help with his math, of course. She hasn't the faintest idea what to fix for supper, and tonight she has to run a Let's Be Lovers party clear out on Harlem Avenue.

She's been diligently following up on all the leads she has accumulated but never pursued, and now she's lined up a party almost every night for the next week. Haskell agreed to a rise in his weekly rent and said he had no problem making a larger contribution toward groceries and other household expenses. If she is very careful with her budget—and assuming nothing major goes wrong with the house—she might be able to achieve some degree of financial independence. Though Vinnie is still handing her cash, she has no idea how long that will continue. But she is trying to take things one step at a time. It's still too early, she believes, to plan a divorce.

The kettle whistles. Jennifer calls again. Myra says, "You know, I don't think she's all that sick."

"Elizabeth?"

"Jennifer. I'll bet she's just looking for attention."

He unwraps a tea bag and drops it into a mug. "She said I took things too personally, that I was too self-absorbed."

"Jennifer?"

"Elizabeth. Oh, I will have to admit that ours was an attraction of opposites, each of us seeing in the other what we lacked in ourselves. I admired her ambition, her drive. She said I put her in mind of the writer Jack Kerouac."

"She knew him?"

"No, of course not. But she had a romanticized idea of him—the wild literary rebel—and she thought I might have the same capacity for invention. Perhaps she was hoping I'd immortalize her in one of my scripts, the way Arthur Miller did Marilyn Monroe." He laughs unhappily. "I guess Elizabeth and I found out the hard way that although opposites may attract, they don't necessarily stick together. But you've already discovered that."

"Meaning…?"

"You and your husband. The first time I saw you together, I thought: how odd. It was obvious—to me, at least—that the two of you were totally mismatched."

"I wouldn't say totally. We agree on a lot of things."

"But deep down, in your soul, you must have known it was impossible—"

Myra grunts with impatience. "I don't get down to that level very often," she says, pouring water and stirring honey into the mug. "I have enough trouble dealing with things on the surface."

"Tell me everything." He holds out his arms, pulls her close and presses his lips to her temple. "You'll feel better not keeping it inside."

"Mommy…?"

Myra jumps, sloshing hot tea over her hand. "Jennifer! I'll be there in a minute!"

❧❧❧

"I'm not inviting Jeremy."

"Don't be silly, Howie. He's your best friend."

"He stinks. I hate him! Brian is my best friend." He glares at her from across the kitchen table, where he and Haskell are working on a papier mache project for school. Myra is writing out the birthday party invitations.

"You've known Jeremy since you were born. And he lives practically next door. This is going to be very awkward."

Haskell signals for her attention and says out of the corner of his mouth, "I would not pursue this if I were you. This is probably some kind of rivalry issue he has to work out by himself."

"I didn't realize you knew so much about children," she says with more than a touch of sarcasm.

"I came across an article on the subject just the other day. I believe it was in the women's pages of the newspaper, though it might have been in the psychology section of Newsweek. Anyway, the article recommended non-interference by an adult unless the child was being victimized."

"Did the article happen to mention anything about Jeremy's mother or what I'm supposed to say to her? We run into each other all the time."

He shrugs and dips another strip of newspaper into the flour-and-water paste. "Perhaps there is nothing to say. After all, this is not your problem. It's between your son and his former friend."

She hates the tone of his voice. It's entirely too reasonable. He's probably right, but when did he get to be such an expert?

"Don't, Brownie," Howie says. The dog is licking paste off his fingers. Copperfield, seated on the table at Haskell's elbow, has a glob of it on his ear.

"You're going to get that stuff all over the place if you're not careful," Myra says, shielding the invitations with her arms as she writes. The party will be held a week from Saturday at the Happie Tymes Pizza Palace from twelve-thirty to three o'clock. Loretta has promised to help out, and Haskell said she could count on him, too. This will be the first birthday party she's ever given without Vinnie around, but if she organizes the activities around a timetable and synchronizes them perfectly, they ought to make it through the afternoon without too much fuss.

In a way, she is looking forward to it. Day by day, she can feel herself getting over him. She can go for hours without even thinking about what he is doing and who he's doing it with. She can hear the familiar clank of a razor on the sink and not be devastated when she sees it's only Haskell walking out of the bathroom. In recovery, is how she considers herself, and this birthday party will be the first real test of her ability to cope.

What Haskell had said about being mismatched was closer to the truth than she cared to admit. Who did she think she was, a girl like her taking up with someone like Vinnie? The wonder of it is that he hadn't pulled something like this years ago.

"When I was in fifth grade," Haskell tells Howie, "I made a model of a pioneer settlement out of papier mache. My teacher put it on display for the whole school to see."

"Were you smart in school?"

"Fairly smart, yes. But where I excelled was in the school pageants and plays."

"You?" Myra says. "I thought you said you were so shy."

"I was—painfully shy. But you see, Myra, children like me have to develop strategies for getting through life. Mine was to invent an alter ego. I projected him to the outside world so that my true self could remain hidden and protected."

She licks the flap of an envelope and seals it. "So who is this alter ego? And do I know him?"

He laughs. "I think I've managed to integrate him pretty well. It's not as schizophrenic as it sounds."

"You seem to have analyzed your childhood pretty thoroughly."

"I did. I spent six and a half years in therapy." His voice is suddenly grim. He sounds like Vinnie does when he tells people he's been to Nam. "I felt I was beginning to make real progress, but then I had to give it up. Elizabeth claimed it was nothing but self-indulgence, paying someone an outrageous sum of money to sit there and listen to my problems. She didn't see why I couldn't simply wake up one morning and decide to be normal."

Frankly, neither does Myra. He could learn a lot just by watching the experts on Oprah and Donahue, and it would not cost him a red cent.

Howie picks up a strip of paste-laden paper. His shirt front is covered with white dots, as is Haskell's cheek. The cat is trying to shake something off his paw. Myra scoops up the invitations and gets them safely out of the way. Then she goes after the globs of paste with a damp sponge. "Honestly," she says, "you guys," and they grin at her sheepishly, like two messy little boys.

∽∽∽

The minute they walk through the doors of the Happie Tymes Pizza Palace, she realizes it was a mistake to have scheduled the party for a Saturday afternoon. A number of other parties are already under way—she counts five long tables of children wearing paper party hats—and dozens of other children appear to be darting around on their own.

"Where should we put the coats?" Haskell calls as they rush to claim a table off to one side of the restaurant. Mechanical puppets in little suits of armor are doing a chipmunk-style version of Jive Talkin' on a raised stage against the far wall. He has to shout over the music to be heard.

There are no chairs, only the backless benches on either side of the table. "I guess we'll have to stuff them under here," Myra calls back.

"What?"

"Under here!"

The music has ended a half second before. A woman in mustard-colored sweat pants and a tee-shirt that reads World's Greatest Grandma turns to stare at her.

Howie starts in right away. He wants tokens to play the bowling game, he wants soda pop, he wants candy.

"Later, Sweetie. Don't you want to wait for your little guests?"

"No, I want—"

"Oh, look! Here comes Aunt Loretta."

"Mom? How come she's wearing sun glasses in here?"

Loretta teeters toward them in her spike heels and skin-tight jeans. She is dressed for a party, all right, but not this one. Myra has taken the precaution of putting on sneakers and cargo pants with pockets large enough to hold her supplies: the list of guests, the timetable, a box of candles, tissues, a comb, money in coin and cash, lip balm, eye drops, and a small bottle of aspirin.

"Where's the birthday boy?" Loretta whispers hoarsely.

"You're not going to poop out on me, I hope." Myra pats her on the arm, assuming a more lavish display of affection would be unwelcome in her condition.

"Hey, my word is my bond. I'm here, right?"

"Was the hangover worth it? Did you have a good time?"

Loretta removes the sun glasses and gives Myra a bleary wink. "You bet."

Myra motions for everyone to gather around and gives them the game plan. "Twelve children and three adults. That's four children each, so Jennifer, I would appreciate your helping out wherever you can."

"Okay, Mom. I could wait by the door for Howie's friends and bring them over when they get here."

"That would be an excellent idea." Myra has secured Jennifer's cooperation with a five dollar bribe and the loan of the white sweater. She asks Haskell to wait with Howie while she and Loretta order lunch. "I think we're right on schedule," she says, checking her timetable and her wristwatch—which seems to have stopped. She looks around for a wall clock. "Does anyone know the time?"

"Twelve thirty-six," Jennifer says, arriving with the first of Howie's guests. She holds up her new digital watch, a Christmas gift from Vinnie.

"It's dumb sitting here," Howie grumbles. "I wanna play the bowling game."

"Later, okay? First we're going to have lunch, then games, then cake, then presents. See? I have it all written down." She grabs Loretta by the elbow and sets off to order the pizzas, hoping that once the party gets going, Howie will perk up. "How long?" she asks the counterman after giving her order: one large cheese and pepperoni, one large cheese and sausage .

"Twenty-five, thirty minutes." He shifts a toothpick to the other side of his mouth and hands her a receipt and a fistful of game tokens. "Watch for your number on the monitor."

She had not expected the pizza to take that long. Pulling out her timetable, she makes a quick revision. "Soda pop!" she says, suddenly inspired. "That'll keep them busy for a while." She orders a pitcher of cola and a pitcher of root beer, and Loretta helps her carry them back to their table.

Several more of Howie's friends have arrived, and Haskell is trying to entertain them by memorizing their names. "Let me see… Jonathan…Joel…Joshua…Kristina Marie…"

"I'm Joshua, he's Joel."

"Mister Calderelli," Kristina Marie says, bouncing in her red high-tops, "can we go play in the jumping room?"

"He's not my father," Howie says.

The lights go down then, and the mechanical puppets once more come to life. They jerk their arms, spin their heads, bleat a Beatles song. Loretta presses her hands to her ears and collapses onto a bench. Jennifer escorts three more children to their table, two boys and a girl wearing a taffeta party dress. She walks up to Myra and says, as soon as the music stops, "I'm not supposed to get myself dirty."

"Well, fine." Myra hands her a plastic cup. Everyone wants the cola, except for the little girl, who asks for ginger ale.

Myra checks her guest list and counts heads. "Who is missing?"

"Brian," Howie says. "I don't wanna wait for him."

"Can we go in the jumping room?"

"In a while," Myra says. "Jennifer? Do you know any games the children could play while we're waiting for the pizza?"

"We could tell who our favorite rock group is." She turns to a pudgy boy with damp-looking hair and asks, "Who's yours?"

While he's thinking about it, someone shouts, "Skinny Puppy!"

"Def Leppard!"

"Anthrax!"

"I remember when rock bands had wholesome names," Myra says to Haskell. "Bread, Cream. The Strawberry Alarm Clock…"

"Dead Kennedys sing a song with the F-word in it."

Kristina Marie folds her hands over her mouth. Howie says, "What's the F-word?"

In an instant, Myra is on her feet and digging into her pockets. "Children! Listen! Here are some game tokens. Go on…go and play!" They grab the tokens from her hands and scatter in every direction. She hands Haskell a ten dollar bill and sends him off to buy more.

Loretta seems to have disappeared, but she shows up moments later with a carafe of white wine.

"I cannot believe you are going to drink that," Myra says.

"Half is for you." Loretta pours the wine and hands her a glass. "I thought you looked a little tense."

"Tense? Don't be silly." She unclamps her jaw. "I think things are going quite well." She takes out her timetable again. Twenty minutes for lunch, an hour or so for games, that left about half an hour for cake and presents. Perfect.

In a while, the children begin straggling back to the table. Myra counts heads again. Still no Brian. "When do we eat?" they keep asking. At long last, their number appears on the monitor.

"Bingo!" Loretta says. She volunteers to go and get the pizzas.

"I gotta pee."

"Shall I take Joel to the bathroom?" Haskell asks.

"Wait a sec. Does anyone else have to go?"

They all raise their hands, except for Howie, who sits forlornly at the head of the table and stares at the front door.

It is decided that Haskell will accompany the boys and Jennifer the girls. Alone with Howie, Myra brushes his hair from his forehead and says, "What's wrong, Honey? Are you upset about Brian?"

He slumps in his chair, ignoring her.

In a few minutes, the children are assembled at the table again and they're grabbing for the pizza, which is too hot to eat. They blow on their slices; they blow on each other's slices; they gargle their pop and slide under the table, laughing. The little girl in the taffeta dress picks up her pizza at one edge and plucks off a morsel of sausage.

Predictably, it plops into her lap. Myra has already jumped to attention, pulling tissues from her pocket. She dabs gingerly at the spot, a mix of grease and tomato sauce, but it's already beginning to set. "Cold water!" she cries, looking around for some.

With a gleam of martyrdom in her eye, the little girl says, "My ma's gonna kill me."

Someone hands Myra an ice cube. Then the lights dim and the music starts up again, and by the time the song is over, the pizza has disappeared and everyone is asking for cake.

"Not yet, children! Not yet!" Her voice has taken on the frantic gaiety of a pediatric nurse. She instructs Haskell to pass out whatever game tokens he has left and sends him off for more.

"What's up with Howie?" Loretta says, watching him amble away with the rest of the scattering children.

"One of his little friends didn't show. He'll get over it." She sits down, rests her elbows on the table and sips her wine, grateful for the temporary respite. "Too bad he wasn't born in the summer. I've always wanted to be able to throw a birthday party on the lawn, with lemonade and tea sandwiches cut into different shapes…"

"I don't think these kids look much like the lemonade and little sandwich crowd. Do you?"

Myra offers a wistful half-smile. "No, I suppose not." She nibbles thoughtfully at a stray crust of pizza and watches the children darting around the restaurant. Kristina Marie skips past, wearing a birthday hat from some other child's party. Jonathan—Joel?—comes back for a swig of pop, wipes his mouth on his sleeve and dashes off again, his crumpled shirttails hanging out of his pants.

The mechanical puppets perform two more numbers, and then the children begin straggling back to the table. They appear flushed and overheated, and Myra hopes no one is going to get sick.

With everyone finally assembled, she brings out the cake, which she has kept safely out of sight until now. She looks around for Haskell. He seems to have disappeared, but then she spots him two tables away, prying something off the sole of his shoe. "We're ready to sing Happy Birthday," she calls, taking the candles out of her pocket and sticking them into the cake. "Seven…eight…and one for good luck." Somehow, the good luck candle has gotten bent in half.

Howie keeps his eyes focused on his belt as everyone sings, but he cheers up a little when Myra sets a big slice of cake in front of him. Then Loretta brings over the pile of gifts, and Haskell helps him open them. "Look, Howie," he says, pushing a Tonka dump truck back and forth on the table, "Isn't this a swell present?"

"Uh-huh." He reaches for the next package.

Really, you would think he could show a little more enthusiasm, especially since everyone is killing themselves for him. Well, it's almost over. She smiles at all the restless children squirming in their seats, picking their noses, squashing cake crumbs and drawing their fingers through the icing. Soon their parents will come and take them away, and then she can go home and collapse.

"Jennifer?" she says, turning to her daughter. "Is it three o'clock yet?"

"It's two-eleven. See?"

"Impossible." She grabs Jennifer's wrist and taps at the watch face. "This must have stopped."

"Don't, Mom, you'll break it."

Loretta moans, "Jesus, my head is killing me."

"You're not thinking of leaving, are you?" Myra tries to keep the panic out of her voice. "Here." She pulls the bottle of aspirin from the pocket of her pants. "Take some."

"Perhaps I should purchase more of those tokens," Haskell says.

"Yes! Tokens!" She hurriedly scrapes together another four dollars and seventy cents, which is all the money she has left. "Go on, boys and girls! Go and play!" She waves her arms like a conductor, orchestrating them out of their seats. Everyone leaves except Howie, who is dragging a GI Joe doll through a rubble of pizza crusts and spilled soda.

"Are you enjoying yourself the least little bit?"

Howie frowns and glances at the door.

Myra grabs some napkins and begins mopping the table. "You know, Sweetie, I think you should reconsider this best friend business with Brian—"

"Mrs. Calderelli! Mrs. Calderelli!" Kristina Marie skips toward her. "Jonathan and Jason were throwing their tokens down the toilet!"

Myra looks out over the swarming sea of children through which Haskell is making his way, holding two boys by their upper arms. One of them is crying. The other keeps saying, "We just wanted to see if we could make them float."

Haskell's face has assumed a look of stern annoyance. It seems he is trying to deliver a lecture, but just then the music starts up again.

Puppets wearing velvet dresses and fairy princess hats sing, *Do you believe in ma-a-a-gic…*

For some reason, Howie is standing on the table now. He's waving his arms and calling to someone who has just walked in the door.

Someone too large to be his friend Brian.

"Dad, Dad!" He scrambles off the table and runs into Vinnie's arms. She sees it in slow motion, Vinnie dropping down, scooping Howie up in one arm, saying something that makes her gloomy little son suddenly shriek with joy. She ditches the soggy wad of napkins under the table as Vinnie and Howie come toward her with a huge box wrapped in silver foil. "Look, Mom! Look what Dad got for me!"

She feels light-headed, dangerously close to crumpling to the floor. The defiant grimace of self-assurance she tries to hold on her face keeps slipping into a crescent of dismay. Haskell stands by her side, one arm wrapped around her for support. They watch Howie tear off the foil paper and pull a deadly looking armored toy vehicle from the box.

"Oh, boy, it's got laser guns and a rocket launcher—" He is overcome, delirious.

Vinnie nods at her. "How's it going?"

"It's…I think…yes, it's very—"

"Terrific," Haskell declares. "Hasn't this been a terrific party, Howie?"

"Uh-huh." He is still salivating over his rocket launcher.

"Right," Myra says. "It's been…terrific."

The boy who was crying now has his fingers around the throat of another child. The little taffeta girl keeps tugging at Myra's arm and saying, "He did. He did. He really, really did."

ஒஒஒ

All evening, she has been on the verge of tears, and now, alone with Haskell in his room, she lets the floodgates open. "Did you see

Howie's face when his father walked in?" she says between sobs. "For all he cared I could have fallen off the earth."

"The absent-parent-as-hero syndrome. I've read it is, unfortunately, a very common malady."

"Vinnie could throw him a party in a bus station—in the toilet of a bus station!—and he would love it."

"It seems so terribly unfair, doesn't it."

She blows her nose. "It stinks."

He runs his finger along the collar of her robe. "Did I ever tell you about my father? After my mother died and I went off to college, he took up with some woman he'd met at a bereavement group, married her weeks later and sent me the news on the back of a postcard. My mother had not even been gone six months."

"Oh, that's awful."

"He wrote on the postcard that at long last he had found true happiness. Well, you can imagine how that made me feel. I wondered what he thought of all those years he'd spent married to my mother. At that point, I did truly consider myself an orphan. It was as if I had lost both of my parents."

"Oh," she says again, "how awful."

Calmer now, she nestles alongside him, resting her head against his shoulder and letting his words drip into her ear. If she is still awake by the time he finishes his story, he will, in his earnest and predictable way, make love to her, and that will allow her to forget for a while her disappointment, the fear and loneliness she cannot seem to escape any other way.

Outside the basement window, snow has begun to fall. Haskell drones out more of his unhappy history, and together they watch the big, sad flakes melting silently down the windowpane. ❧

## SIXTEEN

"Gun control my sweet white ass! You want my opinion? Women in this country ought to be armed to their goddamn teeth."

"Oh, Karen. You don't really believe that."

"The hell I don't. Do you ever read the papers, Janice? Do you listen to the evening news?"

"We all know what goes on in the world. That isn't the point—"

"…and Ladies, here is the perfect undergarment for when you want to let it all hang out…"

"Ooh, naughty, naughty. That come in blue, Myra?"

"Black and pink only. And for those formal occasions when you just can't decide what to wear—voila!—his and hers bikini thongs with matching tuxedo collars and cuffs…"

"Hey, now. Wouldn't Franklin's little patootie look cute in this?"

"You taken a good look at Franklin lately, Charlene? Better order you an extra-large."

"Don't get me wrong. I have nothing against men, but in this day and age, a woman simply cannot be too careful."

"Well, I for one think the world is much too hard on men. Why, most of them are nothing but little boys at heart."

"Dangerous little boys."

"Not true. Like Eddie, for instance. Do you know what turns him on? The smell of cinnamon. He likes me to sprinkle some in my hair before we make love. He says cinnamon reminds him of Christmas, and all the yummy things, and that I'm like the best Christmas cookie he ever ate."

"Awww, how sweet! Isn't that sweet, Charlene?"

"Ronald used to like to pretend that we were still in high school. Couldn't get hard unless he imagined that my father was in the next room."

"Good thing you unloaded him, girl. Who needs those games?"

"…and speaking of games, here is a deck of cards that will liven up any bridge party…"

"Oh, my God!"

"Are these real people?"

"What is that funny looking round thing over there?"

"More wine, Inez?"

"No, thanks. I'm skunked already. I think I'm gonna have to call in sick tomorrow."

"How 'bout we all don't show up? Wouldn't little Mr. Timothy ter Horst have himself a fit about that!"

"He's so busy ogling that new gal in accounting, he probably wouldn't notice."

"So that's why he's been drowning himself in aftershave."

"Smells like horse piss to me."

"Horse piss and mothballs."

"…and speaking of the importance of scent as an aphrodisiac, here is our very own Captive Eight erotic perfume. Go on, try some. Touch it to the pulse points inside your wrists and elbows. That's right. Also in the hollow of the throat and between your breasts…"

"I'd like to see the special guy in Myra's life. I bet he goes around with a smile on his face pretty much all the time."

"Tell the truth, Myra. Do you use this stuff?"

"Certainly I do. I wouldn't sell anything I hadn't tried out personally."

"So what do you recommend? What works best? The Wildfire Oil? The nipple rouge? The banana daiquiri massage cream?"

"Well, I'd have to say it's a matter of personal taste—"

"Hah!"

"—no pun intended. I mean, some couples enjoy rubbing the lotions and creams on one another, and some like parading around in the lingerie, and some like to fool with the toys. Really, it's just whatever turns you on."

"With batteries, or without?"

"Hah, hah!"

"…and fantasy is such an important part of the whole thing. All the experts agree that the brain is our biggest sex organ. These little products just help you along, particularly if you've been with the same partner for a while."

"Me and Patrick have been married almost eighteen years."

"Well, hooray for you, Ruth Ann."

"Things were getting pretty dull in the sex department, especially after I put on a few pounds. But then, a couple of years ago, we managed to turn it around."

"You did? C'mon, girl, spill."

"Well, we started acting out this kind of a game. The Trucker and the Slut. It was Patrick's idea. See, what happens is, I get all decked out in a slinky dress or a pair of tight jeans and a low-cut top. I put on these big earrings and a lot of eye makeup and really red lipstick. Then I drive to somewhere way out, like Prairie View or Gurnee. Find a tavern on the highway, one of those places with a lot of cigarette smoke and guys drinking boilermakers, or whiskey straight up—"

"You drive out there alone?"

"Uh-huh. But Patrick follows in the Blazer. I go into the place first, sit at the bar and nurse a whiskey sour—it's the only drink I can get down without gagging. 'Course, the guys start hitting on me right away. Patrick's watching from a back table, and it's driving him crazy because he knows that I'm not wearing a stitch of underwear."

"Not even in the winter?"

"Uh-uh. Anyhow, when Patrick can't stand it another minute, he comes over and pretends like, Hey, what a co-incidence! Like he knows me from someplace. Then he says he's got that thing I want. I ask him, What thing? and he says, That piece of equipment you ordered. And meanwhile, some other guy is rubbing my shoulder or playing with my fingers, and I'm not paying Patrick much attention. But I can tell he's getting ready to explode. He says something like, This equipment's just right, make a perfect fit for you, and I say, Well, maybe I can take a peek at it. The other guys give him this look, like they're so jealous they could kill, and he's pulling me out the door, practically dragging me into the Blazer. And we, like, you know, do it in the back seat."

"You're putting us on, Ruth Ann, aren't you?"

"Uh-uh. I kind of didn't used to enjoy it, but it's okay now. It's kind of fun."

"You're married to a maniac, you know that? Suppose one of those other guys tried dragging you outside?"

"Oh, Patrick would never let that happen."

"Suppose they got into a fight, knocked him out or something. Then what?"

"Quit it, Karen. You're scaring her."

"But he's using her. Anyone can see that."

"Oh, I don't really see any harm in it. Besides, if I didn't play along, he might go to one of those places by himself and find another girl, someone younger than me, with a better figure."

"You know, Ladies, I think Ruth Ann has expressed a fear that most women have at one time or another. Keeping a man happy at home is the guiding philosophy of Let's Be Lovers. And when he does step out of line...well, have you noticed number twelve ten on your order forms? A beautifully crafted cat 'o nine tails doeskin whip."

"Now there's something I can use!"

"Look, girls, we might as well face facts. Men will never change. It's that short Y chromosome they were born with. Means they're missing a couple of important genes."

"They're never gonna have ovaries, and they're never gonna have common sense."

"Ain't gonna happen, and that's the truth."

"Still, what would we do without them?"

"She's got a point there, Charlene."

"Imagine a world without men."

"I'm trying, but I don't know."

"For one thing, they could close just about all the prisons."

"Yeah, and most of the bars. And Weight Watchers would go out of business in half a minute."

"No Mr. Timmy ter Horst putting his greasy fingers on you."

"Amen to that, Girl."

"No more armies, no more wars—"

"—no more Kennedys!—"

"Praise the Lord."

"...a world without men..."

"Yes, I can honestly see it! No crime. And all these happy fat women." ❧

## *SEVENTEEN*

When he comes for the children on the second Sunday after the birthday party, Vinnie doesn't bring her the usual box of fruits and vegetables. She answers the doorbell, and he swaggers through and just stands there, slouching against the wall until Jennifer and Howie are ready to go. Before he swaggers out, he drops a fifty dollar bill on the hall table. And all he has said to her the whole time is "hullo" and "g'bye."

So when he telephones the next day and tells her to meet him on Wednesday after work at Sue & Ellyn's Snack Shack—because he has to talk to her about something important and he can't do it in the house with the kids and, as he puts it, "that writer guy" around—she knows something is up.

And she's pretty sure she knows what. Unable to stop herself, she keeps replaying that scene from a movie she once saw where the husband takes his bride to a fancy, crowded restaurant and right there on the honeymoon tells her he wants out of the marriage.

So, it is finally, actually going to happen.

As soon as she hangs up the phone with him, she picks it up again and dials Loretta's number. Loretta is the voice of experience about divorce, isn't she? Maybe she'd be able to offer some useful advice.

Her line is busy, and Myra thinks about who else to call.

Her parents? Oh, how she hates to admit it, but they were right all along. Why hadn't she listened all those years ago when they'd station themselves outside the bathroom door while she dressed for their date? "He's no good," they chanted. "He has no future. He's Italian, for God's sake. He'll ruin your life!"

The whole of Tuesday night she spends tossing around in her bed, sleepwalks through the next day, trying to construct the coming scene in her mind. But her imagination will not take her that far. In the end, she sees, she will just have to go it alone: no advice from anyone, no game plan, no script. Before she leaves the house on Wednesday evening, however, she tears a piece of lined paper from Jennifer's composition book and writes out a list of the things she has promised herself she will not do:

*Cry.*
*Raise My Voice.*
*Throw Anything.*
*Beg.*

She folds the sheet of paper and tucks it into her purse, and then she tugs on her hat and gloves and buttons her coat up to her chin. This has to be the worst night of the winter so far. The wind is fierce, blowing sleet from all directions. The streets and sidewalks look deserted, the shop windows are dark, but Sue & Ellyn's Snack Shack is glowing with yellow light. Myra parks in the lot next door and sprints across the icy pavement toward the warmth of the restaurant. Inside the door, she pauses to catch her breath.

"C'mon, babe. You know what I'm talking about..."

Glancing over her shoulder, she sees a young man in a football jacket murmuring into the receiver of the pay telephone, fondling it in his meaty hands. He shifts his eyes in her direction, then goes back to his conversation. A waitress with a row of plates on her arm shoots past. "Comin' up ba-hind you, Miss," she drawls.

"Sorry," Myra says. Watching out for calamity on her left, she nearly knocks into someone on her right, an elderly woman who has gotten up to help her lady friend on with her coat.

She apologizes again. Even this late in the evening the restaurant is a hub of activity. It would be difficult to make a scene here. Probably why Vinnie chose the place.

The calculating bastard.

She should never have put off talking to a lawyer; she understands that now. First thing tomorrow, after she gets the children off to school, she will go through the Yellow Pages and find someone with a name that sounds trustworthy enough to handle her case.

Vinnie is sitting in a booth near the back, hunched over a thick white coffee mug, and he looks up at the same instant she spots him: too late for her to turn and run. He calls her name and flashes a nervous, teeth-only grin. She slides into the booth and pulls off her gloves and hat. She is still shivering a little, though she knows it's more than just the cold weather.

So why is she sipping from that glass of ice water the bus boy has set down in front of her?

Nerves, pure and simple.

"Any trouble getting here?" he asks, lifting the mug and glancing at her.

"No." Her voice is tight. She clears her throat. "No trouble."

"Kids okay?"

"Yes."

"How 'bout your folks?"

She sighs. "They're fine, too." She takes another sip of ice water; it leaves an aftertaste of chlorine on her tongue.

He fiddles with his coffee, puts in more sugar, stirs with a spoon that he leaves in the mug as he drinks. "Cold out, huh?"

Pathetic. Vinnie was about as good at small talk as she was at changing a flat tire. "It's the dead of winter in Chicago," she remarks dryly. "What else can you expect?"

He laughs, a snort. "Yeah."

Their waitress comes over, a rustle of nylon in a cloud of My Sin perfume, and asks for their order.

"Tea," Myra says.

"Gimme a sweet roll, will ya, Hon?"

"What about you, Miss, anything to eat?"

"No—"

"Blueberry pie?"

"No, really—"

"Rice pudding? Jell-O? Cheesecake?"

"Go on, My-ra. Eat something."

"All right," she says, simply to end the discussion. "Cheesecake." Taking another sip of water, she studies the waitress, who is reaching way across the table to gather their menus (an inch closer and she'd fall right into Vinnie's lap). Then she watches him watching her strut away, hips rocking like a boat on choppy water.

"Friendly, isn't she."

He nods, oblivious to the sarcasm. "This is a friendly place."

"Do you come here often?"

He turns a palm over. "Once in a while."

The waitress returns with their order, scribbles out the check and slaps it on the table. "You folks have a real nice evening now," she says. "And if you want more coffee, just whistle." She offers Vinnie a wink.

Myra holds her cup in both hands, letting the heat seep into her fingers. As a child, when she was sick and Grandma Rose would come to take care of her, there was always milky Lipton tea in a chipped ceramic mug. She remembers how she drank in the lukewarm sweetness—along with the fairy tales her grandmother liked to spin—how safe and comforted she felt. But now she is an adult with an obligation to face reality. She brings the cup to her lips and drinks the tea scalding and black, a test of her maturity, her endurance.

"You look a little tired," he remarks.

She says nothing. She is not going to make this easy for him.

"You get any help from that writer guy?"

"Yes, as a matter of fact, I do."

He tilts his head, considering. She's just waiting for him to make some dumb remark about Haskell so she can jump down his throat. But he doesn't. He asks about Howie, if he is doing any better at math, if she's noticed that he's beginning to stutter.

"He does not stutter," she says firmly. "His thoughts get ahead of his words sometimes, that's all. And as far as math is concerned, I'm helping him study his times tables."

"Math is important, you know—"

"Of course I know!" She presses her lips together. *I will not raise my voice.*

He bites into his roll. He doesn't appear to be in any hurry to get on with this. If she doesn't broach the subject, they will be here all night. She takes another hot swallow of tea, and when the burning in her chest subsides she looks directly into his face and says, "Who. Is. She."

Was it her imagination, or did he flinch the tiniest bit?

He plays with some grains of spilled sugar on the table. "What's the difference," he says after a moment, his voice a monotone. "She's someone I know from work."

"One of those fancy, fur-coated tennis players that shop at your store, I suppose."

"What? No, nothing like that. She works in the deli department, sometimes passes out samples to the customers. You know, knockwurst, ham salad..."

Myra thinks of the woman who offered her the jalapeno-flavored cheese spread that horrible day at the Dominick's. She tries to picture her, but the only thing she can recall is a checkered apron, a pair of ordinary hands. "Tell me..." she says slowly, keeping her eyes on his, "...what is it about her you find so wonderful, so irresistible, that you had to up and leave your family for?"

He doesn't offer an answer. He lifts his mug, drinks, sets it down, wipes a palm over his head, rests an elbow on the table. Apparently, she is making him uncomfortable.

Good.

"What kind of samples did she pass out to you?"

"Aw, My-ra, c'mon. You make it sound like—"

"Like what?" She leans closer— to within striking distance, if need be.

He shifts his eyes away. "Look, we used to joke around sometimes, kid each other. She had a nice personality. We'd take our breaks together, once in a while go out for a sandwich. And then she started telling me things. About her life, her troubles. I was a shoulder to cry on." He rolls a wrist, tosses a hand. "It wasn't like I planned for anything to happen." He frowns. "It just did."

She ducks her head, willing back tears. The waitress swings by again with a coffee carafe in each hand. "De-caf or reg-u-lar?" she sings.

He points and she pours, standing in such a way that her breast is only inches from his face. If Myra were not here, she would probably slip him her phone number. Obviously blinded by his good looks, she cannot see what a dangerous character he is.

"Something wrong with the cheesecake?" the waitress asks.

"No." Myra picks up her fork and hacks off the narrow edge.

The waitress gives her a thin smile and sashays away.

"This woman," she says, mashing at the cake with her fork, "this woman with the terrific sense of humor and everything. Does she have a family, too?"

"Yeah. Two boys, teenagers. And a girl around Howie's age."

"And she's divorced, I assume."

"Technically, a widow. Her old man died in some kind of motorcycle accident before the divorce could go through."

"How very convenient." She stares daggers at him. Wouldn't he just love it if she were to drop dead, too. Think how easy it would be: no messy courtroom scenes, no custody arrangements, no lawyers. He'd weep at her grave as if his heart were broken, wait out the briefest period of mourning ever recorded, and rush into marriage with the sample lady. She probably wouldn't want Howie and Jennifer. They'd be given away, like a pair of orphans. Maybe Cara could look after them. Jack and Nettie wouldn't have the time, Lena would send them to church on Sundays, and Loretta was out of the question.

Myra clutches at her stomach. "Oh, God," she moans.

"What's wrong? You sick?"

She shakes her head.

"Maybe you caught something from Jen. Her cold any better?"

"She's fine now."

"Second bad cold she's had this winter. Maybe you ought to start giving her vitamins. Or take her to the doctor—"

"Don't tell me what to do. I'm quite capable of taking care of my own children."

"Sure, sure." He gestures, palms pressing forward. No offense intended, no indeed.

But she is beginning to realize what he's driving at: Jennifer's sicknesses, Howie's stuttering and his low math grades—he doesn't think she is fit to be their mother anymore.

So, not only is he going to divorce her, he's planning to take the children as well.

She cannot believe this is happening. This terrible moment will be imprinted on her brain forever, along with the smells of coffee and fry grease, the clatter of dishes, and the male voice in the booth behind her asking his companion for odds on the Green Bay-Oakland game.

Someone laughs. Myra closes her eyes. She feels his fingers on her wrist, and her eyes spring open again. "You can*not* take Jennifer and Howie," she says, pulling her hand away. Her voice is a slow, deliberate growl.

"What? What're you talking about?'

"I am the *only* person in this whole world they can depend on anymore. No matter what, *I'd* never walk out on them. *I'd* never turn their lives upside down."

"Wait a minute—"

"No, *you* wait a minute, you sorry son of a bitch! I know my rights. You try any fast stuff, I swear I will have my lawyers nail you to the goddamn wall."

She stops for breath. Oh, this feels good, this wave of rage she is riding. All this time, she's been going along and going along, being polite, being reasonable.

Not anymore.

She grabs the glass ashtray on the table: something solid under her fingers. She would like to throw it at his head—never mind what she's written down on her list—see it smash against the wall and break into a thousand angry splinters. Everyone in Sue & Ellyn's Snack Shack would cower under the tables. Someone might call the police. She'd be taken away in restraints, her wild, screaming face all over the ten o'clock news.

"Hey, My-ra, take it easy." He reaches for her hand. She yanks it away again, and this time it knocks against her water glass. The glass teeters for a moment before falling over and spilling its icy contents into Vinnie's lap.

His mouth opens, but no sound emerges. He lifts himself away from the puddle on the seat and stares at her in disbelief. If she had pulled out a gun and shot him, he could not look more surprised.

And here comes the waitress, of course. With a flurry of sympathetic clucks, she mops him up with a large gray rag. Myra sits back and sips her tea. She is growing calmer by the minute, the anger seeming to have run itself out like one of those flash fires that burns the tangled underbrush but leaves the trees intact.

The way ahead is clear for her now. She sees what she has to do.

"You can have the divorce," she says flatly after the waitress has gone. "I won't fight you on that. But Howie and Jennifer stay with me. I will *never* let you take them away."

He tosses a soggy wad of napkins into the ashtray. "Jesus," he says softly. It's clear to her that he never expected this, her standing up for herself, taking control, laying down the law.

"I'm hoping we can get through this in a civilized manner, so that we can put the past behind us and get on with our new lives," she goes on, relishing the sound of those words, their satisfying ring of finality. "We should both sit down with the children and explain everything to them, as honestly as we can. They'll have a lot of questions, of course, and we have to assure them that absolutely none of this is their fault."

He presses his palms into his eyes and wipes them down his face. "My-ra? Would you please tell me what in holy hell you are talking about?"

"As I recall," she says, searching for her fork, which seems to have disappeared in the confusion over the spilled water, "we have been discussing a number of things. The weather. The children. Your lover. And now we've moved on to the subject of our divorce." She pinches off a piece of cheesecake, drops it into her mouth, and licks her thumb.

"Divorce?" He puts his fingers to his temples, as if to keep his head from splitting open. Shadows under his eyes look like bruises he might have suffered in a fistfight. "Who's talking about a divorce?"

"Isn't that the reason you wanted to meet me here? Isn't that the next logical step? You certainly don't expect us to keep going on like this, do you?"

He reaches for her hands, this time locking on to both wrists and looking her squarely in the face. "You don't understand. Everything went sour. Those punk kids of hers, nothing but trouble. That crazy freaking house. My-ra, I don't want no divorce. I just wanna come home." ❧

## EIGHTEEN

"Business certainly does seem to be improving," Haskell remarks. "This is the third night in a row that you're going out to one of those parties." Standing there with a frown on his face and a roll of paper towels under one arm, he seems a little put-upon. Lucy has spit up a hairball on the living room carpet, and Myra's asked him if he wouldn't mind taking care of it.

She herself has been rushing around since four o'clock after spending nearly the whole day at the library. She's managed to get supper together—a canned salmon and frozen vegetable casserole topped with crushed potato chips, pretty much all she had in the house—and now there is the cleaning up. Really, she ought to just leave everything and go. She's supposed to meet Vinnie at seven, and she still has to put on her makeup.

At the restaurant last night—after what he told her had a minute to sink in and she'd regained the power of speech—she asked him if he thought he could just waltz back into her life as if nothing had happened. Things were different now. She'd spent weeks and months without him. She'd had time to think.

He got a kind of guilty, gee-whiz expression on his face then, and he asked her if maybe she decided she didn't love him anymore.

Well, that almost did her in.

Of course she still loved him, had loved him since she first laid eyes on him, though she didn't know it then. She thought it was the flu, her limbs ached so, and a heavy feeling had taken hold in the pit of her stomach. She popped aspirin, drank milky tea; nothing helped until the first time he took her in his arms and gave her the longest, deepest kiss of her life up to that moment. When he was finished, all the pain had gone.

Sitting there with him at Sue & Ellyn's Snack Shack, she had to steady herself against the table to keep from reacting to the misery in his eyes. But then he went on to spoil it, promising that when he came home, they could pick up where they left off and everything would be just fine.

"Honest," he said, touching his fingertips to his chest.

Where had she seen that gesture? On television, those Senate hearings where shifty-eyed men in suits with wide lapels took the Fifth after every other question. That gesture was what made her back off. If he could do this to her once, what guarantee did she have he would not do it again?

She swallowed the words of forgiveness along with the rest of her tea, set down her cup and stared into his eyes. "It's obvious that our marriage needs help, Vinnie. I think we have no option but to go for counseling."

"What, you mean *shrinks*?" His voice rose half an octave. He told her to forget it, karate-chopping the air for emphasis. They glared at each other for a full minute (she'd almost forgotten how ridiculously stubborn he could be) before she gave in and said okay, maybe they'd be able to work this out on their own; do-it-yourself.

That, he agreed to.

So they are meeting tonight at Vinnie's friend's apartment, where he's been staying since moving out of the sample lady's house, and Myra is standing in front of her closet, trying to decide what to wear.

At the library today, she pored over dozens of books and magazine articles on relationships in trouble. She studied case histories and took pages of notes, and still she couldn't really see what any of it had to do with her and Vinnie. As far as she could tell, none of the women had to cope with a household like hers, and most of the men were high-flying executive types who had suddenly crash-landed in some sort of mid-life crisis. The therapists came from either New York or Los Angeles, places that were—in terms of life as most people know it, Myra felt—practically off the planet.

On her way out of the reading room, she happened to spot a small book with a pretty blue cover. The title, *You Say/He Hears,* was rendered in fancy white letters that looked as if they'd been drawn by Martha Stewart with a tube of confectioners icing; and when she read the sub-title—*The Secret to Getting Whatever You Want from Your Guy*—she snatched the book off the shelf with both hands.

The author, a sensible-looking woman with graying hair, laugh lines and a psychology practice in Minneapolis, claimed that all a woman had to do to get what she wanted from the man in her life was to *ask* for it. The trick, apparently, was in mastering the when, the where and the how. All sorts of things had to be taken into consideration: his temperament, the length of his attention span, whether he was more responsive to auditory or visual stimuli, how he related to his mother, what he thought of women like Sandra Day O'Connor, and so on.

Myra read the first two chapters carefully but then had to skim through the rest, and she wishes she'd had more time. There are so many things she needs to toss around in her head, to weigh and consider, but it's already almost six-thirty. Pushing the clothes hangers aside quickly one by one, she finally settles on a pair of dark blue slacks and a cream-colored blouse. Most men are greatly influenced by what a woman wears, according to the Minneapolis psychologist. Myra isn't sure if this is true of Vinnie, but she cannot take any chances. If she wore jeans, he might think she didn't care, and a dress would send the wrong message altogether.

Rushing downstairs, she nearly trips over Haskell, who is bending over the carpet, examining the stain. "Try rubbing a little vinegar on that," she says, reaching into the closet for her coat.

He gets to his feet. "You're looking very nice tonight." He steps into the closet with her and draws her into an embrace. "Will you be home late?"

"The usual time, I suppose." She wishes she didn't feel as if she were doing something immoral, sneaking out to see Vinnie like this. Haskell looks so trusting. She kisses him lightly to avoid smearing her lipstick and asks what the children are doing.

"They're in the kitchen, making brownies from a box mix they found in the pantry."

"Brownies? I just cleaned up in there!"

"I saw nothing wrong with offering this as a reward for finishing their homework. But if you wish, I can settle them in front of the television until bedtime—"

"No, don't do that. Let them make brownies." She puts on her coat and searches the pockets for her keys. "Don't let them go to bed too late. And tell them no more than two brownies apiece."

"Right." He returns his attention to the stain, considering it as if it were a problem in logic.

"Vinegar," she says and hurries out the door.

❦❦❦

Vinnie's friend's apartment is located near Wrigley Field, and on her way down there, she finds herself driving past the neighborhood where they lived after they got married. Impulsively—or maybe from a habit still imprinted in her sub-conscious—she veers off Ridge Avenue and onto Devon. The neighborhood doesn't seem to have changed very much. The coin-op laundry where they used to spend their Saturday mornings is still here; so is the hot dog stand next door and the Mobil station across the street. There's the Catholic school playground with the chain link fence around it and, on the corner, the little drugstore that always had a display of trusses in the window.

Everything looks the same as she remembers. She turns onto Oakley Avenue and, yes, there is the building, halfway up the block. Cruising to a stop at the curb and looking up toward the second floor windows, she half expects to see their old orange tweed curtains and the chain lamp dangling from a hook on the ceiling. But the blue glow from a stranger's television is all that's visible.

When she and Vinnie lived here, they kept their television in the bedroom, which was the nicest room in the apartment. It faced east, and mornings, waking to sunlight poking through cracks in the window shade, she'd stretch her left hand in the air and admire the shine of the gold ring on her finger. Months after the wedding it was still hard for her to believe they had really begun their new life together. Though he had sworn before a judge and a roomful of witnesses to honor and love her forever, she was always a little amazed to wake up and find him lying beside her.

His face in sleep was all innocence—the wariness would not return until a moment or two after he awoke—and she liked to study it feature by feature. Then, because he startled easily, she'd plant a delicate kiss on the white scar beneath his eye and wait with a quickening pulse for his first surly embrace. Sometimes, stirring into wakefulness, he rubbed his eye like a little boy and gave her a crooked smile, and at those moments she would know in her heart she'd done the right thing by becoming his wife.

For a few minutes, she indulges herself in nostalgia. The car radio is tuned to an oldies station, and the song they are playing is one Myra remembers from those early married days: a syrupy tale of young lovers parted by some unnamed tragedy. She waits for the song to end, lets out a ragged sigh, and pulls away from the curb. At the end of the block she stops to let a pregnant woman in a sari cross the street. Turning onto Devon Avenue again, she notices that the little grocery where she used to shop for meat is gone. Now it's a video store, and across the way, where the kosher bakery once stood, a neon sign flashes GYROS-GYROS-GYROS.

∽∽∽

Though she gets to Vinnie's friend's place with no problem, she has to drive around the block four times before she finds a parking space close enough to the building. Lucky for her, because the neighborhood isn't the best. She checks her hair in the rearview mirror and wipes a flake of mascara from her eyelid. How to get what she wants? She's not even sure she knows what she wants, except maybe to go back in time and find out where it went wrong between them. She gets out of the car, locks the door, and walks across the street.

Vinnie's friend lives in one of those flimsy four-plus-one apartment buildings put up cheaply in the sixties. She rings the bell marked "Santino" and waits to be buzzed in. She hopes Steve Santino won't be home. He is a friend of Vinnie's from his Navy days, and she's met him several times. She has also met most of his ex-wives and a number of girlfriends.

Vinnie answers the door in his bare feet. His hair is damp from the shower and his skin has a scrubbed look. "Hey," he says with an edgy half-smile. He doesn't try to kiss her. Taking her coat as politely as a maître de, he invites her inside and asks if she wants a beer.

"Beer would be fine." She sits down on the sofa, a boxy-looking piece of furniture that was popular when she was a child. The wooden coffee table on which he places a can of Schlitz and a bowl of pretzels is missing one of its corners.

"Oops, forgot the glass." He darts back into the kitchen.

"It's okay. I don't need a glass."

"No trouble. Got a clean one someplace."

From where she sits, she can see practically the whole apartment. Miniature kitchen, alcove with a card table and three chairs, slice of the bedroom. A Bears poster is tacked on the living room wall next to the bedroom door.

Steve Santino doesn't seem to be around. "He went out with some girl he met at the hardware store," Vinnie explains, pulling up a chair. "That guy's always got some babe on the line."

"Think he'll ever get married again?"

Vinnie shrugs. "He seems pretty happy with the single life."

"Still works at the 7-Eleven?"

"Yep, manager now. Three stores."

"Really?"

"Yeah."

The conversation sputters to a stop. Vinnie runs a finger around the top of his beer can. Myra picks salt off a pretzel. "I drove by the old neighborhood," she says, "on the way over."

He nods. "Oh."

"It's still there. I mean, the laundry and the gas station and the Catholic school. But the bakery is gone."

"Yeah. Things change, I guess." He drops his head and contemplates his beer.

She studies the poster on the wall, a portrait of Walter Payton running the ball through the end zone. "Is that what happened with us?" she says finally. "Did something change?"

He frowns and looks away. "No, that ain't it. I got into a situation, is all. It happened."

"What? What happened?"

"I already told you. I met this lady. I got involved. I never meant to hurt you."

"And how was walking out on me without a word of explanation supposed not to hurt me?"

He shifts in his chair. "I'm sorry. Okay?"

"Sorry is just not enough, Vinnie. I think I deserve much more than that. I want you to tell me what it was in our marriage that you missed so badly you had to go and find it somewhere else."

Silence again. He finishes his beer, crumples the can and pitches it into the wastebasket.

She folds her hands in her lap. This time, she is not giving in. She's willing to wait all night if she has to.

From somewhere in the building, through the paper-thin walls, comes the sound of a baby crying. Farther off, a telephone rings. Vinnie bends forward, elbows on knees. "Look, My-ra," he says slowly, "I'm not real good at analyzing things. See, I don't have no college degree. I'm not smart. Like I told you, I did it, I was wrong. I'm sorry. What else do you want?"

"I want to know your true feelings. For once in your life, be honest with me."

He pulls in his chin, like a boxer anticipating an upper cut. "What're you saying, I'm a liar?"

"No—"

"I got no feelings?"

"That is not what I meant at all!" Fuming, she gets up and moves over to the window. Why can't she ever have a simple discussion with him, back and forth like normal people? Why does everything have to be Golden Gloves?

In the apartment across the alley, a young girl is swaying, presumably to music, and brushing her long red hair. A huge car with a bad muffler rumbles up the street. Myra snaps the blinds shut. With exquisite patience, she turns from the window and comes back to the sofa, sits down, picks up her glass and takes a measured sip. "You know," she says," drawing circles with her finger in the condensation on the outside of the glass, "I used to think I knew everything about you. But now, I can't honestly say that I know you at all. Do you realize that we have never had a single, deep, meaningful discussion? Ever?"

He glares at her, his features crimped in belligerence. "So?"

"What do you mean, 'so'? Doesn't that sound like a major problem to you?"

"Why should it? Some people like to talk. Talk all the time. Me, I'm an action kind of a guy. Go. Do." He gestures with a couple of punches. "But if you're so hot for this 'meaningful conversation' stuff, why don't you hit on that writer guy you got in the basement. I bet he could talk up a storm for you."

"We are getting off the subject. Forget Haskell."

"Supposing I don't want to. Tell me again how you met him?"

He's trying to start something, but she is not going to give him the satisfaction. She takes another sip of her beer and cradles the glass in her hands. "I've often wondered ," she says, aiming for a neutral tone of voice, "why is it you never talk much about your family? I've always been kind of curious about what was it like for you growing up in your house. I mean, how do you feel about your mother—"

"What's my mother got to do with anything?"

"Well, I read somewhere that the relationship a man has with his mother is fundamental. It almost always influences his relationships with the other women in his life—"

"Whoa! Wait a minute! What're you driving at? This sounds like shrink-talk to me."

"Oh, heaven forbid we should avail ourselves of professional help! It must be a point of honor that no member of the Calderelli family has ever gone for that."

"Damn straight."

Now it is her turn to glare. "You're not interested in finding out what went wrong with our marriage, are you?"

"You're making too much outta this."

"I am?" She clunks her glass down on the coffee table. "Maybe what you need is more time to think about it. Camp out in this dump a little longer with your three-time loser friend, eat Hungry Man frozen dinners every night. See if I care!"

"My-ra, c'mon—"

Leaving him fumbling in mid-sentence, she grabs her coat and flies out the door.

So he has done it to her again, bullied her until she nearly ended up in tears. Oh, he is a closed-off, mean little man and he will never, never change. And to think she threw aside someone like Byron Levine for him. She could have been the wife of a doctor of psychology with a big house and a fancy lifestyle.

Imagine that!

She hurries outside, gets into the car and slams the door, cranks the engine and shifts into reverse. The car behind is awfully close to her bumper. She shifts into drive and turns the wheel, inches forward, then shifts into reverse again.

*Rats...*

There is a tap on her window, and she sees Vinnie standing there in his shirtsleeves, motioning for her to open the door. "C'mon, My-ra. It's freezing out here."

Reluctantly, she hoists her legs over the gearbox. He gets in and eases himself behind the wheel. "Nice car," he says.

She stares through the windshield. Once he has freed the Escort, she will thank him politely and drive home alone. Later, in Haskell's room, she just might pour out the whole sad story, tell him everything, beginning with the night Vinnie nearly ran her down on the way out of that stupid philosophy class, the one she would never have gotten into in the first place if fate had not been gunning for her that day.

With a few twirls of the wheel, he glides the car into the street, drives to the end of the block and makes a right turn. They are heading west on Addison, away from the apartment. Myra fastens her seat belt. "Where are you taking me?" she demands.

"You wanna talk, right? So, let's talk."

"Fine."

"Good."

The radio is still tuned to the oldies station, and now Dion or Frankie or one of those other wavy-haired young men (they must certainly have grandchildren by now) is still searching for his dream lover. Myra has to stop herself from humming along out of habit. Vinnie lowers the volume. He doesn't say anything for a while—words have always been hard for him—but she can tell by the set of his jaw he is trying to collect his thoughts.

Soon, the apartment houses along Addison give way to blocks of factory buildings. A man wearing a camouflage jacket waits at a bus stop. A young couple walking hand in hand turn to go into a tavern. A police car cruises by.

Vinnie says, "One time… I guess I was maybe sixteen, seventeen…my cousin Marco and me went riding in his old man's car. A Buick Electra 225. Guys used to call it a deuce-and-a-quarter, and it was a beautiful machine—you know?—beautiful, like a woman. We cruised all around Rush Street and up North State near the Playboy Mansion, with the top down on this hot summer night…the radio playing something fast and loud…a couple of studs in this choice set of wheels… chicks drooling over us like we was something special…"

He smiles at the memory. "I never knew life could be that good. I thought to myself, yeah, this'll be coming to me. I'll grow up and I'll have it all—" He stops, and then he lets out a weary grunt. "I never figured I'd end up selling fruits and vegetables all day long. You know what I'm saying?"

Myra looks at her hands. "I know what you're saying."

"Like, when I was a kid. I used to live on the edge. Running with my friends, swiping turtles out of Woolworth's, getting into my old man's Canadian Club. That kind of a life kept you on your toes."

"That kind of a life can get you into prison."

"But what I mean is, there was all this excitement. You could feel the blood in your veins, and there was always something gonna happen. Every day was like a whole new adventure, and it never stopped. You hit the street running and you didn't quit until your ma found you and dragged you back home."

"Yes, well, this may all be true. But what has it got to do with us?"

He shakes his head. "I don't know. Maybe nothing." He slumps morosely behind the wheel, which he is steering with one wrist. They are passing rows of squatty bungalows lined up one after the other, and soon the houses begin to get larger, the neighborhoods busier, long rows of shopping centers glowing neon against the night sky.

She says, "I hate it when you drive like that."

He doesn't say anything, but he does put his other hand on the wheel. They have turned onto Milwaukee Avenue now, and soon the glitzy strip of River Road with its bars and restaurants and motels looms ahead. Vinnie says, "We could stop for a drink, if you want."

With the flip of a wrist, she gestures an okay. She doesn't want a drink, but she's getting tired of riding around. Vinnie hangs a left before the next intersection and swings into the parking lot of the Patti-O Motel.

Myra's eyes open with surprise. "If you think I am going in there with you," she says, folding her arms across her chest, "you are truly nuts."

"Don't get excited. I ain't gonna pull nothing. They got a bar off the lobby." He slips the key from the ignition and looks at her crookedly, as if she had grown another eye.

The bar is actually a cocktail lounge called The Snuggery, a cramped little place full of smoke and disco music, although no one is dancing. Couples sit at rickety tables, leaning in close to one another. Myra can't help but wonder how many of them are married, and how many are married to each other.

She takes off her gloves and lays them on the table. Vinnie brings her a glass of white wine and sets down a beer for himself. "So where were we?" he says, rubbing his arms for warmth.

"You were telling me about your career as a juvenile delinquent. But what I think you've been trying to say is that your life has not turned out the way you expected."

"Yeah, you're probably right."

"Might what?"

"No, no." He repeats what he said. To be heard over the music, he has to practically shout in her ear.

"Oh," she says. "But then, I don't know anyone whose dreams all came true."

"So what're you saying? You been disappointed too?"

She shakes her head. "Not that, exactly."

"What then?"

She twirls the stem of her glass, thinking. When she was growing up, little girls saw their futures in their husbands. (How did that rhyme go? ...doctor, lawyer, Indian chief...) Unlike her friend Heidi Pincus, who had set her sights on moving to New York and tap dancing on the Ed Sullivan show, Myra never had any gleaming ambitions of her own. At least, none she can remember.

"I guess I was happy to settle for the ordinary things," she says. "Home, family, an interesting job. I just never thought it would be so much work."

"What?"

"*Work.*"

"Who's a jerk?"

She waves a hand, cancelling his question. "Can't we find someplace quieter?"

They take their drinks out to the lobby, where there are a few empty chairs scattered along the walls. She sits down in one, and he pulls up another close by. Then the desk clerk rushes over and says, "No loitering, folks. Sorry."

"Oh," she says, getting up quickly. "Let's just go back to the apartment."

"Can't. Santino's bringing the bimbo back there at nine. I'm supposed to get lost for a couple hours."

"You folks want a room?"

"We were looking for a quiet place to talk," Myra says primly. "We've been discussing our marriage." She holds up her left hand, but in that harsh light her wedding ring looks trashy, like something she might have picked out of a bargain basket at Walgreen's.

"Number twenty-two." The desk clerk yawns and hands Vinnie the key. "Turn off the lights when you're done."

They make their way down a musty corridor lined with a worn carpet patterned geometrically in brown and green. Vinnie opens the door. Room twenty-two is long and narrow—mostly bed, it seems—with a picture window facing the parking lot and a deflated-looking armchair wedged into one corner. Myra takes the chair, leaving him to perch on the edge of the bed.

It has been a long time since they were alone together in a motel room; in fact, not since before Jennifer was born. On their way home from a trip to the Wisconsin Dells one August night, they'd gotten caught in a sudden storm outside Whitefish Bay and had to take refuge at the Crystal-something Lodge, a rambling wooden structure with a warped front porch sinking into a muddy front lawn. Just running in from the car had soaked them to the skin. In the midst of peeling off their clothes, Vinnie grabbed her by the shoulders from behind and whispered menacingly into her ear, "You know what 'motel' spells backwards?"

Before she could figure out the answer, they were melting into each other, fusing together like strips of hot taffy. They thrashed around on the lumpy double bed while the storm crashed away outside: thunder and lightning and pounding rain. Vinnie was a wild man and Myra was conquered territory, powerless in the face of all that passion. If he had wanted her to, she would have hung by her heels from the chandelier. But there was no chandelier, only two bedside lamps with pink metal bunnies for bases.

In the morning, drawing the curtains aside, she saw the damage. Tree branches littered the street, a piece of the motel roof had blown away, and their bed looked as if the storm had cut a path right through the room.

"Okay," Vinnie says, tossing the room key on the dresser, "where were we?"

Myra removes her coat. (This room seems to be terribly overheated.) "Suppose you tell me about this ex-lover of yours," she says. "Was she pretty?"

He shrugs. "She was okay."

"Well then, what did you see in her?"

He gives a short, unhappy laugh. "It's stupid."

"Tell me anyway."

"Okay, you wanna know? Okay. She had this tattoo, a little purple rose, on her chest. I saw it down her blouse whenever she bent over. So I thought to myself, any broad who'd get herself tattooed might be worth getting to know."

"That was the big attraction?"

He grunts. "I told you it was stupid." He gets up and begins to pace the floor between the dresser and the bed. "Look, My-ra, forget her. It didn't mean nothing. It's finished."

"Vinnie…"

"You were the best goddamn thing that ever happened to me. Honest. That night I first seen you sitting there in that history class—"

"Philosophy. But Vinnie…"

"Whatever. That night, I said to myself, here's a girl that knows things. The right clothes to wear, what to order in a nice restaurant, what to read besides Road and Track. You had class written all over you. And remember? You wouldn't even look at me. You must of thought I was some kind of insect."

"…where was the tattoo?"

"Huh?"

"The tattoo." She unbuttons the top two buttons on her blouse. (Really, this room is stifling!) "Show me where it was."

He points to a place between his left shoulder and breastbone. "Here."

"No," she says. "On me."

He comes closer and leans over her chair. "Right here." He presses his fingers to her upper chest.

Something is happening—she's on fire! She grabs his hand with both of hers and moves it several inches lower. "What was she like in bed?" she demands, her voice sinking to a husky whisper. "Tell me. Tell me all the things she wanted you to do to her."

He squats down next to her, draws an arm across her shoulders, and undoes the remaining buttons on her blouse. "Know what I think?" he says, scooping a breast from her bra as if it were a piece of fruit, "I think you wanna make love." He rolls the nipple between his fingers and then digs deep into her ear with his tongue.

Love?

No, she definitely does not want love. Love was for good girls, wives and mothers, former nuns.

What Myra wants is sex—plain and simple, hot and juicy, lowdown and dirty. And she wants it right this minute.

Oh, does she ever! Throat parched with longing, she murmurs his name.

"Unnnh?" He is still nuzzling her ear, intent it seems on wetting the whole side of her head.

She pushes him away. "Get my bags."

"What? Why?"

She bolts for the door, leaving him kneeling beside her empty chair. "Trunk of the car." She holds the door open. "Bring them both."

The wary look spreads itself over his face, but he stands, pulls the car keys from his pants pocket and goes out. She tears off her blouse and slacks and rushes to the window, plastering herself against it like a lewd decal. She watches as he sorts through the keys, opens the trunk, pulls out her canvas airline bags, sets them down...

He is taking hours— *hours!* She presses her lips against the cold glass and mimes the word: *Hurry.*

He rushes back inside, banging the bags against the doorframe. "You crazy or something? Anyone could of seen you." He whisks the curtains shut and stands there with his fists on his hips. "S' matter with you tonight?"

Even if she could explain, she would not have the time. Opening one of the bags, she begins to pull out lingerie, and lost in the flurry of colorful silken wisps, she feels herself being swept away by lust.

And where, exactly, is her rock-solid core of self-control?

It seems to have vanished. Poof. It's just plain gone.

At the bottom of the bag she locates the blue denim G-string cowboy pouch with the little red zipper on the front. (What is it the brochure says? Something about riding all night.) She dangles it in front of his nose. "I'll bet you'd look like some dangerous dude in this thing," she purrs.

"My-ra, we never use this stuff. If we're gonna do it, why don't we just do it?" He slides his fingers up her thigh and grabs a handful of flesh.

"Humor me," she says, pressing her simmering pelvis into his. She tucks the G-string into his belt and gives him a long, soulful kiss. Then, retracting her tongue, she pushes him into the bathroom and closes the door.

Now she has to work fast. She strips off her underwear and sprinkles on body glitter and Captive Eight perfume. She decides against the lavender peignoir (too sweet) and the French maid costume (too theatrical) and wriggles into the fishnet bodysuit. A fast check in the mirror confirms what she already suspects: in the space of mere minutes, she has transformed herself from an ordinary woman into a shimmering goddess of desire.

Too bad she didn't wear her high heels.

From the second canvas bag she extracts a jar of massage cream and a bottle of scented oil, the rabbit fur glove, an assortment of condoms—edible and otherwise—and a tall black candle in the shape of an erect penis. She places the candle on the nightstand, strikes a match, and turns off the lights.

All that's missing is the music. Lunging across the bed, she flips on the nightstand radio and dials around quickly.

...*ooh, bay-bee, bay-bee, I wan-na-wan-na-wan-na*...

The beat is coarse and thrusting (perfect!), and she turns it up loud. She drapes herself across the pillows, only to spring up one more time, dig through the canvas bag again and bring out the handcuffs: regulation metal, cold and heavy in her hands. She tucks them under her pillow just as the bathroom door opens.

With a hammering heart she watches as he ambles toward the bed, a little wary, a little shy; the flickering candlelight licks deliciously at the muscles of his chest.

"Hey," he says, running his eyes over her inch by inch. He looks absolutely adorable in the G-string. Myra is going to yank that zipper open with her teeth.

In her ears, the radio music is thundering; she can feel the flesh of her inner thighs quivering, as if they were being stabbed by tiny bolts of lightning. And in the midst of it all comes a voice—faint but persistent—laying out for her the difference between good girls and other girls.

In her whole, entire life Myra has never worn a see-through blouse, tight sweater or micro-miniskirt; never excessively glossed her lips, teased her hair or cracked gum; and always she walks with a straight spine, sits with her ankles crossed.

But that girl doesn't seem to be here anymore.

That girl is gone.

And now—pushing her mother's voice away, pulsing insanely with desire—she opens her wanton knees in a wide, wide welcome.

Bad, bad, bad as she can be. ✍

## NINETEEN

Back when she was in the seventh grade, Myra received an invitation to her first boy-and-girl affair, a Halloween party given by the Schroeder twins, Cookie and Candy. She came dressed as a lady pirate in a white blouse with big sleeves, a pair of tall black boots and a flowing cape cut from an old bedspread. Safe behind a black mask, she marched right up to Ian Becker, a boy in whose presence—under ordinary circumstances—she would not have been able to utter a coherent sentence, and asked him to dance.

He kept trying to guess who she was. "Valerie Robinson?" he said, elbows flapping in the funky chicken. "Barbara Stern?"

Smiling coyly, Myra refused to reveal herself, though she did allow Ian to coax her into a corner of the Schroeder's pine-paneled basement and kiss her with his lips parted. Later, when the party was over and she'd removed the mask, he seemed surprised—and relieved. "Oh, Myra," he said. "it's only you." Then, smiling the goofy smile she found so endearing, he threw an arm across her shoulders and walked her home.

That party is what's on her mind this quiet Sunday afternoon with Loretta at Billy Halligan's. They are watching a man who is watching a Bull's game up at the bar. "He bears an awfully close resemblance to a boy I knew in school," Myra says, craning her neck to get a better look. After all these years she can still recall the warm hollow at the back of Ian's neck where she pressed her fingers, the softness of his lips, the little spasms of excitement that ran clear down to her knees.

"Don't even mention men to me," Loretta says. "You wouldn't believe what I been through this week."

Myra, busy with her own thoughts, lets the grammatical error pass. She's had quite a week herself: three nights with Vinnie at the Patti-O Motel, two Let's Be Lovers parties. But she kills the bawdy smirk forming on her lips, drags an expression of what she hopes is sympathy across her face and says softly, "Would you like to tell me about it?"

Loretta stabs a piece of lime with her swizzle stick. Lately, in an attempt at leading a healthier life, she has been drinking tequila with fruit juice. "You don't wanna know the details. All I can say is, this guy seemed normal when he asked me out. Who knew he had a wife, and a talent for boosting fur coats?"

Myra jiggles the ice in her wine spritzer. "Maybe you should be a little more careful about the people you associate with."

"Hey, I'm learning. Okay? Maybe someday I'll luck out and hook up with a decent, upstanding guy like Haskell. When are you gonna unload my good-for-nothing brother and marry him?"

Myra offers a forbearing smile and glances once again at the man at the bar. "Do you suppose I should go up and ask his name?"

"Who? Oh, him. Sure, why not?"

"He probably wouldn't remember me."

"I bet he would. I bet you don't look all that different. Still wearing your hair the same way you did in high school, right?"

She tucks a lock behind one ear. "Maybe I should get it cut."

"Why bother? It'll come back in style some day."

"And I was thinking about getting a makeup make-over, too."

"Hey, what brought this on? You're not having one of those midlife whatchamacallits, are you?"

"Crises? Don't be silly. I'm too young for that." She has a good mind to let Loretta in on what she's been up to. That would open up her eyes and shut her mouth. There is another Myra hidden inside the one everyone thinks they know, and she's itching to be let loose.

Loretta pokes her in the ribs. "Now's your chance, if you're gonna do it." She angles her head toward the man at the bar, who is turning to leave.

Myra grabs her drink before it spills and blurts out, "Ian?" She stands and says, "Ian Becker? Is that you?"

The way he looks at her tells her immediately she has made a huge mistake.

"Well now, Darlin'," he says, appraising her with eyes that are as hard and glittery as a snake's, "I could be anybody you want me to be."

Face burning, Myra backs into her chair and stammers out an apology. "S-sorry. I just thought you were somebody I used to know."

ক⋅ক⋅ক

It's February, and the days are getting noticeably longer, but there still are not enough hours in them to suit her. Afternoons drop without warning into evening, leaving her to rush around like a dervish so she can get herself out the door on time. Those nights when she's not acting the part of the consummate saleswoman and consultant on the arts of love and seduction, she is playing the queen of lewd for Vinnie at the Patti-O. Mornings, she turns back into Howie and Jennifer's mother, a drowsy lady standing at the stove in bathrobe and slippers.

Now it's the quiet part of the afternoon, just before they get home from school, and she is sitting on the couch, attempting to hold an alert expression on her face while Haskell paces from one end of the living room to the other. He is explaining what he calls the narrative strategy for the third act of his play, and she is trying with all her might to appear interested.

But really, she does not have time for this. She has to start supper in a while, her party tonight is on the far edge of Des Plaines, and there's a load of clothes she washed two days ago waiting in the dryer to be folded and put away.

"What I had hoped to accomplish by this point in the play," he says, tapping the rolled up script against his palm, "is a complete reversal of roles."

She stifles a yawn. "I see."

"I wanted the male character to have acquired some of those softer traits which, early on, were so obviously a part of the female character's personality. And I wanted her to abandon her narcissistic tendencies, to become, little by little, more heroic, more outward-looking, more determined and strong."

"So? What's the problem?"

"The problem is they are refusing do what I want them to do. They will let me take them along so far, but past that point they simply will not budge."

He sits down beside her and unrolls the script. From the condition of the text, she can tell how hard he's labored over it. His typewriter was clacking away when she came in last night, and this morning at breakfast he looked as if he hadn't been to bed. His forehead is etched with grooves of consternation, and shiny puffs of skin have appeared beneath his eyes. Myra touches one gently and says, "You sound like you're getting all worked up about this. Can't you just write down what you want them to say and leave it at that?"

He shakes his head. "It doesn't work that way."

"Why not?"

"Because much as I've tried to prevent it, they are turning into fully fledged characters, with desires of their own." He turns to her, eyes roiling with despair. "I can give them the words, but when they say them, they don't really mean them. Sometimes, in my head, I think I can hear them laughing at me." He presses his fingertips to his eyes. "I knew I should never have given them names."

"Seriously?"

"I believe the mistake I made was in trying to transform Yvonne—that is the woman now—from someone like my ex-wife into someone like you."

"Me?"

He reaches for her hand. "You're probably not aware of this, Myra, but you have been an inspiration to me. You've no idea how much I admire you."

"Me?" she says again.

"The way you are with the children, the way you manage all you have to do, always there when people need you. Truly, I am in awe."

"Oh, please." She tries to push the compliment aside, to retrieve her hand. "I think you're exaggerating the importance of—"

"Of being a wife and mother?"

"Well, yes, but—"

"You know something? Elizabeth would have considered you a throwback. She was a high-powered professional, but let me tell you, there were nights she came home and fell apart, collapsed in tears because a meeting had not gone well or a big account threatened to take its business elsewhere."

"I'm sure she was only—"

"Indulging herself. Yes, she could be incredibly childish. And that seems to be Yvonne's problem, as well. She refuses to come to terms with her situation."

"And speaking of the play," Myra says, consulting her wristwatch, "if you want me to help with a read-through, we had better get on with it. I have to leave the house by at least six fifteen."

His shoulders slump pathetically. "Don't tell me you have another party tonight!" He sounds bereft.

Throwing an arm around him, as if that might help hold him together, she promises to try and get away early. Really, she wishes he weren't growing so dependent on her.

He takes her face in his hands. "I'm sorry. I'm being selfish. I know how much your career means to you." He kisses her and murmurs into her hair, "I had hoped that, later, we might...you know..."

"Um," she says. She has not been down to his room since she started this new thing with Vinnie. That makes her feel guilty, and then she feels stupid for feeling guilty. How have things gotten so ridiculously upside down? "Do you want to do this standing or sitting?" she asks.

He looks momentarily perplexed. "Oh, you mean the reading," he says, the light dawning. "Either way. It's entirely up to you."

"Standing, then." She picks up the script and stepping carefully around the dog, who has fallen asleep next to the coffee table, she walks to the center of the room. "I like it better when I have a little space to move around in."

"It's a shame you never took the opportunity to develop your acting talents, Myra. I think you have the instinct for it."

"Yes," she says, scanning the script, already beginning to slip into the role of Yvonne: self-centered bitch-goddess/woman-child. "And you know, Haskell, if I were an important actress, I would want you to write all my roles."

"That's a nice thing to say."

She smiles at him. Lately, she has not had any time to work on his life. The least she can do is help him shore up his confidence. "I'm sure that once you resolve your problems with the third act and finish the play, it will be a great success."

"I hope you're right. I've been promised a reading at the Playwright's Center later this spring." He seems more hopeful now as he gets up from the couch. He runs his finger down the page she is holding. Taking a deep breath, he begins.

"'What does it matter who we were before me met, or what we did? This moment in which we dwell is all we can ever hope to have.'"

"'Ambrose dear, have I ever told you about my first lover, Raul? He was such a sweet and sensitive soul, he could not read the Emancipation Proclamation without weeping.'"

❧❧❧

Nettie calls at five-thirty to report that she thinks she's getting arthritis. "My fingers look funny. Also, I've got a kink in my side."

"Must be a slow day at the store, Ma."

"No one wants to come out in this crummy weather. So what do you think? Should I see a doctor?"

Myra shoos Lucy off the counter and cracks another egg. She's making Denver omelets with her collection of meat and vegetable scraps. (Tomorrow, she'll have to do some serious grocery shopping.) "If you think you need to see a doctor," she says into the mouthpiece of the telephone receiver wedged between her jaw and her shoulder, "then go ahead and make an appointment."

"Ah, what do they know. Charge you a fortune for a bunch of tests, and then they tell you it's nothing but old age."

"Then don't see a doctor."

"Myra! Don't you care?"

"Wait a second." She untangles the telephone cord and crosses to the kitchen table, where Jennifer is signaling for help with her homework.

"Fractions are stupid. Why do we have to learn them?"

Myra does the math in her head. "You forgot to carry the two."

"Was this a bad time to call?"

"I'm a little rushed. I have to leave the house in less than an hour."

"You're always rushing, Myra. I don't know what's gotten into you lately."

Vinnie, she almost says, swallowing a snicker. A few days ago, she brought body paints and camel hair brushes to their rendezvous, and they took turns covering each other with obscene graffiti. "I don't know what you mean, Ma."

"You're not yourself. Remember my cousin Ida from Orlando? You sound the way she did before she tried to poison her husband's pet alligator."

"Why do I have the feeling this is going to be another long story?"

"See? That's what I mean. Edgy she was, like you. Maybe you've got PMS. Maybe you're the one should see a doctor."

Lucy has jumped back onto the counter and is making her way toward the frying pan. "I've got to go," Myra says, lunging for the cat.

"Ah, here's a customer! Talk to you later."

∽∽∽

After thinking it over for several days, consulting a number of magazines and polling a few family members, she decides to have her hair professionally cut, and makes an appointment at Sylvia's Salon de Femme. The beauty parlor is on a side street off Devon Avenue, next to an antiques shop in whose window is a sign that reads: *If you think this stuff is junk, come in and price it.*

While Myra stares at herself in the mirror above a white Formica counter, Sylvia taps a comb against her lip. "Somethin' different, huh? You have a special style in mind?"

"Maybe one of these." She shows her the pictures she's clipped from an issue of Cosmopolitan magazine that Cara left at her house: pouty-mouthed young females modeling hairstyles labeled variously *chic, sleek, sassy, sophisticated* and *seductive*. "I figured it was time I made a few changes."

"Want to do anything about the color, long as you're at it?"

"What's wrong with the color?'

"Mousey." Sylvia grabs a handful of hair. "And you're gettin' a bunch of gray."

"Where?"

She parts the hair and shows her.

"Oh," Myra says. "Oh, boy."

She closes her eyes as Sylvia tilts back the chair and turns on the water. The shop smells sweetly of hair spray and shampoo, with a musty undertone of permanent wave solution. From somewhere in the back, behind a heavy dark curtain, a radio plays Cherry Pink and Apple Blossom White, a Latin-type tune Myra remembers dancing to with her father when she was a little girl.

Sylvia hums as she works suds into her scalp. Myra taps her fingers and grins, thinking of Vinnie last night, flying at her in a purple mask and leather vest. She wore a feather sarong, leading the chase…

"Want to let me in on the joke?" Sylvia says.

"No joke." She pulls her mouth into a straight line. "I was just remembering something."

Sylvia shuts off the water and wraps a pink towel around Myra's head. "Wouldn't be somethin' to do with a man, would it?"

"What makes you think that?"

"Oh, Sugar, I been dealin' with the public long enough. I know a satisfied smile when I see one." She chuckles deep in her throat. "And look at that nice color in your cheeks. I may be wrong, but I think you got a lover-boy tucked away somewhere."

Myra puts a finger to her lips.

Sylvia raises her thinly plucked eyebrows, and then gives a wink of complicity. Her daughter, Verletta, is working on a customer in the next chair, an older lady with a bluish cast to her white hair. Verletta is saying, "Yeah, I know whatcha mean. Gotta get an education if you wanna get somewheres today. World don't need more ditch diggers." She is a thin, pale girl somewhat younger than Myra. Her hair is stringy and bleached out, and her long fingernails are painted a metallic green.

According to Nettie, who has been a customer of the salon for years, both mother and daughter live in the rooms behind the shop with an elderly white dog named Major.

Myra watches in the mirror as Sylvia drags a comb through her wet hair. "That auburn rinse'll be perfect for you. It's a known fact that the sight of a red-headed woman is pretty much guaranteed to nail the heart of a red-blooded man."

"I'd have thought blonde."

"Well, Hon, all I can tell you is, I've had my hair ever color of the rainbow, and it was red always brought 'em begging to my door." She flips the comb around and uses the rattail handle to divide the hair into sections, fixing each with a large silver clamp. Then she picks up the scissors and takes the first cut.

Myra lets out a small gasp as a long lock of hair falls to the floor. "I'm going to love this, aren't I?"

"'Course you are." Sylvia snips away, creating a storm of hair around Myra's shoulders; Myra feels like an animal about to shed an old skin.

In the next chair, Verletta's customer is talking about driving a bus. "Wouldn't that be an interesting job, I always thought. Meeting all kinds of different people every day. And those snappy gray uniforms they wore. Gray was always my best color. But they didn't hire lady bus drivers when I was a young woman."

"World's a whole different place than it used to be," Verletta says, waving a curling iron around the old woman's head. "Apply for a bus driver's job now and see if they try and stop you. Have the whole damn Supreme Court on the case…"

"If you ask me," Sylvia says, "it's kind of risky."

"Driving a bus?"

She puts down the scissors and leans close. "Having a lover-boy. What if someone was to find out?"

Myra shrugs. "Don't cut the bangs too short."

She watches Verletta's curling iron clamp down on a bluish lock, scans the array of equipment spread over the counters: dangerous looking metal rollers, hair clamps and pins, capes, towels, brushes; even the adjustable swivel chair she's sitting in has possibilities.

Oh, yes. What a grand old time she could have with Vinnie in this place!

"Still," Sylvia continues, "it does heat up the blood some, don't it? Takes you away from your ordinary everday self."

"I suppose," Myra says soberly. She is afraid now of breaking down in a snickering fit.

"How old is he?" Sylvia asks.

"Who?"

She clucks impatiently. "You know."

"Forty on his last birthday."

"Married?"

"Definitely."

"Kids?"

She holds up two fingers. Sylvia says, "My, my." She picks up the scissors again and resumes cutting, faster now as Myra's new haircut starts to take shape. "Pardon me for saying this, Sugar, but I never would've figured you for the—" she leans in close again and whispers— "*other woman.*"

Myra bites her lip, fighting down a giggle.

"My second husband, Durwood? I divorced him on account of he couldn't stay away from other women. Verletta wasn't but a little girl at the time."

Myra murmurs sympathetically.

"Strangest thing was, they'd be the dowdiest women I ever laid eyes on. Here I'd be, dressed to perfection with a fresh hairset ever day, and he'd be chasin' after someone named Dorothy or Leona, women who went out in public in their aprons and slippers."

"Men," Myra says without elaborating.

She happens to know that Sylvia herself is no angel. She's been married three or four times and is not above taking a lover here and there. This is the gospel according to Nettie, who has over the years come to know Sylvia's entire life story. Her last husband moved them to Chicago and then abandoned them in the middle of the worst winter in fifty years. It was Nettie's opinion that Sylvia had made a bunch of bad choices in her life and somehow deserved whatever happened to her. She reserved all her sympathy for Verletta, who—as far as anyone could tell—had no life outside of the beauty shop.

Once, Myra invited them to a Let's Be Lovers party that was being held in the neighborhood. She thought she'd be doing them a favor, but both women seemed a little insulted. "Girl, the Good Lord gimme all the equipment I need to have a good time in bed," Sylvia said. And then Verletta got on her soapbox and informed her that she just despised how women thought they had to put on those silly little nothings just to keep a man interested. "Gloria Steinman would die before she'd wear any of that stuff," she declared. The only thing that kept Myra from feeling like a total fool was the fact that she thought she understood the girl and her fear of men, considering all her mother's bad luck.

Now Verletta's customer gets up and checks her hair in the mirror. "Very nice, dear," she says. She pays and waves a cheery good-bye, and the bell over the door jingles with her leaving.

Verletta plunks herself down in the empty chair and lights a cigarette, exhaling two long streams of smoke through her nostrils. "That Mrs. Miller is a sweet old lady, but I just despise how her hairset needs so many little bitty curls."

"Won't she take a perm?"

"Uh-uh. Hair's too fine." She drags on the cigarette, watching Myra in the mirror. "That style is real becoming to you," she says. "Makes you look like a whole 'nother person."

Myra smiles. She thinks so, too.

Someone on the radio announces the time. *Seventeen minutes past one on Chicago's station for musical memories, WJJD.*

"Baby Face," Sylvia says to her daughter, "whyn't you take the Major out for a quick walk before your one-thirty comes in."

Verletta examines her nails. "In a minute."

Sylvia unwinds the cord from the blow dryer and plugs it in. "How 'bout right now? That dog's not gettin' any younger."

Verletta mutters something and pushes out of the chair, disappearing behind the dark curtain. In a few moments, she comes out trailing a leather leash, on the other end of which is the strangest looking animal Myra has ever seen. He's got a bulldog's mean underbite, four long, skinny legs, and the most magnificent set of testicles: two rosy globes suspended delicately between his powerful thighs. The dog lumbers forward to bury his nose in Sylvia's crotch. She bends to rub his chest. "Precious boy," she murmurs, "Mama's precious lil ol' boy."

And all at once an image invades Myra's brain: the beauty shop after hours—curtains drawn tight over the windows, frenzied shadows moving behind them, dancing an obscene cha-cha to the wail of the radio…

She presses her lips together.

…the women naked under plastic capes, the dog leaping at them, jowls shaking and dripping in anticipation…

Squeezing her eyes shut, she digs her nails into her palms, and the image departs.

"Hon?" Sylvia asks. "Are you feelin' okay?"

"Oh, sure," Myra says, trying very hard not to wonder how they would do it with a dog.

Verletta leads Major through the door, and the bell jingles again. Sylvia turns on the blow dryer, aiming hot air at the back of Myra's head. She works quickly with a brush, the flesh of her upper arms quivering. "Just between you and me," she says, "I'm at my wits end with that girl. You'd think she'd have the sense to take on some responsibility for that poor dog without being asked a hundred times. And ol' Major, he just worships her."

"That's how it is sometimes," Myra says. In spite of herself, she's thinking: *older dogs, younger women...* She clears her throat to dissolve the bubble of laughter waiting there to explode.

"Lays his head at her feet while we're watchin' the television, don't even care if she kicks him—"

*Must be into S & M...*

"—he just licks her on the ankle."

*...with a foot fetish?*

Silently, she scolds herself. Trying to halt the slide her mind has gone into, she crosses her arms underneath the cape and grips her ribcage.

There, now. Better.

Sylvia turns off the blow dryer. "You sure nothing's wrong, Hon? Maybe got somethin' there in your eye?"

Myra shakes her head.

If she opens her mouth, she is finished.

Coming over the radio now is the voice of Patsy Cline, her velvety contralto riding on the glossy hum of a slide guitar. Sylvia cries, "Ooh! This here song is my absolute favorite one ever! Don't those words just tear at your heart?" She turns on the blow dryer again and begins to sing along, and her voice trills over the dryer's whine.

"I...fall...to pee-siz...each time I see you a-gin..."

She is wielding the brush around Myra's head as if it were an instrument of chastisement, and Myra—still fighting desperately for control—keeps her eyes glued to the mirror, watching their reflections as they slowly dissolve into two watery blurs. ✥

## *TWENTY*

Lately, she's been finding, she no longer requires much sleep: lucky for her considering that she cannot seem to stay in bed past five a.m. Her dreams now are filled with circuses—clowns, ringmasters, roaring lions, prancing horses—and she is the acrobat dangling from a trapeze or toeing the high wire in the spotlight under the big top.

Tonight, from the audience, comes a string of shouted insults laced with frightening profanities, and they seem to be directed at her. Looking down at her fancy spangled costume, she is shocked to discover that for all it conceals she might as well be wearing Saran wrap. In an attempt to cover herself with her hands (a pathetically futile effort), she loses her balance and falls through the air for a long, long time before being rescued by a pair of outstretched arms.

Strangely enough, the arms belong to little Howie. "Mom...?" he says, setting her down on the sawdust covered floor. "How come I can't whistle when I drink water?"

Startled awake in the darkness, Myra doesn't even attempt to get back to sleep. Sleep is for wimps, and she has much too much to do. After a quick scrub at her teeth, a splash of cold water on her face, and a few rigorous fluffs of her hair, she steps into a pair of sweat pants and gets to work. By the time the children come down for breakfast, the kitchen floor has been swept and scrubbed, Brownie has been fed and walked, a load of laundry has been washed, dried and folded, and two steaming bowls of cereal sit on the table.

Myra brings over a plate of orange slices arranged in a pinwheel design and says to Howie, "Do you have any idea what happens to a wad of bubble gum after it spins around for an hour in a hot dryer?"

He holds up his hands. "I forgot."

"It took me ten minutes to scrape that stuff out of your jeans. *Ten minutes* that I could have spent doing something *productive!*"

"Geez, Mom, he didn't murder anyone. What's the big deal?"

Myra sneers. Depend upon Jennifer to become the benevolently concerned big sister at the exact wrong moment. "And *you*, young lady. Any child who has the *nerve* to borrow her mother's very best blouse—without even *asking!*—and then just *leave* it crumpled up on the floor of her closet…"

Jennifer slumps in her chair. "Geez."

"Later, we are going to discuss this further. We're going to get a few things straightened out. Now finish eating or you'll be late for school."

With that off her chest, she turns back to the stove to prepare Haskell's breakfast. She herself will take only coffee and a slice of lightly buttered whole wheat toast. Too much food weighs her down, makes her thinking fuzzy, and she cannot afford that. She has a pretty good idea of the meaning behind the circus dreams. Each day has become a kind of juggling act, like spinning china plates on long sticks: if she doesn't keep her eye on each and every little detail, the whole thing could easily come crashing down.

These days, she is running on her wits, and regular surges of adrenalin.

After the children have left, Haskell comes upstairs. The heaviness of his tread and the weary way he scrapes his chair back from the table tell her he has spent another night wrestling with the muse. She laces his cereal with a heaping tablespoon of protein powder, steeps a bag of Red Zinger tea, and says, "You look exhausted. You should take a vitamin pill."

He runs his hands up his face and through his hair, leaving it standing in spikes. "I don't need vitamins. I need a headline and creative direction for this new burial vault, and I need it before two this afternoon."

"And if you don't come up with anything by then?"

"I'll probably lose the account. They were not overly pleased with my last project."

She sets his breakfast in front of him. "I don't think I've ever seen an advertisement for a burial vault."

"No reason you would. They appear in trade publications that go to funeral directors and people who operate cemeteries. But what I'm working on now is a tri-fold brochure that will be handed to the bereaved family. The appeal is somewhat different."

Myra thinks she may be able to help him. "Burial vault," she mutters, concentrating. "Funeral…death…departure…deterioration…devastation…. Prevent death's devastating deterioration with—what was the name of the product?"

He shakes his head. "You must never say 'death' or 'deceased person.' It is the Dearly Departed going to their Eternal Rest. Doesn't that have a peaceful ring to it?"

She watches to see if he's joking, but he only grimaces and adds, "Protection through Eternity."

"That sounds good."

"But I've used it before. I need something completely new." He rests his forehead in his fingertips, a study in despair.

She brings her coffee to the table. Closing her eyes, she pictures the cemetery, the open grave, the burial vault ready to receive the gleaming wooden casket…

She almost doesn't hear the telephone.

"Hello? Mrs. Calderelli? This is Tammy Wurbach—the room mother for your daughter's class?—and I'm really, really hoping you'll be able to help us out on Friday, we're going to take the sixth-graders on a field trip to the Art Institute and we need some moms and dads to volunteer as chaperons…"

Myra remembers Tammy Wurbach. She was also the fifth grade room mother, a past president of the PTA, and head of every major fundraising event for the David P. Denton public school. "Friday?" she says.

"For just the morning—we're scheduled to be back early in the afternoon."

"Let me check my calendar." She bites into her toast, chews slowly and takes a sip of coffee. "Well," she says, unable to come up with a decent excuse not to, "I suppose I could block out a few hours—"

"Oh, that is terrific! Just terrific! You would not believe the dickens of a time I'm having trying to find parents who don't work nine to five, and we need more than the usual number for this field trip—our major objective being to keep the kids from messing with the paintings and sculptures?—but I don't suppose you'd know another adult who might be able to come along…"

Myra pictures a funeral, Tammy Wurbach lying in her coffin, lips closed, hands folded gracefully over her heart, but her voice on a tape recorder chattering a mile a minute right up to the instant they slam the lid.

"I know someone," she says, looking at Haskell but thinking of Cara, who would have better sixth-grade field trip survival skills. "I'll call her now."

"Bless you, Mrs. Calderelli. I am so, so relieved! Could you be at the school parking lot by nine o'clock? 'Cause that's when we'll be loading up the buses."

She marks the calendar on the wall next to the phone. "Nine o'clock. Okay."

"And you are definitely bringing another adult?"

"Yes."

"Well, then—"

"Bye." Myra puts down the phone, picking it up a moment later to dial Loretta's number. After four rings, she hears Loretta's voice on an answering machine. *Hey, I'm not here. Leave a message, okay?*

At the beep, Myra says, "You should never say you're not there. It's an open invitation for burglars. Tell Cara to call me as soon as she gets home."

She hangs up, and then Haskell asks, "Is anything the matter? Something about Cara?"

"I've volunteered her to go with me on Jennifer's school field trip."

"You are supposing, I take it, that she hasn't made other plans."

"Cara? Plans? Oh, please. The only thing on her dance card for Fridays is coming over here to do laundry. Between you and me, I'm a little worried about her."

"Really? She seems fine to me. I see no cause for concern."

"You don't know her the way I do. She's too serious about everything, and she has way too many responsibilities. When I was her age, I was having the time of my life, going to parties, and concerts, and all kinds of fun things." But Myra is thinking mostly of her adventures in the cramped back seat of Vinnie's old Chevy. "The point is, she should be kicking up her heels while she has the chance."

"Shouldn't that be her decision?" He picks up a spoon and stirs his cereal. "Maybe she's satisfied with things the way they are."

"Nonsense. At least a trip to the Art Institute will be something different for her to do."

"I'm sure you will have her undying gratitude," he says, lifting the spoon to his lips.

"I am not looking for gratitude. I'm only trying to help. Now where were we?" She gets up to open the shallow drawer next to the sink and rummages for pencil and paper. "Cemetery. An open grave. The mourners standing around, waiting…"

৵৵৵

*"Did you see 'Swamp Thing'?"*

*"Yeah. Wasn't it gross when he ate the guy's liver?"*

*"Yechhh!"*

*"Girls, please talk softly."*

*"And those leeches! Oh, barf!"*

*"Girls!"*

*"Sorry, Miss Halvorsen."*

The school bus jolts merrily along Lake Shore Drive, while Myra takes in the speeding scenery and allows the various conversations of Jennifer's classmates to filter through her consciousness. Cara, sitting next to her, looks fresh-scrubbed and wholesome in her pretty new sweater, a buttery shade of yellow. "I ought to have my head examined for letting you talk me into this," she says. "I should be working on my paper for Renaissance Lit."

"Relax. Enjoy yourself. This might be fun."

The lake this morning is gorgeous, with sunlight twinkling off the water; the sky is a confident shade of blue. This is the kind of late-February morning that can lull a person into believing the worst of winter is over, that can make you want to pack away the snow shovel and haul out the gardening tools.

*"…okay, Scooter, we been hit. Engine number three is out…"*

*"Five. That's five ambulances, if you're counting."*

"Who cares?"

"...I'll feather the propeller. You look for a place to set 'er down..."

"Tyrone, put that thing away."

"Yes, Miss Halvorsen."

"Traffic is really zipping along," Tammy Wurbach says, poking her head around the seat in front. "Looks like we're going to be right on time." She checks her wristwatch and then writes something on a clipboard. Myra would not be surprised if she was also carrying a whistle, a flashlight, and a two-way radio. But she does understand the need to be prepared. When you are dealing with a busload of goofy, gangly sixth graders, anything can happen.

"Do you think we'll be back home before two?" Cara asks.

Myra yawns behind her hand. "I hope so." Last night, after a spectacularly successful Let's Be Lovers party, she met Vinnie for a quickie at the Patti-O Motel. On her way there, she bought a bottle of Cold Duck and was well into her second glass before he showed up. He seemed a little agitated. Maybe he didn't care for her Belle Starr pajamas with the rhinestone-bordered cutouts, or the fact that she pulled a very realistic-looking pistol from her garter and ordered him to drop his pants.

It took her a long time to get him properly worked up, and then he kept saying, "We gotta talk, My-ra. No, really."

Talk? Vinnie? She stabbed his tongue with her own and sank her teeth tenderly into his lower lip. Her lips and fingers did their magic, and by the time she was through with him, he lay sprawled on the bed like a dead man. She checked his pulse before she left.

Now the bus is turning off the Outer Drive and heading for Michigan Avenue, and as soon as it pulls up in front of the building, the children spill out, fifty or more adolescents, all bent and determined to outdo one another for sheer silliness. Two boys goose each other as they walk up the steps to the entrance doors. One of the girls trips over her own purse.

> "It's Gerald's fault, Miss Halvorsen. He pushed me."
>
> "Boys, please!"
>
> "When do we eat?"
>
> "This way, students. No, this way!"

Lagging behind, Myra stops by one of the huge bronze lions guarding the entrance to the art museum. In her junior college days, when she was a regular visitor, she'd touch its cold metal toe for luck before going inside, and she does that now. Back then, she'd be wishing for a passing grade in whatever class she was struggling with. Now, her only desire is to get through today's outing with no major mishap.

In the lobby, the boys and the girls are separated from each other. The teachers divide them further into small, manageable groups and assign two adults to each. Myra and Cara take charge of eight girls. Jennifer is among them, and she's making a point of ignoring her mother. They'd had a disagreement this morning about her outfit, Myra insisting that a skirt or a nice pair of slacks would be more appropriate for a trip downtown than what she was wearing.

Jennifer had screamed, "Oh, Mother, you are so-o-o uncool! You are so-o-o old-fashioned!" Then she jammed her arms into her coat and stormed out the door.

Myra studies Jennifer's coltish legs in their black lace tights (torn Madonna-style at one knee, of course) emerging from a pair of raggedy cut-off jeans. It dawns on her that unless, by some feat of magic, Jennifer turns into the most cooperative child on earth, this will be only the first of many skirmishes to come in the challenging teenage years ahead.

"All right, girls," she says, forcing into her voice a lightness she does not feel, "here we go."

They join the groups of children and adults making their way toward the back of the building and up the wide, curving staircase that leads to the Twentieth Century galleries. "Let's visit the Picassos first, shall we?" says their guide, a hefty woman in her sixties wearing disc-shaped earrings large enough to serve a sandwich on. "Who can tell me what country Señor Picasso comes from?"

"Yugoslavia!"

Jennifer laughs and falls helplessly against her friend Heather, who is making her own fashion statement in a cheesy-looking dress, a leather bomber jacket, and a pair of black flats and white ankle socks. Apparently having trouble keeping the shoes on her feet, she scuffs them along the parquet floor as they move among the paintings, their guide pointing out colors and textures, lines and fragments, in a desperately chirpy voice.

Cara stops before a Cubist masterpiece. "I guess I've never really developed a taste for modern art," she says, wrinkling her nose. "It all seems so weird."

Myra checks the plaque on the wall next to the painting. Leger? No, it's a Duchamp. "When you understand what the artist was trying to do," she tells Cara, "it makes a little more sense."

"Are you saying you actually like this stuff?"

"In a way, I do. I think it's interesting."

She recalls the hours she used to spend here years ago. On Tuesdays and Thursdays, when she had a long break between her English and biology classes, she would come to wander through the galleries, pleasantly lost in the portraits and landscapes and the echoing silence, a stranger to everyone she encountered. She enjoyed that anonymity: it allowed her to be anyone she cared to be. Once, as she was ambling through rooms filled with Monets and Cezannes, a long-haired boy in paint-stained jeans came up to her and said, "Hey, what's your name?" and she responded, in the drizzle of French she knew, "Désolé, je ne sais pas."

She began to develop a kind of proprietary affection for many of the works. The first time she saw the Duchamp, she recognized it instantly from her art appreciation textbook. Eventually she discovered other paintings and sculptures she had seen in that book. Being able to actually walk up to them and touch them with a fingertip gave her a visceral connection to a world outside of the world she knew. Mystery and adventure existed out there—she could almost hear it calling to her from the future—and she decided that someday she would travel to those beautiful street scenes and romantic seascapes. Someday, she would experience them for real.

Unfortunately, she never made it that far. "I used to love coming here," she tells Cara, "but I stopped around the time I met your uncle." She lets out a small sigh over that fact: another sacrifice she had made for love.

"Haskell says that his style of playwriting is like abstract art. He told me he's trying to force the audience into a new awareness by…what does he call it? … *fragmenting reality*. Doesn't that sound exciting—and even a little dangerous?"

"Well, I suppose that's one way of looking at it, but if you read his play—"

"Oh, I have."

"All of it?"

"Of course, all of it. You know, Aunt Myra, I can't pretend to understand everything, but I think Haskell is brilliant."

"Brilliant? He has two people in a lifeboat who may as well be speaking Pig Latin for all the sense they make."

"Maybe you don't understand the symbolism. Haskell says you have to view the play at several levels."

"Did he mention the sub-text?"

"Yes, he did."

She waves her fingers dismissively. "I thought as much."

They make their way through several more galleries filled with colorful abstracts. Myra recognizes a few Kandinskys from her early visits, as well as a Miro, two Mondrians, and the walking stick-figures sculpted by Giacometti. She notices that Cara's attention seems to be wandering, so it'll be up to her to keep the girls in line. But apart from a little giggling and an occasional moony-eyed stare at a passing group of boys, they seem to be behaving themselves. She is glad to see that Heather's shoes are still more or less on her feet.

"Time seems to have weighed heavily on Mr. Dali's mind," their guide says as they gather in a semi-circle before the painting of the melting clocks. While she is delivering a lecture on Surrealism, Myra slips through the doorway into an adjacent gallery, and motions for Cara to follow.

There is a painting she wants to see again. "Over here," she says, advancing toward the far end of the room where a guard in a dark blue uniform eyes her with suspicion, as if she might be a member of the Ma Barker gang.

She comes to a stop in front of a large portrait in a heavy frame: an old lady at her dressing table. The painting is almost exactly as she remembers it. Here is the woman's powder puff, her comb, the vase of dying wildflowers on the tattered dresser cloth. Overdone and a little ghoulish, it always seemed to Myra in her junior-college days like a kind of joke. But for some reason, she doesn't feel like laughing anymore.

"Oh, wow," Cara says. "Look at those legs. They're blue! And that mole on her chin—too much!" She laughs out loud, an echoing guffaw that makes the guard turn his head and Myra suck in her breath.

The old woman in the painting isn't nearly as old as she'd once thought. In fact, she is hardly past middle age. Myra can see that now, and she can see how the artist has etched all the disappointments of the woman's life into her face. Those sad, saggy eyes seem to be asking, *Where have all my pretty years gone? Where have they vanished*?

"Now here is an artist I can understand," Cara says, regarding the portrait with genuine admiration.

Myra turns on her heel and walks briskly past the guard, remarking over her shoulder, "He's okay, I suppose. But really, Cara, he is certainly no Van Gogh."

❧❧❧

The teachers and the room mothers agree on a picnic. "It's such a beautiful day and we figured, wouldn't it be a darn shame to waste all this sunshine? So we're going to park the buses over by the Planetarium and let the children bring their lunches down to the lake."

Myra smiles and nods in Tammy Wurbach's direction. The bus comes to a stop, the doors open, and once again the children come tumbling out, running with their lunch sacks toward the breakers. Reflexively, she calls, "Not too far!"

Cara comes up behind her and drops her jacket on the grass. "Relax, Aunt Myra. Don't you think they'll have enough sense to stop before they hit the water?"

"With sixth graders, you never can tell," Tammy Wurbach chuckles. She sits down next to Cara, opens a knapsack and pulls out a sandwich, a carton of yogurt, a small bunch of grapes, a bag of cookies and a thermos. "I have extra glasses if you want ice tea."

Myra accepts a glass and leans back on her elbows to munch her apple. Cara takes a bite of her sandwich, a heel of white bread smeared with avocado and folded in half. "I guess I'll have to make a quick stop at the grocery before I go home," she says, "or there won't be any supper."

Tammy Wurbach offers Cara some grapes and cookies. "I've packed way too much," she says, and then goes on to talk about some diet she is planning to try. On and on and on.

But the sun is pouring down in golden waves, and Myra can easily tune her out. The air feels so warm she's not even tempted to tell the children to put their coats back on. Shading her eyes, she watches them down by the water, tossing crumbs to the gathering gulls, imagining Jennifer getting rid of her chicken salad sandwich chunk by chunk. She is sorry she hadn't given Jennifer peanut butter and saved the chicken salad for tonight. She could have a picnic supper with Vinnie at the Patti-O, with candles and vodka-spiked lemonade—

And what did he want to talk to her about, anyway?

Was he getting tired of their little arrangement? Maybe tonight she'll come mincing in as the French maid, submissive and compliant. She'll memorize a few words to whisper in his ear. *Désolé*, she thinks. *Chateauneuf*. If you pronounce them with a little growl in your voice, you can make them sound obscene.

"Pardon?" Tammy Wurbach says.

Myra realizes she must have been moving her lips. "Oh, I've been gaining and losing the same five pounds for years," she replies airily. "I think diets are a waste of time."

"Why…yes…"

The hesitation in Tammy Wurbach's voice tells Myra she has missed an important shift in the conversation; but before she can attempt to cover the lapse, she is distracted by the drone of an engine. A small plane banks out of the south, behind the Planetarium, and passes directly overhead.

"I'll bet he's going to land at Meig's Field," Tammy Wurbach says. She sighs heavily and gets a faraway look in her eyes. "Honestly, I wish I was going someplace. We didn't get to take a winter vacation this year—Richard got so busy at work and everything?—and I've been having the worst case of cabin fever, I thought I might die!"

Myra has never taken a winter vacation in her life, and most of the summer is spent helping Vinnie fix whatever's broken around the house and keeping the grass mowed. She wonders where she would go if someone handed her enough money to buy an airplane ticket. Florida? Mexico? New Zealand?

"Haskell says you have to travel in order to appreciate the comforts of home," Cara says, pulling a grape off the bunch Tammy Wurbach gave her and popping it into her mouth. "It doesn't matter where you go. The important thing is to get away."

"That is one of the stupidest things I ever heard," Myra says, feeling suddenly belligerent. "According to that theory, a trip to Peoria is just as good as a trip to Paris."

Cara arches an eyebrow and gives Myra the same kind of look Jennifer gave her when she accused her of being uncool. "You are missing the point."

"Well, then, maybe you could explain it to me in simple words that even I can understand."

"It's a question of changing perspectives, improving your attitude. You know what they say, travel broadens a person."

"Richard and I went to Peoria once, to visit his sister when she was in college down there—she was studying to be a physical education teacher?—well, she always had been good at sports. After she got her degree, she moved to Indianapolis and we went down there once or twice, but then she took a job at a school in Colorado Springs…or maybe it was Denver…"

Her voice is drowned out by the roar of another plane making a runway approach. Myra can see its landing gear as it flies over. Tammy is still talking as the engine noise fades. On the pretext of checking on the children, Myra stands; but really, she feels itchy enough to jump out of her skin. "Those children should not be allowed to throw their lunch to the birds," she says. "It's a shameful waste of perfectly good food."

Cara stretches out in the grass. "I should thank you for making me come today. I guess I really needed the break."

"When I was a child, I was not allowed to waste anything, but especially not food. And speaking of that, how come you're the one who has to do the grocery shopping? Can't Loretta take some responsibility for that, at least?"

"It's difficult to imagine you as a child," Cara says. "Was there ever a time when you weren't so serious and uptight about everything?"

Tammy Wurbach dips a spoon into her yogurt. "No one could ever accuse me of being a serious child. I was the most empty-headed little girl on our street…"

"Some of us feel the need to direct the events of our lives," Myra says to Cara, bathing her words in righteous indignation, "and some of us think whatever happens is okay."

"Like who, for instance?"

"Your mother."

"Haskell says that life is what happens to you while you're making other plans."

Haskell again! Myra will just bet he got those words off of a bumper sticker. She's about to mention that to Cara, when a sudden shout reaches their ears.

"*Oh, no… oh, no!*"

It sounds like it's coming from down by the lake.

Pressing a hand to her chest and hoping that no one has fallen into the water, Myra calls, "What is it? What's wrong!"

"*Look, he's trying to eat it!*"

"*Holy cow! My mother's gonna have a stroke!*"

"*Someone get a stick!*"

Alert as a spaniel, Tammy Wurbach whips out a pair of binoculars and scans the shoreline. Myra chews her lip and wonders if she will be called upon to administer artificial respiration. "W-what has happened?" she asks, her voice trembling.

Tammy Wurbach chuckles. "Oh, my stars and garters…"

Myra wants to rip the binoculars out of her hands. "Will someone please tell me *what* is going *on*?"

"Well, as near as I can figure out, Mrs. Calderelli, some child has lost their shoe."

"Yes…" Myra says, nodding, "…of course…of course…"

She can picture the event unfolding in slow motion: the careless foot dangling the black shoe, the sudden jerk or twist that causes the foot to flip, the shoe making a small arc before landing on the water, the gulls racing toward it…

She has no need to ask whose shoe it is. And, sure enough, here come Jennifer and Heather, laughing and shoving one another up the hill.

"Ohhh…" Heather gasps, "…my Gawd!"

"What is your mother going to say?" Myra demands, eying the dirty white sock on Heather's shoeless left foot. "I should have warned her earlier," she says to Tammy, to Cara. "I knew something like this was going to happen, I could just feel it in my bones..."

"Hey, Aunt Myra, this isn't your fault."

"Why, no," Tammy Wurbach agrees. "It has nothing whatsoever to do with you."

"I feel terrible… just terrible..." Part of her is standing there and wondering when the other part of her is going to stop apologizing.

Heather tries to look contrite.

Jennifer says, "Geez, Mom, chill *out*! It was only a stupid old shoe." ❧

## *TWENTY-ONE*

By Monday, winter is back, March having come in like a lion over the weekend. The ground, which had begun to thaw, is now sending up its chilly dampness, and low gray clouds keep pressing the dampness back into the earth. The house smells musty; the furnace whines on and off, on and off.

Myra's feeling as if she is on the verge of a malady she has no name for, with symptoms she cannot quite describe. The clack of Haskell's typewriter, or the jangle of Brownie's tags, or the occasional squawk from the parrot is enough to rattle her. Late in the afternoon, after having been silent all day, the telephone shrills. She jumps, and nearly drops the chicken she was carrying from the refrigerator to the sink.

"I think I'm coming down with something," she tells Nettie, wedging the receiver against her shoulder and turning on the cold water.

"You went out without a coat that nice day we had, I bet. Caught a chill and now you're getting a cold."

"Colds are caused by viruses, not chills. It is a scientific fact."

"Make yourself a bowl of hot soup, put in plenty of fresh garlic and black pepper."

"What is this? Folk medicine 101?"

"Listen, Myra, I didn't call to argue."

"So, who's arguing? What are you implying?"

"I'll talk to you when you're feeling better."

"Ma?" She hears the phone click. *Hello?*

For a moment, she stands there with the dead receiver on her shoulder and her hands wrist-deep in giblets. In the half-minute it takes her to rinse off and dry her hands and hang up the phone, Lucy has discovered the chicken; and with her fangs sunk into a drumstick, she tries to make off with the whole bird.

Myra lets out a gargle of frustration, seizes the cat and flings her out of the room. Now her damp hands are speckled with gray tabby fur. She rinses them again, passes a forearm across her brow, and turns back to the sink.

This time, it is Ethel who has taken an interest in the chicken. Myra hisses, "Scat!" and claps her hands sharply, but the cat only crouches and closes his eyes, as if he could make himself invisible. She's forgotten how easily intimidated he is. A wave of guilt sweeps over her as she recalls the pathetic rag of starving fur he was the day she found him. Lifting Ethel off the counter and cradling him in her arms, she murmurs words of comfort to him until she feels his muscles relax. Her stomach is tight with the effort to control her anger.

And what is she angry about?

She has no idea.

She sits down and immediately bursts into tears.

A door opens downstairs and then she hears the dim wail of Haskell's phonograph, his tread on the steps. Lost in thought, he wanders into the kitchen and stares out the window over the sink. Myra sets Ethel down and quickly wipes her eyes. Haskell doesn't notice her until she comes to the sink again to wash the fur—white, this time—off her fingers.

"Excuse me," she says, grabbing a towel.

"No, excuse *me*." He seems oddly formal, as if they had run into each other in a public restroom. He looks into her face and asks if anything is the matter.

She sniffles and shakes her head. "I'm getting a cold, I think. And my mother called, and then she hung up on me. And I can't seem to get supper going."

"Tell me what I can do to help," he says, his voice filled with concern. "Shall I set the table? Put up the potatoes?" He looks as innocently eager as a Boy Scout, and every bit as seductive.

She could use a little assistance, but really, she just wants the kitchen to herself right now. Touching him on the arm, she says, "Thanks, but never mind. I'll do it myself."

∽∽∽

Later, fortified with a cold capsule and half a cup of hot tea, she sets off for her Let's Be Lovers party at the home of Rachel Wasserman in Morton Grove. Myra has never met Rachel—Nettie knows the young woman's mother, which is how she got the lead—but she did speak to her on the telephone.

"One time, I had this *caw-stoom* jewelry demonstration," Rachel told her in the vowel-wrenching twang that signified a West Rogers Park upbringing. "Is yours anything like that?"

Myra said, "A little," and did not elaborate.

When she gets to the house, struggling through the doorway with her bags of samples, she sees that Rachel has been discussing wallpaper with her sister, Leah. Swatch books are piled on the bench in the foyer.

"So what do you think?" Rachel says, flipping through the pages of one of the books. "Traditional stripes, or one of these new paisley patterns?"

"Stripes are very masculine," the sister says. "On the other hand…"

Rachel's friends arrive in small groups and she consults each of them about the wallpaper before they take their seats on the sectional couches in the Mediterranean-themed living room. Dressed alike in coordinated clothes, carefully applied makeup and coiffed hair, they chatter animatedly, their various conversations banging up against one another and echoing off the two-story-high ceiling. Myra has to whistle twice for their attention.

None of the young women have any interest in modeling the lingerie, though when Myra holds the garments up against herself and describes their various details, they do listen politely. They giggle at the underwear and titter at the novelties, but when she brings out the appliances, they fall into shocked silence. A few pretend to study the palazzo mural decorating one of the living room walls.

Even though she can sense the whole thing slipping away, Myra keeps at it, using her entire arsenal of quips and jibes, her "free-to-be-me" spiel. But in the middle of explaining the intricacies and pleasures of ben-wah balls, she hears someone say, "I hear grass cloth is going to make a big comeback," and she understands that the evening is beyond rescue.

Rachel buys a bottle of lotion, her sister a set of Adam and Eve toothbrushes. The rest of the women slip silently out the door.

"I guess some nights are better than others," Rachel says sympathetically, helping Myra pack up her samples. "Have you ever considered becoming an *A-vawn* Lady?"

∽∽∽

The cold capsule kicks in on her way home. Since it is barely nine o'clock, she stops at a drug store to call Vinnie; maybe he'd like to meet her at the Patti-O; just for an hour. There is no answer at the apartment, even after she lets the phone ring ten times. Last Friday he canceled out on her; yesterday when he came for the children, she was in the shower, and he didn't even wait around to say hello.

Yes, something is going on, that's for sure, but she cannot worry about that now. An icy drizzle has begun to fall. The streets are getting slippery, and she has to focus every bit of her attention on the road. She drives with exaggerated care, accelerating slowly, braking gently, holding the wheel with both hands and fighting to keep her eyes open. When she reaches her front door at last, she closes her eyes and heaves out a sigh of relief. A big mug of hot tea and a good night's sleep, that's all she needs. Tomorrow, she'll be right as rain.

She will be fine.

The house is silent. She calls Haskell's name, but he is nowhere around. While she's lighting the burner under the kettle, Copperfield sidles up to her and pushes his forehead into her shins. His litter pan is in the laundry room, but the door to the basement is closed. No wonder the cat seems upset.

Well, she is certainly going to have to speak to someone about this. "Come on, boy," she says, opening the door and flipping on the stairwell light. Her voice seems to echo in her ears, as if she were calling from a long way away.

No, it's not only her voice she is hearing. Haskell's phonograph must be playing. She'll ask him if he would like her to make him a cup of tea; as long as she's already put the kettle on, anyway; no trouble. And after what she's been through today, she could use a little companionship, a few words of conversation. (Or more likely—given the man's penchant for delivering lectures on one thing and another—a few thousand words.)

Holding the railing for balance, she makes her way downstairs and raps at his door, which is slightly ajar and falls open at her touch. Light from the hallway slants across the rumpled sofa bed, and Myra can make out a figure moving beneath the sheets. Then Haskell's startled face appears, naked without his glasses. But before she can blurt out an apology for waking him, another face emerges.

A familiar face with blue eyes and round, rosy cheeks.

"Aunt Myra!" Cara cries, clutching the sheet to her chin. "Oh!"

Myra's lips are still trying to form the apology to Haskell when her brain has to suddenly switch gears.

In the struggle she begins to sputter. "But—but—"

Cara pulls the sheet with her as she moves toward her aunt. "Hey, it's all right. Let me explain…"

"I'm—I'm—but—"

"We're going to get married, Haskell and I. We have it all planned. Everything is going to be wonderful."

"—you never—you never *said* anything—"

"I know. Everything just happened so fast, and…"

A noise is starting up now in Myra's head, and in her personal cold-capsule fog it sounds like tornado sirens and fire alarms and church bells rolled into one. She puts her hands over her ears, but the noise keeps growing louder and louder until she thinks her skull will explode.

Haskell gets out of bed then, hitching the wool blanket around his hips like a skirt. "Well," he says wearily, reaching for his glasses, "if no one else is planning to get that highly annoying tea kettle, I suppose that I will have to do it."

And edging cautiously around Myra, he hurries up the stairs.

## *TWENTY-TWO*

Cara is still attempting to explain herself, mouthing her words with exaggerated care and wriggling her fingers in gestures so elaborate she looks as if she might be weaving flax.

But even after Haskell has silenced the shrieking teakettle, Myra is unable to take in the girl's words. She feels chilled and weak, and more than a little queasy. "I don't..." she says, "...I'm not—" and then she turns and lurches up the stairs. Kicking off her shoes, she crawls into bed and pulls the covers over her head. A few hours of sleep, she tells herself before drifting away, but the next time she checks the clock, it's eleven in the morning.

The sun is out.

And where are Jennifer and Howie?

She calls their names and tries to sit up, but the bedding keeps weighing her down. Slowly and laboriously she peels back the coverlet, the blanket, the top sheet. Who has gotten them off to school? Who's fed the animals, walked the dog, emptied the litter pans? There are probably a hundred dirty dishes in the sink and God knows what else on the floor.

Once she's on her feet, she realizes how much better she feels. The nausea seems to be gone, and this wobbly feeling in her legs is probably only due to hunger. Now that she thinks about it, she hasn't had a proper meal in days. A little something to eat, and she will be good as new.

She'll be fine.

So, it was not a cold after all. She will have to mention this to Nettie.

After washing her face and scrubbing the furriness from her teeth, she squints at herself in the mirror. Her skin appears to be a little sallow, but otherwise she doesn't look too bad. And though the comb makes a scraping noise across her scalp, you couldn't really call it a headache. But reaching under the bed for her shoes is an effort; she has to rest a moment. When she looks at the clock again—slowly turning her head and rubbing at the stiffness in her neck—she sees that, somehow, half an hour has gone by.

Maybe she needs to close her eyes for a bit. Then she'll fix a little breakfast and tackle the kitchen, and then she will telephone Cara.

Marry Haskell?

Ridiculous.

Completely, utterly, and totally.

⚜⚜⚜

Someone's calling her name. She would like to answer, but she is at the bottom of a well. Struggling to open her eyes, she says, "*Mmmfph?*"

"I asked if you think you can eat. You really should have something in your stomach."

She rolls her head in the direction of Haskell's voice. If she could organize her thoughts, she would tell him a thing or two.

"I...can make...my own...breakfast," she croaks, raising herself onto an elbow. Her lips feel as if someone has worked on them with sandpaper.

"You've missed breakfast. Also lunch. In fact, it is now a little past suppertime."

She cranks open an eye. The room is dark, and he is standing in the doorway, backlit by the hallway light. "Are you feeling any better?" he says, coming into the room. He's holding a cup of something steaming, which he sets on the nightstand before pressing the back of his hand to her forehead.

"Stop that." She tries to knock the hand away. "I am perfectly fine."

"Your fever seems to be down, anyway." He sits at the edge of the bed and brings the cup to her lips, forcing her to drink: some kind of broth that has the metallic tang of the can it came in. An inferior house brand, no doubt.

"Where are the children? Have they eaten? Have they done their homework?"

"Yes, and yes. Much as it may surprise you, they are doing quite well on their own. Your daughter is helping your son construct a replica of Mount Vesuvius out of mashed potatoes." He turns on the bedside lamp, and the light throws ghastly shadows against the walls.

Shielding her eyes and staring into his face, which looks as bland as ever—not a trace of guilt, no sign he's lost any sleep—she bristles, "How could you!"

"It's a science project, I believe, and they took a solemn oath they would clean up after they were finished—"

"You know perfectly well I don't mean the mashed potatoes volcano. I am talking about my niece."

He blinks and angles his head away from her, as if her question required him to do a series of calculations. "I sense you disapprove of our plans."

"Cara is a child, she's young enough to be your daughter. Of course I disapprove!"

"I fail to see that age has any relevance here."

"You'd have to be blind not to!" She coughs and takes another swallow of the horrible broth. "The girl has never had a real father, and along you come, you take an interest in her that she finds flattering—" She breaks off. "Oh, I should have seen this coming. I should have known."

"You assume there is no reason for the attraction other than my age? Myra, have you forgotten? We used to be lovers, too—"

"We were no such thing! And if you tell that to Cara, I will deny it with my dying breath. We were just…lonely. It was…convenient to be together."

His face falls. He shakes his head slowly and gets to his feet. "I was under the impression that at one time we meant something to one another."

"And how long has this been going on?"

"My love affair with Cara? It was a natural extension of our friendship. You were gone so often, and she was here—"

"How very convenient for you."

"I wish you would stop using that word." He turns to leave.

"Are you going to marry her?"

"Yes."

"No matter what anyone else thinks?"

"Finish the soup. You wouldn't want to become dehydrated."

As soon as he is gone, she drags her legs over the side of the bed. She lets a few moments pass, and then she stands and shuffles into the bathroom. So this is the thanks she gets for taking a perfect stranger into her home. This is what passes for gratitude! She spills the rest of the broth down the sink and puts on a robe over her clothes. If she can't get anywhere with Haskell, maybe Cara will listen to reason. She will call her right now.

But halfway down the stairs, the weakness comes over her again, and she has to sit and take deep breaths to stop the fluttering in her chest.

All right, all right. Maybe she hasn't totally recovered from her illness yet. Maybe the talking-to can wait until tomorrow.

❧❧❧

Morning again.

She jerks herself awake, mumbling the list of things she must do. Clean the kitchen. Call Cara. Try to get hold of Vinnie, who seems to have dropped off the face of the earth. And she has promised Mick Jagger she would drive him to the airport.

Or—wait. That was the dream. Mick had drawn her aside after one of his concerts, put his hand under her elbow and murmured confidentially to her about how much he has been misunderstood as a human being all these years, and could he please explain it to her on their way to O'Hare?

With the dream still in her head, she floats down the stairs, turns into the living room and bumps smack dab into the wing-back chair. Someone has moved it. Someone has moved all the furniture around and hung blankets over everything. Howie, and his infernal tents! He has turned the entire room into a city for moles.

She cannot deal with this now. Let her get a little something to eat, and then she'll be able to—

The minute she sees the state of the kitchen, her appetite disappears. In addition to the expected mess in the sink, bits of Howie's science project—dried mashed potatoes flecked with brown paint—are stuck to the table, the chairs, and the floor. Something has exploded on the stove, and there's a mysterious puddle next to the back door.

Angrily, she calls for the dog, who refuses to show her face. Ethel turns up instead, his tail raised in the shape of a question mark. Myra takes the last slice of American cheese from the package in the refrigerator, breaks off a piece for the cat and eats the rest, washing it down with a glass of water. Then she grabs the bottle of Fantastik and sprays the stove, the table and chairs, the wall behind one of the chairs, and the floor under the table. She fills the sink with suds and then rips off a bunch of paper towels. Just as she has finished mopping up the puddle, the back door opens and Haskell enters, carrying Jennifer in his arms.

"The school called for someone to come and get her," he explains, setting Jennifer down and helping Myra to her feet. "She vomited in gym class."

"It wasn't my fault, Mom. I caught your germs."

They get Jennifer upstairs, and while Myra helps her into bed, Haskell retrieves the thermometer from the medicine chest. "I'm very glad to see that you're feeling better," he says.

"Oh, you know me. Can't stay down for long. Too much to do." She thinks maybe she should apologize for hurting his feelings last night. But then she thinks maybe not: all she did was tell the truth as she saw it. And if the truth hurt, so be it. But she does say how much she appreciates him bringing her daughter home.

"I did what anyone would do, under the circumstances. No need to thank me." He walks out of the room, mumbling something about an appointment downtown.

"Is he mad at you?" Jennifer asks. Her cheeks are flushed, her eyes bright with fever.

"Mad? Don't be silly." She presses her cheek to Jennifer's temple, confirming the thermometer reading of one-hundred-one degrees. "You need Tylenol, and sleep," she says softly, settling her under the covers.

"Don't kiss me, Mom. You'll make me sicker."

"Really? Don't you remember what you told me once, a long time ago? You said, and I quote, 'Mommies don't have germs'."

Jennifer smiles, and Myra blows a kiss in her direction.

Coming downstairs, ready to resume the task of putting the house back together, she almost bangs into the chair again and has to execute a swift pirouette. Then, trying to regain her balance, she nearly topples Angelo's cage. The parrot lets out a startled squawk. Myra says,

"Sorry," and limps into the kitchen. Now she has gone and done something to her knee.

She re-sprays all the surfaces with the cleanser, and while waiting for it to start working she dials Loretta's number. No one is home, and rather than leave a message, she decides to try again later. She needs to speak with Cara directly; it's the only way to make the girl listen to reason.

The dried potato spatter comes off the wall easily enough, but the stuff is really sticking to the table, and while going at it with a rag and her thumbnail, something gives way in her right shoulder. A fiery twinge travels across her back. Sitting down and waiting for the pain to subside, she feels herself getting woozy again.

She moans and lays her head in her hands, and then Lucy jumps into her lap. "I don't have time for a relapse," she tells the cat, who is breathing tuna fumes into Myra's face. "I simply do not have the blankety-blank time!"

In the living room, Angelo lets out a couple of squawks and then: *Goddamn-woof-woof-son-of-a-bitch*!

❧❧❧

Back in her bedroom she tries to rest, but how can she rest with Jennifer running such a high fever, Howie due home any minute, and the house looking like a stage set for the Addams Family? Under the blanket, one of the cats is playing with Myra's toes. In a distant part of the house, Brownie's tags jangle like a restless ghost.

In the pages of her memory, she turns back to that terrible morning years ago when someone forgot to fasten the backyard gate and the dog got out. Myra panicked, of course, put Jennifer in her stroller and went searching the neighborhood, whistling and calling, picturing Brownie lost and confused and wandering farther and farther from home.

Later that afternoon a man telephoned to say the dog had been found, three blocks away. A miracle, she thought, until she remembered the tag Brownie wore with her name spelled out in capital letters. Under that were the words *I Belong To* and then Myra's name and phone number. So it was only a question of time until someone called. She had done all that worrying for nothing.

"We should all wear tags," Brownie says. She has the deep, sensible voice of that television horse, Mister Ed. "Howie and Jennifer and Vinnie and Cara. All of us belong to Myra G. Calderelli—"

Myra twists her head sharply. "*Huh?*"

She sits up and massages the back of her neck. How long has she been dozing? She listens—for voices, cries for help, sounds of things crashing and breaking—but there is only the dull hum of the furnace; dust settling. She closes her eyes. In a while, she will get up and begin again. Just give her another minute…

�����

Now she drifts in and out of sleep, dreams coming and going like towns viewed from a passing train. Was that Jennifer calling? Did Myra bring her a glass of water, or did she only dream it? She thinks she hears a door close, and isn't anyone going to answer that telephone?

Something wet touches her hand; a tail brushes her face. Yawning, she gets out of bed and gropes her way downstairs.

Howie is in the kitchen by himself, standing on a chair in front of the stove and frying an egg in a large, black skillet. The air reeks of cooked butter. "Where is everyone?" she asks, covering her nose and trying not to gag.

"Jennifer's sick."

"I know. Where is Mr. Reed?"

"I dunno."

Myra collapses into a chair. "I don't suppose anyone has fed the cats or the dog."

Howie doesn't answer. He concentrates on his egg, scooping it carefully with a spatula onto a plate and tapping salt over the yolk. "Someone called for you on the telephone."

"Who?"

"I don't remember."

"Think, Howie. Was it a man or a woman?"

"I dunno. I was watching tee-vee." He picks up his knife and fork and begins cutting the egg into squares. "Mom?" he says.

"Yes?"

"Who's gonna take care of me if I get sick?"

"Why, I will, of course. Don't I always take care of you?" She rises slowly from her chair and goes to the refrigerator to get Howie a glass of milk, and then she picks up the phone and dials Cara's number again. "Were you the one who called me today?" she asks as soon as Cara answers.

"Wasn't me," she says in her usual, chipper voice: no trace of guilt or embarrassment from her either. "What's wrong? You sound kind of funny."

"Touch of flu. No biggie. Listen, we need to talk."

There is a brief silence on the other end, and then Cara says, "If you're going to give me a lecture, Aunt Myra, don't bother."

"No lecture. I promise." She arranges her features into a smile that she hopes will register in her tone of voice. "Just a friendly chat between an aunt and her niece."

"Can't it wait until Friday?"

Myra has to think for a moment what day this is. "All right," she says finally, "if you promise not to elope in the meantime."

She hangs up the phone. Well then, she thinks, rolling up her sleeves, no more dilly-dallying. In a series of motions that must by now be imprinted in the fibers of her body, she gets the animals fed and watered and makes a quick sweep of the counters with her sponge. The floor will have to wait until tomorrow—there is only so much she can be expected do right now.

She whistles for the dog. As soon as she opens the back door to let her into the yard, a cold blast of air swoops down her neck and her teeth begin to chatter uncontrollably. "H-Howie," she says, "don't f-forget to let her b-back in."

"Mom? Where are you going?"

"I think I'll have to lie down for another little w-while."

"But who's gonna read me a bedtime story?"

"I'm s-sorry, honey." She staggers out of the room and up the stairs, listening to his forlorn little voice calling after her.

"Mom…?"

ཥཥཥ

"Drop dead."

"You drop dead."

"No, you drop dead!"

"Mo-ther!"

Can it be Saturday already?

Myra rubs her eyes and tries to think. She is wearing the same clothes she had on Monday night, when she got sick. Tuesday…and most of Wednesday…she was—

"Mom! *Mommy!*"

Eyes half open, she pulls the covers aside and rolls out of bed, yelling automatically, "Jennifer! Leave him alone!"

"I'm not doing anything. Oh, he is such a dweeb."

"Am not," Howie whines. "What's a dweeb?"

They are sitting amidst the ruins of the living room in front of the television. On the screen, Oprah is leaning close to a tearful, middle-aged woman, apparently discussing something intimate.

Oprah? Her program is on weekdays.

Therefore, it cannot be Saturday.

Therefore, Howie should not be here.

Myra touches the back of her hand to her daughter's cheek, checking for fever, and demands of her son, "Why are you not at school?"

He shrugs. "Nobody sent me."

Jennifer laughs. "Hah, hah! A real dweeb."

"*...and stuffed inside the toe of one of his loafers,*" the woman is saying, shaking her head sadly and pressing a handkerchief to her nose, "*I found these blue lace panties ...*"

Quickly, Myra flips to another channel. "Here's a movie. Watch this."

"It isn't in color."

"Too bad." She shuffles into the kitchen, where nothing has changed for the better. The stove has grown a new layer of food, and there is a fresh puddle by the back door. The phone rings, and it's Nettie, asking if Myra still remembers her.

"Oh, Ma, I've got the flu. I've been sick all week."

"You poor thing—"

"And I'm in such a mess here. Every time I try to get anything done, I have a relapse. Jennifer is sick, too, and I suppose it's only a question of time before Howie comes down with this."

Her mother *tches* with sympathy. "If it was up to *me*," she says, "I'd be rushing right over. But you know your father. *I* wouldn't catch anything, but he'd get the bug off of me, and you know how it is when *he* gets sick."

Myra sniffles. "So you're not coming?"

"Listen, there were plenty of times I sat up with you when you were little, with cool wash cloths and cough syrup. You forget?"

"I'm not forgetting," she says, but she cannot come up with more than a single memory, and it's not Nettie but Jack, trying to make her a cup of tea while she lay miserable under a heap of blankets. For endless minutes she listened to him rattle around in the kitchen, measuring water into the kettle, turning dials on the stove, opening and shutting cupboard doors. "I couldn't find the honey," he announced, marching into her room at last with the cup and saucer balanced in his upraised hand, "so I mixed in a big spoonful of orange marmalade!"

"Call me when you're feeling better," Nettie says, rushing off the phone, as if contagion could be spread that way.

Meanwhile, Haskell has come into the kitchen. Because he is wearing his overcoat, Myra assumes that he's going out somewhere—until she notices the pajamas and slippers sticking out from beneath the coat. He stands in the middle of the floor with one hand in his pocket and the other pressed against his cheek. "What day is today?" he asks.

"Thursday, I'm pretty sure."

He shakes his head. "I'm having some difficulty thinking sequentially."

"Do you have the weakness in your legs?"

"That appears to be gone, but now my small motor coordination is a little off." He flexes his fingers and then examines a nail.

"I feel like someone is tapping at my ribs with little hammers." She folds her arms across her stomach. "Maybe if we ate, we'd feel better."

From the scraps in the packages of lunchmeat lying in the refrigerator, she constructs two meager sandwiches. Haskell turns on the burner under the kettle, but there's no more tea or even instant soup. Myra supposes this is what it must have been like in London during the second world war, people picking through the debris of their ruined houses, trying to go on with daily life. She takes the bottle of ketchup from the refrigerator door, plops some into two mugs and fills them with the hot water.

As she is handing Haskell the plate with his sandwich, Howie comes barreling past with a box of potato chips under his arm. Without slowing down he cries, "Watch out, Mom!"

"Wait a minute, where are you going with that—" As she turns to grab the chips, she snags her foot on a chair leg, and Haskell reaches out to break her fall.

They stand there, he with his arms around her, she still holding his plate. After a moment, she says, "I'm sorry."

"It's not your fault. Children can be quite dangerous."

"About the other day, I mean. I'm sorry if I said things that hurt you." She puts the plate down but does not try to escape his embrace. "You were helpful to me at a difficult time in my life. You were kind and compassionate, but—"

"But you've found someone else. Is that it?"

"In a manner of speaking, yes."

"I understand."

She rests her head against his chest. "I'm glad you understand." She's not accustomed to leaning on anyone, but she is thinking how good it feels to be able to.

Just for the moment.

∽∽∽

Later, at a few minutes after five, someone opens the back door with a key. Myra hears a rumble of voices, a dog barking, a child's sharp laughter. Though she has been lying in bed—trying to recover her strength after getting the week's worth of dirty laundry sorted—she knows that this is not a dream.

Deep in her chest something begins to unlatch, and she understands immediately: it's Vinnie; he has come home.

She creeps downstairs and watches silently from the kitchen doorway as he puts away the groceries he has brought: a carton of melons and berries out of season; cheeses imported from European countries; a deluxe assortment of crackers; gourmet coffee.

"Hey, leave those alone," he says, grabbing the box of crackers from Jennifer. "That's for your mother."

"Didn't you bring anything for us?"

"Rotten little extortionists." He reaches into his shirt pocket and takes out a package of bubble gum.

Howie leaps at his back. Vinnie grabs him by the pants, flips him around, fakes a few rabbit punches and finishes him off with an upper cut. Howie doubles over, giggling. Jennifer says, "Did you notice? I'm growing out my bangs."

He winks at her. "Nice."

He does not see Myra yet, standing there with her eyes suddenly full of tears. He doesn't notice her until the children nearly bowl her over on their way out of the room, and then he gives her a long, thoughtful stare.

It makes her wonder: how awful does she look?

"I've had the flu," she says, hoping that will explain her appearance, the state of the house, and the reason why there is a striped tail hanging out of an upper cabinet next to the kitchen sink.

"I know," he says. "Howie told me. It's kind of going around."

"Were you the one who called?"

"Didn't he give you the message?"

"He didn't remember."

"Figures." He opens the pantry door and puts away the crackers. "So, where's the writer guy? Still around?"

"He's paid his rent through the end of the month."

"Rent, huh?" He lifts a small honeydew from the grocery carton and turns it in his fingers. "I kind of thought he'd be out of the picture by now."

Myra would like to tell him there has never really been anyone else in the picture, God help her, not for all these long months. But this is not the time for her to be making any confessions. "You do realize that we haven't settled anything yet," she says, picking up the empty carton and setting it next to the back door.

He nods. "If you want, till you're feeling better, I could bunk with Howie."

"We really need to have some long, serious discussions."

"Yeah, yeah..."

"I mean it, Vinnie."

"Well, we tried. But we never had time for—you know—talking." He grins to himself and looks down at his shoes.

"And what's so funny?" she demands, but she knows the images he has in his head: their wild nights at the Patti-O Motel. Those nights are in her head, too.

Will they ever, *ever* be able to live them down?

"Anyway," he says, thumping the melon. "This one here's almost ready. Should be good to eat tomorrow." ଛ

## *TWENTY-THREE*

In the shower the next morning, she finds herself singing the words to Stout Hearted Men, a song she never realized she knew. Its determined, military rhythm is perfectly in tune with her feelings today. Her strength is back, Vinnie is back, everything is settling nicely back to normal, and soon she'll have Cara back on track as well. Turning up the hot water and breathing steam into her sinus cavities, Myra feels the last traces of her illness washing down the drain. When she steps out of the tub, parts of her are scalded pink as shrimp.

Quickly she towels herself dry and pulls on her clothes. What a lot she has to accomplish today! She turns on the nightstand radio (a little music always helps energize her), strips off the bed sheets and replaces them with the new percales she picked up at Sears Roebuck during the January white sale. Vinnie will sleep here tonight—that's definite; and though she has not yet decided if there will be sex, she is certain of one thing: there will be no more Let's Be Lovers fantasy romps.

Sure, it was fun while it lasted—how could it *not* be fun?—but there is simply no place for that unbridled Myra in this tidy double bed.

As she's patting down the top sheet and humming along with the radio (Willie Nelson just can't wait to get on the road again), an idea comes to her. What if she were to go away with Vinnie on a little trip? They could take a leisurely drive—out to Galena, say—and spend the night in one of those quaint bed-and-breakfast places. It would be just the two of them, but they'd be back the next day. And once they were free of responsibilities and distractions, they could bring some things out in the open. They might be able to talk about what they never got around to talking about at the sleazy Patti-O Motel.

Yes, she thinks, picturing the two of them spooning contentedly under an antique quilt: that would be the shot in the arm their marriage needed.

After she gets all the beds made and tidies the bathroom, she spends a good hour cleaning up the disaster area that was once her kitchen. But all the sweeping and scrubbing has been worth the effort. The room sparkles. When Cara arrives, Myra has finished setting the table, decking it out like a picture in a magazine with place mats, napkins, and dishes that match and have no visible chips in them.

"What's the occasion?" Cara asks as she clomps past with the laundry basket.

"Nothing special," Myra replies, wondering when someone will get that girl a decent pair of shoes. "It just feels so good to feel good again, and I want to celebrate."

The melon Vinnie brought her is perfectly ripe. She slices into it, savoring the aroma and listening for noises from downstairs. There is a rap on Haskell's door, the gurgle of a horn from his record player, two voices. He says something, Cara says something; pause; then a ripple of laughter.

She's not liking the sound of this. She scoops coffee grounds into the machine, pours in a full pot of water. Ten cups, but it looks like it's going to be a long afternoon.

Cara comes back into the kitchen and pulls out her chair. "Haskell got us tickets to see the new production at the Belmont Street Theater tonight, and I thought I'd wear my dress. Can I borrow your scarf with the leaf designs on it? Do you think they would look okay together?"

"I suppose so." Myra's voice is cool. She doesn't want her niece to get the idea she approves of any of this.

"The play is a comedy about these two sisters with opposite personalities who take their mother to visit the Grand Old Opry. It's supposed to be really funny."

"Mm-hmm. Have some cheese."

She picks up a wedge. "This is pretty classy stuff, right?"

"Vinnie brought it. He came home last night."

"For good?"

Myra gives a self-satisfied nod. "You bet."

"That's great, Aunt Myra. I mean, if it's what you truly want."

Her lack of enthusiasm gives Myra pause. "And tell me," she says, turning away from the coffee maker and squaring her fists on her hips, "is there any good reason why I should not want him to come home?"

"I don't know. I was under the impression you were getting along pretty well without him."

Myra sits down at the table, shakes out her napkin, and spreads it over her lap. She realizes she has to be careful about how she expresses her thoughts. "Well, okay, I *was* managing without him. Up to a point. But marriage is a complicated business, Cara, especially when children are involved. It's never just a simple matter of black or white—" She waves a hand. "But never mind about me. I want to talk about you. Have you thought this whole thing over carefully?"

Cara dabs cheese on a cracker. "It's a very good play. It won an award."

"You know perfectly well what I'm referring to." She jerks a thumb at the basement door.

Cara fills her cheeks with air. "I suppose now I get the lecture."

"You are much too young to be thinking of marriage."

"I'm the exact same age you were when you met Uncle Vinnie."

"When we *met*. We didn't get *married* until much later. I was old enough to vote by then."

"And I'm old enough to vote right now."

"Because they've gone and changed the law. Anyway, that is totally beside the point. What about your future? Your dreams of making a ton of money?"

"What about it? I can still go to school—"

"And he's so much older than you are!" She stops and then, in a more gentle tone of voice, she asks, "Do you honestly believe he is your Mister Right?"

Cara trains her blue-eyed gaze at Myra's forehead. "Yes," she says, "I do."

A few final grunts emerge from the coffee machine. Myra gets up for the pot. "I always thought you were a sensible child," she says, filling their cups. "I never thought you would pull a stunt like this."

"Stunt?" Cara sounds hurt. "This is no stunt. I went about it very scientifically. I thought you'd be proud of me. First I made a list of all the things I knew about Haskell. And then I divided them into two columns, 'like' and 'dislike'. And guess what? The 'like' side was so much longer. He has such a great way of speaking, don't you think? He knows exactly the right words to use. I could listen to him for days—"

"I'm guessing you probably have."

"And he's so well rounded. He traveled to Africa—"

"Two weeks with the Peace Corps. Big deal."

"He is polite and well mannered. And he thinks I'm beautiful. He called me his Helen of Troy."

"Was he sober when he told you that?"

"He doesn't drink. That's another thing I put in the 'like' column."

Myra pauses and looks directly into Cara's face. "There is one word I haven't heard you mention yet. And it's the single most important thing in any marriage."

She giggles. "Well, you'll have to take my word for this. He's very good at sex."

"That's not the word I meant. Tell me honestly, Cara. Are you in love?"

"Well…sure. Love is when you're happy, right?"

Myra shakes her head. Never has she associated love with happiness. In her experience, love was a malady, filled with as much suffering as sweetness. In the early days of their relationship, if she went more than a day without seeing Vinnie, her whole body would ache with missing him. She recalls the raw feeling after an argument, as if her heart had been scoured with a wire brush. And love meant constant worry. If he was late meeting her, she would picture him dead. If he forgot to call, she would have visions of some thug striking him senseless over the head. "My-ra?" he'd be asking the curvy blonde nurse bandaging his poor head, "My-ra who?"

Oh, how could she survive in the world if he was not in it?

But all at once the phone would ring, or the doorbell, and there he'd be, alive and well after all. It always surprised her how close to despair she had come by then, having just rehearsed her own tragic suicide.

"What has happy got to do with anything?" she says to Cara. "If you were truly in love, you would be miserable at least half the time."

"That makes absolutely no sense."

"Love and sense have nothing to do with one another. It's ridiculous to think you can commit your future to someone based on a list." And briefly she remembers the one she had been drawing up in her head that night in Mr. Karimer's philosophy class when she threw Byron Levine aside without a second thought and cast her lot with Vinnie.

"This is good coffee," Cara says, bluntly changing the subject. Myra knows she has not convinced her niece of anything yet. That dimple near her mouth gives her away. It only shows up when she has her lips pressed together in forbearance.

"Yes, it is good. A specialty brew. Vinnie brought it."

"Trying to get back in your good graces, no doubt."

"Maybe. Probably. But when we were first married, your uncle would come up with the most thoughtful little gifts. For our first anniversary, he brought me a baby olive tree in a clay pot."

"How romantic."

"Actually, I thought it was." She takes a sip of coffee. "Very romantic." She holds the cup in both hands and stares off into space, remembering how, when she unwrapped the olive tree, it put her immediately in mind of the earthy Italian films that Byron Levine used to take her to see, those sexy movie star men with their dangerous, burning eyes. She kept the tree by the sunny bedroom window in their apartment, and on the day they moved to this house, the first thing they did was plant it in their new backyard.

Cara presses a finger into the cracker crumbs on her plate. "Were you a fool for love, Aunt Myra?"

She almost smiles. "I guess you could say I was."

"And would you do it all again?"

She blinks. "You know that is not a fair question to ask me right now."

"So let's say, then, just for the sake of argument, Haskell and I are all weak-kneed and drooling over one another. How long could that last? You can't tell me you still feel the same way about Uncle Vinnie as you used to."

"Situations change, Cara. People get older and wiser, and once you have children, a mortgage, a lot of obligations, it's irresponsible to think of dying for love."

"Just my point. Wild infatuation doesn't last. It can't. So why not go for comfort and security in the first place?"

Myra sets down her cup. "Because there is a good reason for being madly in love with the person you are going to marry, and it's not anything you can relate to right now. But trust me, when you're living together day in and day out, when the roof springs another leak and the dog chews a leg off your new chair, and your son or daughter gets chicken pox and you spend your whole day dabbing them with calamine lotion, you need to remember the way it used to be. Without that, married life and everything that goes with it is nothing but a lot of hard work."

Cara holds up her hands and applauds lightly. "Very nice speech," she says, "but I'm not going to be like you. Haskell and I don't want children or pets or anything that needs taking care of. Not so much as a goldfish. We have no intention of loading ourselves down with unnecessary responsibilities."

"And what will you have in your lives then?"

"Our careers, for one thing. And books, of course. Art, music, the theater…"

"It will still be hard work," Myra says, reaching out a weary arm for the platter of melon slices. "Just living together under the same roof, even if it doesn't leak. It'll take all the strength you've got."

❧❧❧

After Cara has folded the laundry and Myra's helped her load it into the hatch of the Civic, she spends a few minutes alone, clearing away their dishes and thinking about her responsibilities, necessary and otherwise. Then her mother calls to read her an article on the virtues of Vitamin C.

"They say a thousand milligrams a day is not too much," Nettie is reporting, when Myra has to excuse herself to answer the doorbell. Brownie is already barking her head off, naturally, and Angelo chimes in with a few *woof-woofs* of his own.

Locking an arm around the dog, she opens the door to a young man wearing a green parka with an emblem stitched in gold on the pocket. "Hello, there," he says cheerfully and with the too-eager look of the typical door-to-door salesman. "Are you the permanent resident here?"

Without waiting for her answer, he shoves a card into her hand and asks her to check off the magazines she reads most frequently. "I don't need any magazines," she says, trying to give the card back to him.

"This is only a survey, Ma'am. Check off the ones you read now or think you might like to read in the future."

"Oh, well, in that case." She takes the pencil he offers and studies the list while Brownie gets busy sniffing the young man's shoes. "I used to like Good Housekeeping, but I let my subscription lapse. Would that count?"

"I would say, yes."

She marks the appropriate box and then considers the other titles. There seems to be a different magazine for every sort of person, interest, idea and cause on the planet. "I don't know if I can decide about any of the others."

"There must be a few you're curious about. Savvy? Colonial Home? Open Road?" He shifts sideways a step as Brownie begins working her nose around his kneecaps. "Music and Memories? Workbench?"

"I can't seem to make up my mind."

"Here's the deal. Pick any three off this list, and you can get them for half off the cover price. That's sixty months of your three favorite magazines, delivered right to your mailbox, and all you have to do is mark your initials on this line."

"Sixty months?" She does a quick computation. "Five *years*?"

"You could look at it that way."

"Five years is a really long time."

"You pay for thirty months, and you get thirty months for free. How can you pass up such a terrific offer?"

"Let me try to explain. You see, when I was in school, I used to read Seventeen. And later I graduated to Cosmopolitan. I loved that magazine. It gave you advice on fashion and careers, love and romance. It gave you something to strive towards. But then I got married, I had children, and suddenly I couldn't be that Cosmo girl anymore. I still haven't really gotten over it."

"No problem. We have Parents, Working Mother, Pins & Needles—"

"But how can I commit to a magazine for five whole years! Don't you understand? In five years, who knows who I might become!"

She realizes she is speaking too loudly, practically shouting into the young man's face, and the dog is now rooting enthusiastically under his parka. "Yes, Ma'am," he says, backing down the steps, "I'm sure you're right..."

She waves the card. "What about the survey?"

Without giving her an answer, he turns away. From the doorway, Myra and Brownie watch as he flees down the block and out of sight.

⚜⚜⚜

A little before suppertime, Jennifer breezes through the kitchen with her overnight bag on her shoulder and announces that she is sleeping at Heather's house tonight. Myra stops her at the door. "And who gave you permission? You are barely over the flu."

"I'm fine now, see?" She stands with her arms bent like a happy marionette. "But you better check on Howie. He's lying on the floor out there. I think he might be dead."

Myra rushes into the living room. "Sweetie?"

"My stomach hurts," he moans, his face as pale as raw bacon.

Myra gathers him up off the floor and lays him on the couch. She hears the back door closing, Jennifer leaving without even saying goodbye. Then the bathroom door opens and Haskell comes downstairs, toweling his hair. His feet are bare, and he is wearing his overcoat as a robe. "Not another casualty," he says.

"Just when I thought I had everything under control." She sniffs Howie for fever.

"I won't be eating supper at home," he tells her. "I promised Cara we would go to that new Mongolian buffet before the performance."

Myra pulls off her cardigan sweater and covers Howie with it. "Cara is a wonderful girl," she says.

"A fine young woman, yes. You know, Myra, in many ways she reminds me of you."

She thanks him for the compliment, but wonders if there is any truth to it, or if he's just trying to smooth things over. Smooth talker: wasn't that one of the attributes on Cara's list of 'likes'?

"I hope you have a good time tonight," she says, aiming for sincerity. Barring a miracle, it appears he is going to be somewhere in her life indefinitely. She wonders when she stopped remembering what he looked like without his clothes.

As soon as he leaves, the front door opens, and Vinnie comes in, asking what's for supper.

She has not quite finished cleaning up from lunch, and all these comings and goings are making her feel a little faint. "Give me a minute," she says, sitting down on the couch next to Howie and laying her head back.

"What's with the kid?"

"Probably nothing, but who knows?" She closes her eyes, trying to gather enough strength to get up and go into the kitchen. First she has to find a can of ginger ale to settle Howie's stomach. Then she will start on dinner. She's wondering if there is something she can do with sardines and red potatoes, when an odor of garlic begins to waft her way.

Has Vinnie decided to cook for them tonight?

Yes. Yes, he has, bless him. She hears a sizzle, followed shortly by another sizzle, and then the sweet aroma of tomatoes simmering in wine.

To Myra, it is a symphony.

❦❦❦

"Cara? And the writer guy?" Vinnie looks amazed. "Seems like only yesterday she was riding a tricycle down the sidewalk."

"She's the same age I was when I met you."

"So I suppose she's old enough to know what she's doing."

"Don't be ridiculous. Did we know what we were doing?"

Howie says, "Quiet, Mom."

They are putting him to bed after letting him stay up late and drink two cans of pop. Myra plants a kiss on Howie's forehead and follows Vinnie out of the room. "I think you should talk to her."

"What for?"

"Tell her what a mistake she's making. I tried my best, but she refuses to listen to me."

"So maybe you ought to butt out."

"And let her ruin her life?"

"My-ra, how come you always gotta get involved? For once, can't you just let it alone?" He sounds irritated; barely home twenty four hours and already he's starting an argument.

"Sure, I could let it alone," she says. "I could stand back and just let everything fall to pieces."

She steps into the bathroom and shuts the door, a little more firmly than necessary; but by the time she emerges, dressed in her flannel pajamas, she has calmed down a little. She turns into Howie's room to check on him again, touches his cheek, listens for the soft music of his breathing. He is getting to look more like Vinnie every day—the same dark arch of the eyebrows, the same thin curve of the lips—and she wonders about the young female hearts he will probably be breaking as he grows from a boy into a man.

Through the window she watches the full moon casting its watery light over the back yard, in a corner of which stands the gnarled little olive tree. There is a gouge in one side of the trunk from the time Myra lost control of the lawn mower. Several limbs have cracked in windstorms, or because children were swinging from them. Late every spring, just as she has given up hope, the first pale, slender leaves appear; then, toward September, the inedible fruit.

Tangled into the earth are the roots of that dinged-up little tree; and she supposes that, like a marriage, those roots are stronger than the tree itself, but forever hidden from view.

She pulls down the window shade and tiptoes from Howie's room. In their room, Vinnie is lying in bed, staring at the ceiling. Myra climbs in on her side and opens her magazine. *People*. That's one you never really outgrow.

He rubs his eyes. She turns a page. It's as if their nights at the Patti-O Motel never happened; or happened to another couple: two people who looked like them but were not who they were.

"Howie okay?" he says.

"I think so. If he's not better tomorrow, I'll call the doctor."

"Keep him inside anyway. You never can tell."

"All right."

They've had this conversation before, dozens of times. They've had every conversation dozens of times. She turns another page, reads for a moment, and then lays the magazine aside. "Do you remember when we planted the olive tree?" she says.

"The day we moved here."

"Yes."

"What about it?"

"You were digging the hole, and I asked you to watch Jennifer so I could go inside and get her sippy cup. Remember?"

"I think so."

"I want to apologize. I should never have yelled at you."

"What're you talking about?"

"I was so upset. I turned my back for two minutes, and when I came out of the house she was stuffing her mouth with dirt, and you were so busy with the stupid shovel, you didn't even notice."

"That was, what, ten years ago?"

"For days afterward, we barely spoke to one another. It was awful. I was afraid things would never be the same between us."

"So what're you trying to tell me?"

"I'm not sure." She turns on her side to face him. "I feel like, when we had that argument, I was someone else, not the same person I am now."

He is silent for the moment. Then he says, "I never held it against you, if that's what you mean." He reaches across the alley of space between them and takes her hand, gives it a small squeeze, lets it go. "Get some sleep," he says, already beginning to drowse.

"Vinnie?" She raises herself onto an elbow. "I was thinking about maybe taking a little trip, going away for a few days."

"Might be nice. Kids, too?"

"No, not the children." She had envisioned the two of them and a bed and breakfast in Galena, but now she's beginning to realize that it might be a hard sell. Vinnie wasn't much for quaint little inns, antique shop browsing or, for that matter, a four-hour drive to the western edge of Illinois. The rigors of travel tended to make him grumpy, and she would need to work diligently to keep him in a good mood.

It sounded to her like a whole lot of effort, all things considered, and she had no guarantee the trip would end up improving their marriage. In fact, there was a real danger that it might have the opposite effect.

As she's mulling this over, another image begins to take shape, and in her mind's eye she sees a woman in tall boots, striding down a dusty road, heading west: far beyond touristy little Galena into the wide open spaces of Iowa.

The woman is alone—unaccompanied by husband or children, unfettered by the constraints of everyday life. For a moment Myra allows herself to indulge in the fantasy of being that woman. How would it feel, she wonders, to be so utterly free of responsibility? What if she could step into those fearless boots for real...?

Oh, who is she kidding? The unfortunate truth is she has no place in that scenario; she is simply nowhere near brave enough to do anything even remotely like that.

At least, not all on her own.

She lies down again and settles herself under the covers. "What I was thinking," she says, holding onto the image of the brave woman in boots, "is going away with Cara. Just the two of us. Don't you think that a change of scenery could do her a world of good?" Then she describes the place in the advertising brochure: Cedar-something, on the Mighty Mississippi River, where you go to see eagles soaring magnificently through the sky on their journey north after their long winter away.

It would be an adventure, she tells herself, her first adventure ever, not counting those nights she spent cavorting with Vinnie at the Patti-O Motel.

But even as she's speaking, she is wondering what could have put this idea into her head. What makes her think she even wants to go? "Dumb idea, right?" she says, trying to make light of the whole thing.

He offers no reply. His eyes are closed, and she can just imagine the picture he is sketching behind his lids: two daffy dames set loose on the wilderness, creating havoc wherever they go. And sure enough, there he is, drawing back his lips, ready to laugh at her out loud.

But what she hears is not the harsh bark of derision she has expected. No, it's only the gentle putt-putt of his snore—Vinnie's own private melody: the loveliest sound she has heard in a long, long time.

## TWENTY-FOUR

The young woman who answered the telephone at Out In The Open Vacations, Unlimited, is checking to see that she has taken down Myra's information correctly. "So, now, that's two places on the three-day trip leaving a week from Sunday."

"That's right," Myra says.

"Okey-dokey."

"And can you tell me if I'll be needing any special equipment?"

"No, not really. Extra socks, maybe. A poncho, 'case it rains."

"What about first-aid kits…tetanus shots?"

"We have medical supplies at the lodge, but it's a good idea to be current on the booster."

She scribbles the information in the margins of the brochure—which turned up finally in the pantry on top of a box of macaroni and cheese—and studies the photographs, trying to picture herself under that wide blue sky, miles and miles from anywhere, a cold wind burning her face.

"I've never been on this kind of a trip before," she admits.

"Oh, you'll love it, watching those big birds swoop out over the river. Kind of takes your breath away." She sounds sweet and decidedly un-outdoors-womanly, and that gives Myra hope.

"What about snakes?" Myra asks, the thought occurring to her suddenly and sending a shiver up her spine.

The young woman assures her they are still in hibernation. "Don't forget your binoculars," she adds. Myra makes a note and then promises to put her check in the mail. The young woman thanks her and hangs up, and after a moment Myra places the receiver in the cradle. There was still a question or two she would have liked to ask.

Upstairs, she pulls out her suitcases from under the bed. She has two, the large valise that could hold half her wardrobe and the smaller one Vinnie carried the night he walked out. Maybe, by a week from Sunday, she will be able to look at it without experiencing a fresh jolt of grief.

Howie comes in while she's testing the clasps. "Mom..." he says, "are we going away?"

"Well, honey, I am." She tries to keep her voice neutral. "Just for a few days."

His eyes open wide with apprehension. "Are you going to the same place Dad went?"

She can tell that already he is imagining the weeks and months he will be motherless, and she draws him close and sits him down on the bed beside her. "This is not going to be like when Dad went away." She rubs his back, trying to get him to buck up. "I'm leaving next Sunday morning and I will be back Tuesday night after you and Jen are asleep." She takes his hand and counts off the days on his fingers. "You'll help Dad and Mr. Reed take care of things while I'm away, won't you?"

He lifts a shoulder. "What do I hafta do?"

Seeing that she will need to be specific, she recites a short list of chores off the top of her head. "Do you think you can handle that?"

He nods. "What's Jen gonna do?"

"There will be plenty for her."

"Like what?"

This is getting complicated. "I had better make a list," she says.

Howie wants to make out his own list, and she waits while he goes into his room to find a piece of paper and something to write with. This is important, she understands. He is a serious, sensitive child, and if she allows herself to become annoyed—if she mishandles the situation in any way—she may scar him emotionally for the rest of his life.

He comes back into the room and lies down on his stomach on the floor next to her bed. "How do you spell 'bird seed'?" he asks.

Patiently, she gives him the letters as he presses them into the paper with a teal-colored crayon. When he is done, he looks up at her soberly and says, "Mom? Will you remember me in five years?"

"Oh, sweetie. How can you ask such a question?" She presses a hand to her heart. "Of course I will."

"Will you remember me in seven years?"

She picks him up off the floor and draws him into her arms. "Howie, you are my child, my flesh and blood, my heart and soul. You are a part of who I am. I will love and remember you always." She plants a kiss on his temple, releases him and goes back to figuring out what to pack. She opens a drawer in her dresser to rummage for woolen socks.

"Mom…?"

"Mm-hmm?"

"Knock-knock."

She smiles absently. "Who's there?"

"See?" He is grinning so hard it looks as if his ears might fall off. "You forgot me already!"

❧❧❧

A week from Sunday…

That does not give her a whole lot of time. She has to finish the laundry and at least make a dent in the pile of ironing. There are also a few bills that need to be paid. And isn't Brownie overdue for her rabies shot? (Too bad Dr. Thornberry can't work on people, too. It would be so convenient if she could get her tetanus booster from him at the same time.) She will need to do some cooking and freezing, which means some serious grocery shopping, and that means she had better get to the coupon drawer, which she's been neglecting for far too long.

She empties the drawer onto the kitchen table, tosses the coupons that have expired and sorts the rest into five stacks: cleaning and laundry products, health and beauty aids, real food, pet food, junk food. This system, which over the years she has perfected almost to an art, has allowed her to save hundreds of dollars and at the same time keep the family properly nourished and groomed. She's almost done with the sorting when the back door suddenly swings open and Haskell comes in on a blast of chilly March wind.

"Uh-oh," he says, as the coupons go flying in all directions. As usual, he is loaded down with parcels: more books, a rolled-up rug, and a skinny wooden implement that looks like a back scratcher.

Helping him gather the scattered coupons, she waves away his apology. "Listen, I have a favor to ask."

"Anything. Name it and it's yours." He sounds suspiciously giddy. If she didn't know better, she would say he'd been drinking. Or maybe he *is* drunk…on love.

"I'm going away for a few days, and I'm taking Cara with me. And since she will probably ask your opinion, I want you to say what a good idea you think it is."

"I take it, then, that she is not very enthusiastic about going."

"She doesn't know. At least, not yet."

"Doesn't know? Isn't that a bit presumptuous of you? What about her classes?"

"I have it all figured out. Her college will be on spring break, no problem there. But Howie and Jennifer will still be in school, so you'll have to be on stand-by during the day. Vinnie will take over at night."

"Ah, yes. Vinnie." He plucks a coupon out of the dog's water dish, wipes it on his sleeve and hands it to her. "I noticed he was home again."

"Sorry. I guess I should have warned you." She examines the coupon—forty cents off a box of tampons—and sets it on one of the stacks.

"You needn't apologize. In fact, we had a surprisingly pleasant conversation over breakfast today."

"Vinnie? Talked to you?"

"I think I may have misjudged him. I have to admit, he does seem like a fairly decent fellow."

"Did you discuss anyone—I mean, anything—in particular?"

"Your name did not come up, if that's a concern. No, the topic of conversation was playwriting. I was explaining my difficulties with Act Three."

She takes another coupon from him. "The same problem you had before?"

"My characters still refuse to speak to one another. They have spent the previous two acts dissecting their lives, probing, analyzing, agonizing. They've discussed every subject from quantum physics to bodily excretions, made love and come close to murder…"

"In other words," she says impatiently, "they've put each other through the wringer."

"Exactly. But when I found I could not get either one of them to utter a single coherent sentence, I began to sense that the problem was organic, that I had failed to set up the earlier scenes properly. And if that was true, then the whole project was doomed."

"What was it you wanted them to say?"

He frowns, thinking. "Something significant. Something that would throw the characters into relief and force the audience into a new awareness of their own lives and the world around them."

He goes on for a few minutes while she nods and *tches*, feigning interest. "Well," she says at last, anxious to keep any more of the afternoon from slipping away, "you'll probably figure out the answer eventually."

"Oh, I have figured it out. And I must credit your husband. He gave me a suggestion that has opened up a door and shown me the way out of my dilemma."

"Vinnie?"

"He said that perhaps the reason my characters would not speak was that they had nothing left to say."

"He told you that?"

"Not in so many words. But that was the gist of it. And I sensed immediately he was correct."

"But Vinnie doesn't know a single thing about the theater. And except for parent night productions at the children's school, he's never even seen a real play."

"No matter. I trust his instincts. I've been pondering all day, and the light has finally dawned." He seizes the edges of the table and leans across it, as if arriving at some kind of finish line. "I have decided," he says, nearly screaming into her face, "that I will render the entire last act in *pantomime*!"

She tries to imagine this. No scenery, no costumes, no music, and now no words. "Won't that be a little risky? What if the audience doesn't get it?"

"Not get it? Of course they'll get it!" He sits down in a chair, leans back and massages his chin. "The actors will need to be carefully coached, but the lighting direction will help to amplify their gestures. And I think the audience will be able to extrapolate from what has gone before—"

"What're you guys doing, having a fight?" Jennifer has come into the room. She opens the refrigerator and stares inside. "How come there's never anything to eat?"

"We are having a discussion about the theater," Myra says pointedly. "If you're hungry, you can finish the potato salad."

Jennifer wrinkles her nose. "Who ate all the pickles? I bet Howie did, the little pig."

"Actually," Haskell says, "I was up all night working, and about two a.m. I had this craving. I'm afraid I am the culprit who finished the pickles."

"Mr. Reed accepts your apology."

Jennifer's face turns pink. "Sor-ry!" She closes the refrigerator door and slinks out of the room.

He pinches the bridge of his nose. "Where was I?"

"Something about extrapolating?" Myra is digging through the coupons. Somewhere she has one for a jar of Vlasic kosher dills.

"Yes, well…" He stares off into space, then rises abruptly. "I had better get to work."

"Will you tell Cara what I asked?"

"If you insist. I will tell her what a wonderful thing it will be to run off with you to…?"

"Cedar Point." She says it the way she might have said Paris, France. "We're going to see eagles."

"Eagles?" he says, gathering his parcels. "I was under the impression the group had broken up and that their lead singer was recording on his own."

"No, no. Not *the* Eagles." She flaps her arms. "Eagles."

"In the wilderness?"

"What's the matter? Don't you think women can handle the wilderness?"

"I am sure you can do anything you put your minds to. It's just that I never knew you were the outdoors type."

"There is a lot about me you don't know." She picks up a coupon for raisins and puts it on the real food stack. "There's a lot about me no one knows."

"I do not doubt that at all."

Myra points to the back scratcher. "And what is that thing?"

"This is a replica of a South American fertility goddess. Peruvian, probably." He turns the stick so she can see the figure carved into the side. "I bought it for Cara."

"Really? I thought she wasn't interested in having children."

"Next term she plans to take a seminar in comparative religions, and I thought…I thought—"

"Oh, forget it," Myra says, dismissing him with a wave of her fingers.

She returns her attention to the coupons, studying each one, putting it in the proper stack, marking the item down on her grocery list. Marginally aware of the television droning in the next room, the dog and one of the cats dozing together in a patch of sunlight, she sighs with the contentment of the moment and picks up a coupon for Big Mixx.

The advertising says the cereal has no artificial colors, but it makes no mention of artificial flavors. Or sugar. In fact, the stuff might have enough sugar to qualify as junk food. On the other hand, it does have a good combination of whole grains. She holds the coupon in her fingers and chews her lower lip.

The clock ticks.

It's a simple decision, but she cannot seem to make it, cannot just lay the coupon down in one place or the other and move on to the next simple decision. It's as if something has short-circuited in her brain.

And now she understands what has come from so many years of bogging herself down in so much stupid, meaningless detail. This is why she will never become the sort of person who is able to extrapolate, or discuss quantum physics, or study comparative religion. She will not even be able—and here she thinks of Vinnie and Haskell at breakfast today—to offer pragmatic insights into knotty problems.

She closes her eyes. Slowly she crumples the Big Mixx cereal coupon in her fist and lets it drop to the floor. A moment later, she hears the cat pounce upon it, and then a soft *thwack-thwack-thwack* as he bats it around the floor.

⌘⌘⌘

On Friday night, when she gets back from her Let's Be Lovers party, everyone is in bed, but Myra is so wired she can't even think of sleep. The party went exceptionally well. The women had all been participants in a seminar on self-reliance that was sponsored by the local chapter of a national organization of female professionals. She met a social worker, a carpenter, a realtor, a metal sculptor, several women with consulting businesses like hers, and a few who were still mapping out their careers. One of them was getting married for the second time, and the others had organized the gathering on her behalf.

The bride-to-be selected a number of wispy garments for her trousseau and several appliances, and all the others bought merchandise as well. Just as the party seemed to be breaking up and Myra was tallying her sales, someone brought out champagne and cake. Then a male stripper arrived, and the place went up for grabs.

Dreamily, she kicks off her shoes and puts her coat in the closet. One-Eyed Jacks is the late movie. Myra tunes it in and sets up her ironing board in front of the television set. While she drags the iron back and forth over Vinnie's white shirt, she thinks of all the clever remarks the women made to one another, the way she joined in as if she had gone through the seminar with them and learned what they'd learned. And that dancer: all bronzed muscles and gleaming teeth—how perfect he was! (Too perfect, said the carpenter, to be straight.)

She is so lost in thought she barely hears Vinnie call her name.

"How come you're up in the middle of the night?" he says, poking his head into the room and squinting against the light before padding into the kitchen. Myra hears water run, the refrigerator door open and close. He comes back, chewing something, and sits down on the couch.

"I'm sorry if I disturbed you." She pokes the tip of the iron in and out of the spaces between the shirt buttons. "I have a lot to do before I leave."

He grunts. He hasn't said much about the trip one way or the other, but she can tell he doesn't think it's such a hot idea.

On the screen, Brando tilts back his hat and mumbles at someone. Myra sighs. "Wasn't he handsome?"

"You seen him lately? He turned into a fat old man."

There is a bitter edge to his voice that puts her on alert. She turns to him and says gently, "Why don't you go back to bed. You have to get up so early."

He rubs his hands over his face. "Yeah, well, I'm not sleeping too good lately. I got things on my mind."

She is not going to ask him what. There's no telling where a simple question like that might lead. She finishes ironing the collar, shakes out the shirt and puts it on a hanger, then spreads another shirt over the board and picks up the iron again.

After a few moments of silence, he reaches for the plug and pulls it from the wall. "Talk to me, My-ra. I gotta know something. I gotta know if anything went on between you and…"—he gestures with his head toward the kitchen—"…him."

Still feeling a residual boldness from the party tonight, she sets the iron down and stares directly into his eyes. "You have no right to question my behavior."

"Maybe not. But I'm asking anyway."

She could flat out lie, and he would have to believe her. He had been so wrong in what he'd done, was so utterly and undeniably the guilty party, he would not dare dispute whatever she told him. But a lie is something she'd have to wake up with every day for the rest of her life, and she is not willing to shoulder that burden.

Forcing herself to keep her head up and not look away, she says, "For a short time, when I thought our marriage was over, Haskell and I had a…relationship. I'm not proud of it, but I don't apologize for it either. And you may as well know something else, Vinnie. I was so angry at you, I got rid of all your records and magazines. And your bottle and ashtray collections. And your sports memorabilia. And, you may have noticed, the turquoise chair."

She can tell he's upset because his left eye is twitching, though it's difficult to tell which of her revelations is bothering him the most. He wipes a hand over his mouth and says, "The Sinatra, too?"

"Yes, the Sinatra, too. And you know what? I am not sorry. Not a bit."

She plugs the iron back into the wall and begins running it briskly over the cloth, though it has cooled off some and isn't having much effect on the wrinkles. Thinking about her struggles during the long months of Vinnie's absence is beginning to fray her mantle of self-assurance. A tear escapes her eye and lands on the shirt; it makes a little hissing noise as the iron slides over it.

"So…the writer guy…" He has come up behind her and is talking into her ear, his voice low and slightly menacing. "…was he any good?"

She continues ironing. "Yes, he was. More than adequate."

"He don't look the type. I mean, to be a lady killer."

"Looks can deceive. And he has managed to sweep our niece off her feet, you know."

"Yeah, I know." He clamps a hand on her shoulder, and his breath is now a heat on her neck. "So…you like his moves better than mine?"

She tries to squirm away, but he takes her earlobe in his teeth and imprisons her with his other arm, locking it across her waist like a steel bar.

Helpless, she melts into him, her knees barely able to support her. She turns off the iron as she twists to face him, and they sink, scrambling, to the carpet. Grinding away in her head is the male stripper, his hard limbs and rippled torso. But the face is Vinnie's: the smooth olive skin, the little white scar, the sweet damaged nose.

Almost as soon as he enters her, she comes, grabbing on to him and holding fast as if she were a boat in danger of being carried away on a wild, storm-tossed sea. With a long groan, he slumps against her and then, in deference to his greater weight, rolls onto his side. She is still wearing her clothes, more or less. Her slacks are now hugging her ankles.

"All right," she says, nuzzling the damp hair above his ear, "you're the best. You are definitely the best."

He gives her his gangster's laugh, the one with the leer running through it, and strokes her butt. A moment later, he barks out a laugh.

She lifts her head. "What is so funny?"

"I just thought of something. When the writer guy and Cara get married, you know what's gonna happen, don't you?"

Myra settles her head back against his chest. "No, tell me."

"That walking encyclopedia is gonna be our brand new nephew." ✺

## *TWENTY-FIVE*

On the Sunday morning of their departure, Nettie and Jack show up half an hour early to drive them to the bus station. Myra is still rushing around with her lists, making sure she has not overlooked anything. "There's coffee, if you want any," she tells her parents, tucking another pair of socks into her suitcase.

Nettie says no thanks, they had the Grand Slam breakfast at Denny's. Jack wanders into the kitchen, where Vinnie is busy rustling up bacon and eggs. They can hear him banging pans on the stove, rumbling commands. Nettie cocks her head in the direction of his voice. "I hope he came crawling back," she says, settling into the couch. "I hope you made him grovel, but good."

"Sure, Ma. He wore out the knees on a pair of pants, groveling."

Her mother turns down the corners of her mouth. "You're too easy, Myra. Who could have guessed that such a stubborn little girl would grow up to be such a big pushover."

Nettie is wrong; she doesn't know the whole story. But Myra grits her teeth, determined not to argue.

"I bet he didn't offer you so much as an apology," she goes on. "And how come you're running off with Cara if everything is so wonderful with him?"

"This trip has nothing to do with Vinnie. I just need some time away."

"So what would be wrong with a few days in Miami? Or Las Vegas? One of my customers went on a charter deal, paid less than a hundred dollars for the plane—round trip, yet!—and got the hotel for free…"

Myra snaps the suitcase shut and sets it by the front door. She has decided to take the smaller one after all.

"…of course, the silly woman lost a thousand dollars at the roulette table, but still…"

"This will be an adventure, Ma. Doesn't every woman need a little adventure in her life?" She takes her red quilted jacket out of the closet and lays it over the arm of the wing-back chair, and puts her purse and her gloves on the seat.

Nettie chuckles. "I remember, when you were little, you used to do the same thing. Line up your clothes and shoes and schoolbooks. Every night, with the shoes facing the door. Daddy and I got such a kick out of it!" She shakes her head and sighs. "Ah, Myra, you always had to have everything in order."

"Please, Ma, don't exaggerate."

"With the blouse already inside the sweater so you could save maybe a half a minute!" She laughs again, a titter with a snort at the end.

"I was probably going through a stage." Countering the impulse to check her list again, she picks up the lint roller instead and cleans the dog fur off her jacket. Then the doorbell rings, and Cara and Loretta come in. Cara greets Nettie with a hug, while Loretta staggers into the kitchen, muttering something about coffee. Another big Saturday night, Myra supposes.

"Don't forget your binoculars, Aunt Myra." Cara is wearing hers around her neck, along with a blue and orange striped scarf that matches her hat, and those big boots. Adventurous young outdoorswoman: yes, she truly looks the part.

Myra's boots are thin, with little heels, more suitable for walking through a shopping mall than a wilderness. And she has no binoculars, only the opera glasses that Haskell lent her. Well, they will just have to do.

She lifts the binoculars off Cara's neck. "These look very professional," she says. "Where did you get them?"

"They belong to Tim and Joey. They use them to spy on the girls in the building across the alley from us."

The binoculars are heavy. Myra peers through the eyepieces, training her sights on the kitchen. Loretta passes in and out of view, a cloud of dark hair. She adjusts the focus, and there is Vinnie, looking flushed and busy and entirely too cheerful for a man whose future includes three days of housework and child care.

Last night, for old time's sake, they went to the Tip Tap Lounge. She had the idea that going back to the beginning might help them figure out where on the long road that was their marriage they had taken a wrong turn. So they sat in the back booth they used to sit in, fed coins to the juke box and played their favorite songs, drank a few beers, even tried a little surreptitious necking. But it felt forced, uncomfortable. And anyway, where was the thrill in doing what nobody would consider illegal or immoral in the first place?

The sad fact was, they were too old to ever go back. The people they used to be did not exist anymore.

Turning the binoculars the other way, she sees the kitchen from a distance, in tableau. Here is her father showing Howie a trick with a fork and a napkin, Jennifer reaching toward Vinnie for her plate. The back door opens and Haskell comes in with the fat bundle of Sunday newspapers under his arm, and then Cara appears at his side and whispers into his ear.

Quickly, Myra turns the binoculars the other way again, nearly dropping them in her haste.

"Shame on you," Nettie says, getting up from the sofa, "spying on your own family." She bats at her slacks, trying to brush the fur away.

Myra puts down the binoculars and hands her mother the lint roller. "You should know better than to wear navy blue in this house."

"So sue me, I forgot." She trails Myra into the kitchen but stops in the doorway to send a snarling glance in Vinnie's direction, let him know that Nettie Greenburg is no mush-heart, no pushover.

He pours coffee into a mug and hands it to her. "Taste this," he says. "We just started carrying it at the store, special gourmet blend."

Nettie sniffs warily, then sips.

"You like, I'll bring some for you." He winks at Myra and goes back to frying eggs. Give him credit, he knows how to handle a tough customer.

Now Howie is tearing through the papers in search of the comics, and Haskell is trying to help him. Loretta and Jennifer are having a heart-to-heart about the length of their fingernails. Jack tugs at Cara's sleeve. "Did you hear the one about Harry and Edna and the Plotnick diamond?"

His joke is lost in the confusion of dishes and newspapers, in the noisy scramble of voices. It is such a heart-warming scene it might have come from the pages of Family Circle magazine.

How can Myra even think of leaving?

But almost before she knows it, Jack is checking his watch, rising from the table, and in an excessively hearty tone of voice that reminds her of the ringmaster on Bozo's Circus, he says, "Okay, boys and girls, time to hit the road."

Howie starts to whimper. "How come I can't go, too?"

Jennifer says, "Bring me back a present."

"They don't have gift shops in the wilderness."

"Okay, an eagle feather. I'll make one of those cool headbands."

Haskell comes forward to point out that it is a federal offense to be in possession of an eagle feather, punishable by a fine or imprisonment, or both.

Vinnie chucks Howie under the chin. "C'mon, champ. Let's send Mom off with a smile."

Howie takes a breath, screws up his face, and lets loose a howl of desolation. This is killing him. Years from now he'll be spilling out his tragic story on Oprah, telling her of his many childhood traumas and that dreadful, dreadful woman he used to call his mother.

"Oh, Howie." Myra strokes the back of his head and bends to put her arm around him. Vinnie is also holding him; the three of them appear to be locked together, like a piece of modern sculpture.

Then a horn toots. Myra stands. Vinnie snags an arm around her shoulders and squeezes hard. She tries to return the hug, but Howie is still between them, wiping his nose on the hem of her sweater.

"Take care of yourself," Vinnie says. He looks as if he also might break down. He gives her a quick kiss, which lands on the corner of her mouth.

"There's cold roast chicken in the fridge for tonight," she says, moving toward the front door, "and chili for tomorrow. The load in the dryer is just underwear, so you can get it anytime. And don't forget to give Ethel his pill—"

"Bye, Mom." Jennifer offers her cheek. "Have fun."

"—keep the dog's water dish filled, and please, please pick up after yourselves—"

"We're going to be late, Aunt Myra."

"—and I don't want to hear that there's been any fighting. Jen? Howie? Is that clear?"

"We will all be fine," Haskell says. "You needn't worry about a thing."

Not worry?

Might as well tell a cat not to shed.

She puts on her jacket and picks up the suitcase, and over the flurry of voices she hears Angelo calling his mournful, three-note farewell.

*Good-bye-ee…good-bye-ee. Woof-woof.*

Walking through the front door, she discovers a silvery fairyland. An overnight storm has caught the rain and frozen it in motion. Ice drips like tinsel from bare branches, glazes everything up and down the street.

"Careful," Nettie calls from the car, "you can break your neck on that sidewalk."

Myra holds on to the railing and picks her way down the steps. She slides into the back seat next to Cara, who is blowing a last kiss toward the house. Framed in the living room window, like a portrait of an alternative family, Haskell, Vinnie and the children are waving goodbye.

"Tell me again the reason why we're going," Cara says as Jack pulls away from the curb and crawls up the street. He makes a full stop at the intersection, even though there is no stop sign, a fact which Nettie does not hesitate to point out to him.

"You're such a fan of the environment," Myra answers over the ensuing argument from the front seat, "I thought you would be drooling at the chance to see it this close up."

"Know what I think, Aunt Myra? You just want to get me away from Haskell so you can talk me out of marrying him. But it won't work."

"I wouldn't think of trying to change your mind," she says, a little too innocently. "And please do me a favor. Don't call me 'Aunt.' For the next three days I don't want to be anyone's relative."

Nettie twists around in her seat. "What's this? You're divorcing the whole family?"

"Oh, Ma. Please. This has nothing to do with family. I want to see what it feels like to be just me." And for the briefest instant she wonders who, exactly, that might be.

The streets are quiet, traffic sparse. Sunlight glints off the frozen tree branches, making them appear as if they'd been dipped in silver paint. Jack has turned the heat in the car too high, and Myra feels drowsy, like someone moving in a dream toward some beautiful but perilous destination. She feels as if she might wake up any minute to the familiar clatter of her ordinary life and its exhausting, maddening demands.

Jack's voice squeezes into her reverie. "Children, we have arrived!" He eases the car into a space across the street from the bus station and lets the engine idle.

Myra looks around. The Loop is practically deserted. A few homeless people shuffle along Dearborn Street, shapeless gray bundles of despair. She gets out of the car, thanks her parents and promises to call when she gets back.

"Where is your hat?" Nettie says.

Myra points to her suitcase. "In here."

"You'll catch a cold, nothing on your head—"

Jack drives away before Myra can counter with the virus argument. Cara tosses the flap of her scarf over her shoulder. "I can't believe we're actually going through with this. Can you?"

Myra admits that it's hard for her, too, but here they are, standing alone on the sidewalk in air so still and bright it seems as if a shout might be enough to shatter it. They turn and walk to the corner.

"It's not too late to change our minds, you know."

"We are not changing our minds, Cara. We're going to see eagles and enjoy the outdoors and have a wonderful time. And when we come home, we will have interesting stories to tell."

"Sure. How I caught pneumonia sitting in a swamp out in the middle of nowhere—"

"We're going to be fine." Myra sets her jaw. "Just fine."

"If you say so. *Myra*." Cara giggles. "Can I call you *My*, for short?"

They stop at the corner and wait for the traffic light to change. Myra puts her suitcase down and for a moment, without its weight, she feels like a ship without ballast. She grabs a lamppost for support. A man digging through a garbage container pauses to stare at her.

"Are you all right?" Cara says.

"Of course I am." She rifles through her pockets until she finds some quarters to give to the man. "Just that, without the children or Vinnie, it seems so strange. I'm not used to this."

"Me, neither. I miss Haskell already."

"I can't get over the feeling that I'm forgetting something… Oh, I know! The deli slices I bought last week. I'll bet they've gone bad by now. I'd better call home before we get on the bus."

"Wait a minute." Cara gives Myra her quirky, dimpled grin. "Do you honestly believe everyone is going to poison themselves if you aren't around to supervise every morsel they put into their mouths?"

She shakes her head. "I guess I'm being silly."

"Your family has got to learn to get along without you once in a while."

"Yes, well...I suppose this will be good training."

"And, anyway, Haskell is there. Between him and Uncle Vinnie, they ought to be able to figure out what to do about the lunch meat."

"You're right." She tries to smile.

The light turns green, and she picks up the suitcase again, but as they're stepping off the curb, a taxi making a quick right turn veers into their path.

"Careful!" Myra shouts, grabbing Cara by the elbow and yanking her back to the curb. "You could get killed!"

"I saw him, you know," Cara says calmly. "But thank you very much anyway."

"You are very welcome."

"And promise me that you're not going to spend the next three days rescuing me from one thing and another. Please?"

Myra nods. "Okay. Promise." This time, she does manage a smile. And taking a deep breath and another step forward, she lets the girl go.

## END

Made in the USA
Lexington, KY
11 December 2014